# NORA ROBERTS

# MIDNIGHT SHADOWS

Includes *Night Shield* & *Hidden Star*

**SILHOUETTE**™

Recycling programs for this product may not exist in your area.

Midnight Shadows

ISBN-13: 978-1-335-42596-6

Copyright © 2022 by Harlequin Enterprises ULC

Night Shield
First published in 2000. This edition published in 2022.
Copyright © 2000 by Nora Roberts

Hidden Star
First published in 1997. This edition published in 2022.
Copyright © 1997 by Nora Roberts

For questions and comments about the quality of this book, please contact us at CustomerService@Harlequin.com.

Silhouette
22 Adelaide St. West, 41st Floor
Toronto, Ontario M5H 4E3, Canada
www.Harlequin.com

**Printed and bound in Barcelona, Spain by CPI Black Print**

# CONTENTS

# NIGHT SHIELD

For tough guys with soft hearts

# Chapter 1

He didn't like cops.

His attitude had deep roots, and stemmed from spending his formative years dodging them, outrunning them—usually—or being hassled by them when his feet weren't fast enough.

He'd picked his share of pockets by the time he'd turned twelve and knew the best and most lucrative channels for turning a hot watch into cold cash.

He'd learned back then that knowing what time it was couldn't buy happiness, but the twenty bucks the watch brought in paid for a nice slice of the happiness pie. And twenty bucks cannily wagered swelled into sixty at three-to-one.

The same year he'd turned twelve, he'd invested his carefully hoarded takes and winnings in a small gambling enterprise that centered around point spreads and indulged his interest in sports.

He was a businessman at heart.

He hadn't run with gangs. First of all he'd never had the urge to join groups, and more importantly he didn't care for the pecking order such organizations required. Someone had to be in charge—and he preferred it to be himself.

Some people might say Jonah Blackhawk had a problem with authority.

They would be right.

He supposed the tide had turned right after he'd turned thirteen. His gambling interests had grown nicely—a little too nicely to suit certain more established syndicates.

He'd been warned off in the accepted way—he'd had the hell beat out of him. Jonah acknowledged the bruised kidneys, split lip and blackened eyes as a business risk. But before he could make his decision to move territories or dig in, he'd been busted. And busted solid.

Cops were a great deal more of an annoyance than business rivals.

But the cop who'd hauled his arrogant butt in had been different. Jonah had never pinned down what exactly separated this cop from the others in the line of shields and rule books. So, instead of being tossed into juvie—to which he was no stranger—he'd found himself yanked into programs, youth centers, counseling.

Oh, he'd squirmed and snapped in his own cold-blooded way, but this cop had a grip like a bear trap and hadn't let go. The sheer tenacity had been a shock. No one had held on to him before. Jonah had found himself rehabilitated almost despite himself, at least enough to see there were certain advantages to, if not working in the system, at least working the system.

Now, at thirty, no one would call him a pillar of Denver's community, but he was a legitimate businessman whose enterprises turned a solid profit and allowed him a lifestyle the hustling street kid couldn't have dreamed of.

He owed the cop, and he always paid his debts.

Otherwise, he'd have chosen to be chained naked and honey-smeared to a hill of fire ants rather than sit tamely in the outer office of the commissioner of police of Denver.

Even if the commissioner was Boyd Fletcher.

Jonah didn't pace. Nervous motion was wasted motion and gave too much away. The woman manning the station outside the commissioner's double doors was young, attractive with a very interesting and wanton mass of curling red hair. But he didn't flirt. It wasn't the wedding ring on her finger that stopped him as much as her proximity to Boyd, and through him, the long blue line.

He sat, patient and still, in one of the hunter-green chairs in the waiting area, a tall man with a long-legged, tough build wearing a three-thousand-dollar jacket over a twenty-dollar T-shirt. His hair was raven-black, rain straight and thick. That and the pale gold of his skin, the whiplash of cheekbones were gifts from his Apache great-grandfather.

The cool, clear green eyes might have been a legacy from his Irish great-grandmother, who'd given the Apache man three sons.

Jonah knew little of his family history. His own parents had been more interested in fighting with each other over the last beer in the six-pack than tucking their only son in with bedtime stories. Occasionally Jonah's father had boasted about his lineage, but Jonah had never been sure what was fact and what was convenient fiction.

And didn't really give a damn.

You were what you made yourself.

That was a lesson Boyd Fletcher had taught him. For that alone, Jonah would have walked on hot coals for him.

"Mr. Blackhawk? The commissioner will see you now."

She offered a polite smile as she rose to get the door. And she'd taken a good, long look at the commissioner's ten o'clock appointment—a wedding ring didn't strike a woman blind, after all. Something about him made her tongue want to hang out, and at the same time made her want to run for cover.

His eyes warned a woman he'd be dangerous. He had a dangerous way of moving as well, she mused. Graceful and sleek as a cat. A woman could weave some very interesting fantasies about a man like that—and fantasies were probably the safest way to be involved with him.

Then he flicked her a smile, so full of power and charm she wanted to sigh like a teenager.

"Thanks."

She rolled her eyes as she shut the door behind him. "Oh boy, are you welcome."

"Jonah." Boyd was already up and coming around his desk. One hand gripped Jonah's while the other gave Jonah's shoulder a hard squeeze in a kind of male hug. "Thanks for coming."

"Hard to refuse a request from the commissioner."

The first time Jonah had met Boyd, Boyd had been a lieutenant. His hair had been a dark, streaked gold, and his office small, cramped and glass walled.

Now Boyd's hair was deep, solid silver, and his office spacious. The glass wall was a wide window that looked out on Denver and the mountains that ringed it.

Some things change, Jonah thought, then looked into Boyd's steady bottle-green eyes. And some don't.

"Black coffee suit you?"

"Always did."

"Have a seat." Boyd gestured to a chair then walked over

to his coffee machine. He'd insisted on one of his own to save himself the annoyance of buzzing an assistant every time he wanted a hit. "Sorry I kept you waiting. I had a call to finish up. Politics," he muttered as he poured two mugs with rich black coffee. "Can't stand them."

Jonah said nothing, but the corner of his lips quirked.

"And no smart remarks about me being a damn politician at this stage of my game."

"Never crossed my mind." Jonah accepted the coffee. "To say it."

"You always were a sharp kid." Boyd sat on a chair beside Jonah's rather than behind the desk. He let out a long sigh. "Never used to think I'd ride a desk."

"Miss the streets?"

"Every day. But you do what you do, then you do the next thing. How's the new club?"

"It's good. We draw a respectable crowd. Lots of gold cards. They need them," Jonah added as he sipped his coffee. "We hose them on the designer drinks."

"That so? And here I was thinking of bringing Cilla by for an evening out."

"You bring your wife, you get drinks and dinner on the house—is that allowed?"

Boyd hesitated, tapped his finger against his mug. "We'll see. I have a little problem, Jonah, I think you might be able to help me with."

"If I can."

"We've had a series of burglaries the last couple of months. Mostly high dollar, easily liquidated stuff. Jewelry, small electronics, cash."

"Same area?"

"No, across the board. Single family homes out in the

burbs, downtown apartments, condos. We've had six hits in just under eight weeks. Very slick, very clean."

"Well, what can I do for you?" Jonah rested his mug on his knee. "B and E was never my thing." His smile flashed. "According to my record."

"I always wondered about that." But Boyd lifted a hand, waved it away. "The marks are as varied as the locations of the hits. Young couples, older couples, singles. But they all have one thing in common. They were all at a club on the night of the burglary."

Jonah's eyes narrowed, the only change of expression. "One of mine?"

"In five out of the six, yours."

Jonah drank his coffee, looked out the wide window at the hard blue sky. The tone of his voice remained pleasant, casual. But his eyes had gone cold. "Are you asking me if I'm involved?"

"No, Jonah, I'm not asking you if you're involved. We've been beyond that for a long time." Boyd waited a beat. The boy was—always had been—touchy. "Or I have."

With a nod, Jonah rose. He walked back to the coffeemaker, set down his cup. There weren't many people who mattered enough to him that he cared what they thought of him. Boyd mattered.

"Someone's using my place to scope marks," he said with his back to Boyd. "I don't like it."

"I didn't think you would."

"Which place?"

"The new one. Blackhawk's."

He nodded again. "Higher end clientele. Likely a bigger disposable income than the crowd at a sports bar like Fast Break." He turned back. "What do you want from me, Fletch?"

"I'd like your cooperation. And I'd like you to agree to work with the investigating team. Most specifically with the detective in charge."

Jonah swore, and in a rare show of agitation, raked his fingers through his hair. "You want me to rub shoulders with cops, set them loose in my place?"

Boyd didn't bother to hide his amusement. "Jonah, they've already been in your place."

"Not while I was there." Of that, he could be sure. He could sense cop at half a mile, while he was running in the other direction in the dark.

And had.

"No, apparently not. Some of us work during daylight hours."

"Why?"

With a half laugh, Boyd stretched out his legs. "Did I ever tell you I met Cilla when we were both on night shift?"

"No more than twenty or thirty times."

"Same smart mouth. I always liked that about you."

"That's not what you said when you threatened to staple it shut."

"Nothing wrong with your memory, either. I could use your help, Jonah." Boyd's voice went soft, serious. "I'd appreciate it."

He'd avoided prisons all his life, Jonah thought. Until Boyd. The man had built a prison around him of loyalty and trust and affection. "You've got it—for what it's worth."

"It's worth a great deal to me." He rose, offered his hand to Jonah again. "Right on time," he said as his phone rang. "Get yourself some more coffee. I want you to meet the detective in charge of the case."

He rounded the desk, picked up the receiver. "Yes, Paula. Good. We're ready." This time he sat at the desk. "I have a lot of faith in this particular cop. The detective shield's fairly new, but it was well earned."

"A rookie detective. Perfect." Resigned, Jonah poured more coffee. He didn't bobble the pot when the door opened, but his mind jumped. He supposed it was a pleasant thing to realize he could still be surprised.

She was a long-legged, lanky blonde with eyes like prime whiskey. She wore her hair in a straight, sleek tail down the middle of her back over a trim, well-cut jacket the color of steel.

When she flicked those eyes over him, her wide, pretty mouth stayed serious and unsmiling.

Jonah realized he'd have noticed the face first, so classy and fine-boned, then he'd have noticed the cop. The package might have been distracting, but he'd have made her.

"Commissioner." She had a voice like her eyes, deep and dark and potent.

"Detective. You're prompt. Jonah, this is—"

"You don't have to introduce her." Casually Jonah sipped fresh coffee. "She has your wife's eyes and your jaw. Nice to meet you, Detective Fletcher."

"Mr. Blackhawk."

She'd seen him before. Once, she recalled, when her father had gone to one of his high school baseball games and she'd tagged along. She remembered being impressed by his gutsy, nearly violent, base running.

She also knew his history and wasn't quite as trusting of former delinquents as her father. And, though she hated to admit it, she was a little jealous of their relationship.

"Do you want some coffee, Ally?"

"No, sir." He was her father, but she didn't sit until the commissioner gestured to a chair.

Boyd spread his hands. "I thought we'd be more comfortable having this meeting here. Ally, Jonah's agreed to cooperate with the investigation. I've given him the overview. I leave it to you to fill in the necessary details."

"Six burglaries in a period of under eight weeks. Estimated cumulative loss in the ballpark of eight hundred thousand dollars. They go for easily fenced items, heavy on the jewelry. However, in one case a victim's Porsche was stolen from the garage. Three of the homes had security systems. They were disengaged. There have been no signs of break-in. In each case the residence was empty at the time of the burglary."

Jonah crossed the room, sat. "I've already got that much—except for the Porsche. So, you've got someone who can boost cars as well as lift locks, and likely has a channel to turn over a variety of merchandise."

"None of the goods have turned up through any of the known channels in Denver. The operation's well organized and efficient. We suspect there are at least two, probably three or more people involved. Your club's been the main source."

"And?"

"Two of your employees at Blackhawk's have criminal records. William Sloan and Frances Cummings."

Jonah's eyes went cold, but didn't flicker. "Will ran numbers, and did his time. He's been out and clean for five years. Frannie worked the stroll, and it's her business why. Now she tends bar instead of johns. Don't you believe in rehabilitation, Detective Fletcher?"

"I believe your club is being used as a pool to hook fish, and I intend to check all the lines. Logic indicates someone on the inside's baiting the hook."

"I know the people who work for me." He shot Boyd a furious look. "Damn it, Fletch."

"Jonah, hear us out."

"I don't want my people hassled because they tripped over the law at some point in their lives."

"No one's going to hassle your people. Or you," Ally added. Though you did plenty of tripping of your own, she thought. "If we'd wanted to interview them, we would have. We don't need your permission or your cooperation to question potential suspects."

"You move them from my people to suspects very smoothly."

"If you believe they're innocent, why worry?"

"Okay, simmer down." Boyd stayed behind the desk, rubbed the back of his neck. "You're in an awkward and difficult position, Jonah. We appreciate that," he said pointedly with a subtle lift of his eyebrows for his daughter. "The goal is to root out whoever's in charge of this organization and put an end to it. They're using you."

"I don't want Will and Frannie yanked down into interrogation."

"That's not our intention." So he had a hot button, Ally mused. Friendship? Loyalty? Or maybe he had a thing going with the ex-hooker. It would be part of the job to find out. "We don't want to alert anyone on the inside to the investigation. We need to find out who's targeting the marks, and how. We want you to put a cop on the inside."

"I'm on the inside," he reminded her.

"Then you should be able to make room for another waitress. I can start tonight."

Jonah let out a short laugh, turned to Boyd. "You want your daughter working tables in my club?"

Ally got to her feet, slowly. "The commissioner wants one of his detectives undercover at your club. And this is my case."

Jonah rose, as well. "Let's clear this up. I don't give a damn whose case it is. Your father asked me to cooperate, so I will. Is this what you want me to do?" he asked Boyd.

"It is, for now."

"Fine. She can start tonight. Five o'clock, my office at Blackhawk's. We'll go over what you need to know."

"I owe you for this, Jonah."

"You'll never owe me for anything." He walked to the door, stopped, shot a glance over his shoulder. "Oh, Detective? Waitresses at Blackhawk's wear black. Black shirt or sweater, black skirt. Short black skirt," he added, then let himself out.

Ally pursed her lips, and for the first time since she'd come into the room relaxed enough to slip her hands casually into her pockets. "I don't think I like your friend, Dad."

"He'll grow on you."

"What, like mold? No," she corrected. "He's too cool for that. I might end up with a little skin of ice, though. You're sure of him?"

"As sure as I am of you."

And that, she thought, said it all. "Whoever's set up these B and E's has brains, connections and guts. I'd say your pal there has all three." She lifted her shoulders. "Still, if I can't trust your judgment, whose can I trust?"

Boyd grinned. "Your mother always liked him."

"Well then, I'm half in love already." That wiped the grin off his face, she noted with amusement. "I'm still going to have a couple of men under as customers."

"That's your call."

"It's been five days since the last hit. They're working too well not to want to move again soon."

She strode toward the coffeepot, changed her mind and

strode away again. "They might not use his club next time, it's not a given. We can't cover every damn club in the city."

"So, you focus your energy on Blackhawk's. That's smart, and it's logical. One step at a time, Allison."

"I know. I learned that from the best. I guess the first step is to go dig up a short black skirt."

Boyd winced as she walked to the door. "Not too short."

Ally had the eight-to-four shift at the precinct, and even if she left on the dot and sprinted the four blocks from the station to her apartment, she couldn't get home before 4:10 p.m.

She knew. She'd timed it.

And leaving at exactly four was as rare as finding diamonds in the mud. But damned if she wanted to be late for her next meeting with Blackhawk.

It was a matter of pride and principle.

She slammed into her apartment at 4:11 p.m.—thanks to the delay of a last-minute briefing by her lieutenant—and peeled off her jacket as she raced to the bedroom.

Blackhawk's was a good twenty minutes away at a brisk jog—and half again that much if she attempted to drive in rush-hour traffic.

It was only her second undercover assignment behind her detective's shield. She had no intention of screwing it up.

She released her shoulder harness and tossed it onto the bed. Her apartment was simple and uncluttered, mostly because she wasn't there long enough for it to be otherwise. The house where she'd grown up was still home, the station house was second on that list of priorities, and the apartment where she slept, occasionally ate and even more rarely loitered, was a far down third.

She'd always wanted to be a cop. She hadn't made a big deal of it. It simply was her dream.

She yanked open her closet door and pushed through a selection of clothes—designer dresses, tailored jackets and basketball jerseys—in search of a suitable black skirt.

If she could manage a quick change, she might actually have time to slap together a sandwich or stuff a handful of cookies into her mouth before she raced out again.

She pulled out a skirt, winced at the length when she held it up, then tossed that on the bed as well to dig through her dresser for a pair of black hose.

If she was going to wear a skirt that barely covered her butt, she would damn well cover the rest with solid, opaque black.

Tonight could be the night, she thought as she stripped off her trousers. She had to stay calm about it, cool, controlled.

She would use Jonah Blackhawk, but she would not be distracted by him.

She knew a great deal about him through her father, and she'd made it her business to find out more. As a kid he'd had light fingers, quick feet and a nimble brain. She could almost admire a boy with barely twelve years under his belt who'd managed to organize a sports' betting syndicate. Almost.

And she supposed she could come close to admiring someone who'd turned those beginnings around—at least on the surface—and made himself into a successful businessman.

The fact was she'd been in his sports' bar and had enjoyed the atmosphere, the service and the truly superior margaritas Fast Break provided.

The place had a terrific selection of pinball machines,

she recalled. Unless someone had broken her record in the last six months, her initials were still in the number one slot on Double Play.

She really should make time to get back there and defend her championship status.

But that was beside the point, she reminded herself. Right now the point was Jonah Blackhawk.

Maybe his feathers were ruffled because she'd made it clear that two of his employees were on her short list of suspects. Well, that was too bad. Her father wanted her to trust the man, so she'd do her best to trust him.

As far as she could throw him.

By 4:20 p.m., she was dressed in black—turtleneck, skirt, hose. She shoved through the shoes on the floor of her closet and found a suitable pair of low heels.

With a nod to vanity, she dragged the clip out of her hair, brushed it, clipped it back again. Then she closed her eyes and tried to think like a waitress in an upscale club.

Lipstick, perfume, earrings. An attractive waitress made more tips, and tips had to be a goal. She took the time for them, then studied the results in the mirror.

Sexy, she supposed, certainly feminine and in a satisfactory way, practical. And there was no place to hide her weapon.

Damn it. She hissed out a breath, and settled on stuffing her nine millimeter in an oversize shoulder bag. She tossed on a black leather jacket as a concession to the brisk spring evening, then bolted for the door.

There was enough time to drive to the club if she got straight down to the garage and hit all the lights on green.

She pulled open the door. Swore.

"Dennis, what are you doing?"

Dennis Overton held up a bottle of California Chardonnay and offered a big, cheerful smile. "Just in the neighborhood. Thought we could have a drink."

"I'm on my way out."

"Fine." He shifted the bottle, tried to take her hand. "I'll go with you."

"Dennis." She didn't want to hurt him. Not again. He'd been so devastated when she'd broken things off two months before. And all his phone calls, pop-ins, run-intos since then had ended badly. "We've been through all this."

"Come on, Ally. Just a couple of hours. I miss you."

He had that sad, basset hound look in his eyes, that pleading smile on his lips. It had worked once, she reminded herself. More than once. But she remembered how those same eyes could blaze with wild and misplaced jealousy, snap with barely controlled fury.

She'd cared for him once, enough to forgive him his accusations, to try to work through his mood swings, enough to feel guilty over ending it.

She cared enough now to strap her temper at this last invasion of her time and her space. "I'm sorry, Dennis. I'm in a hurry."

Still smiling, he blocked her way. "Give me five minutes. One drink for old times' sake, Ally?"

"I don't have five minutes."

The smile vanished, and that old, dark gleam leaped into his eyes. "You never had time for me when I needed it. It was always what you wanted and when you wanted it."

"That's right. You're well rid of me."

"You're going to see someone else, aren't you? Brushing me off so you can run off to be with another man."

"What if I am." Enough, she thought, was way past enough. "It's no business of yours where I go, what I do, whom I see. That's what you can't seem to get straight. But you're going to have to work harder at it, Dennis, because I'm sick of this. Stop coming here."

He grabbed her arm before she could walk by. "I want to talk to you."

She didn't jerk free, only stared down at his hand, then shifted her gaze, icy as February, to his eyes. "Don't push it. Now step back."

"What're you going to do? Shoot me? Arrest me? Call your daddy, the saint of the police, to lock me up?"

"I'm going to ask you, one more time, to step back. Step way back, Dennis, and do it now."

His mood swung again, fast and smooth as a revolving door. "I'm sorry. Ally, I'm sorry." His eyes went damp and his mouth trembled. "I'm upset, that's all. Just give me another chance. I just need another chance. I'll make it work this time."

She pried his fingers off her arm. "It never worked. Go home, Dennis. I've got nothing for you."

She walked away without looking back, bleeding inside because she had to. Bleeding inside because she could.

# Chapter 2

Ally hit the doors of Blackhawk's at 5:05 p.m. One strike against her, she thought and took an extra minute to smooth down her hair, catch her breath. She'd decided against the drive after all and had run the ten blocks. Not such a distance, she thought, but the heels she wore were a far cry from track shoes.

She stepped inside, took stock.

The bar was a long, gleaming black slab that curved into a snug semicircle and offered plenty of room for a troop of chrome stools with thick, black leather cushions. Mirrored panels of black and silver ran down the rear wall, tossed back reflections and shapes.

Comfort, she decided, as well as style. It said, sit down, relax and plunk down your money.

There were plenty of people to do so. Apparently happy hour was under way, and every stool was occupied. Those who sat at the bar, or kicked back at the chrome tables, drank and nibbled to the tune of recorded music kept low enough to encourage conversation.

Most of the patrons were the suit-and-tie crowd with briefcases dumped at their feet. The business brigade, she concluded, who'd managed to slip out of the office a little early, or were using the club as a meeting arena to discuss deals or close them.

Two waitresses worked the tables. Both wore black, but she noted with a hiss through her teeth that they wore slacks rather than skirts.

A man was working the bar—young, handsome and openly flirting with the trio of women on stools at the far end. She wondered when Frances Cummings came on shift. She'd need to get work schedules from Blackhawk.

"You look a little lost."

Ally shifted her gaze and studied the man who approached her with an easy smile. Brown hair, brown eyes, trim beard. Five-ten, maybe one-fifty. His dark suit was well cut, his gray tie neatly knotted.

William Sloan looked a great deal more presentable tonight than he had for his last mug shot.

"I hope not." Deciding a little agitation fit the role, Ally shifted her shoulder bag and offered a nervous smile. "I'm Allison. I'm supposed to see Mr. Blackhawk at five. I guess I'm late."

"Couple of minutes. Don't worry about it. Will Sloan." He offered a hand, gave hers a quick, brotherly squeeze. "The man told me to keep an eye out for you. I'll take you up."

"Thanks. Great place," she commented.

"You bet. The man's in charge, and he wants the best. I'll give you a quick go-through." With a hand on her back, Will led her through the bar area, into a wide room with more tables, a two-level stage and a dance floor.

Silver ceilings, she mused, glancing up, set with pinpoint lights that blinked and shimmered. The tables were black squares on pedestals that rose out of a smoky silver floor with those same little lights twinkling under the surface, like stars behind clouds.

The art was modern, towering canvases splashed or streaked with wild colors, odd, intriguing wall sculptures fashioned from metals or textiles.

The tables were bare but for a slim metal cylindrical lamp with cut-outs in the shape of crescent moons.

Deco meets the third millennium, she decided. Jonah Blackhawk had built himself a very classy joint.

"You work clubs before?"

She'd already decided how to play it and rolled her eyes. "Nothing like this. Pretty fancy."

"The man wanted class. The man gets class." He turned down a corridor, then punched a code into a control panel. "Watch this."

When a panel in the wall slid open, he wiggled his eyebrows. "Cool, huh?"

"Major." She stepped in with him, watched him reenter the code.

"Any of us who've got to do business on the second level get a code. You won't have to worry about it. So, you new in Denver?"

"No, actually I grew up here."

"No bull? Me, too. I've been hanging with the man since we were kids. Life sure was different then."

The door opened again, directly into Jonah's office. It was a large space, split into business and pleasure with an area to one side devoted to a long leather sofa in his signature color, two sink-into-me armchairs and a wide-screen TV where a night baseball game was being battled out in silence.

Automatically she checked the stats in the top corner of the screen. Yankees at home against Toronto. Bottom of the first. Two out, one on. No score.

The focus on sports didn't surprise her, but the floor-to-ceiling shelves of books did.

She shifted her attention to the business area. It appeared to be as ruthlessly efficient as the rest of the room was indulgent. The workstation held a computer and phone. Across from it stood a monitor that showed the club area. The single window was shielded with blinds, and the blinds were tightly shut. The carpet was cozily thick and stone-gray.

Jonah sat at the desk, his back to the wall, and held up a hand as he completed a call. "I'll get back to you on that. No, not before tomorrow." He lifted a brow as if amused by what was said to him. "You'll just have to wait."

He hung up, sat back in his chair. "Hello, Allison. Thanks, Will."

"No problem. Catch you later, Allison."

"Thanks a lot."

Jonah waited until the elevator door shut. "You're late."

"I know. It was unavoidable." She turned to the monitor giving him an opportunity to skim his gaze down her back, over those long legs.

Very nice, he thought. Very nice indeed.

"You have security cameras throughout the public areas?"

"I like to know what's going on in my place."

She just bet he did. "Do you keep the tapes?"

"We turn them over every three days."

"I'd like to see what you've got." Because her back was to him, she allowed her gaze to slide over and check the action in Yankee Stadium. Toronto brought one home on a line drive bullet. "It'll help to study the tapes."

"For that you'll need a warrant."

She glanced back over her shoulder. He'd changed into a suit—black and, to her expert eye, of Italian cut. "I thought you'd agreed to cooperate."

"To a point. You're here, aren't you?" His phone rang and was ignored. "Why don't you sit down? We'll work out a game plan."

"The game plan's simple." And she didn't sit. "I pose as a waitress, talk to customers and staff. I keep my eyes open and do my job. You keep out of my way and do yours."

"Wrong plan. I don't have to keep out of anyone's way in my place. Now, ever worked a club?"

"No."

"Ever waited tables?"

"No." His cool, patient look irked. "What's the big deal. You take the order, you put in the order, you serve the order. I'm not a moron."

He smiled now, that quick, powerful strike. "I imagine it seems that way when you've spent your life on the other side of it. You're about to get an education, Detective. Head waitress on your shift is Beth. She'll help train you. Until you've got a handle on it, you'll bus tables. That means—"

"I know what busing tables involves."

"Fine, I've put you on six to two. You get a fifteen-minute break every two hours. No drinking during shift. Any of the customers get overly friendly or out of line, you report to me or to Will."

"I can handle myself."

"You're not a cop here. Somebody puts hands on you in an inappropriate way, you report to me or to Will."

"You get a lot of that?"

"Only from the women. They can't keep their hands off me."

"Ha-ha."

Out of the corner of his eye, he noted the Yankees ended the inning on a strikeout. "No, we don't get a lot of it, but it happens. Some guys cross lines when they drink. They only cross them in my place once. The crowd starts getting thick after eight. Entertainment starts at nine. You'll be busy."

He got to his feet, walked to her, walked around her. "You've got a nice cover over the cop in you. You have to look hard to see it. I like the skirt."

She waited until he'd come around and they were face-to-face. "I'll need work schedules for all employees. Or do I need a warrant?"

"No, I can help you out there." He liked the scent of her. Cool and clearly female. "I'll have printouts for you by closing. Anyone I hire who I don't know personally—and even some I do—goes through a full background check. Not everyone here's been lucky enough to come from a nice, tidy family and live a nice, tidy life."

Jonah picked up a remote, switched the angle of the cameras so the bar area popped on screen. "Kid just coming off shift at the bar? Grew up with his grandparents when his mother ran off. Got into a little trouble when he was fifteen."

"And what kind of trouble was that?"

"Got tagged with a joint in his pocket. He straightened out, they sealed the records, but he was up front with me when he wanted the job. He's putting himself through night school."

At the moment she wasn't interested in the young man going off shift at the bar. She kept her eyes on Jonah. "Is everyone up front with you?"

"The smart ones are. That's Beth." He tapped the screen.

Ally saw a little brunette, about thirty, come in through a door behind the bar.

"Bastard she was married to used to kick her around. She can't weigh a hundred pounds. She's got three kids at home. Sixteen, twelve and ten. She's been working for me on and off about five years, used to come in every couple weeks with a black eye or split lip. She took the kids and left him two years ago."

"Is he leaving her alone?"

Jonah shifted his gaze to Ally's. "He was persuaded to relocate."

"I see." And she did. Jonah Blackhawk looked after his own. She couldn't fault him for it. "Did he relocate in one piece?"

"Mostly. I'll take you down. You can leave your bag up here if you want."

"No, thanks."

He pushed the button for the elevator. "I assume you've got your gun in there. Keep it in there. There's a secure employee area off the bar. You can lock it up in there. This shift Beth and Frannie have keys. Will and I have keys or codes for all areas at all times."

"Tight ship, Blackhawk."

"That's right. What's the cover?" he asked as they stepped into the elevator. "How'd I meet you?"

"I needed a job, you gave me a job." She shrugged. "Keep it simple. I caught you at your sports bar."

"Know anything about sports?"

She sent him a smile. "Anything that takes place off a field, a court or outside an arena is just marking time."

"Where have you been all my life?" He took her arm as they stepped out on the main floor. "So, Jays or Yankees?"

"Yankees have stronger bats this season and rule the

long ball, but their gloves are sloppy. The Jays chip away with reliable base hits, and their infield's a ballet of guts and efficiency. I go for guts and efficiency over the power stroke every time."

"Is that a baseball statement, or a life statement?"

"Blackhawk, baseball is life."

"Now you've done it. We have to get married."

"My heart's all aflutter," she said dryly and turned to scan the bar area. The noise level had bumped up several notches. They were two and three deep at the curved black slab now, the after-work, before-dinner crowd.

For some it was unwind time, she thought, for others a casual mating ritual. But for someone, it was a hunt.

People were so careless, she mused. She saw men leaning on the bar, back pockets ripe for picking. More than one handbag hung vulnerable on the back of a stool or chair. Coats and jackets, some likely to have car or house keys in their pockets, were tossed aside.

"Nobody ever thinks it can happen to them," Ally murmured, then tapped Jonah's arm, inclined her head. "Check out the guy at the bar—six down, with the news anchor hair and teeth."

Amused, Jonah tagged the guy from Ally's description and watched him flash his wallet, choked with bills and credit cards.

"He's trying to lure the redhead there, or her pretty blond friend. Doesn't matter which. Odds are he hits with the blonde," Jonah concluded.

"Why?"

"Call it a hunch." He looked down at Ally. "Wanna bet?"

"You don't have a license for gambling on the premises." As she watched, the blonde sidled over and batted her lashes at the man with the wallet. "Good call."

"It was easy. And so's the blonde." He steered Ally back toward the club area where Beth and Will huddled over the reservation book at a black podium.

"Hey, boss." Beth plucked the pencil out of her thick curls and made a note in the book. "Looks like we're turning most tables over twice tonight. Big dinner crowd for midweek."

"Good thing I brought you some help. Beth Dickerman, Allison Fletcher. She needs training."

"Ah, another victim." Beth shot out a hand. "Nice to meet you, Allison."

"Ally. Thanks."

"You show her the ropes, Beth. She'll bus tables until you figure she can wait them."

"We'll whip her into shape. Come on with me, Ally. I'll get you set up. Got any experience in food services?" she asked as she plowed through the crowd.

"Well, I eat."

Beth let out a bright cackle of a laugh. "Welcome to my world. Frannie, this is Ally, new waitress in training. Frannie's captain of the bar here."

"Nice to meetcha," Frannie called out, flipped a smile, dumping ice into a blender with one hand and shooting soda into a glass with the other.

"And that gorgeous specimen down the other end of the bar's Pete."

The big shouldered black man sent them a wink as he measured Kahlúa into a short glass.

"Now, no flirting with Pete, 'cause he's my man and nobody else's. That right, Pete?"

"You're the one for me, sugar lips."

With another laugh, Beth unlocked a door marked Employees Only. "Pete's got a beautiful wife and a baby on the way. We just tease. Now, if you need to get in here for any reason—hey, Jan."

"Hey, Beth." The curvy brunette on the other side of the door had her waist-length hair pulled back with combs from a lovely, heart-shaped face. Ally gauged her as mid-twenties, and a fashion plate. She'd gone for a skirt the approximate size of a table napkin, and a clingy shirt with small silver buttons. Silver winked at her wrists, ears and throat as she freshened her lipstick in a mirror.

"This is Ally. Fresh meat."

"Oh, yeah." The smile when she turned was friendly enough, but there was a measuring gleam in her eye. One female sizing up another, and the competition.

"Jan works the bar area," Beth explained. "But she'll pinch hit in the club if we need her." There was a wild burst of laughter from outside the door. "Tom-toms are beating."

"I'd better get out there." Jan tied a short, many-pocketed black apron at her waist. "Good luck, Ally, and welcome aboard."

"Thanks. Everybody's so friendly," Ally said to Beth when Jan strolled out.

"You get to be kind of a family when you work for Jonah. He's a good boss." She pulled an apron out of a closet. "You work your butt off for him, but he lets you know he notices and that he appreciates. Makes a difference. Here, you'll need this."

"Have you worked for him long?"

"About six years, give or take. I handled tables at Fast Break, his sports bar. And when he opened the club here, he asked me if I wanted to switch. It's a classy place, and closer to home. You can leave your purse in here." She opened a narrow locker. "You reset the combination by spinning around zero twice."

"Great." Ally set her purse inside, palming her beeper out of it and hooking it on the waist of her skirt under the apron. She shut the locker, set the combination. "I guess that's it."

"You want to freshen up or anything?"

"No, I'm fine. A little nervous, I guess."

"Don't worry. In a few hours your feet are going to ache so bad you won't think about nerves."

Beth was right. About the feet anyway. By ten, Ally felt she'd hiked twenty miles in the wrong shoes, and lifted approximately three tons of trays loaded with dirty dishes.

She could have marched the trail from table to kitchen in her sleep.

The live band was considerably louder than the recorded music that had played until just after nine. The crowd shouted above it, crammed the dance floor and jammed together at the tables.

Ally piled dishes on trays and watched the crowd. There were plenty of designer clothes, expensive watches, cell phones and leather briefcases. She saw a woman flash a lightning bolt diamond engagement ring for three friends.

Plenty of money here, she noted. And plenty of marks.

Hefting the loaded tray, she headed off for the kitchen, detouring toward an attractive couple when the man signaled her.

"Sweetheart, can you get me and my lovely companion a refill here?"

She leaned closer, pasted on her sweetest smile and made a quiet and crude suggestion.

The man only grinned. "Cops have such filthy mouths."

"Next case I'm going to be the one sitting on my butt, Hickman, while you work out," Ally replied. "See anything I should know about?"

"Nothing's popped yet." He grabbed the hand of the woman sitting next to him. "But Carson and I are in love."

Lydia Carson gave Hickman's hand a vicious squeeze. "In your dreams."

"Just keep your eyes open." She aimed a stare at Hickman's glass. "And that'd better be club soda."

"She's so strict," she heard Hickman murmur as she walked away.

"Beth, table...ah, sixteen's looking for a refill."

"I'm on it. You're doing good, Ally. Go dump those and take your break."

"You don't have to tell me twice."

The kitchen was a madhouse, full of noise and shouted orders and heat. Gratefully Ally set down her tray, then lifted her eyebrows as she spotted Frannie slipping out the back door.

Ally stalled for ten seconds, then followed.

Frannie was already leaning against the outside wall and taking her first drag from a cigarette. She blew out smoke with a long, relieved sigh. "Break time?"

"Yeah. I thought I'd grab some air."

"Zoo in there tonight. Blackhawk's really packs them in." She pulled the cigarettes out of her pocket, offered them.

"No, thanks. I don't smoke."

"Good for you. I can't kick it. No smoking in the employee lounge. Jonah gives me a break and lets me use his office if the weather's lousy. So how's your first night?"

"My feet are killing me."

"Occupational hazard. First paycheck you buy yourself one of those bubbling footbath things. Put some eucalyptus in it and go straight to heaven."

"I'll do that."

An attractive woman, Ally noted, though the lines around

Frannie's eyes made her look older than twenty-eight. She kept her dark red hair cut short and the makeup subtle. Her nails were short and unpainted, her hands ringless. Like the rest of the staff, she wore black, and finished off the simple shirt and slacks with sturdy yet trendy black shoes.

The only touch of flash was the silver hoops that swung at her ears.

"How'd you get into tending bar?" Ally asked her.

Frannie hesitated, then puffed on her cigarette. "I guess I hung out at bars a lot, and when there came a time I was looking for what you could call gainful employment, Jonah asked me if I wanted a job. Trained me over at Fast Break. It's good work. You need a decent memory and people skills. You interested?"

"I'd better see if I make it through one shift busing before I start raising my sights."

"You look like you can handle whatever comes along."

Ally smiled into Frannie's considering eyes. "You think so?"

"Observation's one of those people skills. And on short observation you don't strike me as the type who expects to make waiting tables her life's work."

"Gotta start somewhere. And paying the rent's a priority."

"Don't I know it." Though Frannie had already calculated that Ally's shoes equaled half a month's rent on her own apartment. "Well, if you want to climb the ladder, Jonah's the one to give you a boost. You'd have figured that."

Frannie dropped the cigarette, crushed out the butt. "Gotta get back. Pete pouts if I go over break."

The ex-hooker, Ally decided, was proprietary when it came to Jonah. They were probably lovers, she thought as she went back inside. When you factored in his defensive attitude toward her, it added up.

As lover, as trusted employee, Frannie was in a prime position to cull out marks, to pass the information along. The bar faced the entrance. Whoever went in or out passed by her station.

People handed her credit cards, and the name and account number led to addresses.

It would pay to look at her most closely.

Jonah was doing his own looking. From his office, from the floor. He knew enough about cons, short and long, to calculate who the targets might be. He pegged three possibilities that would have topped his list if he'd been running the game. And since he'd also spotted the cops at table sixteen, he wandered over.

"Everything all right tonight?"

The woman beamed up at him, swept back her short swing of streaky blond hair with one hand. "Everything's terrific. It's the first night on the town Bob and I have managed in weeks with work keeping both of us so busy."

"I'm glad you picked my place." Jonah laid a friendly hand on Bob's shoulder, leaned down. "Next time ditch the cop shoes. Dead giveaway. Enjoy your evening."

He thought he heard the woman snort out a laugh as he walked away.

He headed for the table Ally was busy cleaning. "How you holding up?"

"I haven't broken any of your dishes yet."

"And now you want a raise?"

"I'm going to stick with my day job, thanks all the same. I'd rather clean up the streets than tables." Absently she pressed a hand to the ache in the small of her back.

"We go back to bar food at eleven, so the busing slows down."

"Hallelujah."

He laid a hand on her arm before she could lift the tray. "You corner Frannie outside?"

"Excuse me?"

"She went out, you went out, she came in, you came in."

"I'm doing my job. However, I resisted shining a light in her eyes and smacking her in the face with my rubber hose. Now let me get on with it."

She hefted the tray, shoved past him.

"By the way, Allison."

She stopped, a snarl working up her throat. "What?"

"The power ball trounced your guts and efficiency. Eight to two."

"One game doesn't a season make." She jerked up her chin and strode off. On her way by the dance floor, a man reached out and gave her butt a hopeful pat. As Jonah watched she stopped dead in her tracks, turned slowly and gave him one, long icy look. The man stepped back, lifted his hands in apology and quickly melted into the dancers.

"Handles herself," Beth said from beside him.

"Yeah. Yeah, she does."

"Pulls her weight, too, and doesn't whine about it. I like your girlfriend, Jonah."

He was too surprised to comment and only stared when Beth hustled away.

He let out a short laugh and shook his head. Oh, that one had slipped by him. Right on by him.

Last call was enough to make Ally all but weep with gratitude. She'd been on her feet since eight that morning. Her fondest wish was to go home, fall into bed and sleep for the precious five hours she had before starting it all over again.

"Go on home," Beth ordered. "We'll go over closing tomorrow night. You did fine."

"Thanks. I mean it."

"Will, let Ally into the lounge, will you?"

"No problem. Nice crowd tonight. Nothing I like better than a crowded club. Want a drink before you head out?"

"Not unless I can stick my feet in it."

He chuckled, patted her back. "Frannie, pour me one, will you?"

"Already on it."

"I like a brandy at the end of a shift. One glass of the good stuff. You change your mind," he said as he unlocked the door. "Just pull up a stool. The man, he doesn't charge employees for an end of shift drink."

He went off, whistling through his teeth.

Ally shoved her apron into her locker, pulled out her bag and jacket. She was just putting the jacket on when Jan breezed in. "Heading out? You look beat. Me, I'm just hitting stride this time of night."

"My stride hit me about an hour ago." Ally paused at the door. "Don't your feet hurt?"

"Nah. I got arches of steel. And most guys tip better if you walk around on skinny heels." She bent to run a hand up her leg. "I believe in using what works."

"Yeah. Well, good night."

Ally stepped out of the lounge, shutting the door behind her, and bumped solidly into Jonah.

"Where'd you park?" he asked her.

"I didn't. I walked." Ran, she remembered, but it came to the same thing.

"I'll drive you home."

"I can walk. It's not far."

"It's two in the morning. A block is too far."

"For heaven's sake, Blackhawk, I'm a cop."

"So naturally, bullets bounce off you."

Before she could argue, he caught her chin in his hand. The gesture, the firm grip of his fingers, shocked her to silence. "You're not a cop at the moment," he murmured. "You're a female employee and the daughter of a friend. I'll drive you home."

"Fine. Dandy. My feet hurt anyway."

She started to shove his hand away, but he beat her to it and shifted his grip to her arm.

"Night, boss," Beth called out, grinning at them as they passed. "Get that girl off her feet."

"That's my plan. Later, Will. Night, Frannie."

Suspicion was buzzing in Ally's brain as Will lifted his brandy snifter and Frannie watched her with quiet and serious eyes.

"What was that?" Ally demanded when they stepped out in the cool air. "What exactly was that?"

"That was me saying good-night to friends and employees. I'm parked across the street."

"Excuse me, my feet have gone numb, not my brain. You gave those people the very distinct impression that we have a thing here."

"That's right. I didn't consider it, either, until Beth made some remark earlier. It simplifies things."

She stopped beside a sleek black Jaguar. "Just how do you figure that having people think there's a personal thing between us simplifies anything?"

"And you call yourself a detective." He unlocked the passenger door, opened it. "You're a beautiful blonde with legs up to your ears. I hire you, out of the blue, when you have basically no experience. The first assumption from people who know me is I'm attracted to you. The second would be you're attracted to me. Add all those together and you end up with romance. Or at least sex. Are you going to get in?"

"You haven't explained how those deductions equal simple."

"If people think we're involved they won't think twice if I give you a little leeway, if you come up to my office. They'll be friendlier."

Ally said nothing while she let it run through her head. Then she nodded. "All right. There's an advantage to it."

Going with impulse he shifted, boxed her in between his body and the car door. There was a light breeze, just enough to stir her scent. There was a three-quarter moon, bright enough to sprinkle silver into her eyes. The moment, he decided, seemed to call for it.

"Could be more than one advantage to it."

The thrill that sprinted straight up her spine irritated her. "Oh, you're going to want to step back, Blackhawk."

"Beth's at the window of the bar, and she's got a romantic heart despite everything that's happened to her. She's hoping for a moment here. A long, slow kiss, the kind that slides over melting sighs and heats the blood."

His hands came to her hips as he spoke, rode up to just under her breasts. Her mouth went dry and the ache in her belly was a wide stretch of longing.

"You're going to have to disappoint her."

Jonah skimmed his gaze down to her mouth. "She's not the only one." But he released her, stepped back. "Don't worry, Detective. I never hit on cops, or daughters of friends."

"Then I guess I've got a double shield against your wild and irresistible charms."

"Good thing for both of us, because I sure as hell like the look of you. You getting in?"

"Yeah, I'm getting in." She got into the car and waited until the door shut before letting out the long, painful breath she'd been holding.

Wherever that spurt of lust inside her had come from, it would just have to go away again. Cool off, she ordered herself, but her heart was bumping madly against her rib cage. Cool off and focus on the job.

Jonah slid in beside her, annoyed that his pulse wasn't quite steady. "Where to?" When she rattled off the address, he shoved the key into the ignition and aimed one hot look at her. "That's a damn mile. Why the hell did you walk?"

"Because it was rush hour. It's quicker. And it's ten blocks."

"That's just stupid."

She had a response for that. The venom of it scalded her tongue as she rounded on him. She didn't even recognize the vibration of her beeper for several seconds, mistaking it for the vibration of rage.

She yanked it from her skirt, checked the number. "Damn it. Damn it." From her purse she pulled out her cell phone and quickly dialed. "Detective Fletcher. Yeah, I got it. I'm on my way."

Calming herself, she shoved the phone back into her purse. "Since you're determined to play cabdriver, let's get going. I've got another B and E."

"Give me the address."

"Just take me home so I can get my car."

"Give me the address, Allison. Why waste time?"

# Chapter 3

Jonah dropped her off in front of an attractive, ranch-style home in an upscale development convenient to the freeway. In reasonable traffic, the commute to downtown would take under twenty minutes.

The Chamberses, Ally discovered, were an attractive, upscale couple, both lawyers in their early thirties, child-less professionals, who spent their comfortable income on the good life.

Wine, wardrobe, jewelry, art and music.

"They got my diamond earrings, and my Cartier tank watch." Maggie Chambers rubbed her eyes as she sat in what was left of her sprawling great room. "We haven't gone through everything, but there were Dalí and Picasso lithographs on that wall there. And in that niche there was an Erté sculpture we bought at an auction two years ago. Joe collected cuff links. I don't know how many pairs he had offhand, but he had diamond ones, and ruby for his birthstone and several antique pairs."

"They're insured." Her husband reached out to take her hand, squeeze it.

"It doesn't matter. It's not the same. Those thugs were in our house. In our house, Joe, and they've taken our things. Damn it, they stole my car. My brand-new BMW, and it didn't have five thousand miles on it. I loved that stupid car."

"Mrs. Chambers, I know it's hard."

Maggie Chambers whipped her gaze toward Ally. "Have you ever been robbed, Detective?"

"No." Ally set her notebook on her knee a moment. "But I've worked plenty of burglaries, robberies, muggings."

"It's not the same."

"Maggie, she's just doing her job."

"I know. I'm sorry. I know." She covered her face with her hands, drew air in, slowly let it out. "I've got the shakes, that's all. I don't want to stay here tonight."

"We don't have to. We'll go to a hotel. How much more do you need, Detective…was it Fletcher?"

"Yes. Just a few more questions. You said both of you were out all evening."

"Yeah, Maggie won a case today, and we decided to go out and celebrate. She's been piled under for more than a month. We went to the Starfire club with some friends." As he spoke, he rubbed soothing circles over his wife's back. "Drinks, dinner, a little dancing. Like we told the other policeman, we didn't get home until nearly two."

"Does anyone other than the two of you have a key?"

"Our housekeeper."

"Would she also have the security code?"

"Sure." Joe started to speak, then blinked, stuttered. "Oh, listen, Carol's been cleaning for us for nearly ten years. She's practically family."

"It's just procedure, Mr. Chambers. Could I have her full name and address, for the record?"

She took them through the entire evening, looking for a connection, a contact, anything that struck a chord. But for the Chamberses it had been nothing more than an entertaining evening out, until they'd walked back in their own front door.

When Ally left them, she had a partial list of stolen items, with a promise for the complete as well as the insurance information. The crime scene unit was still working, but she'd gone over the scene herself. She didn't expect the miracle of fingerprints or dropped clues.

The moon had set, but the stars were out and brilliant. The wind had picked up to dance down the street in little whirls and gusts. The neighborhood was hushed, the houses dark. Those who lived here had long since been tucked in for the night.

She doubted the canvass was going to turn up any handy eyewitnesses.

Jonah was leaning against the hood of his car, drinking what appeared to be a cup of takeout coffee with one of the uniforms.

When she approached the car, Jonah held out the half cup he had left. "Thanks."

"You can have a whole one. There's a twenty-four-hour place a few blocks down."

"This is fine," she replied, taking the cup. "Officer, you and your partner were first on scene?"

"Yes, ma'am."

"I'll need your report on my desk by eleven hundred."

With a brisk nod, the officer headed for his car. Ally sipped the coffee, then turned to Jonah and handed him the cup. "You didn't have to wait. I can get a ride home in one of the radio cars."

"I have a stake here." He opened the car door. "Were they at my place?"

"Now why would you ask me when we both know you just got finished pumping that uniform?"

"Hey, I bought the coffee." He handed it back to her, then walked around to the driver's side. "So, the perps picked their marks at the Starfire tonight. Have they hit there before?"

"No, you're still the only repeater. They'll come back to you." She shut her exhausted eyes. "It's just a matter of time."

"Well, that makes me feel lots better. What kind of take did they get?"

"BMW roadster out of the garage, some art, high-end electronics and heavy on the jewelry."

"Don't these people have safes?"

"These did, a small one in the walk-in closet of the master suite. Of course they had the combination for it written down on a piece of paper in the desk."

"That'll discourage the criminal element."

"They had a security system, which they swear they engaged when they left— though the wife didn't look quite so sure of that. Anyway, the point is they felt secure. Nice house, nice neighborhood. People get sloppy." Eyes still closed, she circled her head, cracking out the tension. "They're both lawyers."

"Well, hell then, what do we care?"

She was tired enough to laugh. "Watch it, ace. My aunt is district attorney in Urbana."

"You going to drink that coffee or just hold on to it?"

"What? Oh, no, here, I don't want anymore. It'll just keep me awake."

He doubted a tanker truck of coffee could keep her awake much longer. Her voice was going thick, adding, he thought, to the in-the-gut sexiness of it. Fatigue had her unguarded enough to tilt her face toward him as she tried to find a comfortable resting spot. Her eyes were shut, her lips soft and just parted.

He had a feeling he knew exactly how they'd taste. Warm and soft. Ripe with sleep.

At a stop sign, he put the car in neutral, engaged the emergency brake, then leaned over her to press the mechanism that lowered her seat back.

She jerked up, rapped her head smartly against his. Even as he swore she slapped a hand on his chest.

"Back off!"

"Relax, Fletcher, I'm not jumping you. I like my women awake when we make love. I'm putting your seat back. If you're going to sleep, you might as well get as close to horizontal as we can manage."

"I'm all right." Mortified, but all right, she thought. "I wasn't sleeping."

He put a hand on her forehead, shoved her back. "Shut up, Allison."

"I wasn't sleeping. I was thinking."

"Think tomorrow. You're brain-dead." He glanced over at her as he started to drive again. "How many hours have you been on duty?"

"That's math, I can't do math if I'm brain-dead." She gave up and yawned. "I'm on eight to fours."

"It's closing in on 4:00 a.m., that gives you twenty hours. Why don't you put in for night shift until this is over, or do you have a death wish?"

"It's not my only case." She'd already decided to talk

to her lieutenant. She couldn't give her best to the job on a couple of hours sleep a night. But it wasn't any of Jonah's business how she ran her life.

"I guess Denver's not safe without you on the job."

She might have been tired, but she still had a pretty good ear for sarcasm. "That's right, Blackhawk. Without my watchful eye, the city's in chaos. It's a heavy burden but, well, somebody's got to shoulder it. Just pull up at the corner. My building's only a half a block down."

He ignored her, drove through the light and pulled smoothly to the curb in front of her building. "Okay. Thanks." She reached down to retrieve her bag from the floor.

He was already out of the car, skirting around the hood. Maybe it was fatigue that had her reacting so slowly, as if she were moving through syrup instead of air. But he had the outside handle of the door seconds before she had the inside handle.

For about five seconds they battled for control. Then with a halfhearted snarl, Ally let him open the door for her. "What are you, from another century? Do I look incapable of operating the complex mechanism of a car door?"

"No. You look tired."

"Well, I am. So good night."

"I'll walk you up."

"Get a grip."

But he fell into step beside her, and damn him, reached the door one pace ahead of her. Saying nothing, merely watching her with those impossibly clear green eyes, he held it open for her.

"I'll have to curtsy in a minute," she muttered under her breath.

He grinned at her back, then crossed to the lobby elevators with her, sliding his hands into his pockets.

"I can make it from here."

"I'll take you to your door."

"It's not a damn date."

"Lack of sleep's making you irritable." He stepped into the elevator with her. "No, wait, you're always irritable. My mistake."

"I don't like you." She jabbed the button for the fourth floor.

"Thank God you cleared that up. I was afraid you were falling for me."

The movement of the elevator tipped her already shaky balance. She swayed, and he closed a hand over her arm.

"Cut it out."

"No."

She jerked at her arm. He tightened his grip. "Don't embarrass yourself, Fletcher. You're asleep on your feet. What's your apartment number?"

He was right, and it was stupid to pretend otherwise, and foolish to take it out on him. "Four-oh-nine. Let me go, will you? I'll be all right after a couple hours' sleep."

"I don't doubt it." But he held on to her when the elevator opened.

"You're not coming in."

"Well, there go my plans to toss you over my shoulder, dump you in bed and have my wicked way with you. Next time. Key?"

"What?"

Her burnt-honey eyes were blurry, the delicate skin beneath them bruised. The wave of tenderness that swept inside him was a complete surprise, and far from comfortable. "Honey, give me your key."

"Oh. I'm punchy." She dug it out of her jacket pocket. "And don't call me honey."

"I meant Detective Honey." He heard her snicker as he unlocked her door. He pulled the key back out of the lock, took her hand, dropped it in and closed her fingers around it. "Good night."

"Yeah. Thanks for the lift." Because it seemed the thing to do, she closed the door in his face.

Hell of a face, she thought as she stumbled toward the bedroom. Face that dangerous ought to be registered as a weapon. A woman who trusted a face like that got exactly what she deserved.

And probably enjoyed every minute of it.

Ally stripped off her jacket, whimpering a little as she pried off her shoes. She set her alarm, then fell facedown and fully clothed on the bed. And was instantly asleep.

Four and a half hours later, she was finishing up her morning meeting in the conference room at her station house. And her fourth cup of coffee.

"We'll canvass the neighborhood," Ally said. "We could get lucky. In that kind of development, people tend to look out for each other. Some sort of vehicle was necessary to get the perpetrators to the Chamberses', and to transport at least some of the stolen goods. The sports car they boosted wouldn't hold that much. We have a full description of the car, and the APB's out on it."

Lieutenant Kiniki nodded. He was a toughly built man in his mid-forties who enjoyed the way command sat on his shoulders. "The Starfire's a new pool for them. I want two men over there to check out the setup. Soft clothes," he added, indicating he wanted his detectives to dress casually rather than in suit jackets. "Let's keep it low-key."

"Hickman and Carson are canvassing pawn shops, pressuring known fences." Ally glanced toward her two associates.

"Nothing there." Hickman lifted his hands. "Lydia and I've got a couple of good sources, and we've put the heat on. Nobody knows anything. My take is that whoever's running this has an outside channel."

"Keep the heat on," Kiniki ordered. "What about the insurance angle?"

"It doesn't play out," Ally told him. "We've got nine hits and five different insurance companies. We're still trying to find a connection, but so far that's a dead end. We've got no common links between the victims that carry through," she went on. "Out of the nine, we've got four different banks, three different brokerage houses, nine different doctors, nine different places of employment."

She rubbed the ache at the back of her neck and went down her list. "Two of the women go to the same hair salon—different operators, different schedules. They use different cleaning services, different mechanics. Now two of the targets used the same caterer in the last six months, and we're running that. But it doesn't look like a hook. The only common link so far is a night on the town."

"Give me the rundown on Blackhawk's," Kiniki ordered.

"The place does a hell of a business," Ally began. "Pulls in a big crowd, and the crowd varies, though it's heavy on the upwardly mobile. Couples, singles on the prowl, groups. He's got good security."

Absently Ally rubbed her eyes, then remembered herself and lowered them. "He's got cameras, and I'm working on getting the security tapes. Sloan is the floater. He works the public areas, has access to everything. There are six tables in the bar area and thirty-two in the club. People push them together if they get friendly. There's a coat check but not everybody bothers with it. I couldn't count the number of handbags left on tables when the dancing started."

"People mill," Lydia added. "Especially the younger customers. It's a regular meeting ground for them, and they tend to table hop. Lots of sex vibes." She gave Hickman a bland look when he chortled. "It's a sexy place. People get careless when their blood's hot. There's a ripple when Blackhawk comes through."

"A ripple?" Hickman repeated. "Is that a technical term?"

"The women watch him. They don't watch their bags."

"That's accurate." Ally walked over to the board where the list of victims and stolen items were posted. "Every hit involved a woman. There are no single men on the list. The female's the prime target. What's a woman carry in her purse?"

"That," Hickman said, "is one of life's most complex mysteries."

"Her keys," Ally continued. "Her wallet—with ID, credit cards. Pictures of her kids if she has them. None of the victims had children at home. If we break this down to its basic element, we're looking first for a pickpocket. Somebody with good fingers who can get what he needs out of a bag, then put it back before the victim knows she's been hit. Do an imprint of the key, make a copy."

"If you pick the pocket, why put the stuff back?" Hickman asked.

"Keep the victim unaware, buy more time. A woman goes into the bathroom, she takes her purse. If she reaches in for her lipstick and doesn't find her wallet, she's going to send up an alarm. This way, the house is hit and the perpetrators are out before the victims get home. Whatever time they get home."

She turned back to the board. "Twelve-thirty, one-fifteen, twelve-ten, and so on. Somebody at the club alerts the burglars when the victims call for their check. Somebody's on the inside, or a regular and repeat customer. At Blackhawk's the average time between calling for the check and leaving the club was about twenty minutes."

"We have two other clubs involved now, besides Blackhawk's." Kiniki's brow furrowed. "We'll need stakeouts on all of them."

"Yes, sir. But Blackhawk's is where they'll come back. That's the money tree."

"Find a way to cut down the tree, Fletcher." He got to his feet. "And take some personal time today. Get some sleep."

She took him up on it and curled up on the small sofa in the coffee room, leaving word that she was to be notified when the reports she was waiting for came in.

She got ninety minutes and felt very close to human when Hickman shook her shoulder.

"Did you steal my cheese bagel?"

"What?" She pushed herself up, shoved back her hair.

"You like cheese bagels. I had one. It's gone. I'm detecting."

Shaking off sleep, she dug her clip out of her pocket and pulled back her hair. "It didn't have your name on it."

"Did, too."

She circled her shoulders. "Is your name Pineview Bakery? Besides I only ate half of it." She checked her watch. "The first-on-scene reports in yet?"

"Yeah, and so's your warrant."

"Great." She swung to her feet, adjusted her weapon harness. "I'll be in the field."

"I want a cheese bagel back in that box by end of shift."

"I only ate half of it," she called out and stopped by her desk for the paperwork. Scanning it, ignoring the backwash of noise from the detectives' bull pen, she hitched her harness into a more comfortable position, then shrugged into her jacket.

She glanced up when the noise became a murmur, and watched her father walk in. Like Blackhawk, she thought, this was a man who created ripples.

She knew a few of her fellow officers harbored some resentment over her rapid rise to detective. There were mutters now and then, just loud enough for her to hear, about favoritism and oiling the ranks.

She'd earned her badge and knew it. Ally was too proud of her father and too secure in her own abilities to let mutters worry her.

"Commissioner."

"Detective. Got a minute?"

"A couple." She pulled her shoulder bag from her bottom desk drawer. "Can we walk and talk? I'm on my way out. Got a warrant to serve on Jonah Blackhawk."

"Ah." He stepped back to let her pass, and his eyes scanned the room. If there were any mutters, they would wait until he was well out of range.

"Stairs okay with you?" she asked. "I didn't have time to work out this morning."

"I think I can keep up with you. What's the warrant?"

"To confiscate and view Blackhawk's security tapes. He got pissy about it yesterday. I seem to put his back up."

Boyd pushed open the door to the stairwell, then angled his head to study his daughter's back as she passed through. "I seem to detect a few ruffled feathers on yours."

"Okay, good eye. We put each other's backs up."

"I figured you would. You both like to do things your own way."

"Why would I want to do them someone else's way?"

"Exactly." Boyd skimmed a hand down the long, sleek tail of her hair. His little girl had always had a mind of her own, and a very hard head around it. "Speaking of ruffled feathers, I have a meeting with the mayor in an hour."

"Better you than me," Ally said cheerfully as she jogged down the stairs.

"What can you tell me about last night's break-in?"

"Same M.O. They hit a real treasure trove with the Chamberses. Mrs. Chambers got me the loss list this morning. The woman's efficient. They were fully insured—value of stolen items comes to a solid two hundred and twenty-five thousand."

"That's the biggest haul so far."

"Yeah. I'm hoping it makes them cocky. They took some art this time. I don't know if it was dumb luck or somebody knew what they had when they saw it. They have to have somewhere to keep the goods before they turn them. Big enough for a car."

"A decent chop shop could have a car dismantled and turned in a couple hours."

"Yeah, but…" She started to push open the next door herself, but her father beat her to it. It reminded her oddly, and not entirely happily, of Jonah.

"But?" he prompted as they crossed the lobby.

"I don't think that's the route. Somebody likes nice things. Somebody has really good taste. At the second hit, they took a collection of rare books, but they left an antique clock. It was appraised at five thousand, but it was dead ugly. It's like they said, please, don't insult us. There've been other cars at other scenes, but they've only taken two. Cool cars."

"Burglars with standards."

"Yeah, I think so." When they stepped outside she blinked against the brilliant sunlight until she pulled out her shaded glasses. "And a kind of arrogance. Arrogance is a mistake. That's going to turn it my way."

"I hope so. The pressure's on, Ally." He walked her to her car, opened the door for her in a way that made her frown and think of Jonah again. "We're getting press, the kind that makes the mayor uncomfortable."

"In my best judgment they won't wait more than a week. They're rolling now. They'll come back to Blackhawk's."

"They got a bigger slice of pie from the new place."

"Blackhawk's is reliable. Once I spend a few nights under there, I'll start recognizing faces. I'll pin him, Dad."

"I believe it." He bent down to kiss her cheek. "And I'll handle the mayor."

"I believe it." She slid behind the wheel. "Question."

"Ask it."

"You've known Jonah Blackhawk for what, like fifteen years?"

"Seventeen."

"How come you never had him over to the house? You know, for dinner or football afternoons or one of your world-famous cookouts?"

"He wouldn't come. Always acknowledged the invitation, thanked me and said he was busy."

"Seventeen years." Idly she tapped her fingers on the steering wheel. "That's a lot of busy. Well, some people don't like socializing with cops."

"Some people," Boyd told her, "draw lines and never believe they have the right to cross them. He'd meet me at the station house." The memory made Boyd grin. "He didn't like it, but he'd do it. He'd meet me for coffee or a beer, at the gym. But he'd never come to my home. He'd consider that crossing the line. I've never convinced him otherwise."

"Funny, he strikes me as being a man who considers himself good enough for anything, or anyone."

"There are a lot of twists and pockets in Jonah. And very little about him that's simple."

# Chapter 4

She called ahead, and had to admit she was surprised when Jonah answered the phone in his office.

"It's Fletcher. I didn't think you were much on daylight hours."

"I'm not. Some days are exceptions. What can I do for you, Detective?"

"You can come downstairs and let me in. I'll be there in ten minutes."

"I'm not going anywhere." He waited a beat. "So, what are you wearing?"

She hated herself for laughing, and hoped she managed to smother most of it. "My badge," she told him and flicked the phone off.

Jonah hung up, sat back and entertained himself by imagining Allison Fletcher wearing her badge, and nothing else. The image came through, entirely too clear, entirely too appealing, and had him shoving back from the desk.

He had no business imagining Boyd's daughter naked. No business, he reminded himself, fantasizing about Boyd's daughter in any way whatsoever. Or wondering how her mouth would taste. Or what scent he'd find on the flesh just under the line of that very stubborn jaw.

God, he wanted to sink his teeth there, right there. Just once.

Forbidden fruit, he told himself and paced since there was no one to see. She was forbidden fruit and therefore all the more alluring. She wasn't even his type. Maybe he liked leggy blondes. Maybe he liked leggy blondes with brains and a strong backbone. But he preferred friendlier women.

Friendlier, unarmed women, he thought, amusing himself.

He hadn't been able to get her out of his head, and the clearest most compelling picture had been the yielding and temporary, he was certain, fragility of her when she'd fallen asleep in his car.

Well, he'd always been a sucker for the needy, he reminded himself, as he pulled up the blinds on his office window. Which should solve his problem over Allison. Despite that short interlude of vulnerability early that morning, needy was one thing the gorgeous detective wasn't.

She had a use for him, again temporary. And when the job was done, they'd both go back to their separate corners in their separate worlds. And that would be the end of that.

He saw her pull up in front of the club. At least she'd had the sense to drive, he noted, and wasn't hiking all over Denver today.

He took his time going down to let her in.

"Good morning, Detective." He looked around her, studied the flashy lines of the classic red-and-white Stingray.

"Nice car. Is that the new police issue? Oh wait, what was I thinking? Your daddy's loaded."

"If you think you can razz me over a car, you're going to be disappointed. Nobody razzes like a precinct full of cops."

"I'll practice. Nice threads," he commented and rubbed the lapel of her subtly patterned brown jacket between his thumb and forefinger. "Very nice."

"So we both like Italian designers. We can compare wardrobes later."

Because he knew it would irritate her, because he enjoyed the way the gold highlighted her eyes when he irritated her, he shifted, blocking her before she could step inside. "Let me see the badge."

"Come off it, Blackhawk."

"No. Let's see it."

Eyes narrowed behind her sunglasses, she pulled her badge out of her pocket, pushed it close to his face. "See it?"

"Yes. Badge number 31628. I'll buy myself a lottery ticket and play your numbers."

"Here's something else you might want to look at." She took out the warrant, held it up.

"Fast work." He'd expected no less. "Come on up. I've been reviewing the tapes. You look rested," he said as they walked to his elevator.

"I am."

"Any progress?"

"The investigation is ongoing."

"Hmm, policy line." He gestured her into the elevator. "We seem to be spending a lot of time in these. Close quarters."

"You could do your heart a favor and take the stairs."

"My heart's never caused me any problems. How about yours?"

"Whole and healthy, thanks." She walked out when the doors opened. "Wow, you actually let the sunlight in here. I'm shocked. Let's have the tapes. I'll give a receipt."

She wasn't wearing perfume today, he noted. Just soap and skin. Odd how erotic that simplicity could be. "In a hurry?"

"Clock's ticking."

He strolled into an adjoining room. After a small internal battle, Ally walked over to the doorway. It was a small bedroom. Small, she noted, because it was two-thirds bed. A black pool of bed, unframed and on a raised platform.

Curious, she looked up and was mildly disappointed there wasn't a mirror on the ceiling.

"It would be too obvious," Jonah told her when her gaze skimmed back to his.

"The bed's already a statement. An obvious one."

"But not vain."

"Hmm." To amuse herself she poked around the room. On the walls were a number of framed black-and-white photographs. Arty, interesting, and all stark or shadowy night scenes.

She recognized a couple of the artists, pursed her lips. So the man had a good eye for art, and decent taste, she admitted.

"I've got this print." She tapped a finger against a study of an ancient man in a ragged straw hat sleeping on a cracked concrete stoop, a paper bag still clutched in his hand. "Shade Colby. I like his work."

"So do I. And his wife's. Bryan Mitchell. That's one of hers beside it. The old couple holding hands on the bench at the bus stop."

"Quite a contrast, despair and hope."

"Life's full of both."

"Apparently."

She wandered. There was a closet, closed, an exit door, securely locked, and what she assumed was a bath or washroom just beyond. She thought of the sex vibes Lydia Carson had referred to. Oh, yeah, this room had plenty of them. It all but smoked with them.

"So, what's through there?" She jerked a thumb at another door. Instead of answering he gestured, inviting her to see for herself.

She opened the door, let out a long sigh of pleasure. "Now we're talking." The fully equipped gym was a great deal more appealing to her than a lake-size bed.

He watched as she trailed her fingers over machines, picked up free weights, doing a few absent curls as she roamed. Very telling, he thought, that she'd given the bed a sneer, and was all but dewy-eyed over his Nautilus.

"You got a sauna?" Envy curled inside her as she pressed her nose to a little window of a wooden door and peered into the room beyond.

"Want to try it out?"

She turned her head enough to slide her gaze in his direction. And the sneer was back. "This is pretty elaborate when you could be at a full-service health club in two minutes."

"Health clubs have members—that's the first strike. They also have regular hours. Strike two. And I don't like using someone else's equipment."

"Strike three. You're a very particular man, Blackhawk."

"That's right." He took a bottle of water out of a clear-fronted bar fridge. "Want one?"

"No." She replaced the free weight, moved back to the

doorway. "Well, thanks for the tour. Now, the tapes, Blackhawk."

"Yeah, clock's ticking." He unscrewed the top of the bottle, took a casual sip. "You know what I like about night work, Detective Fletcher?"

She looked deliberately toward the bed, then back at him. "Oh, I think I can figure it out."

"Well, there's that, but what I really like about night work is that it's always whatever time you want it to be. My favorite's the three o'clock hour. For most people, that's the hard time. If they don't sleep through it, that's the time the mind wakes up and starts worrying about what they did or didn't do that day, or what they'll do or not do the next. And the next, and right up until life's over."

"And you don't worry about yesterday or tomorrow."

"You miss a lot of the now doing that. There's only so much now to go around."

"I don't have a lot of the now to stand around philosophizing with you."

"Take a minute." He crossed to her, leaning on one jamb as she leaned on the other. "A lot of people who come into my place are night people—or those who want to remember when they were. Most have jobs now, the kind of jobs that pay well and make them responsible citizens."

She took the water bottle from his hand, drank. "Your job pays well."

He grinned. That quick jab was just one of the things that attracted him to her. "You saying I'm not a responsible citizen? My lawyers and accountants would disagree. However, my point is that people come in here to forget about their responsibilities for a while. To forget the clock's ticking and they have to punch in at 9:00 a.m. I give them a place without clocks—at least till last call."

"And this means?" She passed the bottle back to him.

"Forget about the facts a minute. Look at the shadows. You're hunting night people."

And he was one of them, she thought. Very much one of the night people, with his black mane of hair and cool, cat's eyes. "I'm not arguing with that."

"But are you thinking like them? They've picked their prey, and when they move, they move fast. It would be less risky, give them more time to study the lay of the land, if they waited to make the hit during the day. Stake out the mark, learn their patterns—when do they leave for the office, when do they get back? These guys could probably nail it down in a couple of days."

He lifted the bottle, drank. "That would be more efficient. Why don't they play it that way?"

"Because they're arrogant."

"Yeah, but that's only the top layer. Go down."

"They like the kick, the rush."

"Exactly. They're hungry, and they like the thrill of working in the dark."

It irked almost as much as it intrigued her that his thought process so closely followed her own. "You think that hasn't occurred to me before?"

"I figure it has, but I wonder if you've factored in that people who live at night are always more dangerous than people who live during the day."

"Does that include you?"

"Damn right."

"So warned." She started to turn away, then stopped, stared down at the hand he'd shot out to grip her arm. "What's your problem, Blackhawk?"

"I haven't figured it out yet. Why didn't you send a uniform over here to pick up the tapes?"

"Because it's my case."

"No."

"No, it's not my case?"

"No, that's not the reason. I'm crowding you." He edged forward to prove it. "Why haven't you decked me?"

"I don't make a habit of punching out civilians." She angled her chin when he nudged her back against the doorjamb. "But I can make an exception."

"Your pulse is jumping."

"It tends to when I'm irritated." Aroused, she'd nearly said aroused because that was the word that came into her head. That was the sensation sliding through her body. And enough was enough.

She shifted, a smooth move that should have planted her elbow in his gut and moved him aside. But he countered, just as smoothly, and changed his grip so that his fingers wrapped tight around her wrist. Instinctively she pivoted, started to hook her foot behind his to take him down.

He adjusted his weight, used it to plaster her back against the door. She told herself it was annoyance that quickened her breathing, and not the way the lines of his body pressed against the lines of hers.

She bunched the hand at her side into a fist, calculated the wisdom of using it for one short-armed punch to the face, and decided sarcasm was a more potent weapon against him.

"Next time, ask me if I want to dance. I'm not in the mood to—" She broke off when she saw something sharp come into his eyes, something reckless that had her already rapid pulse tripping to a faster rate.

She forgot self-defense, forgot the fist she still held ready. "Damn it, Blackhawk, back off. What do you want from me?"

"The hell with it." He forgot the rules, forgot the consequences of breaking them. All he could see was her. "The hell with it, let's find out."

He let the bottle drop, and the water that remained in it spilled unnoticed on the bedroom rug. He wanted his hands on her, both his hands, and used them to hold her arms over her head as his mouth came down on hers.

He felt her body jerk against his. Protest or invitation, he didn't care. One way or the other, he was bound to be damned for this single outrageous act. So he might as well make the most of it.

He used his teeth on her, the way he'd already imagined, scraping them along the long line of her lower lip. Freeing the warmth, the softness of it to him, then absorbing it. She made some sound, something that seemed to claw up from her throat and was every bit as primitive as the need that raged through him.

The scent of her—cool soap and skin—the flavor of her, such a contrast of ripeness and heat, overwhelmed him, stirred every hunger he'd ever known.

When his hands took her, fingers sliding down, gripping her hips, he was ready to feed those hungers, to take what he craved without a second thought.

Then his hand bumped over her weapon.

He jerked back as if she'd drawn it and shot him.

What was he doing? What in God's name was he doing?

She said nothing, only stared at him with eyes that had gone blurry at the edges. Her arms remained over her head, as if his hands still pinned them there.

Her body quaked.

"That was a mistake," she managed to say.

"I know it."

"A really serious mistake."

With her eyes open, she fisted her hands in his hair and dragged his mouth back to hers.

This time it was his body that jerked, and the shock of it vibrated through her, down to the bone. He'd savaged her mouth with that first mad kiss, and she wanted him to do it again. He would damn well do it again until her system stopped screaming.

She couldn't breathe without breathing him, and every desperate gulp of air was like the pump of a drug. The power of it charged through her while their lips and tongues warred.

With one violent move, he yanked her shirt out of the waistband of her slacks, then snaked his hand beneath until it closed over her breast.

The groan came from both of them.

"The minute I saw you." He tore his mouth from hers to feast on her throat. "The first minute I saw you."

"I know." She wanted his mouth again, had to have it. "I know."

He started to drag her jacket off, had it halfway down her arms when sanity began to pound against madness. The madness urged him to take her—why shouldn't he?—fast and hard. To take what he needed, the way he needed it, and please himself.

"Ally." He said her name, and the old-fashioned sweetness of it clicked reality back into place.

She saw him step back—though he didn't move, she saw the deliberate distance he built between them by the change in his eyes. Those fascinating and clear green eyes.

"Okay." She sucked in a breath. "Okay, okay." In an almost absent move she patted his shoulder until he did indeed step back. "That was…whoa." She sidestepped, paced away into his office. "Okay, that was…something."

"Something or other."

"I need a minute for my mind to clear." She'd never had passion slam into her with a force that blanked the mind. But she'd have to worry about that, deal with that later. Right now it was essential she find her balance.

"We probably both knew that was in there. And it's probably best we got it out," she said.

To give himself a moment he bent down, picked up the empty water bottle, set it aside. Then he dipped his hands into his pockets because they weren't altogether steady, and followed her into the office.

"I'll agree with the first part and reserve judgment on the second. What do we do now?"

"Now we…get over it."

Just like that? he thought. She'd cut him off at the knees, and now he was supposed to just hobble away and get over it?

"Fine." Pride iced his voice. He walked over, took three tapes out of his desk drawer. "I believe these satisfy your warrant."

Her palms were sweaty, but she couldn't sacrifice the dignity she was trying to rebuild by wiping them off. She took the tapes, slipped them into her shoulder bag. "I'll give you a receipt."

"Forget it."

"I'll give you a receipt," she repeated, and took out a pad. "It's procedure."

"We wouldn't want to tamper with procedure." He held out his hand, accepting the copy she offered. "Don't let me keep you, Fletcher. Clock's ticking."

She strode to the door, yanked it open. Dignity be damned, she decided and spun back. "You can save the attitude. You made the first move, I made the second. That's an even slate to me, and now it's done."

"Honey—make that Detective Honey, if we were done, we'd both be feeling a lot better right now."

"Yeah, well. We'll live with it," she muttered and sacrificed dignity for satisfaction by slamming the door.

Ally wasn't cut out to be a waitress. She was sure of it when, during her second shift at Blackhawk's, she poured the drink Beth had allowed her to serve over the head of the idiot customer who grabbed her butt and invited her to engage in a sexual act that was illegal in several states.

The customer had objected, rather strongly, to her response, but before she could flatten him, Will had appeared like smoke between them. She'd had to stand passively and be rescued.

It had grated for hours.

But if she was sure of her lack of waitress potential after her second shift, she was desperate to shed her cover by the third.

She wanted action. And not the kind that required her to serve wild wings in demon sauce and take orders for drinks called tornadoes to young executives on the make.

Twenty minutes into her third night at Blackhawk's had given her a profound respect for those who served and cleared and tolerated impatience, lousy tips and lewd propositions.

"I hate people." Ally waited for her drink order at the bar while Pete drew a beer off tap.

"Ah, no, you don't."

"Yes. Yes, I do. I really do. They're rude, annoying, oblivious. And all of them are jammed into Blackhawk's."

"And it's only six-thirty."

"Please. Six thirty-five. Every minute counts." She glanced back at Jan who worked the bar area, all but dancing between tables as she cleared, served and played up her assets. "How does she do it?"

"Some are born for it, Blondie. You'll excuse my saying so, but you're not. Not that you don't do the job, but you don't have the passion."

She rolled her eyes. "I don't have the arches, either." She started to lift the tray, eyes tracking the room as always, then she let it drop again when she spotted the man coming in the front door.

"Oh, hell. Pete, ask Jan to get this order to table eight club side. I have to do something."

"Ally, what're you doing here?"

It was all Dennis got out of his mouth before Ally grabbed his arm and hauled him through the bar, into the kitchen and out the back door. "Damn it, Dennis. Damn it!"

"What's the matter? What did you drag me out here for?" He put on his best baffled look, but she'd seen it before. She'd seen the whole routine before.

"I'm on the job. You'll blow my cover, for God's sake. I told you what would happen if you started following me again."

"I don't know what you're talking about." His injured air had worked on her once. More than once.

"You listen to me." She stepped close, jabbed a finger in his chest. "Listen hard, Dennis. We're done. We have been done for months. There's no chance that's going to change, and every chance, if you keep hassling me, I'll slap a restraining order on your butt and make your life a living hell."

His mouth thinned, his eyebrows lowered, the way she knew they did when he was backed into a corner. "This is a public place. All I did was walk into a public place. I'm entitled to buy a drink in a bar when I'm in the mood."

"You're not entitled to follow me, or to jeopardize my cover in a police investigation. You crossed the line, and I'm calling the D.A.'s office in the morning."

"You don't have to do that. Come on, Ally. How was I supposed to know you were on the job here? I just happened to pass by and—"

"Don't lie to me." She balled her hand into a fist, then in frustration tapped it against her own temple as she turned away. "Don't lie."

"I just miss you so much. I think about you all the time. I can't help it. I know I shouldn't have followed you. I didn't mean to. I was just hoping we could talk, that's all. Come on, baby." He took her shoulders, buried his face in her hair in a way that made her skin crawl. "If we could just talk."

"Don't...touch me." She hunched her shoulders, started to pull away, but he wrapped his arms around her, one hard squeeze of possession.

"Don't pull away. You know it makes me crazy when you go cold like that."

She could have had him flat on his back with her foot on his throat in two moves. She didn't want it to come to that. "Dennis, don't make me hurt you. Just leave me alone. Take your hands off me and leave me alone or it's going to be so much worse than it already is."

"No. It'll be better. I swear, it'll be better. You just have to take me back, and things'll be the way they used to be."

"No. They won't." She stiffened, braced to break the hold. "Let me go."

Light spilled out of the kitchen door as it opened. "I'd advise you to do what the lady asked," Jonah warned. "And do it fast."

She closed her eyes, felt temper and embarrassment rise up under the frustration. "I can handle this."

"Maybe, but you won't. This is my place. Take your hands off her."

"We're having a private conversation." Dennis turned, but pulled Ally with him.

"Not anymore. Go inside, Ally."

"This is none of your business." Dennis's voice rose, cracked. It was a tenor she'd heard before. "Just butt out."

"That wasn't the right response."

She moved now, breaking free and stepping between the men when Jonah moved forward. There was a gleam in his eye that worried her, like a flash of lightning against thin ice. "Don't. Please."

Anger wouldn't have stopped him, nor would an order. But the plea in her eyes, the weariness in them, did. "Go back inside," he said again, but quietly as he laid a hand on her shoulder.

"So that's the way it is." Dennis lifted bunched fists. "There's nobody else. That's what you told me. No, there was nobody else. Just another lie. Just one more of your lies. You've been sleeping with him all along, haven't you? Lying bitch."

Jonah moved like a snake. She'd seen street fights before. Had broken up her share while in uniform. She only had time to swear and leap forward, but Jonah already had Dennis up against the wall.

"Stop it," she said again and grabbed his arm to try to pull him off. She might as well have tried to shove aside a mountain.

He shot her one steely look. "No." He said it casually, like a shrug. Then he plowed his fist into Dennis's belly. "I don't like men who push women around or call them names." His voice stayed cool and steady as he delivered a second blow. "I won't tolerate it in my place. You got that?"

He let go, stepped back, and Dennis collapsed in a heap at his feet. "I think he got it."

"Great. Wonderful." While Dennis moaned, Ally pressed her fingers to her eyes. "You just gut-punched an assistant district attorney."

"And your point would be?"

"Help me get him up."

"No." Before she could try to haul Dennis to his feet, Jonah took her arm. "He walked in on his own, he'll walk away on his own."

"I can't leave him here, curled up like a damn shrimp on the pavement."

"He'll get up. Right, Dennis?" Elegant and unruffled in black, Jonah crouched down beside the groaning man. "You're going to get up, you're going to walk away. And you're not going to come back here in this lifetime. You're going to stay very far away from Allison. In fact, if you find out that by some mischance you're breathing the same air, you'll hold your breath and run in the opposite direction."

Dennis struggled to his hands and knees, retched. Tears swam in his eyes, but behind them was a rage that drilled in his head like a diamond bit. "You're welcome to her." Pain radiated through him as he stumbled to his feet. "She'll use you, then toss you aside. Just like she did me. You're welcome to her," he repeated, then limped away.

"Looks like you're all mine now." Jonah straightened, flicked fingers down his shirt as if removing some pesky lint. "But if you're going to start using me, I'd prefer we do it inside."

"It's not funny."

"No." He studied her face, the shadowed eyes and the pity in them. "I can see that. I'm sorry. Why don't you come inside, take a few minutes up in my office until you're feeling steadier."

"I'm okay." But she turned away, dragged the clip out of her hair as if it were suddenly too tight. "I don't want to talk about it now."

"All right." He put his hands on her shoulders, used his thumbs to press at the tension. "Take a minute anyway."

"I hate having him touch me, and I feel lousy because I hate it. I don't think it jeopardized the cover."

"No. According to Pete, some dude walked in, you flipped and dragged him out."

"Anybody asks, I'll keep it close to the truth. Ex-boyfriend who's hassling me."

"Then stop worrying." He turned her around. "And stop feeling guilty. You're not responsible for other people's feelings."

"Sure you are, when you help make them. Anyway." She lifted a hand to the one he still rested on her shoulder, patted it. "Thanks. I could have handled him, but thanks."

"You're welcome."

He couldn't stop himself from leaning into her, drawing her close. He watched her lashes lower, her mouth lift to his. And was a breath away from tasting her when the light spilled over them.

"Oh. Sorry." Frannie stood, framed in the door where kitchen noise clattered, a lighter in one hand, a cigarette at the ready in the other.

"No." Ally broke away, furious with herself for forgetting her priorities. "I was just going back in. I'm already late." She flicked one look at Jonah then hurried back inside.

Frannie waited until the door swung shut, then stepped over to lean back against the wall. She flicked on her lighter. "Well," she said.

"Well."

She blew out smoke on a sigh. "She's beautiful."

"Yes, she is."

"Smart, too. It comes across."

"Yeah."

"Just your type."

This time he angled his head. "You think so?"

"Sure." The tip of her cigarette glowed as she lifted it to her lips. "Classy. Class shows. She suits you."

It troubled him, more than he'd imagined it would, to dance around the truth with an old friend. "We'll see how well we fit."

Frannie moved a shoulder. But she'd already seen. They fit like lock and key. "Was there trouble with that suit?"

Jonah glanced in the direction Dennis had taken. "Nothing major. An ex who doesn't like being an ex."

"Figured it was something like that. Well, if it matters, I like her."

"It matters, Frannie." He walked to her, touched a hand to her cheek. "You matter, and always have."

# Chapter 5

Six days after the Chamberses' burglary, Ally stood in her lieutenant's office. To save time, she'd already changed into her waitress gear for the evening. She had her badge in the pocket of her trousers and her clutch piece strapped just above her ankle.

"We haven't been able to trace one single piece of stolen property." She knew it wasn't what he wanted to hear. "There's no news on the street. Even Hickman's bottomless sources are dry. Whoever's pushing the buttons on this is smart, private and patient."

"You've been inside Blackhawk's for a week."

"Yes, sir. I can't tell you any more than I could the first day. Between the security tapes and my own in-the-field observations I've tagged several regulars. But nobody pops. On the upside, my cover's secure."

"Fortunately. Shut the door, Detective."

Her stomach sank a little, but she did so and stood in

the glass box of his office with the noise from the bull pen humming behind the clear wall.

"On the matter of Dennis Overton."

She'd known it was coming. Once she'd made the complaint to the D.A.'s office, it was inevitable that some of the flak would scatter into her own house.

"I regret the incident, Lieutenant. However, the way it ultimately played out added to my cover rather than detracting from it."

"That's not my concern. Why didn't you report his behavior previously to the D.A.? To me?"

They both heard the unspoken *To your father*.

"It was personal business, and until this last incident, on my personal time. I believed I could handle it without involving my superiors or Dennis's."

He understood the defensive stance, because he understood her. "I've spoken with the district attorney. In your complaint to him you state that Overton has, over a period of time beginning the first week of April, harassed you with phone calls both here and at home, has staked out your apartment, followed you on and off duty."

"He didn't interfere with the job," she began, then wisely closed her mouth when her lieutenant stared at her.

Kiniki set aside a copy of her written statement, folded his hands on it. "Contacting you against your stated wishes when you're on duty, as well as when you're off, interferes. Are you unaware of the stalking laws, Detective?"

"No, sir. When it became apparent that the subject would not desist in his behavior, could not be discouraged and could potentially interfere with this investigation, I reported his behavior to his superior."

"You haven't filed charges."

"No, sir."

"Nor have you, as yet, requested a restraining order."

"I believe a reprimand from his superior is sufficient."

"That, or being knocked back by Jonah Blackhawk?"

She opened her mouth, closed it again. She hadn't mentioned that part of the incident to the D.A.

"Overton claims that Blackhawk attacked him, unprovoked, in a fit of jealous rage."

"Oh, for God's sake." The words, and the disgust in them, were out before she could stop them. She yanked at her hair once, then bit down on control. "That is completely inaccurate. I didn't detail the incident, Lieutenant. It didn't seem necessary. But if Dennis insists on making trouble here, I'll write out a full report."

"Do it. I want a copy on my desk by tomorrow afternoon."

"He could lose his job."

"Is that your problem?"

"No." She blew out a breath. "No, sir. Lieutenant, Dennis and I dated for a period of three months." She hated this, bringing her personal life into her superior's office. "We were…intimate, briefly. He began to display—hell."

She dropped the copspeak, approached the desk. "He got possessive, jealous, irrational. If I was late or had to cancel, he'd accuse me of being with another man. It got way out of hand, and when I broke things off he'd come by or call. Full of apologies and promises to be different. When I didn't go for it, he'd either get nasty or fall apart. Lieutenant, I slept with him. Part of this situation is my doing."

Kiniki waited a moment, pulling on his bottom lip while he studied her. "That's one of the few stupid remarks I've ever heard you make. If a victim came to you describing this situation, would you tell her it was her doing?" When she didn't answer, he nodded. "I didn't think so. You would follow procedure. Follow it now."

"Yes, sir."

"Ally…" He'd known her since she was five. He tried to keep the personal separate as religiously as she. But there were times… "Have you told your father about this?"

"I don't want to bring him into it. Respectfully, sir, I'd prefer you didn't discuss it with him."

"That's your choice. The wrong one, but yours. I'll agree to it if I have your word that if Overton so much as breathes within ten feet of you, you report it to me." He cocked his head when her lips quivered. "That's amusing?"

"No, sir. Yes." She let go of the cop-to-cop stand. "Jonah made nearly the same statement, Uncle Lou. I guess it's… sweet. In a manly sort of way, of course."

"Always had the smartest mouth. Go on, get out of here. And get me something on these burglaries."

Since most waitresses-in-training didn't drive classic Corvettes, Ally was in the habit of parking two blocks away and walking the rest of the distance to Blackhawk's.

It gave her time to shift gears, to appreciate what spring brought to Denver. She'd always loved the city, the way the buildings, silver towers, rode into the sky. She loved seeing the mountains go from winter-white to those steely jags laced by snow and forest.

And though she enjoyed the mountains, had spent many wonderful days in her parents' cabin, she preferred to view them from city streets. Her city.

Her city had scarred-booted cowboys walking down the same streets with Armani-clad executives. It was about cattle and commerce and nightlife. It was about the wild, coated with a sheen or polish but not quite tamed.

The East would never hold the same appeal for her.

And when spring was in full, balmy life, when the sun beamed on the white-tipped peaks that guarded Denver, when the air was thin and bright, there was no place like it in the world.

She stepped out of the city, and into Blackhawk's.

Jonah was at the bar, the far end, leaning casually, sipping what she knew was his habitual sparkling water and listening to one of his regular customers complain about his day.

Those light and beautiful green eyes pinned her the minute she walked in, stayed steady, stayed level and gave away nothing.

He hadn't touched her since the night behind the club, and had said little. It was best that way, she told herself. Mix duty and lust and you end up compromising one and being burnt by the other.

But it was frustrating to see him night after night, to remain just close enough to maintain illusions and not be able to take a complete step forward or back.

And to want him, the way she'd never wanted anyone else.

She shrugged out of her jacket and got to work.

It was killing him, by inches. Jonah knew what it was to want a woman, to have one stir blood and loins and spin images in the mind. It could be a kind of hunger that slowly churned in the belly, gnawing there until it was finally satisfied.

This was a hunger, his desire for Ally. But there was nothing of the slow churning in it. This was sharp, constant and painful.

No other woman had ever caused him pain.

He carried the taste of her inside him. He couldn't rid himself of it. That alone was infuriating. It gave her an advantage he'd never allowed another to have over him. The fact that she didn't appear to know it didn't negate the weakness.

Where you were weak, you were vulnerable.

He wanted the investigation over. He wanted her back in her own life, her own world so he could regain his balance in his.

Then he remembered the way she'd erupted against him, the way her mouth had scorched over his, and her hands fisted in his hair. And he began to worry he'd never find his feet firmly planted again.

"Good thing we don't have a cop around."

Jonah's fingers tightened on his glass, but his eyes were mild as he turned to Frannie. "What?"

She pulled a beer, poured a bump, then served it. "A guy could get arrested for looking at a woman that way. I think it's called intent or something. What you intend is pretty clear, at least when she's not looking."

"Really?" And that, he realized, was another worry. "Then I'd better watch myself."

"She's doing plenty of watching," Frannie murmured as he walked away.

"The man's got trouble on the brain," Will commented. He liked coming over to Frannie's end of the bar so he could get a whiff of her hair or maybe work a smile out of her.

"He's got woman on the brain. And he's not altogether easy with this one." She winked at him and squirted a glass of the soft drink Will drank by the gallon during working hours.

"Women never trouble the man."

"This one does."

"Well." He sipped his drink, scanned the bar crowd. "She's a looker."

"That's not it. Looks are surface stuff. This one's got him down in the gut."

"You think?" Will tugged on his little beard. He didn't understand women, and didn't pretend to. To him they were simply amazing creatures of staggering power and wonderful shapes.

"I know." She patted Will's hand and had his heart throbbing in his throat.

"Two margaritas, frozen with salt, two house drafts and a club soda with lime." Jan set down her tray and walked her fingers up Will's arm in a teasing, tickling motion. "Hey, big guy."

He blushed. He always did. "Hey, Jan. I better do a round in the club."

He hurried off and had Frannie shaking her head at Jan. "You shouldn't tease him like that."

"I can't help it. He's so sweet." She flipped her hair back. "Listen, there's this party tonight. I'm going by after closing. Want to tag along?"

"After closing I'm going to be home, in my own little bed, dreaming of Brad Pitt."

"Dreaming never gets you anywhere."

"Don't I know it," Frannie muttered and sent the blender whirling.

Allison carried a full tray of empties, and had two tables worth of drink orders in the pad tucked in her bar apron. Only thirty minutes into shift, she thought. It was going to be a long night. Longer, she realized when she spotted Jonah coming toward her.

"Allison, I'd like to speak with you." About something,

anything. Five minutes alone with you might do it. Pitiful.
"Would you come up to my office on your break?"

"Problem?"

"No," he lied. "No problem."

"Fine, but you'd better tell Will. He guards your cave like a wolf."

"Take your break now. Come up with me."

"Can't, thirsty people waiting. But I'll shake loose as soon as I can if it's important." She walked away quickly because she'd heard it, that underlying heat that told her what he wanted with her had nothing to do with duty.

She stopped at her station beside Pete and ordered herself to settle down. Since he was in the middle of entertaining three of the stool-sitters with a long, complicated joke, she took the time to rest her feet and study the people scattered at table and bar.

A twentysomething couple who looked like they were on the leading edge of an argument. Three suits with ties loosened arguing baseball. A flirtation, in its early stages, starting to cook between a lone woman and the better-looking of a pair of guys at the bar. Lots of eye contact and smiles.

Another couple at a table laughing together over some private joke, holding hands, she noted, flirting some even though the hands wore wedding rings. Well married, happy and financially secure if the designer handbag on the back of the woman's chair and the matching shoes were any indication.

At the next table another couple sat having a quiet conversation that seemed to please them both. There was an intimacy there as well, Ally noted. Body language, gestures, the smiling looks over sips of wine.

She envied that…comfort, she supposed, of having someone who could sit across the table in a crowded place and focus on her, care about what she said, or what she didn't have to say.

It was what her parents had—that innate rhythm and respect that added real dimension to love and attraction.

If it was lovely to watch, she wondered, how much more lovely must it be to experience?

Brooding over it, she listened to the laughter break out at Pete's punch line. She placed her orders, listening absently to the chatter around her, scanning, always scanning the movements, the faces.

She watched the hand-holding couple signal Jan, and the woman pointing to an item on the bar menu when the waitress moved to the table to take the order. Bending down, Jan waved a hand in front of her mouth, rolled her eyes and made the woman laugh.

"The hotter the better," the woman claimed. "We don't have a club table until eight, so there's plenty of time to cool down."

When Jan had scribbled down the order and moved off, Ally found herself smiling at the way the man brought the woman's hand to his mouth and nipped at her knuckles.

If it hadn't been for that kernel of envy that kept her attention focused on them, she might have missed it. As it was, it took her several seconds to note the picture had changed.

The woman's bag still hung over the back of her chair, but at a different angle, and the outside zipper pocket wasn't quite closed.

Ally came to attention, her first thought to focus on Jan. Then she saw it. The second woman sitting with her back to the first, still smiling at her companion. While under the table, smooth and unhurried, she slipped a set of keys into the purse she held on her lap.

Bingo.

"You gone to the moon, Ally?" Pete tapped a finger on her shoulder. "I don't think anybody's waiting for vodka tonics up there."

"No, I'm right here."

As the woman rose, tucked her purse under her arm, Ally lifted her tray.

Five-four, she thought. A hundred and twenty. Brown hair, brown eyes. Late thirties with an olive complexion and strong features. And just now heading toward the ladies' room.

Rather than break cover, she hurried into the club, spotted Will and shoved the tray at him. "Sorry, table eight's waiting for these. Tell Jonah I need to speak with him. I have to do something."

"But hey."

"I have to do something," she repeated and walked briskly toward the restrooms.

Inside, she scanned the bottom of the stalls, located the right shoes. Making a wax mold of the keys, Ally concluded and turned to one of the sinks. She ran water while she watched the shoes. It would only take a few minutes, but she'd need privacy.

Satisfied, Ally walked out.

"Ally? I got tables filling up here. Where's your tray?"

"Sorry." She shot Beth an apologetic smile. "Little emergency. I'll get on it."

She moved quickly, catching the eye of one of her team members and pausing by the table. "White female, late thirties. Brown and brown. She'll be coming out of the ladies' room in a minute. Navy jacket and slacks. She's sitting in the bar area with a white male, early forties, gray and blue in a green sweater. Keep them in sight, but don't move in. We handle it just like we outlined."

She walked back to the bar to pick up another tray as a prop. The man in the green sweater was paying the tab. Cash. He looked relaxed, but Ally noted he checked his watch and glanced back toward the restrooms.

The woman came back in, but rather than taking her seat, stood between the tables and reached down for the short, black cape she'd draped over the chair. For a matter of seconds, her body blocked the view, then she straightened, beamed at her companion and handed him the cape.

Smart hands, Ally thought. Very smart hands.

When Jonah turned the corner of the bar, she inclined her head and let her gaze slide over to the couple preparing to leave, then back to him.

Casually she crossed over and ran a hand affectionately up and down Jonah's arm. "I've got two officers to tag them. We want them to get through the setup, all the way through. I want to give it some time before I alert the targets. When I do, I need your office."

"All right."

"We need to keep business as usual down here. If you'll hang around, I can let you know when I want to move. You can tell Beth you need me for something so she can juggle tables. I don't want any alarms going off."

"Just let me know. I'll take care of it."

"Let me have the code for your elevator. In case I need to take them up without you." She leaned in, her face tilted to his.

"Two, seven..." He leaned down, brushed his lips over hers. "Five, eight, five. Got it?"

"Yeah, I got it. See if you can keep attention off me until I move the targets out of the bar."

Her energy was up, but her mind was cool. She waited fifteen minutes. When the female target rose to use the restroom, Ally slipped in with her.

"Excuse me." After a quick check of the stalls, Ally pulled her badge out of her pocket. "I'm Detective Fletcher, Denver P.D."

The woman took a quick, instinctive step in retreat. "What's this about?"

"I need your help with an investigation. I'd like to speak with you and your husband. If you'd come with me."

"I haven't done anything."

"No, ma'am. I'll explain it all to you. There's a private office upstairs. If we could move up there as quietly as possible? I'd appreciate your cooperation."

"I'm not going anywhere without Don."

"I'll get your husband. If you'd walk back out, turn to the left, and wait in the corridor."

"I want to know what this is about."

"I'll explain it to both of you." Ally took the woman's arm to hurry her along. "Please. Just a few moments of your time."

"I don't want any trouble."

"Please wait here. I'll get your husband." Because she didn't trust the woman to stay put long, Ally moved fast. She paused at the couple's table, picked up empty glasses.

"Sir? Your wife's back there. She asked if you could come back for a minute."

"Sure. Is she okay?"

"She's fine."

Ally crossed to the bar, set down the empties. Then ducked quickly back into the corridor.

"Detective Fletcher," she said with a quick flash of her

badge as the man joined her. "I need to speak with you and your wife in private." She was already keying in the code.

"She won't say what it's about. Don, I don't see why—"

"I appreciate your cooperation," Ally said again and all but shoved them both into the elevator.

"I don't appreciate being bullied by the police," the woman said with an edge of nerves in her voice.

"Lynn, calm down. It's okay."

"I'm sorry to be abrupt." Ally stepped into Jonah's office, gestured to the chairs. "If you'd have a seat, I'll fill you in."

Lynn crossed her arms, hugged her elbows tight. "I don't want to sit down."

Have it your way, sister, Ally thought. "I'm investigating a series of burglaries in and around Denver during the last several weeks."

The woman sniffed. "Do we look like burglars?"

"No, ma'am. You look like a nice, well-established, upper-class couple. Which has been, to date, the main target of this burglary ring. And less than twenty minutes ago, a woman we suspect is part of that ring lifted your keys out of your purse."

"That's impossible. My purse has been right with me all night." As if to prove it, she started to unzip the pocket. Ally snagged her wrist.

"Please don't touch your keys."

"How can I touch them if they're not there?" the woman argued.

"Lynn, shut up. Come on." He squeezed his wife's shoulder. "What's going on?" he asked Ally.

"We believe molds are made of the keys. They're replaced and the targeted victim remains unaware. Then their house is broken into and their belongings are stolen. We'd like to prevent that from happening to you. Now sit down."

Authority snapped in her voice this time. Visibly shaken, the woman lowered herself into a chair.

"If I could have your names please."

"Don and Lynn—Mr. and Mrs. Barnes."

"Mr. Barnes, would you give me your address?"

He swallowed, sat on the arm of his wife's chair and rattled it off while Ally noted it down. "Do you mean someone's in our house right now? Robbing us right now?"

"I don't believe they can move quite that quickly." In her mind she was calculating the drive time. "Is there anyone at that address right now?"

"No. It's just us. Man." Barnes ran a hand through his hair. "Man, this is weird."

"I'm going to call in your address and begin setting up a stakeout. Give me a second."

She picked up the phone as the elevator doors opened, and Jonah walked it. "I've got it covered here," she told him.

"I'm sure you do. Mr. and Mrs....?"

"Barnes," the man answered. "Don and Lynn Barnes."

"Don, can I offer you and your wife something to drink? I realize this is very inconvenient and upsetting for you."

"I could use a shot. A good stiff bourbon, I think."

"Can't blame you. And Lynn?"

"I..." She lifted a hand, dropped it. "I just can't... I don't understand."

"Maybe a little brandy." Jonah turned away, opened a panel in the wall to reveal a small, well-stocked bar. "You can put yourselves in Detective Fletcher's capable hands," he continued and he chose bottles and glasses. "And meanwhile, we'll try to keep you as comfortable as possible."

"Thanks." Lynn took the brandy from him. "Thank you so much."

"Mr. Barnes." A little miffed at how smoothly Jonah had settled ruffled feathers, she yanked the man's attention back to her. "We have units on the way to your house right now. Can you describe your house for me? The layout, doors, windows?"

"Sure." He laughed, a little shakily. "Hell, I'm an architect."

He gave her a clear picture, which she relayed to the team before she began to set up the coordinates for the stakeout.

"You have dinner reservations here tonight?" Ally asked them.

"Yeah. Eight o'clock. We're making a night of it," he said with a sour smile.

Ally checked her watch. "They'll think they have plenty of time." She wanted them to go back down, to finish their time at the bar, go into dinner and present the appearance of normality. And one look at the woman's face told her it was a long shot.

"Mrs. Barnes. Lynn." Ally came back around the desk, sat on the edge of it. "We're going to stop these people. They won't take your things or damage your home. But I need you to help me out here. I need you and your husband to go back down, to try to get through the evening as if nothing was wrong. If you could hold on for another hour, I think we could wrap this up."

"I want to go home."

"We'll get you there. Give me an hour. It's possible that a member of the organization is assigned to keep an eye on you. You've already been away from your table nearly twenty minutes. We'll cover that, but we can't cover another hour. We don't want to scare these people off."

"If they're scared off, they won't break into my house."

"No, just into someone else's the next time."

"Give me a minute with her, okay." Barnes got up, took his wife's hands. "Come on, Lynn. Hell, it's an adventure. We'll eat out on the story for years. Come on, let's go— let's just go downstairs and get drunk."

"Jonah, go with them. Ah, pass the word that those— what was it—the wild wings you ordered didn't sit too well after all. You're fine now, but you were feeling a little sick. Blackhawk's will cover your bar bill, right?"

"Naturally." Jonah offered Lynn his hand to help her to her feet. "And the dinner tab. I'll take you down. You just needed to stretch out for a few minutes, and I offered to take you and your husband up to my office until you felt better. Good enough?" he asked Ally as he pressed for the elevator.

"Perfect. I need to make a couple more calls, then I'll be down. I'm going to have to cut out before end of shift. I've had a family emergency."

"Good luck with it," he told her, and led the Barneses away.

# Chapter 6

She got the key from Jonah and went straight to the employee lounge for her bag. She ran straight out, doing no more than waving a hand when Frannie called out to her from behind the bar.

She was trusting Jonah to answer any questions. No one could do it better, she thought as she raced the blocks to her car. A simple word, a shrug from him and that would be that. No one pumped a man like Jonah Blackhawk.

She had to get to Federal Heights before everything went down.

At first she thought she was seeing things. But the night was clear and cool and her vision excellent. There was no mistaking the fact that all four of her tires were slashed.

She swore, kicked viciously at the mangled rubber. A hell of a time, she thought, one hell of a time for Dennis Overton to get nasty. Digging into her bag she pulled out her cell phone and called for a radio car.

Time wasted, was all she could think. Two minutes, five minutes ticking away while she paced the sidewalk and waited. She had her badge out and her teeth clenched when the patrol car pulled up.

"Got some trouble, Detective?"

"Yeah. Hit the sirens, head north on 25. I'll tell you when to go silent."

"You got it. What's going down?"

She settled into the back behind the two uniforms, itching to have her hands on the wheel and her foot on the gas. "I'll fill you in." She took her weapon and harness out of her bag, and felt more herself the minute she strapped it on.

"Call for a tow truck, will you? I don't want to leave my car on the street like that."

"Shame about that. Nice car."

"Yeah." She forgot about it as they screamed up the interstate.

A block from the Barneses' address, she hopped out of the car, and arrowed straight to Hickman. "Give me the story."

"They took their time getting here. Balou and Dietz had the first leg of the tail and said they drove like solid citizens, kept under the speed limit, signaled for turns. Woman riding shotgun, made a call on a cell phone. He turned over the tail to me and Carson when they got on 36. They stopped for gas. The woman gets in the back. They're driving a nice, suburban minivan. She's doing something back there, but I couldn't get close enough to see."

"Making the keys. I bet you two weeks' pay she's got the works for it in the van."

"Do I look like I take sucker bets?" He glanced down the quiet street. "Anyhow, we had a unit here, waiting. The suspects were observed parking the van a block down from the target address. They strolled up the street, walked right up to the door, unlocked it and went in like they owned the place."

"Barnes said they have a security system."

"Alarm didn't trip. They've been inside about ten minutes now. Lieutenant's waiting for you. We've got the area blocked off, the house surrounded."

"Then let's move in and wrap this up."

He grinned, handed her a walkie-talkie. "Saddle up."

"God, I love cowboy talk."

They moved fast, kept low. She spotted the cops positioned on the street, behind trees, in shadows, hunched in cars.

"Glad you could join the party, Detective." Kiniki nodded toward the house. "Ballsy, aren't they?"

Lights gleamed, a homey glow against windows on the first and second floor. While Ally watched, she saw a faint shadow move behind the lower window.

"Dietz and Balou are covering the back. We've got them closed in. What's your play?"

Ally reached in her pocket, pulled out keys. "We move in on all sides, and go in the front. When we move, pull one of the radio cars across the driveway. Let's block that route."

"Call it."

She lifted the walkie-talkie, to establish positioning and give the orders. And all hell broke loose.

Three gunshots blasted the air, the return fire slamming into the echoes. Even as Ally drew her own weapon, voices shouted through the walkie-talkies.

"Dietz is down! Officer down! Shooter's male, heading east on foot. Officer down!"

Cops rushed the house. Ally hit the door first, went in low. Blood pounded in her ears as she swept the area with her weapon. Hickman took her back, and at her signal headed up the stairs while she turned right.

Someone was shouting. She heard it like a buzz in the brain. Lights flashed on.

The house opened out like a fan. She brought the lay-out Barnes had described into her mind as she and the rest of the team spread out. At each doorway she led with eyes and weapon, following training while her breath came short and shallow.

There was more gunfire from outside, muffled pops. She started to turn in that direction and saw the sliding door on what looked like a small solarium wasn't quite shut.

She caught a scent, very female, and following instinct turned away from the shouts and bolted for the door.

She saw the woman, just the silhouette of her, running hard toward a line of ornamental trees. "Police! Stop where you are!"

She would replay it a dozen times. The woman continued to run. Weapon drawn, Ally raced after her, calling out the warning, shouting her position and situation into her hand unit.

She heard calls from behind her, running feet.

They'd cut her off, Ally thought. Cut her off even before she reached the six-foot fence that closed in the property.

Nowhere to go.

She gained ground, caught both the scent of perfume and panic sweat the woman left on the air. Moonlight picked her out of the shadows, the swing of her dark hair, the stream of the short, black cape.

And when, on the run, the woman turned, the moonlight bounced off the chrome plating of the revolver in her hand.

Ally saw her lift it, felt with a kind of detached shock the heat of the bullet that whined past her own head.

"Drop your weapon! Drop it now!"

And as the woman pivoted, and the gun jerked in her hand, Ally fired.

Ally saw the woman stagger, heard the thud as the gun fell from her hand, and heard a kind of sighing gasp. But what she would remember, what seemed to burn on her brain like acid on glass, was the dark stain that bloomed between the woman's breasts even as she dropped.

It was bone-deep training that had her rushing forward, stepping on the woman's gun. "Suspect down," she said into her hand unit as she crouched to check for a pulse. Her voice didn't shake, and neither did she. Not yet.

It was Hickman who got to her first. She heard his voice like something carried on the crest of a wave of churning water. Her head was full of sound, a rushing liquid sound.

"Are you hit? Ally, are you hit?"

His hands were already moving over her, tugging at her jacket to check for injury.

"Call an ambulance." Her lips were stiff, they felt wooden, splintered. She reached forward, crossing her hands over each other, pressing the heels of them on the woman's chest.

"On the way. Come on. Get up."

"She needs pressure on this wound. She needs an ambulance."

"Ally." He holstered his own weapon. "You can't do anything for her. She's dead."

She didn't let herself be sick. She made herself stand and watch as the wounded officer and the woman's partner were loaded into ambulances. She made herself watch when the woman was zipped into a thick black bag.

"Detective Fletcher."

And she made herself turn, face her lieutenant. "Sir. Can you tell me Dietz's condition?"

"I'm on my way to the hospital. We'll know more later."

She rubbed the back of her hand over her mouth. "The suspect?"

"Paramedics said he'll make it. It'll be a couple of hours at least before we can question him."

"Am I...will I be allowed to be in on the interrogation?"

"It's still your case." He took her arm to draw her away. "Ally, listen to me. I know what it feels like. Ask yourself now, right now, if you could have done anything differently."

"I don't know."

"Hickman was behind you, and Carson was coming in from the left. I haven't spoken with her as yet, but Hickman's report is you identified yourself, ordered her to stop. She turned and fired. You ordered her to drop her weapon, and she prepared to fire again. You had no choice. That's what I expect to hear from you during the standard inquiry tomorrow morning. Do you want me to call your father?"

"No. Please. I'll talk to him tomorrow, after the inquiry."

"Then go home, get some rest. I'll let you know about Dietz."

"Sir, unless I'm relieved of duty, I'd rather go to the hospital. Stand by for Dietz, and be on hand to question the suspect when we're cleared to do so."

It would be better for her, he thought, to do what came next. "You can ride with me."

Panic was like an animal clawing at his throat. He'd never felt anything like it before. Jonah told himself it was just hospitals that did it to him. He'd always detested them. The smell of them brought back the last hideous months of his father's life, and made him all too aware that a turn here, a turn there in a different direction might have damned him to experience the same fate his father had at fifty years old.

His source had assured him that Ally wasn't hurt. But all he knew for certain was that something had gone very wrong at the bust and she was at the hospital. That had been enough to have him heading straight out. Just to see for himself, he thought.

He found her, slumped in a chair, in the hallway of Intensive Care. The panic digging into his throat released.

She'd taken the clip out of her hair as he knew she did when she was tense or tired. The gilt curtain of hair fanned down the side of her face, concealing it. But the tired slouch, the hands she gripped together on her knees, told him what to expect.

He stepped in front of her, crouched down and saw, as he'd known he would, pale skin and dark, bruised eyes.

"Hey." He gave in to the need to lay his hand over hers. "Bad day?"

"Pretty bad." It seemed like wires were crossed in her brain. She didn't think to wonder why he was there. "One of my team's in critical condition. They don't know if he'll make it till morning."

"I'm sorry."

"Yeah, me, too. The doctors won't let us talk to the son of a bitch who shot him. Male suspect identified as Richard Fricks. He's sleeping comfortably under a nice haze of drugs while Dietz fights for his life, and his wife's down in the chapel praying for it."

She wanted to close her eyes, to go into the dark, but kept them open and on his. "And for a bonus, I killed a woman tonight. One shot through the heart. Like she was a target I aced at practice."

Her hands trembled once under his, then fisted.

"Yeah, that's a pretty bad day. Come on."

"Come where?"

"Home, I'm taking you home." When she looked at him blankly, he pulled her to her feet. She felt featherlight, her hands fragile as glass. "There's nothing you can do here now, Ally."

She closed her eyes, groped for a breath. "That's what Hickman said at the scene. There's nothing you can do. Looks like you're both right."

She let him lead her to the elevator. There was no point in staying, or arguing or pretending she wanted to be alone. "I can…get a ride."

"You've got one."

No, she thought, no point in arguing, or in resisting the supporting arm he slipped around her waist. "How did you know to come here?"

"A cop came by to take the Barneses home. I got enough out of him to know there'd been trouble, and where you were. Why isn't your father with you?"

"He doesn't know. I'll tell him about it tomorrow."

"What the hell's wrong with you?"

She blinked, like a woman coming out of a dark room into the light. "What?"

He pulled her out of the elevator, across the hospital lobby. "Do you want him to hear about this from someone else? To not hear your voice, hear you tell him you're not hurt? What are you thinking?"

"I… I wasn't thinking. You're right." She fumbled in her purse for her phone as they crossed the lot. "I need a minute. I just need a minute."

She got into the car, steadying herself, steadying her breathing. "Okay," she whispered it to herself as Jonah started the car. She punched in the number, waited through the first ring, then heard her mother's voice.

"Mom." Her breath hitched. She bore down, holding a hand over the phone until she was sure her voice would be normal. "I'm fine. Everything okay there? Uh-huh. Listen, I'm on my way home, and I need to speak to Dad a minute. Yeah, that's right. Cop talk. Thanks."

Now she closed her eyes, listened to her mother call out, heard the warm mix of their laughter before her father's voice sounded in her ear.

"Ally? What's up?"

"Dad." Her voice wanted to crack but she refused to let it. "Don't say anything to upset Mom."

There was a pause. "All right."

"I'm okay. I'm not hurt, and I'm on my way home. It went down tonight, and things went wrong. Ah, one of the team was wounded, and he's in the hospital. One of the suspects is in there, too. We'll know more tomorrow on both."

"You're all right? Allison?"

"Yes, I wasn't hurt. Dad. Dad, I had to fire my weapon. They were armed. Both suspects were armed and opened fire. She wouldn't... I killed her."

"I'll be there in ten minutes."

"No, please. Stay with Mom. You'll have to tell her and she's going to be upset. I need to... I just need to go home and—tomorrow, okay? Can we talk about it tomorrow? I'm so tired now."

"If that's what you want."

"It is. I promise, I'm all right."

"Ally, who went down?"

"Dietz. Len Dietz." She lifted her free hand, pressed her fingers to her lips. They didn't feel stiff now, but soft. Painfully soft. "He's critical. The lieutenant's still at the hospital."

"I'll contact him. Try to get some sleep. But you call, anytime, if you change your mind. I can be there. We both can."

"I know. I'll call you in the morning. I think it'll be easier in the morning. I love you."

She broke the connection, let the phone slide into her purse. She opened her eyes and saw they were already in front of her apartment. "Thanks for..."

Jonah said nothing, simply got out, came around to her door. Opening it, he held out a hand for hers. "I can't seem to get my thoughts lined up. What time is it?"

"It doesn't matter. Give me your key."

"Oh, yeah, the traditionalist." She dug it out, unaware her other hand was clutching his like a lifeline. "I'm going to start expecting flowers next."

She walked through the lobby, to the elevator. "It seems like there's something I have to do. I can't get a rope around what it is, though. There should be something I have to do. We identified her. She had ID anyway. Madeline Fricks. Madeline Ellen Fricks," she murmured, floating like a dream out of the elevator. "Age thirty-seven. She had an address in... Englewood. Somebody's checking it out. I should be checking it out."

He unlocked the door, drew her inside. "Sit down, Ally."

"Yeah, I could sit down." She looked blankly around the living room. It was just the way she'd left it that morning. Nothing had changed. Why did it seem as if everything had changed?

Jonah solved the matter by picking her up and carrying her toward the bedroom.

"Where are we going?"

"You're going to lie down. Got anything to drink around here?"

"Stuff."

"Fine. I'll go find some stuff." He laid her on the bed.

"I'll be okay."

"That's right." He left her to hunt through the kitchen. In a narrow cupboard he found an unopened bottle of brandy. He broke the seal, poured three fingers. When he brought it back, she was sitting up in the bed, her knees rammed into her chest, her arms roped around them.

"I've got the shakes." She kept her face pressed to her knees. "If I had something to do, I wouldn't have the shakes."

"Here's what you need to do." He sat on the bed, cupped a hand under her chin and lifted it. "Drink this."

She took the first sip obediently when he lifted the glass to her lips. Then she coughed and turned her head away. "I hate brandy. Somebody gave me that last Christmas, God knows why. I meant to…" She trailed off, began to rock.

"Have some more. Come on, Fletcher, take your medicine."

He gave her little choice but to gulp down another swallow. Her eyes watered and color flooded her cheeks. "We had the place closed in, surrounded the house, cordoned off the area in a three-block radius. They couldn't have gotten through. They had no place to run."

She needed to talk through it. Jonah set the brandy aside. "But they ran anyway."

"We were just about to move in, and he—Fricks—came out the back, already firing. He hit Dietz with two rounds. Some of us went around the back, covering both sides. Some of us went in the front. I was first in, Hickman was behind me. We spread out, started the sweep."

She could still see it in her head. Moving through, fast and steady, the lights blazing.

"I could hear more gunfire, and shouting from outside. I nearly turned back, thinking they were both out of the house and running—that they were together. But I saw—there's this bump-out sunroom deal on the house, and the sliding door leading out wasn't closed, not all the way closed. I spotted her as soon as I stepped out. Going in the opposite direction as her partner. Splitting us up, I guess. I called out, told her to stop. I was in pursuit and she fired a round. Sloppy shot. I ordered her to stop, to drop her weapon. I didn't see she had a choice. Where the hell could she go? But she spun around."

"She spun around," Ally repeated. "The moon was very bright, very bright and it was on her face, in her eyes, shining on the gun. And I shot her."

"Did you have a choice?"

Her lips trembled open. "No. In my head that's clear. Jonah, that's so clear. I've gone over it, step after step, a dozen times already. But they don't prepare you for what it's like. They can't. They can't tell you how it feels."

The first tear spilled over and she wiped it impatiently away. "I don't even know what I'm crying for. Or who."

"It doesn't matter." He put his arms around her, drew her head down on his shoulder and held her while she wept.

And while she wept he went back over what she'd told him.

Sloppy shot, she'd said, almost skimming over the fact that someone had tried to kill her. Yet she wept because she'd had no choice but to take a life.

Cops. He turned his cheek against her hair. He'd never understand cops.

She slept for two hours, dropping into oblivion like a stone in a pool, and staying deep at the bottom. When she woke, she was wrapped around him in the dark.

She lay still a moment, orienting herself, while his heart

beat strong and steady under her palm. With her eyes open and her mind clearing she went through a mental check-list. She had a vague headache, but nothing major—just a hangover from the crying jag. There was a stronger feeling of embarrassment, but she thought she could live with that, too.

She wiggled her toes and discovered she was barefoot. And her ankle holster was gone.

So, she realized, was her shoulder harness.

He'd disarmed her, she thought, in more ways than one. She'd blubbered out her story, cried on his shoulder and was now wrapped around him in the dark. Worse than all of that was realizing she wanted to stay there.

Believing him asleep she started to inch away.

"Feel any better?"

She didn't jolt, but it was close. "Yeah. Considerably. I guess I owe you."

"I guess you do."

In the dark he found her mouth with his and sank in.

Soft, unexpectedly soft. Warm, deliciously warm. Yes, she wanted to stay there, and so she opened for him, sliding her hand from his heart to his face, yielding when he turned his body to press hers into the mattress.

The good solid weight of him, the hard lines of his body, the drugging heat of his mouth was exactly what she wanted. Her arms came around him, holding him there as he had held her in tears and in sleep.

He gave himself the moment, the dark taste of her mouth, the sleepy sigh she made, the feminine give of her beneath him. He'd lain beside her, his body alert, his mind restless while hers slept. Wanting her, wanting her so it was like a fever in the blood.

Yet when she woke, he found himself drowning in tenderness.

Yet when she surrendered, he found himself unwilling, unable, to take.

He drew back, skimmed a thumb over the curve of her cheek. "Bad timing," he said and rolled off the bed.

"I…" She cleared her throat. Her body had just started to ache, her mind had just started to float. Now she floundered free. "Look, if you have some weird idea that you were taking advantage, you're wrong."

"Am I?"

"I know how to say yes or no. And while I appreciate you bringing me home, hearing me out and not leaving me alone, I'm not grateful enough for any of that to pay you back with sex. I think too much of myself. Hell, I think too much of sex."

He laughed, sat on the edge of the bed again. "You do feel better."

"I said I did. So." She slid over, tossing her hair back and nuzzling his throat.

His pulse tripped and a fireball burst in his belly. "That's tempting." He was lucky to be able to breathe, and still casually patted her hand and got to his feet. "But no thanks."

Insult came first, and something vile nearly spilled off her tongue. Because it made her think of Dennis, she yanked herself back. "Okay. Mind if I ask why? Under the current circumstances, that seems like a reasonable question."

"Two reasons."

He switched on the bedside light, watched her eyes narrow in defense. And the look of her slammed into him like a fist in the throat.

"God. You're beautiful."

A little thrill jumped up her spine. "And that's why you don't want to make love with me?"

"I want you. Enough that it's starting to hurt. That ticks me off."

Idly he took the ends of her hair, wrapped a length of it around his hand, released it. "You're on my mind, Ally, too often for comfort. I like to be comfortable. So reason one is that I haven't decided if I want to get tangled up with you. If I do half of the very interesting things I have in mind to do with you, I'm going to be tangled."

She sat back on her heels. "I imagine you know how to cut line when you want to."

"I've never had any trouble before. You're trouble. It's that simple."

Insult and annoyance had vanished. "This is fascinating. Here I had you pegged as somebody who took what he wanted when he wanted it, and the hell with the consequences."

"No. I prefer calculating, then eliminating consequences. Then I take what I want."

"In other words, I make you nervous."

"Oh, yeah. Go ahead and grin," he said with a nod. "I can't blame you."

She laughed, lifted her eyebrows. "You said there were two reasons. What's the second?"

"That's easy." He stepped to the bed, bent down and caught her chin in his hand. "I don't like cops," he said, and brushed his lips lightly over hers.

When he would have leaned away from the kiss, she leaned in, sliding up so that her body rubbed over his. She felt his body quiver, and nothing had ever been more satisfying.

"Yeah, you're trouble," he muttered. "I'm leaving."

"Coward."

"Okay, that stings, but I'll get over it." He walked over to shrug on the jacket he'd tossed onto a chair, slip his feet back into his shoes.

She didn't just feel better, Ally realized. She felt fabulous. Invincible. "Why don't you come on back here and fight like a man."

He glanced at her. She knelt on the side of the bed, her eyes dark and challenging, her hair a tumble of gold around her face and shoulders.

The taste of her was still sizzling on his tongue.

But he shook his head, walked to the door. Tormented himself with one last look. "I'm going to hate both of us in the morning," he told her, then strode away while her laughter followed him.

# Chapter 7

Ally was up at six and ready to roll out the door at seven. She nearly rolled right over her parents, who were at her front door.

"Mom." She flicked her eyes up to her father, started to speak, but her mother already had her caught in a hard hug. "Mom," she said again. "I'm all right."

"Indulge me." Cilla held on, tight, heart pressed to heart, cheek pressed to cheek.

Stupid, Cilla thought, so stupid to have kept it together all night and to feel herself falling apart now that her child was in her arms.

She couldn't, wouldn't allow it.

"Okay." She laid her lips on Ally's temple for a moment, then drew back far enough to study her daughter's face.

"I had to see for myself. You're lucky your father held me off this long."

"I didn't want you to worry."

"It's my job to worry. And I believe in doing a job well."

Ally watched her mother's lips curve, saw the tears willed away. And knew it cost her. "You do everything well."

Cilla O'Roarke Fletcher's eyes were the same golden-brown as her daughter's, her short sweep of hair a luxuriant black that suited her angular features and smoky voice.

"But I've got worry down to a science," she said.

Since they were almost of identical heights, Ally had only to shift closer to kiss Cilla's cheek. "Well, you can take a break. I'm fine. Really."

"I suppose you look it."

"Come on inside. I can make some more coffee."

"No, you're on your way out. I just needed to see you." To touch you, Cilla thought. My baby. "I'm heading into work. I'm interviewing a new sales manager at KHIP. Your dad's dropping me off. You can use my car today."

"How did you know I needed a car?"

"I have connections," Boyd told her. "You should have yours back by midafternoon."

"I would've handled it." Ally shut the door behind her, frowned.

"Meaning you would have handled the car, and Overton and the tangle of bureaucracy," Cilla put in. "I hope I didn't raise a daughter who's ungrateful, and who expects her father to stand back with his hands in his pockets when something happens to her." Cilla tilted her head, lifted her brows. "I'd be very disappointed if I had."

Boyd grinned, slipped an arm around Cilla's shoulders and pressed his lips to her hair.

"Good one," Ally muttered, properly chastised. "Thank you, Dad."

"You're welcome, Allison."

"Now, which one of us is going to go beat the tar out of Dennis Overton?" Cilla rubbed her hands together. "Or can we all do it? In which case, I get to go first."

"She has violent tendencies," Ally pointed out.

"Tell me about it. Down, girl," he told Cilla. "Let the system work. Now... Detective." Boyd draped his arm around his daughter's shoulders as they walked to the elevator. "You're to report to the hospital first. There's a suspect who needs to be questioned."

"The inquiry into the shooting?"

"Will proceed this morning. You'll need to give your statement and file your report. By ten hundred. Detective Hickman filed his last night, which gives a very clear picture. You don't have anything to worry about."

"I'm not worried. I know I did what I had to do. It gave me some bad moments last night." She blew out a breath. "Some pretty bad ones. But I'm okay with it now. As okay as it gets, I guess."

"You shouldn't have been alone last night," Cilla said.

"Actually I had...a friend with me for a while."

Boyd opened his mouth, shut it again. After Ally's call the night before, he'd contacted Kiniki immediately. He knew that Jonah had driven Ally home from the hospital, so he had a good idea just who the friend was.

But he had no idea how he felt about it.

Ally pulled into the hospital visitors' lot, circled until she found a space. She spotted Hickman as she set the locks and alarm.

"Nice ride," he commented, hands in pockets, eyes squinted into slits against the brilliant sunshine. "Not every cop's got herself a Mercedes as a backup vehicle."

"It's my mother's."

"You've got some mother." He'd seen Cilla, so he knew it was true. "So, how's it going?"

"Okay." She fell into step beside him. "Look, I know you already filed your report on last night's incident. I appreciate you getting it in so fast and backing me up."

"It happened the way it happened. If it smooths any edges for you, you should know that you fired about a split hair before I did. If I'd been in the lead instead of you, I'd've been the one to take her out."

"Thanks. Any word on Dietz?"

"Still critical." Hickman's expression darkened. "He made it through the night, so that's hopeful. I want a round with the son of a bitch who put him here."

"Get in line."

"You know how you want to play it?"

"I've been thinking about it." They moved together across the lobby to the bank of elevators. "She made a call from her cell phone—that puts at least one other person in on the deal. I say two. Whoever's inside the club, and somebody pushing the buttons, organizing. Our guy here shot a cop, so he knows he's going down hard. His wife's dead, his operation's broken and he's looking at death row."

"Doesn't give him much incentive to talk. You going to deal him a life sentence?"

"That's the road. Let's make sure he walks it."

She showed her badge to the uniform on guard at Fricks's door, walked through.

Fricks lay in bed, his skin pale, slightly gray. His eyes were blurred, but open. His gaze passed over Ally and Hickman, then returned to contemplate the ceiling.

"I have nothing to say. I want a lawyer."

"Well, that makes our job easier." Hickman walked over

to the bed, pursed his lips. "Doesn't look like a cop killer, does he, Fletcher?"

"He's not. Yet. Dietz might make it. Of course, this guy here's still looking at being strapped to a table and being put down like a sick dog. Nighttime B and E, burglary, possession of an unregistered weapon, assault with a deadly, attempted murder of a police officer." She moved her shoulders. "And plenty more where that came from."

"I have nothing to say."

"Then shut up," she suggested. "Why try to help yourself? Trust a lawyer to take care of everything. But... I'm not in the mood to make deals with lawyers. How about you, Hickman?"

"Nope, can't say that's my mood at this time."

"We're not in the mood," Ally repeated. "Not when we have a fellow officer fighting for his life up in Intensive Care. That really puts us off lawyers who look for ways to wiggle cop killers out of the noose. Right, Hickman?"

"Yeah, puts me right off. I don't see any reason we should give this guy any kind of a break. I say let him hang for it all by himself."

"Well, we ought to look at the big picture, though. Show a little compassion. He lost his wife last night." She watched the ripple of pain run over Fricks's face before he closed his eyes.

There, she thought, was the key to him.

"That's rough. His wife's dead, and he's lying here shot up and looking at a death sentence." Ally lifted her shoulders, let them fall. "Maybe he's not thinking how other people, people who helped put him in this situation could walk away clean. Clean, and rich, while he's twisting in the wind on a very short rope. And his wife gets put in the ground."

She leaned over the bed. "But he ought to be thinking about it. Of course maybe he didn't love his wife."

"Don't talk to me about Madeline." His voice wavered. "She was my heart."

"Really. I'm touched. That touches me. Now that might not hold any weight with Hickman here, but me, I've got a soft spot for true love. Since I do, I'm going to tell you you ought to be thinking how you can help yourself now, because if you were her heart, she wouldn't want you to go down for this alone."

His eyes flickered, then closed.

"You ought to be thinking that if you cooperate and tell us what we want to know, we'll go to the D.A. and press for a little leniency. Show some remorse now, Richard, reach out. That'll go a long way toward keeping you off a table in a little room a few years down the road."

"I talk, I'm already dead."

Ally shot Hickman a glance. "You'll get protection."

Fricks's eyes were still closed, but tears began to leak out of them. "I loved my wife."

"I know you did." Ally lowered the bed guard so she could sit beside him.

Intimacy now, she thought. Sympathy. And infused her voice with both. "I saw you together at Blackhawk's. The way you looked at each other tells me you had something special between you."

"She she's gone."

"But you tried to save her, didn't you, Richard? You ran out of the house first, to cover for her. That's why you're in this jam. She loved you. She'd want you to help yourself. She'd want you to go on living, to do whatever you had to do to go on. Richard, you tried to save her last night, drawing the cops off her so she could get away. You did what you could. Now you've got to save yourself."

"No one was supposed to get hurt. The guns were just a precaution, to scare anybody off if something went wrong."

"That's right. You didn't plan on this. I believe that. That'll make a difference how this all comes out for you. Things just got out of control."

"Nothing ever went wrong before. She panicked. That's all. She just panicked, and I couldn't think of anything else to do."

"You didn't mean to hurt anybody." Ally kept her voice quiet, compassionate, even while the image of Dietz, bleeding on the ground, ran through her mind. "You just wanted to give her time to get away." She took a moment while he wept.

"How'd you get past the alarm systems?"

"I've got a knack for electronics." He took the tissues she handed him, wiped his eyes. "I worked in security. People don't always remember to set their alarms anyway. But when they did, I could usually disarm them. If I couldn't, it was a wash and we walked away. Where have they put Madeline? Where is she?"

"We'll talk about that. Help me out here, and I'll do what I can to arrange for you to see her. Who called you from the club, Richard, to tell you something was wrong with the Barneses? Was it the same person Madeline called from the car?"

He let out a sobbing breath, shook his head. "I want immunity."

Hickman let out a snort, made a move to draw Ally off the bed, make her the protector. "The son of a bitch wants immunity. You're bending over backward to help him out, and he wants a walk. Screw him. Let him hang."

"Hold on. Just hold on. Can't you see the man's upset? Lying here like this, he can't even make arrangements for his wife's funeral."

"She—" Fricks turned his head away, and his chest heaved once. "She wanted to be cremated. It was important to her."

"We can help you arrange that. We can help you give her what she wanted. You have to give us something back."

"Immunity."

"Listen, Richard. You can't ask for the moon and stars on this one. Now I could make you promises, but I'm being straight with you. Best I can do is leniency."

"We don't need him, Ally." Hickman picked up the chart at the foot of the bed, scanned it. "We got him cold, and we'll pick up the rest of the pieces within a couple of days."

"He's right." Ally let out a sigh, looked back at Fricks. "A couple of days, maybe less, we'll have all the answers. But if you save us some time, some trouble, prove you're remorseful over shooting that cop, I can promise to go to bat for you. We know there are other people involved. It's just a matter of time before we get to them. Help me out, I'll help you. I'll help you do what you need to do for Madeline. That's fair."

"It was her brother." He said it between his teeth, then opened his eyes. They were no longer blurry, no longer wet, but burning dry with hate. "He talked her into it. He could talk her into anything. It was going to be an adventure, exciting. He set it up, all of it. He's the reason she's dead."

"Where is he?"

"He has a house down in Littleton. Big house on the lake. His name's Matthew Lyle, and he'll be coming after me for what happened to Madeline. He's crazy. I tell you he's crazy, and he's obsessed with her. He'll kill me."

"Okay, don't worry. He won't get near you." Ally took out her notebook. "Tell me more about Matthew Lyle."

At four that afternoon, Jonah was settled behind his desk, trying to work. He was furious with himself for calling Ally three times, twice at home, once at the station. And equally furious she'd made no attempt to get back to him.

He'd decided he'd made a very big mistake by walking out of her apartment instead of staying with her in the dark, in the bed, instead of taking what he wanted.

It was a mistake he'd have to live with, and he was certain he could live with it more comfortably than live with the options.

All he wanted now was the simple courtesy of information. Damn it, she owed him that. He'd let her into his life, into his business, let her work side by side with his friends while she deceived them. While he deceived them.

Now, by God, he wanted answers.

He snatched the phone up again just as the elevator doors slid open. And Ally walked through.

"I still had your code."

Saying nothing, he replaced the receiver. She was dressed for work, he noted. Cop work. "I'll make a note to have it changed."

Her eyebrows rose but she continued across the room and dropped comfortably into the chair across from his desk. "I figured you'd want an update."

"You figured correctly."

Something was in his craw, she noted. They'd get to that later. "Fricks rolled over on his brother-in-law. Matthew Lyle, aka Lyle Matthews, aka Lyle Delaney. Computer crimes mostly, with some assaults. He's got a long sheet, but most of the charges were dumped. Insufficient evidence, deals. Did some psych time, though. He's cleared out. We hit his place a couple of hours ago, and he's gone."

She paused long enough to rub her eyes. "Didn't have time to take everything with him. The house was packed with stolen goods. From what it looks like they've turned very little, if anything. Place looked like an auction house. Oh, and you're going to be short a waitress tonight."

"I didn't think you'd be reporting for work tonight."

"No, I didn't mean me. Jan. According to Fricks, she and Lyle are..." She lifted a hand, crossed two fingers. "Very close. She's the inside man. Scanned for the marks, passed the credit card number to Lyle via beeper. The Fricks move in, she helps cover for them while they lift the keys. Then she alerts them with another code when the targets call for their check. Gives the Fricks time to finish up, clear out. Very smooth all in all."

"Have you got her?"

"No, doesn't look like she went home last night. My guess is she went straight to Lyle, and they went under together. We will get her. We'll get them both."

"I don't doubt it. I suppose that ends your association with Blackhawk's."

"Looks like." She rose, wandered to the window. He had the blinds shut today, so she tapped a slat up, looked out. "I'll need to interview your people. I thought they'd feel more comfortable if I did it here. Do you have any problem with me using your office for it?"

"No."

"Great. I'll start with you. Get it out of the way." She came back to sit, took out her notepad. "Tell me what you know about Jan."

"She's worked here about a year. She was good at her job, a favorite with a number of the regulars. Had a knack for remembering names. She was reliable and efficient."

"Did you have a personal relationship with her?"

"No."

"But you're aware she lives in the same apartment building as Frannie?"

"Is that against the law?"

"How did you come to hire her?"

"She applied for the job. Frannie has nothing to do with this."

"I didn't say she did." Ally took a photo out of her bag. "Have you ever seen this man in here?"

Jonah glanced at the police photo of a dark-haired man of about thirty. "No."

"See him anywhere else?"

"No. Is this Lyle?"

"That's right. Why are you angry with me?"

"Irritated," he corrected coolly. "I'd classify it as irritated. I don't care to be interrogated by the police."

"I'm a cop, Jonah. That's a fact." She put the photo back into her bag. "I've got a job to finish. That's another fact. And I'm hung up on you, there's fact number three. Now maybe all of that irritates you, but that's the way it is. I'd like to start the interviews now."

He got to his feet as she did. "You're right. It all irritates me."

"There you go. I'd appreciate it if you'd send Will up now. And stay downstairs. I might need to speak with you again."

He came around the desk. Her eyes narrowed, flashed a cold warning as he approached her. They stayed level and cool when he gripped the lapels of her jacket and hauled her to her toes.

A dozen desires, all of them impossible, ran through his mind. "You push too many of my buttons," he muttered, and releasing her, walked away.

"Same goes." But she said it quietly, after he'd gone.

"So…" Frannie lit a cigarette, peered at Ally through the haze of smoke. "You're a cop. I might've figured it if Jonah hadn't been with you. He doesn't like cops any more than I do."

Frannie had put on an attitude, Ally noted, and nodded. "Now, there's breaking news. Listen, let's make this as painless as possible for everyone. You've got the rundown on the burglary ring, how the club was used, Jan's part in it."

"I've got what you've decided to tell me now that you're wearing your badge."

"That's right. And that's all you need. How long have you known her?"

"About a year and a half, I guess. I ran into her in the laundry room of my apartment building. She was waiting tables in a bar. I worked in a bar." Frannie lifted her shoulders. "We hung out together now and again. I liked her well enough. When Jonah opened this place, I helped get her a job. Does that make me an accessory?"

"No, it makes you a jerk for copping an attitude with me. She ever mention a boyfriend?"

"She liked men, and men liked her."

"Frannie." Ally shifted, decided to play another angle. "Maybe you don't like cops, but there's one on the critical list right now, and he's a friend of mine. They're still not sure he'll make it. He's got two kids and a wife who loves him. Another woman's dead. Somebody loved her, too. You want to go a round with me on personal business, fine. Let's just get this done first."

Frannie made a little shrugging movement again. "She talked about this one guy sometimes. Never told me his name. Liked to be mysterious about it. But she said things like pretty soon she wouldn't be hauling trays and bagging tips."

She got up, crossed over to open the panel to the bar in a way that told Ally she was very at home in Jonah's space. She pulled out a soft drink, twisted off the cap. "I figured it was talk. She liked to talk big about men. Conquests, you know?"

"Did you ever see her with this guy?" Ally nudged the photo across the desk.

Sipping from the bottle, Frannie walked back, studied the photo. "Maybe. Yeah." Frannie scratched her jaw. "I saw them come into the building together a couple of times. Didn't seem like her type is what I thought. He's kinda short, a little pudgy. Ordinary. Jan, she went more for flash. Studs with platinum cards was her usual type."

Catching herself, Frannie shook her head, dropped into a chair. "That sounds hard. I liked her. Look, she's young, maybe a little foolish. But she's not mean."

"You might want to keep in mind that she used you, Jonah, and this place. Now, did she ever mention anyplace they went together? Any plans?"

"No…well, she might've said something about a place on a lake. I didn't pay much attention when she started bragging. Most of it was just air."

Ally questioned her for another fifteen minutes, but didn't jiggle anything loose.

"Okay. If you think of anything, I'd appreciate a call." Rising, Ally offered Frannie a card.

"Sure." Frannie skimmed her eyes over it. "Detective Fletcher."

"Would you ask Beth to come up, please?"

"Why the hell don't you leave her alone? She doesn't know anything."

"But I have such a good time intimidating and threatening potential witnesses." She came around the desk, sat on the corner. "Okay, there's the bell. Go ahead with your personal round."

"I don't like the way you came in here, the way you used

us and spied on us. I know how it works. You did a background check on everybody, pried into all our lives and sat in judgment. I guess you're sorry it turned out to be Jan instead of the former hooker."

"You're wrong. I like you."

Off balance, Frannie sat again. "Bull."

"Why shouldn't I like you? You got yourself out of a spiral that only goes down. You've got a legitimate job, and you're good at it. The only problem I have with you is Jonah."

"What do you mean, Jonah?"

"You've got a relationship with him. I'm attracted to him. That's makes you a personal problem for me."

Baffled now, Frannie took out another cigarette. "I don't get you. You mean it about Jonah?" she said after a minute. "You've got a thing for him?"

"It looks like. But the problem's mine. Like I said, I like you. In fact, I admire the way you turned your life around. I never had to do that, never had to face those kinds of things, make those kind of choices. I'd like to think I'd do as well as you have if I had."

"Damn it." Frannie pushed to her feet, paced the room. "Damn it," she repeated. "Okay, first. I don't have a relationship with Jonah. Not like you mean. Never did. He never bought me when I was for sale, and he never touched me that way when I was free. Even when I offered."

Though a fine sense of relief ran through her, Ally kept her voice mild. "Is he blind or stupid?"

Frannie stopped pacing, took a long, hard look. "I don't want to like you. You're sure making it tough not to. I love him. A long time ago, I loved him…different than I do now. We grew up together, more or less. I mean we've known each other since we were kids. Me and Jonah and Will, we go back."

"I know. It shows."

"When I was working corners, Jonah'd come by sometimes, pay me for the night. Then he'd take me for coffee or something to eat. And that was it." Frannie's eyes softened. "He always was a sucker."

"Are we talking about the same man?"

"If he cares about you, that's it. He'll keep pulling you up no matter how many times you fall down again. Bite his hand, he'll just ignore you and haul you up. You can't fight that. You can't fight that kind of thing for long. I didn't make it easy for him."

With a sigh, she walked over to sit again, picked up the soft drink, finished it off. "A few years ago, I was scraping the bottom of the gutter. I'd been on the stroll since I was fifteen. By the time I hit twenty I was used up. So I figured what the hell, let's just get out of this whole mess. I started to slash my wrists. Seemed just dramatic enough."

She held out a hand, turned it over to expose the scar on the inside of her left wrist. "Only got to the one, and didn't do such a hot job on it."

"What stopped you?"

"First? The blood. Really put me off the idea," she said with a surprisingly cheerful laugh. "Anyway, I'm standing there in this filthy bathroom, stoned, bleeding, and I got scared. Really scared. I called Jonah. I don't know what would've happened if I hadn't reached him, if he hadn't come. He got me to the hospital, then he got me into detox."

She sat back, tracing a finger over the scar as if it brought the memory back with more clarity. "Then he asked me something he'd asked me a hundred times before. He asked me if I wanted a life. This time I said yes. Then he helped me make one.

"Along the way, I thought I should pay him back, and I offered what I was used to offering men. It was the only time he ever really got pissed off." She smiled a little. "He thought more of me than I did of myself. Nobody else ever had. If I knew anything about Jan, or this business, I'd tell you. Because he'd want me to, and there's nothing I wouldn't do for him."

"From where I'm standing, you both got a good deal."

"I've never once had a man look at me the way I've seen him look at you."

"Then you've got your eyes shut." It was Ally's turn to smile. "Keep them open tonight when Will asks for his after-closing brandy."

"Will? Come on."

"Keep your eyes open," Ally said again. "Are we square here?"

"Yeah, sure. I guess." Confused, Frannie got to her feet again.

"Ask Beth to come up. Just give me five minutes to find my brass knuckles."

With a half laugh, Frannie went to the elevator. After pushing the button, she glanced back. "Will knows what I was."

"I guess he knows what you are, too."

She wrapped up the last interview by seven, circled her shoulders and wondered if there was a possibility of food anytime in her near future.

The clock told her she was officially off duty, and since she had nothing to add to the current status of the case, her reports and follow-ups could wait till morning.

Still, she helped herself to the use of Jonah's phone, checking in, giving updates. She was sitting quietly at his desk when he came in.

"Dietz. The cop who was shot last night. They've upgraded his condition from critical to serious." Closing her eyes, she pressed her fingers against them. "It looks like he's going to make it."

"I'm glad to hear it."

"Yeah." She pulled the clip out of her hair, ran her fingers through it. "It sure fills this big hole in my gut. I appreciate the use of your office. I can tell you that the rest of your people aren't suspects, at this time."

"At this time."

"I can't give you more than that, Blackhawk. All evidence points to the fact that Jan and Jan alone worked the inside. It's the best I can do."

She tossed the clip on his desk. "Now, I've got something else to say."

"Which is?"

"I'm off duty. Can I have a drink?"

"I happen to have a club just downstairs."

"I was thinking of a private drink. From your private bar." She gestured toward the panel. "If you could spare a glass of wine. I noticed a nice sauvignon blanc in there."

He turned toward the panel, opened it, selected the bottle. "Why don't you join me?"

"I'm still on duty. I don't drink during working hours."

"I noticed that. Don't drink, don't smoke, don't hit on the customers. During working hours," she added.

He turned back, the glass of pale gold wine in his hand. And watched her take off her jacket.

"I hope you don't mind," she said, then shrugged out of her holster. "I find it awkward to seduce men when I'm wearing my weapon."

She laid it on his desk, then walked toward him.

# Chapter 8

She might have taken off her gun, Jonah thought, but she wasn't unarmed. A woman with eyes as potent as whiskey and a voice like smoke would never be without a weapon.

Worse, she knew it. That longbow mouth was curved up, just a little, like a cat's when the canary cage was open. He didn't much care for his role as target.

"Your wine." He held out the glass, a deliberate move to keep an arm-span of distance between then. "And though I appreciate the thought, I don't have time for a seduction at the moment."

"Oh, it shouldn't take very long."

She imagined he'd devastated countless women with that careless, almost absent dismissal. For her, it was only a challenge she had every confidence of meeting.

She took the wine, and moved right in, grabbing a fistful of his shirt to hold him in place. "I really like the look of you, Blackhawk. Hot mouth, cool eyes." She took a sip of wine, watching him over the rim. "I want to see more."

His senses went blade sharp. The muscles of his belly tied themselves into a dozen hard and tangled knots. "You get right to it, don't you?"

"You said you were in a hurry." She rose on her toes to nip her teeth into his bottom lip, and sliced a jagged line of need straight through him. "So I'm picking up the pace."

"I don't like sexually aggressive women."

Her laugh was low, mocking. "You don't like cops, either."

"That's exactly right."

"Then this is going to be very unpleasant for you. That's a shame." She leaned in, skimmed her tongue up the side of his neck. "I want you to touch me. I want you to put your hands on me."

He kept them at his sides, but in his mind they were already ripping at her shirt, already taking. "Like I said, it's a nice offer, but—"

"I can feel your heart pounding." She shook her hair back, and the scent of it slithered into his system. "I can feel the way you want me, the same way I want you."

"Some of us learn to shelve certain wants."

She saw the change in his eyes, the faintest deepening of green. Dead giveaway, she thought. "And some of us don't." She took another sip of wine, then moved forward, walking him backward. "I guess I'm going to have to get rough."

Mortified she'd put him in retreat, he stopped short, nearly groaning when her body bumped his. "You're going to embarrass yourself. Drink your wine, Detective Fletcher, and go home."

She imagined he thought his voice was clipped, dismissive. But it was thick and strained. And his heart was a fury under her fist.

"What is that answer you're always giving me? No. Yes, that's it." She drained her glass so the wine pumped in with the reckless power surging through her. "No," she said again and, tossing the glass aside, hooked a hand in the waistband of his trousers.

Aroused and furious, he retreated again. "Cut it out."

"Make me." She threw her head back, then leaped, arms wrapping around his neck, legs vised around his waist. "Come on and make me. You've got plenty of moves."

Her mouth swooped down to tease his, and she tasted a wild, wonderful mix of desire and temper. "Take me down," she whispered, raking her hands through his hair. "Finish it. Finish me."

His blood was raging. The taste of her, hot and female with the faint zip of wine, was on his tongue. "You're asking for trouble."

"So…" She rubbed her lips over his, as if imprinting her flavor on him. "Give it to me."

Control snapped. He could hear it echo in his head like the violent crack of hammer against stone. He gripped her hair, wrapping it around his hand, yanking it back so that she let out a little gasp as her head flew back.

"The line's crossed." His eyes weren't cool now. They simmered, as if a bolt of lightning had struck a pool. "You'll give me everything I want. What you don't give, I'll take. That's the deal."

Her breath was already quickened. "Done."

His gaze lowered to the long, vulnerable curve of her throat. Then he set his teeth on her.

Her body jerked against his as the shock of that threat of pain, that lance of pleasure stabbed into her. Then she was falling, clinging to him as she tumbled into the shadows, into the dark.

She lost her breath when she hit the bed, lost her grip when his body covered hers. Then, for a moment, when he tore her shirt open, she lost her mind.

Floundering for balance, she threw an arm up. Her knuckles thudded against the bedspread, then her fingers dug in. "Wait."

"No."

His mouth was on her breast, ravaging tender flesh with lips and teeth and tongue. She fought for air, fought to find the power that had been hers just moments before. Instead she found herself spinning past control, past reason.

His hands were on her, as she had demanded. And they were hard and fast, ruthlessly exploiting weakness, secrets she hadn't known she'd possessed.

Then his mouth came back to hers, hot and greedy. The low sound in her throat was equal parts terror and triumph. Leaping recklessly toward the heat, she met demand with demand.

She went wild beneath him. Writhing, bucking, reaching. He'd wanted nothing less. If he was to sin, he would sin fully, and reap all the pleasure before the punishment.

Her skin seemed to burn under his hands, his mouth. He craved. The long, clean lines of her. The taut and ready strength. The delicate give of curves.

He rolled with her over the wide pool of the bed, taking what and how he wanted.

She tugged at his shirt, sending buttons flying, then letting out a sound of feral delight when flesh met flesh. When he dragged her to her knees, she trembled. But there was nothing of fear left in her.

She could see his eyes, the predatory gleam of them,

from the backwash of light from the office. She let out a ragged breath as she ran her hands up his chest, into his hair.

"More," she told him, and crushed her mouth to his.

And there was more.

Lightning quick flashes of unbearable ecstasy. Gusts of shuddering desperation. And a flood of needs that swamped them both.

He tugged the slacks down her hips, following the path of exposed flesh with his mouth until she was shuddering and mindlessly murmuring his name in that hoarse, erotic voice he couldn't get out of head.

His teeth scraped her inner thigh, sent the strong muscles quivering. When she arched, opened, he feasted on her.

She cried out as the orgasm ripped through her, fisted her hands in the bedclothes and let each glorious aftershock batter her until her system wept with the pleasure of it. Heat swarmed up her body, through her, and she embraced it, reveled in the breathless power of what they made together.

"Now. Jonah."

"No."

He couldn't get enough of her. Each time he thought desperation would overpower him, he found something new to tantalize him. The subtle flare of her hips, the narrow dip of her waist. He wanted to feel the bite of her nails on him again, hear that choked cry of release when he dragged her over the next edge.

Her breath was sobbing, his own so clogged in his lungs he thought they would burst from it. He moved up her again while her hands raced over him and her body bucked.

He could see her eyes, and nothing else. Just the dark glint of them, watching him as he rose over her. He held back for one quivering instant, then plunged.

Here was everything. The thought stabbed through him then shattered in his brain as she closed hot and tight around him.

She rose to him, fell with him, the slick slide of bodies mating. Sighed with him as pleasure shimmered. Her heart thundered against his, beat for beat. Their breath mixed, drawing him deeper so that his mouth was on hers, another link, as they moved together.

The tempo quickened so that the slide became a slap, and sighs broke into gasps and moans. Her hips pistoned as he pounded into her. As sensations staggered her, she raked her nails down his back, dug them into his hips. Urging him on even as she was swamped by the next crest.

He felt himself slip—a glorious feeling of surrender— and with his face buried in the tumbled mass of her hair, he fell.

It was over for him. He knew it the minute his system leveled and his mind began to work again. He'd never get over her. Never get past her. With one sweep, she'd destroyed a lifetime of careful avoidance.

Now he was stupidly, helplessly, irretrievably in love with her.

Nothing could be more impossible or more dangerous.

She could slice him to pieces. No one had ever been allowed to have that kind of control or power over him. He didn't mean to let that change now.

He needed some sort of defense, and determined to start building it, he rolled away from her.

She simply rolled with him, stretched that long, limber body of hers over his and said, "Mmmmm."

Another time he might have laughed, or at least felt that knee-jerk of pure male satisfaction. Instead he felt a light trip of panic.

"Well, you got what you wanted, Fletcher."

Instead of being insulted, which would have given him a little room to regroup, she just nuzzled his neck. "Damn right."

To please herself she hooked a leg around him, then shifted to straddle him and slick back her hair. "I like your body, Blackhawk. All tough and rangy and taut." She trailed a finger over his chest, admiring the contrast of her skin against his. "It looks good on you."

He twirled a lock of her hair around his finger. "Yours too," he said dryly.

She leaned down until they were nose to nose. "Now that we're all cozy and complimentary, how about doing me a favor?"

"And that would be?"

"Food. I'm starving."

"Want a menu?"

"No. Umm." She tilted her head, teased his mouth with hers. "Just something that's on it. Maybe you could send down for something." She trailed her lips down to his jaw, back up to his mouth. "And we could, you know, fuel up. Mind if I grab a shower?"

"No." He rolled her onto her back. "But you'll have to wait until I'm done with you."

"Oh?" She smiled. "Well, a deal's a deal."

And when he was done with her, she staggered more than walked into the bathroom. She closed the door, leaned back against it and let out a long puff of breath.

She'd never had to work harder to maintain a careless, sophisticated image. Then again, she'd never had anyone turn her inside out and leave her jittering like a mass of jelly before.

Not that she was complaining, Ally told herself as she rubbed the heel of her hand over her heart. But her idea that sex was simply a pleasant occupation between two consenting adults who, hopefully, cared about each other had been forever shattered.

Pleasant didn't begin to describe making love with Jonah Blackhawk.

Waiting for her system to level again, she scanned the bathroom. He'd indulged himself here, she noted, with the deep, why-don't-you-join-me whirlpool tub in his customary jet-black. Though it looked tempting, she thought she'd settle for the separate shower enclosed by seeded glass.

The sink was a wide scoop in a sheer black counter. Nothing stood on it, no pieces of him left out for the casual eye to study. Just as there were no pieces, no odds and ends, memorabilia or personal photographs in his office or bedroom.

She was tempted to poke in the cabinet, rifle through a couple of the drawers—what kind of shaving cream did he use? What brand of toothpaste?—but it seemed so pitifully obvious.

Instead she crossed the white tiles and studied her own face in the mirror. Her eyes were soft, her mouth still swollen from that wonderful assault of his. There were a number of faint bruises shadowing her skin.

All in all, she decided she looked just the way she felt. Like a woman happily used.

But what did he see when he looked at her? she wondered. When he looked at her in that cool, distant way? He wanted her, she could have no doubts about that. But did he feel nothing else?

Did he think she hadn't noticed the way he'd drawn back

from her both times, after passion had been spent? As if his need for…separation was as deep as his desire.

And why was she letting it hurt her? It was such a *female* reaction.

"Well, I am a female, damn it," she muttered and turned to switch on the shower.

If he thought he was going to get away with nudging her back whenever he pleased, he was very much mistaken. The man was not going to rock her to her toes then stroll away while she was still teetering.

She stuck her head under the spray, mumbling to herself.

She expected a lot more give-and-take in a relationship. And if he couldn't trouble himself to give her a little affection along with the heat, well then he could…

She trailed off, winced.

She sounded like Dennis, she thought. Or at least close enough.

At least she could stop that before she dug herself a hole too deep to crawl out of.

The only relationship she had with Jonah was a physical one, and she herself had insisted on it. Both of them knew the ground rules and were smart enough not to need them spelled out.

If she needed to mix emotion in with desire, that was fine. That was okay. But it was also her problem.

Satisfied she'd solved the matter in her own mind, she turned off the taps, turned for a towel.

And let out one wild yelp when she saw Jonah holding one out for her.

"Most people sing in the shower," he commented. "You're the first I've come across who talks to herself in the shower."

"I was not." She snatched the towel.

"Okay, it was more unintelligible mumbling."

"Fine. Most people knock before they come into an occupied bathroom."

"I did, but you couldn't hear me because you were talking to yourself. I thought you might want this." He held up his other hand, and the black silk robe that dangled from his fingers.

"Yeah. Thanks." She wrapped the towel around herself, anchored it with a hand between her breasts.

"Dinner'll be up in a minute." Idly he skimmed a fingertip down her arm, sliding water over flesh.

"Good. I need to get my weapon off your desk."

"I moved it." Frowning now, he traced the curve of her shoulder. "I put it in the bedroom. The door's closed. They'll just leave the tray on my desk."

"Works for me." When she felt the brush of his finger over her collarbone, she released her hold on the towel, let it fall to her feet. "Is this what you're looking for?"

"I shouldn't want you again already." Eyes on hers, he backed her against the wall. "I shouldn't need you again."

"Then walk away." She tugged down the zipper on the trousers he'd pulled on. "Who's stopping you?"

He closed a hand around her throat. Though the pulse under his fingers jumped, she merely lifted her chin and dared him.

"Tell me you want me," he demanded. "Say my name, and that you want me."

"Jonah." She took the first step onto a bridge she knew could burn away under her feet. "I've never wanted anyone the way I want you." Her breath hitched as she drew it in, but her eyes remained steady. "Give it back to me."

"Allison." He lowered his forehead to hers, in a gesture so weary and sweet, she reached out to comfort him. "I can't think for wanting you. Just you," he murmured, then took her mouth, took her body. Desperately.

"I gotta say," Ally commented as she ate like a starving wolf, "you've got a really good kitchen. A lot of clubs, the food's mediocre at best. But yours, um…" She licked barbecue sauce from her thumb. "It's first-class."

She shook her head when he picked up the wine to top off her glass. "No, uh-uh. I'm driving."

"Stay." Another rule broken, he thought. He never asked a woman to stay.

"I would if I could." Smiling she tugged on the lapel of the borrowed robe. "But I don't have a change for tomorrow, and I'm back on eight-to-fours. As it is I'm going to have to borrow a shirt from you to get home. You did a number on mine."

He did no more than pick up his own glass, but she felt him retreat. "Ask me to come back tomorrow and stay."

He looked back at her. "Come back tomorrow and stay."

"Okay. Look at that! Look at that! That runner was safe."

"Out. By a half step," Jonah corrected, amused that she'd nearly come off the sofa when the play on the wide screen caught her eye.

"Bull. You watch the instant replay. They hit the bag at the same time. Tie goes to the runner. See? Manager's coming out. Give him hell. Anyway—"

Satisfied the requisite argument would proceed over a controversial call, she turned her attention back to Jonah. She smiled, rubbed her bare feet intimately against his hip. "Pretty good deal from my point of view. Good sex, good food and a ball game."

"To some…" He reached down to trace a finger up her instep. "Paradise."

"Since we're in paradise, can I ask you something really important?"

"All right."

"Are you going to eat all those fries?"

He grinned at her, shoved the plate in her direction, then leaned over to answer the phone. "Blackhawk. Yes." He held out the portable receiver. "For you, Detective."

"I left this number when I logged out," she told him, and took the phone. "Fletcher." She straightened on the sofa, and her eyes went flat. "Where? I'm on my way."

She was already on her feet when she tossed the receiver on the hook. "They found Jan."

"Where is she?"

"On her way to the morgue. I have to go."

"I'm going with you."

"There's no point in it."

"She worked for me," he said simply and walked into the bedroom.

Jonah had seen and done a great deal. In the first half of his life, he'd thought he'd seen and done everything. He'd seen death, but he'd never seen it stripped bare in cold, antiseptic surroundings.

He looked through the glass at the young woman and felt nothing but raw pity.

"I can verify ID," Ally said beside him. "But it's cleaner procedure if the visual comes from somebody else who knew her. Is that Janet Norton?"

"Yes."

She nodded to the technician behind the glass, and he lowered the blinds. "I don't know how long I'll be."

"I'll wait."

"There's coffee, down this corridor and to the left. It's

crap, but it's usually hot and strong." She reached for the door, hesitated. "Listen, if you change your mind and want to go, just go."

"I'll wait," he said again.

It didn't take her long. When she came out he was sitting in one of the molded plastic chairs at the end of the hallway. Her footsteps clicked on the linoleum, and the clicks echoed.

"Nothing much to do until the autopsy report's in."

"How did she die?" When Ally shook her head he got to his feet. "How? It can't be that big a dent in the rules to tell me."

"She was stabbed. Multiple wounds, by what appears to be a long bladed knife with a serrated edge. Her body was dumped on the side of the road off southbound 85, just a few miles outside of Denver. He threw her purse out with her. He wanted us to find her and ID her quickly."

"And that's it for you? Just identify her and put another piece in the puzzle?"

She didn't snap back. She recognized the chill in his eyes as temper on a short leash, and her own was straining.

"Let's get out of here." Ally headed out. She wanted to fill her lungs with fresh air. "From the number of wounds, it appears she was killed with considerable rage."

"Where's yours?" He shoved the door open. "Or don't you feel any?"

She strode out ahead of him. "Don't slap at me."

He grabbed her arm, whirled her around. She led with her fist and pulled it an inch from his jaw. "You want rage." She shoved away from him. "I'll give you some rage. From the looks of things she was getting sliced to pieces while I was rolling around on the sheets with you. Now ask how I feel?"

He caught her before she got to the car and wrenched the door open. "I'm sorry."

She tried to shrug him off, then push him away, but when she spun around snarling he just wrapped his arms around her.

"I'm sorry." He said it quietly, pressing his lips to her hair. "I was out of line. We both know it wouldn't have made any difference where we were or what we were doing. This would have happened."

"No, it wouldn't have made any difference. And still, two people are dead." She drew away. "I can't afford rage. Can you understand that?"

"Yes." He took the clip out of her hair, rubbed the back of her neck. "I'd like to go home with you. I'd like to be with you tonight."

"Good, because that's what I'd like, too."

She slid into the car, waiting for him to climb into the passenger seat. They both needed to set aside the rage, she knew, and the guilt. "I have to get up really early."

He smiled at her. "I don't."

"Okay." She pulled out of the lot. "That means you get to make up the bed and do the dishes. That's the deal."

"Does it also mean that you make the coffee?"

"It does."

"I'll take the deal."

When she reached her building, she pulled into the underground garage. "Tomorrow might be a long one," she told him. "Does it matter what time I get to your place?"

"No." He got out of the car, came around to her side, then held out his hand for her keys.

"So what, did you take like a charm-school course or something?"

"Top of my class. I have a plaque." He pressed the button for the elevator. "Now some women are insecure and find the simple courtesy of a man opening doors for them or pulling out their chair, whatever, troubling. Naturally you're secure enough in your own power and femininity not to be troubled."

"Naturally," she agreed, and rolled her eyes as he gestured her into the elevator. Then he took her hand and made her smile.

"I like your style, Blackhawk. I haven't been able to pin it down, not exactly, but I like it." She angled her head to study him. "You used to play baseball, right?"

"That and your father kept me in high school."

"Basketball was my game. You ever shoot hoops?"

"Now and then."

"Want to shoot some with me, on Sunday?"

"I might." He walked out of the elevator with her. "What time?"

"Oh, let's say two. I'll pick you up. We can go—" She broke off, shifting in front of him fast and pulling her weapon. "Keep back. Don't touch anything."

He saw it now. The fresh scrape and pry marks on the door. She used two fingers on the knob, turned it, then booted the door open with her foot. She went in low, slapping the lights on, starting her sweep even as Jonah stepped in front of her.

"Get back. What are you crazy?"

"One of the things I learned in charm school was not to use a woman as a shield."

"This woman happens to be the one with the badge, and the gun."

"I noticed. Besides." He'd already scanned the debris of the room. "He's long gone."

She knew it, felt it, but there were rules and procedure.

"Well, pardon the hell out of me while I play cop and make sure. Don't touch anything," she said again, and stepping over a broken lamp, checked the rest of the apartment.

She was swearing in a low, steady voice as she headed for the phone.

"Your old friend Dennis?" Jonah asked.

"Maybe, but I don't think so. Lyle was heading south out of Denver." She jabbed her fingers into the keypad on the phone. "I think I just found out what he was doing here. This is Detective Fletcher. I've had a break-in."

Even before the crime scene unit arrived, Ally snapped on protective gloves and began to do inventory. Her stereo components, good ones, hadn't been stolen. But they had been smashed. Her laptop computer and the small TV that stood above the stereo had received the same treatment.

Every table lamp in the place—including the antique bookkeeper's light she'd bought for her desk—was broken. Her sofa had a long gash from end to end, and the guts of it spilled out in nasty puffs.

He'd poured the half gallon of paint she'd bought then had never gotten around to using, in the middle of her bed.

Over the bed, he'd slopped a message in the same paint.

Try To Sleep At Night

"He blames me for his sister's death. He knows I was the one. How does he know?"

"Jan," Jonah said from behind her. "She has to be the one who warned them something was wrong that night," he continued when Ally turned. "You got the Barneses back to their table, but they were still both gone for an unusual amount of time. They were nervous, upset. She picked up on it."

"Maybe." She nodded as she walked back out of the bedroom. "It was enough to make her start thinking. Worrying. She didn't notice when I left. She was busy, but Frannie did. She might have mentioned it to Jan in passing."

She picked her way through the living room, into the kitchen. "So she called it off, but just a little too late. Too late to save his sister. Doesn't look like he bothered much in here. Nothing worth smashing. I guess—" She broke off, walked slowly to the counter. "Oh, God."

When she turned her eyes were wide and horrified. "My bread knife." She laid her fingertips on the knife block, with one empty slot. "Long blade with serrated edge. God, Jonah. He killed her with my own knife."

# *Chapter 9*

She wasn't going to let it shake her. She couldn't. For a cop, she reminded herself, nerves were as costly as rage and just as dangerous. The break-in at her apartment was a direct, and personal, attack. Her only choice was to stand up to it, maintain her objectivity, and do the job she'd sworn to do.

When the crime scene unit had left, adding their wreckage to what Lyle had left behind him, she hadn't argued with Jonah. He'd told her to pack what she thought she needed.

She was moving in with him until it was over.

Neither of them talked about the giant step they were taking; they told themselves it was simply a logical and convenient arrangement.

Then they had slept, tangled together, for what was left of the night.

"We've doubled the guards on Fricks," Kiniki told her at the morning briefing. "Lyle can't get to him."

"He's too smart to try." Ally stood in her lieutenant's office, hands in pockets. The horror had dulled, and the thin edge of fear was over. "He can wait, and he will. He's not in any hurry to pay Fricks back for what he might see as his part in his sister's death."

Behind the glass wall of Kiniki's office, the phones in the bull pen rang, and detectives went about the business of the day. Ally put herself into the mind of a dead woman she'd known for a matter of days.

"Jan Norton was easy. It was all an adventure to her, romantic, exciting. She was with him, and thought she was safe with him. The canvass of my building turned up two neighbors who saw a couple fitting Lyle's and Jan's description enter the building at around eight o'clock. Holding hands," she added. "She helped him trash my place, then once they were on the road again, he killed her. She stopped having a purpose."

She'd had plenty of time to think it through, lying awake through the darkest hours of the night in Jonah's bed. "He doesn't do anything without a purpose. There's a lot of anger in him for what he sees as the privileged class. There's a pattern in his background, in his previous arrests. All of them involve crimes against wealth—the hacking, the burglaries. Even the assaults were against wealthy superiors at his job when he held a computer programming position."

She pulled her hands out of her pockets, ticked off her fingers. "Wealth, authority, authority, wealth. They're synonymous to him, and both need to be taken down a peg. He's smarter than they are. Why should they have the easy life?"

In her mind she flipped through the steadily growing file of data on Matthew Lyle. "He grew up on the bottom rung of lower middle class. Not quite poor, but never really comfortable. His father had a history of unemployment. Always moving from one job to another. His stepfather was arrogant and domineering. Lyle followed the same patterns. The supervisors and coworkers I've been able to contact all said the same basic thing. He's brilliant with tech stuff, but not great socially. He's arrogant, belligerent and a loner. He came from a broken home, and both of his parents are dead. The only person he was ever close to was his sister."

Ally walked to the glass wall, looked out. "His sister played into his weaknesses, fed his monumental ego. One enabled the other. Now she's gone, and he's got no one but himself."

"Where would he go?"

"Not far," Ally calculated. "He's not finished yet. He has me to deal with, the Barneses, Blackhawk."

"I think your instincts are on target. We've put Mr. and Mrs. Barnes in a safe house. That leaves you, and Blackhawk."

She turned back. "I don't intend to take any unnecessary chances. But I have to keep visible, maintain a routine or he'll just go under and wait me out. He has my name, my address. He's probably got a reasonable description. He wants me to know it. To sweat it."

"We'll stake out your building."

"He may come back there. He doesn't want to just pick me off. It's not personal enough. And I don't think I'll be his first target."

"Blackhawk?"

"Yeah, in order of importance, Jonah's next. And as for Blackhawk, he's not cooperating."

And it still irked that he'd dismissed her idea of arranging protection.

"We can keep a couple of men on him, at a distance."

"You could keep them two miles away, and he'd spot them. Then he'd lose them on principle. Lieutenant, I'm... close to him. He trusts me. I can take care of it."

"You have an investigation to run, Detective, and your own butt to cover."

"I can do a considerable amount of all three at his club. And the fact is, I believe we might lure Lyle out, push him into making a move if he sees me with Blackhawk routinely."

"It's doubtful he knows you killed his sister. We've had a lid on that since the incident."

"But he knows I was part of the operation, the part inside the club. That Blackhawk and I worked together and started the steps that caused his sister's death."

"Agreed. I'm putting two men on Blackhawk, for the next seventy-two hours. Then we'll reevaluate."

"Yes, sir."

"On a different matter, you're aware that Dennis Overton's fingerprints were found on your hubcaps, your wheel wells. A search of his car turned up a recently purchased hunting knife. The lab work isn't back, but there were bits of tire rubber on the blade. He's been fired from the district attorney's office. They'd like to file formal charges."

"Sir—"

"Toughen your spine, Fletcher. If you don't file charges, he can walk. If you do, the D.A. will recommend psych evaluation. He needs it. Or do you want to wait until he shifts his obsession from you to somebody else?"

"No. No, I don't. I'll take care of it."

"Do it now. One lunatic out there after one of my detectives is enough."

The fact that he was right didn't make it any easier. Ally

walked out to the squad room, plopped down at her desk and decided she deserved at least thirty seconds to brood.

She'd made mistakes with Dennis, right from the beginning. Hadn't paid enough attention, hadn't picked up on the cues. None of that was any excuse for his behavior, but it did weigh into her part in triggering it.

"What's the problem, Fletcher? The boss ream you?"

She glanced up at Hickman who made himself at home with his butt on the edge of her desk. "No. I'm about to ream somebody."

He bit into his midmorning Danish. "That usually puts me in a pretty chipper mood."

"That's because you're a heartless jerk."

"I love it when you flatter me."

"If I tell you you're a brainless moron, would you do me a favor?"

He took another bite, sprinkled crumbs on her desk. "My life for you, baby."

"I have to file on Dennis Overton. When the warrant comes through, would you pick him up? He knows you. It might be a little easier on him."

"Sure. Ally, he's not worth the regrets."

"I know it." She got to her feet, pulled her jacket from the back of her chair. Then she smiled, broke off a corner of his Danish and popped it into her mouth. "You're ugly, too."

"Girl of my dreams. Marry me."

Grateful Hickman knew how to lighten her mood, Ally headed out.

Two hours later she was walking into her father's office.

He met her at the door this time, ran his hands up and down her arms while he studied her face. Then he simply pulled her into his embrace.

"Good to see you," he murmured.

She burrowed in, let herself absorb his strength, his stability. "You're always there, you and Mom. No matter what, you're right there. I just wanted to say that first."

"She's worried about you."

"I know. I'm sorry for it. Listen." She gave him an extra squeeze, then drew back. "I know you're up-to-date, but I wanted you to know I'm okay. And I'm handling it. Lyle can't wait long to make a move. He's got nobody now. Everything we've got on him indicates he needs somebody, a woman, to admire him, feed his ego, play his games with him. Alone, he'll break."

"I agree. And it's my assessment that it's a woman he'll want most to punish. You're elected."

"Agreed. He's already made his first big mistake by breaking into my place. He exposed himself. He left prints everywhere. His grief, his anger, pushed him to show me what he is and what he wants. Using my knife to kill Jan, that was his way of saying it could have been me."

"So far we have no argument. Why are you alone?"

"He won't move on me during the day. He works at night. I'm not going to take stupid chances, Dad. That's a promise. I wanted you to know I've filed charges against Dennis."

"Good. I don't want you hassled, and I don't want you distracted. I went by your apartment this morning."

"I've got some serious redecorating to do."

"You can't stay there. Come home for a few days. Until this is closed."

"I've, ah, already made arrangements." She tucked her hands into her pockets, rocked back on her heels. This part, she thought, would be tricky. "I'm staying at Blackhawk's."

"You can't bunk in a club," he began. Then it hit him, a sneaky jab to the solar plexus. "Oh." Boyd ran a hand through his hair, walked to his desk. Shook his head, walked to the coffeepot. "You, ah... Hell."

"I'm sleeping with Jonah."

His back still to her, Boyd lifted a hand, waved it from side to side. Acknowledging the signal, Ally closed her mouth and waited.

"You're a grown woman." He got that much out, then set the coffeepot back down. "Damn it."

"Is that a comment on my age, or my relationship with Blackhawk?"

"Both." He turned back. She was so lovely, he thought, this woman who'd come from him.

"Do you have anything against him?"

"You're my daughter. He's a man. There you go. Don't grin at me when I'm having a paternal crisis."

Obediently she folded her lips. "Sorry."

"If you don't mind, I think I'll imagine you and Jonah are spending your time together discussing great works of literature and playing gin rummy."

"Whatever gets you through, Dad. I'd like to bring him to the Sunday barbecue."

"He won't come."

"Oh, yes." Ally smiled thinly. "He will."

She spent the rest of her shift doing follow-ups on the case and dealing with the threads of two others assigned to her. She closed one on sexual assault, opened another on armed robbery.

She parked her car in a secured lot and backtracked the block and a half to Blackhawk's.

She spotted the stakeout car from the end of the block, and had no doubt Jonah had tagged it, as well.

The first person she saw when she walked into the club was Hickman sitting hunched at the bar. She figured she could have spotted his black eye from a block away, as well.

She went to him, tapped a finger under his chin and studied his face while he sulked. "Who popped you?"

"Your good friend and general jerk-face Dennis Overton."

"You're kidding. He resisted?"

"Ran like a jackrabbit." He glanced toward Frannie, tapped his glass for a refill. "Had to chase him down. Before I could cuff him, he caught me." He picked up his dwindling beer, sipped morosely. "Now I'm wearing this, and I've taken about all the razzing I'm going to."

"Sorry, Hickman." To prove it, she leaned over and touched her lips to the swollen bruise. When she leaned back, she noticed Jonah had turned the corner into the bar. He merely lifted a brow at seeing her with her arm around Hickman's shoulders, then signaled to Will.

"I never figured him for a rabbit." With a heavy sigh, Hickman scooped up a handful of bar nuts. "Then I take him down and got this." He shifted on the stool to show her the hole in the knee of his trousers. "And he's flopping around like a landed trout, and crying like a baby."

"Oh, God."

"One ounce, one ounce of sympathy in his direction, Fletcher, and I'll pop you myself." Instead Hickman began popping the nuts into his mouth. "He swings back and his elbow catches me, right here, right on the cheekbone. I saw whole planets erupt. Stupid son of a bitch can do his crying in a cage tonight. What the hell'd you ever see in him?"

"Beats me. Frannie, put my pal's drinks on my tab, will you?"

"I'm switching to the imported stuff then."

She laughed, then glanced over her shoulder when Will came up behind her.

"Never used to have cops in here." But he said it with

an easy smile, and winked at Frannie. "You want some ice on that eye, Officer?"

Hickman shook his head. "Nah." He used his good one to give Will the once-over. "You got a problem with cops?"

"Not in about five years. Say, is Sergeant Maloney still down at the sixty-third? He busted me twice. Was always straight about it."

Amused, Hickman turned around on the stool. "Yeah, he's still there. Still working vice, too."

"You see him, you tell him, Will Sloan said hi. He was always square with me."

"I'll be sure to do that."

"Anyway, the man says I should have some dinner sent out to your friends in the Ford across the street. Figures they'll get hungry sitting out there all night twiddling their thumbs."

"I'm sure they'll appreciate that," Ally said dryly.

"Least we can do." Giving Hickman a friendly slap on the back, Will headed toward the kitchen.

"I've got a couple of things to do." Ally gave Hickman's black eye another look. "Put some ice on that," she advised, then made her way into the club area to track down Beth.

"Got a minute?"

Beth continued to key in codes on the register. "It's Friday night, we're booked solid. And we're a couple of waitresses short."

Ally acknowledged the sting of the cool tone, but didn't back down. "I can wait until your break."

"I don't know when I'll be able to take one. We're busy."

"I'll wait. I won't take up much of your time."

"Suit yourself." Without a glance at her, Beth strode away.

"She's feeling pretty raw," Will commented.

Ally turned around. "Are you everywhere?"

"Mostly." He lifted his shoulders. "That's my job. She trained Jan like, you know, she trained you. I guess we're all pretty shaken up about what happened."

"And blaming me?"

"I don't. You were doing your job. That's how it works. Beth, she'll come around. She thinks too much of the man not to. You want me to get you a table? Band's going to start in about an hour, and it's a hot one so there won't be a square inch of free space if you wait."

"No, I don't need a table."

"Give a yell if you change your mind."

"Will." She touched his arm before he could walk away. "Thanks."

He gave her a wide, easy smile. "No problem. I got nothing but respect for cops. In the last five years."

Beth made her wait an hour, and Ally was having her eardrums rattled by the band's second number, when the head waitress quickly strode up to her.

"I've got ten minutes. You can have five of them. That'll have to be enough."

"Fine." She had to lift her voice to a shout. "Can we go back in the employee lounge, or would you rather yell at each other right here?"

Saying nothing, Beth spun around and marched out of the club area. She unlocked the door to the lounge, walked to the sofa and, sitting, took off her shoes.

"More questions, Detective Fletcher?"

Ally closed the door and shut off the worst of the racket behind it. "I'll keep it brief and to the point. You're aware of what happened to Jan?"

"Yes. I'm very aware of it."

"Her next of kin have been notified," Ally said in the

same flat tone. "Her parents will be in Denver tomorrow, and would like her things. I'd like to box up whatever she might have in her locker, and have it available for them. It would be easier on them that way."

Beth's lips trembled, and she looked away. "I don't have the combination to her lock."

"I do. She had it written down in her address book."

"Then do what you have to do. You don't need me."

"I need a witness. I'd appreciate it if you'd verify that I list any and all items in her work locker, that I put nothing in from the outside, or misappropriate any of her property."

"That's all it is to you? All what happened to her is to you? Another bit of business?"

"The sooner I cover every bit of business, the sooner we find the man who did this to her."

"She was nothing to you. None of us were. You lied to us."

"Yes, I lied. And since under the same circumstances I'd lie again, I can't apologize for it."

Ally walked to the locker, spun the combination lock. "To your knowledge did anyone have the combination to this except Janet Norton?"

"No."

Ally removed the lock, opened the door. As she scanned the contents, she took a large evidence bag from her purse.

"It smells like her." Beth's voice trembled, then broke. "You can smell her perfume. Whatever she did, she didn't deserve to be killed, to be thrown out on the side of the road like trash."

"No, she didn't. I want the man who did it to her to pay as much as you do. More."

"Why?"

"Because there has to be justice, or there's nothing. Because her parents loved her, and their hearts are broken. Because I can smell her perfume. Cosmetic bag," Ally snapped out, grabbing the hot-pink case, yanking the zipper. "Two lipsticks, powder compact, three eyeliner pencils—"

She broke off when Beth touched her arm. "Let me help you. I'll write it down."

She took a tissue out of her pocket, wiped her eyes, then stuffed it away again to take out her pad. "I liked you, you see. I liked who I thought you were. It was a kind of an insult to find out you were someone else."

"Now you know. Maybe we can start from here."

"Maybe." Beth pulled out her pencil and began to write.

Ally ordered a light meal at the bar and kept her eye on Jonah. His Friday night crowd was thick and they were rowdy. The longer she sat, watching, listening, the more she began to see the myriad problems of keeping him safe.

She saw just as many problems convincing him he needed to make adjustments in his lifestyle until Matthew Lyle was in custody.

Because she considered herself on duty, she stuck with coffee. And when the caffeine started to jiggle her system, switched to bottled water.

When the inactivity threatened to drive her mad, she informed Frannie she was going to help out with the bar tables and grabbed a tray.

"I believe I fired you," Jonah said as she hauled a tray of empties to the bar.

"No, you didn't. I quit. House draft and a bump, Pete, campari and soda, Merlot with ice on the side and the complimentary ginger ale for the designated driver."

"You got it, Blondie."

"Go upstairs, get off your feet. You're tired."

Ally merely narrowed her eyes at Jonah's orders. "Pete, this guy's making insulting remarks about my looks. And he just put his hand on my butt."

"I'll break his face for you, honey, just as soon as I have a free hand."

"My new boyfriend here has biceps like oil tankers," Ally warned Jonah, and executed a stylish hair flip. "So you better watch your step, pretty boy."

He grabbed her chin, lifted her to her toes by it, then kissed her until her eyes threatened to roll back in her head. "I'm not paying you," he said mildly and strolled away.

"I'd work for that kind of tip," the woman on the stool beside her commented. "Anytime, anywhere."

"Yeah." Ally let out a long breath. "Who wouldn't?"

She worked through last call, then grabbed a table in the club and put her feet up while the band broke down and the staff prepared for closing.

And sitting, fell asleep.

Jonah sat across from her while the club went quiet.

"Anything I can do for you before I head out?"

He glanced up at Will. "No. Thanks."

"Guess she's worn-out."

"She'll bounce back."

"Well…" Will jiggled the change in his pockets. "I'm just going to have my nightcap, then head home. I'll see Frannie off and lock up. See you tomorrow."

The man was sunk, was all Will could think as he walked back to the bar. Who could've figured it? The man was sunk, and over a cop.

"A cop." Will slid onto a stool. On cue, Frannie set down his nightly brandy. "The man's hooked on the cop."

"You just clued into that?"

"I guess." He tugged on his beard. "You think it'll work out?"

"I'm no judge of romantic relationships. They look good together, though, and they won't be able to run over each other since both of them have heads like bricks."

"She conked out in there." Will jerked his head toward the club, then sipped his brandy. "He's just sitting, watching her sleep. I think you can mostly tell what's going on in a man by the way he watches a woman."

And because he caught himself watching Frannie as she mopped up the bar, he flushed and stared down at his drink as if the brandy suddenly contained the solution to a very complex problem.

But she caught it, this time she caught it because she was looking for it. She continued to wipe the bar dry as she inventoried her reaction. A nice little tug, she realized, and just a little heat to go with it.

She hadn't felt—or hadn't let herself—feel either for a man in a very, very long time.

"I guess you're heading home," she said casually.

"I guess. You?"

"I was thinking about ordering a pizza and watching this horror movie marathon on cable."

He smiled over at her. "You always had a thing for monster movies."

"Yeah. Nothing like giant tarantulas or blood-sucking vampires to chase away your troubles. Still… It's not a lot of fun by myself. You up for it?"

"Up for—" Brandy sloshed over the rim of his snifter and onto her clean bar. "Sorry. Damn. I'm clumsy."

"No, you're not." She slid the cloth over the spilled brandy, then looked him dead in the eye. "Do you want to split a pizza with me, Will, and watch old black-and-white monster movies, and neck on my sofa?"

"I— You—" He'd have gotten to his feet if he could have felt them. "Are you talking to me?"

She smiled, spread her cloth over the rim of the bar sink. "I'll get my jacket."

"I'll get it." He pushed to his feet, relieved when they held him upright. "Frannie?"

"Yes, Will?"

"I think you're beautiful. I just wanted to say that right out in case I'm too nervous later and forget."

"If you forget later, I'll remind you."

"Yeah. Okay. Good. I'll get your jacket," he said, and leaving her grinning, dashed off.

Jonah waited until the club was empty, until he heard Will and Frannie call out their good-nights. He rose, leaving Ally sleeping as he checked the locks and alarms himself. His heels clicked on the silver floor as he crossed it to go backstage. He chose the light pattern and music loop that suited his mood and set them.

Satisfied, he went back to Ally and bending down, kissed her awake.

She floated to the surface on the taste of him. Warm, a little rough, and very ready. When she opened her eyes, it was as though a thousand stars were twinkling against the night.

"Jonah."

"Dance with me." His mouth continued to nibble on hers as he lifted her to her feet.

She already was. Before the clouds cleared from her brain, she was moving with him, body molded to body as music rippled around them.

"The Platters." She stroked her cheek against his. "That's so weird."

"You don't like it? I can put on something else."

"No, I love it." She angled her head to give his lips freer access to her neck. "This number, it's my parents' song. 'Only You.' You know my mother was a night shift DJ at KHIP before she was station manager there. This is the song she played over the radio for my father the night she agreed to marry him. It's a nice story."

"I've heard pieces of it."

"You should see the way they look at each other when they dance to this. It's beautiful."

She dipped her fingers into his hair as they glided over the stars in the floor. "Very smooth," she whispered. "You're very smooth, Blackhawk. I should've figured it." She turned her head on his shoulder, watched the lights gleam. "Is everyone gone?"

"Yes." There's only you, he thought, brushing his lips over her hair. Only you.

# Chapter 10

For the first time in weeks Ally woke without the need to jump out of bed and rush into the day.

Glorious Sunday.

Since Saturday night at Blackhawk's had been more crowded than the night before, she'd spent most of the time on her feet, and all of it mentally on duty.

Jonah might have shrugged off the guards outside the club, but she didn't think he'd take having her standing as his shield quite so casually.

Some things were best left undisclosed and undiscussed.

Besides, they were doing each other a favor. She couldn't stay in her apartment until it was cleaned out and refurnished. He was giving her a comfortable place to stay, and she was giving him a bodyguard. To her, it was a fair and rational deal.

And the deal had a distinctively superior side benefit. Intent on indulging in it, she ran her hand over his chest and began to nibble on the body she was more than happy to shield and protect.

He shot awake, fully aroused, with her mouth hot and greedy on his.

"Let me. Let me." Exhilarated, she chanted it, already straddling him, already riding. She hadn't known her blood could leap so fast, that her own needs could bolt from lazy to desperate in one hammer beat of the heart.

She took him in, surrounded him, her own body shuddering and bowing back as the sharp claws of pleasure raked her.

He kept the bedroom dark. It was all shadows and movement as he reared up to wrap his arms around her. Possession. It drove them both. He found her mouth, her throat, her breast, fed the hunger she'd unleashed in him before he could think, before he could do anything but feel.

Her release came like a whiplash, snapping and slicing the system. And when she melted against him, he laid her back. Began to love her.

A kiss, soft as the shadows. A touch, tender as the night. When she reached for him, he took her hands, cupping them together and bringing them to his lips in a gesture that had something rich, something sumptuous sliding through her to tangle with needs still raw.

"Now let me."

This was different. This was patient and sweet and slow. A fire banked and left to simmer with light.

She yielded herself, a surrender as powerful as seduction. He was murmuring to her, quiet words that stirred the soul even as he stirred her blood. As her breathing thickened she floated on the thin and delicate layers of silky sensations.

The brush of his fingertips, of his hair, the warmth of

his lips, the glide of his tongue urged her higher, gradually higher. As the rise of desire became a deep and liquid yearning that spread to an aching need, she moaned his name.

He slid her over the first satin edge.

He needed to touch her this way, to take her this way. He needed, at least in the shadows, to have the right to. Here, she could belong to him.

Her arms came around him as he sank into a kiss, took it deep, fathoms deeper, until he was lost in it. And lost, he slipped inside her, held there linked, and desperately, helplessly in love.

When at last they lay quiet, she turned her face into his throat, wanting the taste of him to linger just a little longer. "No, don't move," she whispered. "Not yet."

Her body was gold, pulsing gold. She would have sworn even the dark had gilt edges.

"It's still night." She stroked her hands down his back, up again. "As long as we're like this, it's still night."

"It can be night for as long as you want."

Her lips curved against him. "Just a little longer." She sighed again, content to hold and be held. "I was going to get up and use your equipment, but then…well, there you were, and it just seemed like a much better idea to use you."

"Good thinking." He closed his eyes and kept her close.

She let the morning slide away, enjoyed a fast, hard workout with him in his gym while they argued over sports highlights that flashed by on the portable TV.

They shared a breakfast of bagels and coffee, along with the Sunday paper, while spread out lazily in bed. Natural, normal, almost domestic habits, Ally thought as they dressed for the day.

Not that a man like Blackhawk could or should be domesticated. But a slow, uncomplicated Sunday morning was a nice change of pace.

She sat on the side of the bed and laced up her ancient high-tops. Jonah tugged on a T-shirt, studied the endless line of her legs.

"Is your plan to wear those little shorts to distract me from whipping your excellent ass on the court?"

She lifted both eyebrows. "Please. With my innate skill I don't need such pitiful ploys."

"Good, because once I start a game, nothing distracts me until my opponent is crushed."

She stood, rolled strong shoulders shown to advantage in the sleeveless jersey. "We'll see who's crushed, Blackhawk, when the buzzer sounds. Now are you going to stand around here bragging, or are you ready to rock and roll?"

"More than ready, Detective Honey."

She waited until they were in his car. She thought the timing best. Besides, the longer she waited to bring it up, the shorter amount of time he'd have to argue with her.

Casually, she stretched out her legs and prepared to enjoy the ride. And smirked, just a little, when she saw his gaze shift, and slide down the length of her legs.

"So, are you ever going to let me drive this machine?"

Jonah switched on the engine. "No."

"I can handle it."

"Then buy your own Jag. Where's the court where you want to go down in inglorious defeat?"

"You mean where's the court where I plan to beat you into a whimpering pulp of humiliation? I'll give you directions. Of course, if I were driving, I could just take us there."

He merely flicked her a pitying glance, then slipped on his sunglasses. "Where's the court, Fletcher?"

"Out near Cherry Lake."

"Why the hell do you want to shoot hoops way out there? There are a half-dozen gyms around here."

"It's too nice a day to play indoors. Of course if you're afraid of a little fresh air…"

He reversed, and drove out of the parking lot.

"What do you do besides use that gorgeous equipment in your apartment over the club when you have a free day?" she asked him.

"Catch a game, check out a gallery." He sent her a slow smile. "Pick up women."

She tipped down her own sunglasses, peered at him over the tops. "What kind of game?"

"Depends on the season. If it's got a ball or a puck, I'll probably watch it."

"Me, too. I've got no resistance. What kind of gallery?"

"Whatever appeals at the time."

"You've got some great art. In the club and in your apartment."

"I like it."

"So… What kind of women?"

"The easy kind."

She laughed and tucked her glasses back in place. "You calling me easy, ace?"

"No, you're work. I like a change of pace now and again."

"Lucky me. You've got a lot of books," she commented. She studied his profile, the sexy, angular lines of it, the way the dark glasses concealed the fascinating contrast of those eyes of pure, light green. "It's hard to picture you curling up with a good book."

"Stretching out," he said, correcting her. "Women curl up with books, guys stretch out."

"Oh, I see. That's entirely different. This is your exit

coming up. You'll take the two-two-five. And watch your speed. The traffic cops just love to nail pretty boys like you in their hot cars."

"I have pull in the police department."

"You think I'm going to fix a ticket for you when you won't even let me drive this thing?"

"It so happens I know the police commissioner."

As soon as he said it, it clicked.

"You said out in Cherry Lake?"

"That's right."

He got off the first exit and pulled into a convenience store parking lot.

"Problem?"

"Your family lives in Cherry Lake."

"That's right. And they have a basketball court—well half court. It was all we could push my parents into, even though my brothers and I campaigned pretty hard. They also have a barbecue pit, which my father puts to very good use. We try to get together a couple Sundays a month."

"Why didn't you tell me we were going to your parents'?"

She recognized the tone: anger, ruthlessly tethered. "What difference does it make?"

"I'm not intruding on your family." He shoved the car in Reverse again. "I'll drop you off. You can get a ride back when you're done."

"Hold on." She reached over, switched off the ignition. If he was angry, fine, they'd fight. But she'd be damned if he'd freeze her out. "What do you mean intruding? We're going to shoot some baskets, eat some steak. You don't need an engraved invitation."

"I'm not spending Sunday afternoon with your family."

"With a cop's family."

He pulled his sunglasses off, tossed them aside. "That has nothing to do with it."

"Then what does? I'm good enough to sleep with, but I'm not good enough for this?"

"That's ridiculous." He shoved out of the car, stalked to the end of the lot and stared out on a narrow grassy area.

"Then tell me something that isn't ridiculous." She marched up to him, jabbed his shoulder. "Why are you so angry that I want you to spend a few hours with my family?"

"You conned me into this, Allison. That's first."

"Why should I have to con you into it? Why is it, Jonah, that you've known my father for more than half your life but you've never accepted a single invitation to our home?"

"Because it's his home, and I have no place there. Because I owe him. I'm sleeping with his daughter, for God's sake."

"I'm aware of that. So is he. What? Do you think he's going to dig out his police issue and shoot you between the eyes when you walk in the door?"

"This isn't a joke. It's so easy for you, isn't it?"

Here's the heat, she thought, pumping.

"Everything was always just right in your world. Solid, balanced and steady. You have no idea what mine was before he came into it, and what it would be now if he hadn't. This is not the way I intend to pay him back."

"No, you pay him back by insulting him. By refusing to acknowledge your relationship with me, as if it was something to be ashamed of. You think I don't know what your life was like? You think my world was so rarefied, Blackhawk. I'm the daughter of a cop. There's nothing you've seen I haven't, through his eyes. And now my own."

She drilled a finger in his chest. "Don't you talk up to

me, and don't you talk down. Wherever, however each of us started, we're on level ground now. And you'd better remember it."

He grabbed her hand. "Stop poking at me."

"I'd like to flatten you."

"Same goes."

He walked away, waiting until he was sure he had some level of control again. Her mention of shame had gotten through. He could be angry with himself for falling in love with her. But he wouldn't be ashamed of it.

"I'll make you a deal. You get rid of the tail." He gestured to the shadow car that had pulled in a minute behind them. "And we'll take a couple of hours at your parents'."

"Give me a second."

She walked to the dark sedan, leaned in and had a short conversation with the driver. She had her hands in her pockets as she strode back over to Jonah.

"I cut them loose for the rest of the afternoon. It's the best I can do." She circled her shoulders. Apologies always tensed her up. "Look, I'm sorry I played it this way. I should have done it straight and we could have argued about it back at your place."

"You didn't play it straight because you knew I wouldn't be here to argue with."

"Okay, you're right." She threw up her hands in defeat. "Sorry again. My family's important to me. I'm involved with you. It just follows that I want you to feel comfortable with them."

"Comfort might be asking a little too much. But I'm not ashamed of my relationship with you. I don't want you to think I am."

"Fair enough. Jonah, it would mean a lot to me if you'd give it a try this afternoon."

"It's easier to argue with you when you're being obnoxious."

"Now see, that's what my brother Bryant always says. You'll get along fine." Hoping to soften things, she hooked her arm with his. "There's one thing, though," she began as they walked back to the car.

"What thing?"

"This deal at the house today? It's a little…more than I might have indicated. Sort of a kind of reunion. It's just that there'll be more people, that's all," she said quickly. "Aunts and uncles and cousins from back East, and my father's old partner and her family. It's really better for you this way," she insisted when he balled a fist and tapped it against her chin. "It's more a horde than a group, so nobody'll even notice you. Hey, why don't you let me drive the rest of the way?"

"Why don't I knock you unconscious and you can ride in the trunk the rest of the way?"

"Never mind. It was just a thought." She strolled around the car, reached for the door handle. But he beat her to it. It made her laugh and turn and take his face in her hands.

"You're a real case, Blackhawk." She gave him a noisy kiss, then climbed in. When he joined her, she leaned over, rubbed her knuckles over his cheek. "They're just people. Really nice people."

"I don't doubt it."

"Jonah. An hour. If you're uncomfortable being there after an hour, just tell me. I'll make an excuse and we'll go. No questions. Deal?"

"If I'm uncomfortable in an hour, I'll go. You stay with your family. That's the way it should be, so that's the deal."

"All right." She settled back, secured her belt. "Why don't I give you a quick rundown so you know the players?

There's Aunt Natalie and her husband—Ryan Piasecki. She runs some of the interests of Fletcher Industries, but her real baby is Lady's Choice."

"Underwear?"

"Lingerie. Don't be a peasant."

"Terrific catalogues."

"Which you peruse for fashion's sake."

"Hell no. There are half-naked women in there."

She laughed, relieved they'd passed the crisis point. "Moving right along. Uncle Ry's an arson inspector in Urbana. They have three kids, fourteen, twelve and eight, if my math's right. Then there's my mother's sister, Aunt Deborah—Urbana's district attorney—her husband, Gage Guthrie."

"The Guthrie who has more money than the national treasury?"

"So rumor has it. Four kids for them. Sixteen, fourteen, twelve and ten. Like steps." She made upward motions with her hand. "Then there's Captain Althea Grayson, Dad's former partner, and her husband Colt Nightshade. Private Investigator. More of a troubleshooter really. Sort of a loose cannon. You'll like him. They have two kids, one of each, fifteen and twelve. No, thirteen now."

"So basically, I'm spending the afternoon with a teenage baseball team."

"They're fun," she promised him. "You don't like kids?"

"I have no idea. My exposure to their species has been limited."

"This exit," she told him. "Well, it won't be limited after today. I think you might have met my brothers somewhere along the line. Bryant's in Fletcher Industries. I guess he's a kind of troubleshooter, too. Does a lot of traveling and nailing butts to the wall. He loves it. And Keenan's a firefighter. We visited my aunt Natalie right after she hooked up with Uncle Ry, and Keen, he fell for the big red truck. That was it for him. Left at the next light. That wraps it up."

"I have a headache."

"No, you don't. Right at the corner, left two blocks down."

He'd already gotten a solid impression of the neighborhood. Stable, rich and exclusive with its big, beautiful houses on big, beautiful grounds. It gave him an itch between the shoulder blades he'd never be able to explain.

He was comfortable in the city, where the streets reminded him he'd overcome something, and the faces that crowded him were anonymous. But here, with the majestic trees, the sloped lawns, green and lush with approaching summer, the explosion of flowers and rambling old homes, he wasn't just a stranger.

He was an intruder.

"That one there, on the left, the cedar and river rock, with the zigzagging decks. I guess everyone's here already. Looks like a parking lot."

The double driveway was packed. The house itself was a huge and unique study of rooflines, jutting decks, wide expanses of glass, all accented by trees and flowering bushes with a meandering slate path ribboning up the gentle hill.

"I've reassessed the deal," Jonah told her. "I'm adding exotic sexual favors. I think this deserves them."

"Fine. I'll take 'em."

She reached for the door, but his arm shot out, pinned her back against the seat. She only laughed and rolled her eyes. "Okay, okay, we'll discuss exotic sexual favors later. Unless you're demanding a down payment on them here and now."

"Yeah, that'll put a cap on it." He jerked open his door,

but before he could walk around the car, there was a war whoop, and a pretty young girl with a pixie cap of dark hair raced down the hill.

She grabbed Ally in a bear hug the minute she was out of the car. "There you are! Everyone's here. Sam already pushed Mick into the pool and Bing chased your neighbor's cat up a tree. Keenan got him down and my mom's inside putting something on the scratches. Hi."

She beamed a hundred-watt smile at Jonah. "I'm Addy Guthrie. You must be Jonah. Aunt Cilla said you were coming with Ally. You own a nightclub? What kind of music do you have?"

"She does shut up twice a year, for five minutes. We time it." Ally wrapped an arm around her cousin's neck and squeezed. "Sam is in the Piasecki branch, Mick is Addy's brother. And Bing is our family dog who has no manners whatsoever, so he fits in very well. Don't worry about re-membering any of that, or you really will have a headache."

She reached out to take his hand, but Addy beat her to it. "Can I come to your club? We're not going home until Wednesday. Thursday if nagging works. I mean what's one more day? Gosh, you're really tall, aren't you? He looks great, too," she added peering around him to her cousin. "Nice job, Allison."

"Shut up, Addy."

"Somebody's always saying that to me."

Charmed despite himself, Jonah smiled at her. "Do you listen?"

"Absolutely not."

The noise level rose—screams, shouts. A couple of gan-gly teenagers of indeterminate sex raced by armed with enormous water guns. He saw a woman with a sunny sweep of hair in deep conversation with a striking redhead. A group of men—some stripped to the waist—battled it out brutally on a blacktopped basketball court. Another group of young people, dripping wet, raided a table loaded with food.

"Pool's around the other side of the house," Ally explained. "It's glassed in so we can use it all year."

One of the men on court pivoted, drove through the line of defense and dunked the ball. Then he caught sight of Ally, and deserted the field.

She met him halfway, shouting with laughter when he plucked her off her feet. "Put me down, moron. You're sweaty."

"So would you be if you were leading your team to a second consecutive victory." But he dropped her on her feet, wiped his hand on his jeans, then held it out to Jonah. "I'm Bryant, Ally's far superior brother. Glad you could make it. Want a beer?"

"Yes, actually."

Bryant eyed Jonah, measuring size and build. "You play any round ball?"

"Occasionally."

"Great, we're going to need fresh meat. Shirts and skins. Ally, get the man a beer while I finish trouncing these pansies."

"Come on inside." In a show of sympathy, Ally rubbed a hand up and down Jonah's arm. "Get your bearings. It's too confusing to try to meet everyone at once."

She drew him up onto a deck, where yet another table was spread with food and an enormous metal trough was filled with ice and cold drinks. She plucked out two beers and went in through the atrium doors.

The kitchen was spacious, broken up into family areas with counters and a banquette. In one corner a dark-haired man was trying to tug away from a dark-haired woman. "I'll live, Aunt Deb. Mom, get her off me."

"Don't be a baby." With her head stuck in the refrigerator, Cilla swore. "We're going to run out of ice. I knew it. Didn't I tell him we'd run out of ice?"

"Hold still, Keenan." Deborah covered the scratches with a gauze pad, taped it neatly. "There, now you can have a lollipop."

"I'm surrounded by smart alecks. Hey, speaking of which, here's Ally."

"Aunt Deb." Ally hurried over to hug her aunt, then reached over and grazed her knuckles over Keenan's cheek. "Hi, hero. This is Jonah Blackhawk. Jonah, my aunt, Deborah, my brother, Keenan. You've met my mother."

"Yes. Nice to see you again, Mrs. Fletcher."

A small army chose that moment to pour in through the door, full of shouted complaints and chased by an unbelievably large and ugly dog.

Ally was immediately absorbed into them. And before he could defend himself, so was Jonah.

Jonah intended to leave at the end of the hour. A deal was a deal. His plan was to make some polite conversation, keep as far out of the way as humanly possible, then fade back into his car and back into the city where he knew the rules.

And somehow, he was stripped out of his shirt and going elbow to gut in a vicious game of basketball with Ally's uncles, cousins, brothers. In the heat of competition, he lost track of intentions.

But he damn well knew it was Ally herself who stomped on his instep and cost him game point.

She was fast and sneaky, he conceded that as he ripped the ball away from an opponent and gave her one deadly glare. But she hadn't grown up on the streets where a single basket could mean a buck for a burger against a painfully empty stomach.

That made him faster. And sneakier.

"I like him." Natalie ignored her son's bloodcurdling scream of revenge and tucked an arm through Althea's.

"He was a hard-ass, but Boyd always liked him. Ouch, he plays dirty."

"What other way is there? Whoa, Ryan's going to be limping tomorrow. Serves him right," Natalie said with a laugh. "Taking on a guy half his age. Nice butt."

"Ry's? I've always thought so."

"Keep your eye off my husband, Captain. I was referring to our Ally's young man."

"Does Ryan know you ogle young men?"

"Naturally. We have a system."

"Well, I am forced to agree. Ally's young man has a very nice butt. Oh, ouch, that had to hurt."

"I think I could take him," Natalie murmured, then laughed at Althea's arch look. "In basketball. Get your mind out of the gutter." She swung an arm over her old friend's shoulder. "Let's go get some wine and pump Cilla for info on this new and very interesting situation."

"You read my mind."

"I know nothing, I say nothing," Cilla claimed as she poured another bag of ice into the trough. "Go away."

"It's the first guy she's brought to one of the family deals," Natalie pointed out.

Cilla merely straightened and mimed zipping her own lips.

"Give it up," Deborah advised. "I've been interrogating her for a half hour, and I got zero."

"You lawyers are too soft." Althea moved forward, grabbing Cilla by the collar. "Now a good cop knows how to get to the truth. Spill it, O'Roarke."

"Do your worst, copper, I ain't no stool pigeon. Besides, I don't know anything yet. But I will," she murmured as she saw Ally dragging Jonah toward the deck. "Clear out, give me five minutes."

"It's nothing," Jonah insisted.

"It's blood. Rules of the house. If it bleeds, it gets mopped up."

"Ah, another victim." Cilla rubbed her hands together as her friends and relations conveniently scattered. "Bring him on."

"His face ran into something."

"Your fist," Jonah said with some bitterness. "Guarding the goal doesn't include left jabs."

"Around here it does."

"Let's see." Wisely Cilla kept her expression sober as she studied Jonah's bleeding lip. "Not so bad. Ally, go help your father."

"But I—"

"Go help your father," Cilla repeated, and snagging Jonah's hand dragged him up to the deck and into the kitchen. "Now let's see, where did I put my instruments of torture?"

"Mrs. Fletcher."

"Cilla. Sit down, and button it up. Whining is severely punished around here." She gathered up a damp cloth, ice and antiseptic. "Punched you, did she?"

"Yes, she did."

"Takes after her father. Sit," she ordered again and jabbed a finger into his bare stomach until he obeyed. "I appreciate your restraint in not hitting her back."

"I don't hit women." He winced when she dabbed at the cut.

"Good to know. She's a handful. Are you up to that?"

"I beg your pardon?"

"Is it just sex, or are you up for the whole package?"

He wasn't sure which shocked him more, the question or the sudden sting of antiseptic. He swore, ripely, then clenched his teeth. "Sorry."

"I've heard the word before. Was that your answer?"

"Mrs. Fletcher."

"Cilla." She leaned in close, then smiled into his eyes. Good eyes, she thought. Steady, clear. "I've embarrassed you. I didn't expect to. Almost done here. Hold this ice on it a minute."

She slid onto the bench across from him, crossed her arms on the table. By her calculations, she had two minutes tops before someone burst in the door and interrupted. "Boyd didn't think you would come today. I did. Allison is relentless when she's set her mind on something."

"Tell me about it."

"I don't know your mind, Jonah. But I know something about you, and I know what I see. So I want to tell you something."

"I didn't intend to stay this long—"

"Hush," she said mildly. "A lifetime ago. Nearly your lifetime ago, I met this cop. This irritating, fascinating, hardheaded cop. I didn't want to be interested. I certainly didn't want to be involved. My mother was a cop, and she died in the line of duty. I've never gotten over it. Not really."

She had to take a breath to steady herself, because it was perfectly true. "The last thing I wanted, the last thing I figured was good for me, was to find myself tangled up with a cop. I know how they think, what they are, what they risk.

God, I didn't want that in my life. And here I am, a lifetime later. The wife of one, the mother of one."

She glanced out the window, caught sight of her husband, then her daughter. "Strange, isn't it, the way things turn out? It isn't easy, but I wouldn't give up a moment of it. Not one moment."

She patted the hand he'd laid on the table, then rose. "I'm glad you came today."

"Why?"

"Because it gave me a chance to see you and Ally together. It gave me a chance to look at you, close. An opportunity you haven't given me more than twice in, what is it, Jonah, seventeen years? And I like what I see."

Leaving him speechless, she turned to the fridge and pulled out a platter of burger patties. "Would you mind taking these to Boyd? If we don't feed the kids every couple of hours, it gets ugly."

"All right." He took the platter, struggled with himself while she just smiled at him out of the eyes Ally had inherited. "She's a lot like you, too."

"She inherited all of my and Boyd's most annoying qualities. Funny how that works." She rose on her toes, gently touched her lips to the wound at the corner of his mouth. "That comes with the treatment."

"Thanks." He shifted the tray, searched for something to say. No one in his life had ever kissed him where it hurt. "I have to get back to the city. Thank you for everything."

"You're welcome. You're welcome anytime, Jonah."

She smiled to herself as he went out. "Your turn at the plate, Boyd," she murmured. "Make it count."

# Chapter 11

"It's all in the wrist," Boyd claimed, flipping a burger.

"I thought you said it was all in the timing." Ally stood, thumbs tucked into her pockets while her brother Bryant looked on, his elbow comfortably hooked on her shoulder.

"Timing is, of course, essential. There are many, many subtle aspects to the art of the barbecue."

"But when do we eat?" Bryant demanded.

"Two minutes if you're going for a burger. Another ten if you're holding out for steak." He peered through the billowing smoke as Jonah cut across the yard with a platter. "Looks like we have more supplies on the way."

"How about a burger, then steak?"

"You're tenth in line, I believe, for burger requests, son. Take a number." Boyd flipped another, sent it sizzling, then furrowed his brow as he caught sight of his wife on the side deck.

Dancing in place, she waved her arms, pointed at Jonah,

pointed at Boyd, circled her fingers. He got the drift, and though he winced inwardly, gave a subtle shrug of acknowledgment.

*Okay, okay, I'll talk to him. Damn it.*

Cilla only smiled, then wagged her finger back and forth. *And I won't hurt him. Sheesh.*

"Just set down the fresh rations, Jonah." Boyd jerked a thumb toward the high table beside the pit. "How's the lip?"

"I'll live." Jonah sent Ally a steely stare. "Especially since despite unsportsmanlike conduct by the opposing guard, I made the basket. And won."

"Lucky shot. We'll have a rematch after we eat."

"She loses," Bryant commented, "she demands a rematch. She wins, she rubs it in your face for days."

"And your point would be?" Ally fluttered her lashes at him.

"Mom would never let me hit her, because she was a girl." Bryant gave Ally's ear one hard tug. "I've always found that grossly unfair."

"Big deal. You just beat up on Keenan."

"Yeah." Instantly Bryant's face brightened. "Those were the days. I'm planning on punching on him later, for old times' sake."

"Can I watch? Like I used to."

"Naturally."

"Please. Your mother and I like to maintain the illusion we raised three well-balanced, competent adults. Don't shatter our dreams. Jonah, you haven't seen my workshop, have you?" At his daughter's answering snort, Boyd winged an eyebrow at her. "No comments. Bryant, this is a moment."

"Is it?"

"A monumental moment. I am passing the sacred tongs and spatula to you."

"Wait a minute, wait a minute." Ally elbowed her brother aside. "Why can't I do it?"

"Ah." Boyd held a hand to his heart. "How many times have I heard you say those very words in our long and exciting life together?"

Amused and fascinated by the family dynamics, Jonah watched mutiny settle over Ally's face. "Well, why can't I?"

"Allison, my treasure, there are some things a man must pass to his son. Son." Boyd laid a hand on Bryant's shoulder. "I'm trusting you with the Fletcher reputation. Don't let me down."

"Dad." Bryant wiped an imaginary tear from his eye. "I'm overwhelmed. Honored. I swear to uphold the family name, no matter what the cost."

"Take these." Boyd held out the barbecue tools. "Today, you are a man."

"That bites," Ally muttered as Boyd swung an arm around Jonah's shoulder.

"You're just a girl." Bryant leered and rubbed the tools together. "Live with it."

"She'll make him pay for that," Boyd murmured. "So, how are things?"

"Well enough." How the hell was Jonah supposed to make a quiet escape when someone or other was always dragging him somewhere? "I appreciate the hospitality today. I'm going to have to get back to the club."

"A business like that doesn't give you a lot of free time, especially in the early years." Still he steered Jonah toward a wooden structure in the far corner of the yard. "Know anything about power tools?"

"They make a great deal of noise."

Boyd gave a hoot of laughter and opened the door of the workshop. "What do you think?"

The garage-size room was full of tables, machines, shelves, tools, stacks of wood. There appeared to be a number of projects in progress, but Jonah couldn't tell what they were, or what they were intended to be.

"Impressive," he decided, diplomatically. "What do you do here?"

"I make a great deal of noise. Other than that, I haven't figured it out. I helped Keenan build a birdhouse about ten years ago. Came out pretty good. Cilla started buying me tools. Boy toys, she calls them."

He ran his hand over the guard of a skill saw. "Then I needed a place to keep them. Before I knew it, I had a fully equipped workshop. I think it was all a ploy to get me out of her hair."

"Pretty clever."

"That she is." They stood for a moment, hands in pockets, soberly studying the tools. "Okay, let's get this over with so we can both relax and get something to eat. What's going on with you and my daughter?"

Jonah couldn't say it was unexpected, but it still made his stomach clench. "We're seeing each other."

With a nod, Boyd walked over to a small square refrigerator and took out two beers. He twisted off the tops, held one out to Jonah. "And?"

Jonah tipped back the beer, then gave Boyd a level look. "What do you want me to say?"

"The truth. Though I realize what you'd like to say is that it's none of my business."

"Of course it's your business. She's your daughter."

"There we have no argument." Deciding to get comfortable, Boyd boosted himself up on a worktable. "There's a matter of intent, Jonah. I'm asking what you intend in regard to my daughter."

"I don't have any intentions. I should never have touched her. I know that."

"Really." Intrigued, Boyd cocked his head. "Mind explaining that?"

"What do you want from me? Damn it." Giving into frustration, Jonah dragged a hand through his hair.

"The first time you asked me that, in almost that same tone, you were thirteen. Your lip was bleeding then, too."

Jonah steadied himself. "I remember."

"I've never known you to forget anything, which means you'll remember what I said to you then, but I'll say it again. What do you want from *you,* Jonah?"

"I've got what I want. A decent life run in a way I can respect and enjoy. And I know why I have it. I know what I owe you, Fletch. Everything. Everything I've got, everything I am started with you. You opened doors for me, you took me on when you had no reason to."

"Whoa." Genuinely shocked, Boyd held up a hand. "Hold on."

"You changed my life. You gave me a life. I know where I'd be if it wasn't for you. I had no right to take advantage of that."

"You're sure putting a lot on me here," Boyd said quietly. "What I did, Jonah, was see a street kid with potential. And I hassled him."

Emotion swirled into Jonah's eyes. "You made me."

"Oh, Jonah, no, I didn't. You made yourself. Though God knows I'm proud to have played a part in it."

Boyd slid off the table, wandered the shop. Whatever he'd expected from this talk, it hadn't been to have his emotions stirred. To feel very much like a father being given a precious gift by a son.

"If you feel there's a debt, then pay it off now by being

straight with me." He turned back. "Are you involved with Ally because she's mine?"

"In spite of it," Jonah corrected. "I stopped thinking about her being yours. If I hadn't, I wouldn't be involved with her."

It was the answer he wanted, so Boyd nodded. The boy's suffering, he thought, and couldn't find it in himself to be overly sorry about it. "Define involved."

"For God's sake, Fletch." Jonah took a long gulp of beer.

"I don't mean that area." Boyd spoke quickly, took a deep drink himself. "Let's just leave that particular area behind a firmly locked door so we don't have to punch each other."

"Fine. Good."

"I meant, what are your feelings for her?"

"I care about her."

Boyd waited a beat, nodded again. "Okay."

Jonah swore. Boyd had asked him to play straight, and he was circling. "I'm in love with her. Damn it." He closed his eyes, imagined flinging the bottle against the wall, shattering glass. It didn't help. "I'm sorry." Jonah opened his eyes again, got a slippery grip on control. "But that's as straight as it gets."

"Yeah, I'd say so."

"You know what I'm built on. You can't think I'm good enough for her."

"Of course you're not," Boyd said simply, and noticed those clear green eyes didn't so much as flicker. "She's my little girl, Jonah. No one's good enough for her. But knowing what you're built on, I'd say you're pretty close. I wonder why that surprises you. The one area I don't recall you ever being low in is esteem."

"I'm over my head here," Jonah murmured. "It's been a long time since I've been over my head in anything."

"Women do that to you. The right woman, you never really surface again. She's beautiful, isn't she?"

"Yes. She blinds me."

"She's also smart, and she's strong, and she knows how to deal with what's dished out."

Absently, Jonah rubbed his thumb over his sore lip. "No argument."

"Then my advice to you is to play it straight with her, too. She won't let you get away with less, not for long."

"She isn't looking for anything else from me."

"You keep thinking that, son." At ease again, Boyd crossed to Jonah, laid a hand on his shoulder. "There's just one thing," he said as they started toward the door. "If you hurt her, I'll take you out. They'll never find your body."

"Well, I feel better now."

"Good. So, how do you like your steak?"

Ally saw them come out of the workshop and relaxed for the first time since the moment she'd watched them go in. Her father had his arm swung companionably around Jonah's shoulder. It looked as if they'd done no more than share a friendly beer and grunt over the power tools.

If her father had done any poking or prying into her relationship with Jonah, at least he hadn't drilled any embarrassing holes.

She liked seeing them together, liked very much witnessing the very real bond of affection and mutual respect. Her family was paramount in her life, and though she would have given her heart where her heart yearned, it would never have settled with full happiness on a man her family couldn't love.

She bobbled the bowl of potato salad, would have dropped it if Cilla hadn't made the grab.

"Butter fingers," Cilla said and set the bowl on the deck table.

"Mom."

"Hmm? We're going to run out of ice again."

"I'm in love with Jonah."

"I know, baby. Who's not blocked in? I need somebody to get some ice."

"How can you know?" Ally grabbed her mother's wrist before Cilla could go to the deck rail and shout for an ice run. "I just figured it out this second."

"Because I know you, and I see the way you are with him." Gently, she smoothed a hand over Ally's hair. "Scared or happy?"

"Both."

"Good." Cilla turned, sighed once, then kissed Ally on each cheek. "That's perfect." She slipped an arm around Ally's waist, turned to the rail. "I like him."

"Me, too. I really like who he is."

Cilla tipped her head toward her daughter's. "It's nice, isn't it, having the family together like this."

"It's wonderful. Jonah and I had a fight about coming here today."

"Looks like you won."

"Yeah. We're going to have another fight when I tell him we're getting married."

"You're your father's daughter. My money's on you."

"Place your bets," Ally suggested, and walked down the steps, crossed the lawn. It was a calculated move. She didn't mind being calculating, not when she had a point to make.

She strolled up to her father and Jonah, cupped Jonah's face in her hands and pressed her lips hard to his. He hissed, reminding her about his sore mouth. But she just laughed, shook back her hair.

"Suck it in, tough guy," she suggested and kissed him again.

His hands came to her waist, fused there, drawing her up on her toes that intimate inch.

"Dad?" She eased back down. "Mom needs more ice."

"She's just saying that to make me look bad." Boyd scanned the yard, homed in on his target. "Keenan! Go get your mother more ice."

"So…" As her father chased down her brother, Ally linked her hands at the back of Jonah's neck. "What were you talking about with my father?"

"Man stuff. What are you doing?" he demanded as she brushed her lips over his again.

"If you have to ask, I must not be doing it right."

"I'm outnumbered here, Allison. Are you trying to coax your family into stomping me into dust?"

"Don't worry. We're very big on kissing in my family."

"I noticed. Still." He drew her back.

"You've got this quietly proper streak. It's really cute. Are you having a good time?"

"Except for a couple of minor incidents," he said, deliberately tapping his finger on the corner of his mouth. "You have a nice family."

"They're great. You forget sometimes how steadying, how comforting it is to have them. How much you depend on them for a hundred little things. My cousins will remember coming out here when they were kids, or all of us piling into that gorgeous gothic fortress of Uncle Gage's, or trooping up to the mountains to…"

"What?"

"Wait. Give me a minute." She had his hand and squeezed it as she shut her eyes and let the pieces of the puzzle tumble together. "You're drawn back," she murmured.

"You're always drawn back to memories, and places where you were happy with the people who mean the most. That's why people are always going back to visit their hometown, or driving by the house where they grew up." She paused and opened her eyes as a new thought hit her. "Where did he grow up?"

She tapped a fist against Jonah's chest. "Where did he and his sister grow up? Where did they live together? Where was he happy? He has to go somewhere, has to find a place to hide, to plan. He's gone home."

She spun around and raced for the house.

She was already dialing the kitchen phone when Jonah caught up with her. "What are you doing?"

"My job. Stupid, stupid, not to think of it before! Carmichael? It's Fletcher. I need you to do a check for me. I need an address—Matthew Lyle's old address, addresses maybe. Going back to when he was a kid. There's, ah…"

She paused, forced it into focus. "He was born in Iowa, and they moved around some. I can't remember when he came to Denver. The parents are dead. Yeah, you can reach me at this number." She recited it. "Or my cell phone. Thanks."

"You think he's gone back home?"

"He needs to feel close to his sister to feel safe, to feel powerful." Allison paced the kitchen as she tried to remember details of the file. "The psych profile tags him as dependent on her, even as he sees himself as her protector. She's his only real consistency, the only constant in his life. Parents divorced, kids got bounced around. Mother remarried, bounced around some more. Stepfather was…damn."

She pressed her fingers to her temple as if to push out the memory. "Ex-Marine. Very gung ho, and apparently very tough on the pudgy nerd and his devoted sister. Part of the whole authority complex comes from this instability of family life, ineffective father, the passive mother, the stern stepfather. Rocky foundations," she said as she paced.

"Lyle was bright, high IQ, but he was emotionally and socially inept. Except with his sister. His biggest trouble with the law was right after she got married. He got sloppy, careless. He was angry."

She checked her watch, urging Carmichael to hurry. "She stood by him, and it appears whatever rift there might have been between them was healed."

She leaped on the phone when it rang. "Fletcher. Yeah, what have you got?" She snatched up a pencil, began to scribble on the pad by the phone. "No, nothing out of state. He needs to stay close. Hold on." She covered the mouthpiece with her hand. "Do me a favor, Blackhawk. Would you tell my father I need to talk to him for a minute?"

It took more than a minute. She moved into her father's office, booted up his computer. With him beside her, and Carmichael on the phone, they worked through the files, picked through Matthew Lyle's history.

"See, ten years ago he was listing a P.O. Box as his address. He kept that listing for six years, even though he had a house on the lake. Bought that house nine years ago, the same year his sister married Fricks. But he held on to the P.O. Box."

"And his sister lists the same P.O. Box as her address through the same period."

"But where did they live? I'm going to go in and pin Fricks down on this one." Then she pursed her lips, considered. "Carmichael, you up for another run? See what you can find me on property in the Denver metro area listed under the names Madeline Lyle or Madeline Matthews. Run Matthew and Lyle Madeline, too."

"Good move," Boyd approved. "Good thinking."

"He likes to own things," Ally noted. "Possessions are very important to him. If he stuck in the same spot for six years, more or less, he'd want his own place—or one for his sister."

She straightened in the chair. "Did you just say bingo? Carmichael, I think I love you. Yeah, yeah. All right. I've got it. I'll let you know. Really. Thanks."

She hung up, jumped out of the chair. "Lyle Madeline owns a condo in the center of downtown."

"Good work, Detective. Contact your lieutenant and assemble your team. And, Ally," Boyd added, "I want in."

"Commissioner, I'm sure we can make room for you."


It ran like clockwork. Within two hours the building was surrounded, the stairways and exits blocked. Using hand signals a dozen cops wearing Kevlar vests ranged the hallway outside of Matthew Lyle's two-level condo.

Ally had the floor plan in her head, every inch of the blueprint she'd studied. She gave the nod, and the two officers beside her hit the door with the battering ram.

She went in first, went in low.

A stream of men rushed by her and up the stairs to her right. Others fanned out to the rooms at her left. It took less than ten minutes to determine the condo was empty.

"He's been staying here." Ally gestured to the dishes in the sink. She dipped a finger into the dirt of an ornamental lemon tree potted by the kitchen window. "Damp. He's tending house. He'll be back."

In a bedroom upstairs they found three handguns, an assault rifle and a case of ammunition. "Be prepared," Ally murmured. "I see extra clips for a nine millimeter, but I don't see the nine millimeter, so he's armed."

"Detective Fletcher?" One of her team backed out of the closet, holding a long bladed knife with gloved fingers. "Looks like our murder weapon."

"Bag it." She picked up a black-and-silver matchbook from the dresser. "Blackhawk's." She shifted her eyes to her father. "That's his target. The only question is when."

Night had fallen when Ally confronted Jonah in his office. The man was mule stubborn, she thought. And more, he was just plain wrong.

"You close down for twenty-four hours. Forty-eight tops."

"No."

"I can close you down."

"No, you can't. And if you wrangle it, it'll take you longer than the forty-eight hours, which makes the entire process moot."

She dropped into a chair. It was important to stay calm, she reminded herself. Vital to stay in control. She hissed out a breath, then a stream of violent and inventive oaths.

"I don't believe your last suggestion is possible, regardless of my strength and flexibility."

She bolted forward. "Listen to me."

"No, you listen to me." His voice was quiet, cool, inflexible. "I could do what you're asking. What's to stop him from waiting me out? I close down, he goes under. I open, he surfaces. We could play that game indefinitely. I prefer running my own game, on my own turf."

"I'm not going to say you don't have a point, because you do. But we'll nail him within two days. I promise you. All you have to do is shut the place down, take a little vacation. My parents have a great place in the mountains."

"Would you be coming with me?"

"Of course not. I have to stay here and close this thing."

"You stay. I stay."

"You're a civilian."

"Exactly, and until this is a police state, I have a right to run my business and come and go as I please."

She wanted to tear at her hair, but knew that would just amuse him. "It's my job to keep you alive to run your business."

He got to his feet. "Is that what you think? Are you my shield, Ally? Is that why you've been wearing your gun until we're up here behind locked doors? Is that why you keep it within reach even when we are here?"

He came around the desk, even as she cursed herself for the slip. "I don't like the implications of that."

She met him toe to toe. "You're a target."

"So are you."

"This is a waste of time."

He spun her around before she could stalk to the elevator. "You will not stand in front of me." He said it slowly, distinctly, with that rare glint of ready temper in his eyes. "Understand that."

"Don't tell me how to do my job."

"Don't tell me how to live my life."

She threw her head back, released a muffled scream. "All right. Okay. Forget it. We do it the hard way. Here's the deal. Twenty-four-hour guards outside. Cops in soft clothes in the bar and club areas at all times. You take on undercover officers as kitchen and wait help."

"I don't like that deal."

"Tough. Take it or leave it. Leave it and I pull strings and have you slapped into protective custody so fast even a slick customer like you won't be able to slide through the knots. I can do it, Blackhawk, and I will. My father will help me do it, because he cares about you. Please." She grabbed him by the lapels. "Do it for me."

"Forty-eight hours," he agreed. "And in the meantime, I put out word on the street I'm looking for him."

"Don't—"

"That's the deal. It's fair."

"All right. That's the deal."

"Now, what would you like to bet that I can go downstairs right now and pick out every cop you've already planted?"

She puffed out her cheeks, then showed her teeth in a smile. "No bet. I don't suppose I can convince you to stay up here tonight?"

He traced a fingertip down the center of her body. "I will if you will."

"That's what I figured." Sometimes compromise, however annoying, was the only out. "Hold that thought until closing."

"That I have no problem with." He walked over to call for the elevator. "Tonight, or tomorrow night."

"Yeah. It's just as likely, more really, that they'll take him at the condo. But if he slips through the net, or senses anything, it'll be here. And it'll be soon."

"Will's got good eyes. He'll know what to look for."

"I don't want you, or any of your people, taking chances. If he's spotted, you tell me." She glanced over, caught him studying her. "What?"

"Nothing." But he traced his fingers over her cheek. "When you've closed this down, can you take any time?"

"What do you mean time?"

"A few days. Away. Somewhere away."

"I might be talked into that. Do you have anywhere in mind?"

"No. Pick it."

"Well, aren't you open-minded and daring? I'll start thinking." She took a step out of the elevator, already shifting her focus, but he took her arm.

"Ally?"

"Yeah."

There was too much to say. Entirely too much to feel. And it wasn't the time, not the time to play it straight or any other way. "Later. We'll get into it later."

## Chapter 12

Traditionally business at Blackhawk's was light on Sunday nights. There was no live music as a lure, and the first day of the work week loomed heavily.

Ally decided a great many people in Denver were taking advantage of the gorgeous weather and mild evening, and most who strolled in out of the night lingered an hour or more over their drinks or bowls of guacamole and chips.

She watched the entrance, checked the exits, studied faces and counted heads. Throughout the evening she slipped into the lounge at regular intervals to check in with the stakeout at Lyle's condo.

An hour before closing, and still he hadn't been spotted.

Itchy, she roamed the floor, checking faces, watching doors. The crowd was thinning out, and she imagined there'd be no more than a scatter of customers left by last call.

Where was he? she asked herself. Where the hell was he? He'd run out of places to hide.

"Detective." Jonah danced his fingers over her shoulder. "I thought you'd be interested to know one of my sources reports a man fitting Lyle's description has been asking questions about me."

"When?" She gripped his arm and pulled him toward the alcove. "Where?"

"Tonight, actually. At my other place."

"Fast Break?" She swore, whipped out her phone. "We didn't put anyone there. They never hit there. It's not his style."

"I'd say that holds true." He laid a hand over hers before she could dial the phone. "The bartender there just got in touch. Apparently Lyle—I assume it was Lyle though he was wearing glasses and sporting a beard—dropped into Fast Break a few hours ago, loitered at the bar, started asking if I ever came in."

"Hold on." Ally tapped his hand away and put her call through. "Balou? Cut a pair of uniforms loose from the condo. Tell them to see the bartender at Fast Break. The address is…"

She looked at Jonah, repeated the address he gave her. "Lyle was in there tonight. He's reported to be wearing a beard and glasses. Make sure that gets out."

She disconnected, looked back at Jonah.

"As I was saying," he continued, "my man didn't think anything of it initially, then it started to bother him. He says Lyle was jumpy. Hung around about a half hour then said to tell me he'd see me around."

"His center's crumbling. He's psyching himself up to move." She wanted Jonah out of the way. "Look, why don't you go up, give your man another call. Let him know a couple of cops are on their way."

"Do I look like I'd fall for that lame a con?"

He strolled away from her to check on a table of customers who were preparing to leave.

The shouts came from the kitchen, followed by an explosive crash of dishes. Ally had her gun out, bolting for the door when it burst open.

He'd ditched the glasses, and the beard was a thin and scraggly dusting over his chin. But she saw she'd been right. He'd psyched himself up. His eyes were wide and wild.

And he had the barrel of the nine millimeter pressed to the soft underside of Beth's jaw.

"Don't move! Don't anybody move!" he shouted over the screams, the rush of running feet as customers scattered.

"Stay calm. Everybody stay calm." She sidestepped, kept her gun trained on him, her eyes trained on him. Forced herself to block out Beth's terrified face. "Lyle, take it easy. You want to let her go."

"I'll kill her. I'll blow her head off."

"You do that, I kill you. Think, you need to think. Where does that get you?"

"Put your gun down. Drop it, kick it over here, or she's dead."

"I'm not going to do that. And neither are any of the other cops in here. You know how many weapons you have aimed at you right now, Lyle? Look around. Do a count. It's over. Save yourself."

"I'll kill her." His gaze jittered around the room, bounced off guns. "Then I'll kill you. That'll be enough."

Someone was sobbing. Out of the corner of her eye she could see the bar area where civilians were being rushed outside to safety.

"You want to live, don't you? Madeline would want you to live."

"Don't you say her name! Don't you say my sister's

name!" He shoved the gun harder against Beth's throat and made her cry out.

No place to run, Ally thought. His sister had had no place to run, and still she'd turned and fired.

"She loved you." Ally edged closer, keeping his focus on her. If she could get him to lower the gun, a few inches, get him to shift it toward her. Away from Beth. "She died for you."

"She was all I had! I got nothing to lose now. I want the cop who killed her, and I want Blackhawk. Now! Right now or she dies!"

Out of the corner of her eye, Ally saw Jonah move forward. "Look at me!" She shouted the words. "I'm the one who killed your sister."

He screamed, one long howl as he jerked the gun away from Beth, swung it toward Ally. There was a burst of gunfire, a blur of movement, wails of terror.

With fear locked in her throat, Ally rushed forward to where Jonah lay tangled with Lyle. Blood coated them both.

"Damn you! Damn, are you crazy?" With urgent hands she began to pat him down, looking for wounds. He'd thrown himself at the gun. In front of the gun.

He was breathing. She held on to that. He was breathing, and she would make sure he kept on breathing. "Jonah. Oh, God."

"I'm all right. Stop poking at me."

"All right? You jumped into cross fire. You nearly got yourself killed."

"You, too." He looked past her to where the starry floor was cracked an inch from where she'd stood.

"I'm wearing a vest."

"And that takes care of your hard head, too?" He sat back as a cop turned Lyle over.

"He's gone."

Jonah spared Lyle's face one glance, then looked into Ally's eyes. "I'd like to calm my customers down."

"You're not calming anyone down." Ally rose with him. "You've got blood all over you. Is all of it his?"

"Mostly."

"What do you mean mostly?"

"I'm going to deal with my customers and my people." He held her at arm's length before she could snatch at him again. "Do your job, and let me do mine."

He turned away to take Beth from the female officer who was holding her. "Come on, Beth, come on with me. Everything's all right now."

Ally pressed her fingers to her eyes then looked down at what was left of Matthew Lyle. "Yeah, everything's dandy."


"Slipped in the back," Hickman told her while they sat in the nearly empty club. The civilians were gone, the body had been removed and the crime scene unit was packing up.

She wondered idly what time it was, and how soon she could fall on her face and tune the world out. "He stopped being smart," she said. "He stopped thinking."

"You got that right," Hickman agreed. "Got himself one of those white kitchen uniforms, slapped on a wig and glasses. Before the cop who spotted him could call in or move, all hell broke loose."

"He didn't think we were smart enough to close him in. I saw his face when he spotted all the cops. Pure shock. My guess? He figured on breaking in here, taking Jonah down, me if I was around, then he's got hostages. He'd demand we turn over the cop who killed his sister. He really figured we'd do it, and he'd get out."

"Arrogant. Speaking of which, it was pretty cocky, telling him you were the one he wanted."

"I don't know why he didn't spot me in the first place."

"You look different." Hickman scanned a look up, then down. "Very un-Fletcherlike."

"Give me a break, Hickman. I look how I look. I'll tell you how it was. He came in here for Jonah. When he looked at me, all he saw was cop—no face, no form, just another cop. He didn't put me together with the one who'd worked here."

"Maybe." He got to his feet. "I guess we'll never know." He glanced over at the starburst crack in the floor. "Too bad about that—classy floor. Bet it'll cost an arm and two legs to fix it."

"Maybe he'll leave it like that. Conversation piece. Draw a crowd."

"Yeah." The idea tickled Hickman. "We'd've taken him out right away, you know, but he would've gotten that shot off anyway. At that range, the vest would've stopped the bullet. Probably. But one way or the other, if the shot hadn't been deflected, you'd have been seriously hurt."

Absently she rubbed a hand between her breasts, imagined the breathless pain. "You ever taken one in the vest?"

"Nope, but Deloy did. Had himself a softball-size bruise." Hickman held up his hands, made a circle. "Knocked him clean off his feet, too, and tossed him back like a rag doll. Ended up with a concussion where his head hit the pavement. That has to hurt."

"I'll take it over a bullet."

"Any day of the week. I'm going home." He got to his feet. "See you tomorrow."

"Yeah. Nice work."

"Back at you. Oh, your guy's in the kitchen, getting patched up."

"What do you mean patched up?"

"Caught a little friendly fire. Just a nick."

"He's shot? *Shot?* Why didn't anyone tell me?"

Hickman didn't bother to answer. She was already gone.

Ally slammed into the kitchen, her eyes dark and furious when she saw Jonah at one of the worktables, stripped to the waist, calmly drinking a brandy while Will rolled gauze over his upper arm.

"Hold it. Just hold it. Let me see that." She slapped Will away, unwound the gauze and poked at the long shallow cut until Jonah pushed her face up with the heel of his hand on her chin.

"Ouch," he said.

"Put that drink down, you're going to the hospital."

He kept his eyes on hers, lifted the brandy. Sipped. "No."

"No, my butt. What is this? Some idiot, male, macho deal? You've been shot."

"Not really. Grazed is more the accepted term. Now if you don't mind, Will's got a kinder touch with this than you. I'd like him to finish so he can go home."

"It could get infected."

"I could get hit by a truck, but I don't intend for either to happen."

"It's okay, Ally, really." Playing peacemaker, Will patted her shoulder before picking up the gauze again. "I cleaned it real good. We got some worse in the old days, didn't we, Jonah?"

"Sure did. Looks like I'm another scar up on you now."

"Well, isn't that nice?" Ally grabbed the brandy, glugged.

"I thought you hated brandy."

"I do."

"Why don't you get a glass of wine," Will suggested. "I'm nearly done here."

"I'm fine. I'm okay." Ally blew out a breath. Now, she thought, after everything, her hands wanted to shake.

"Damn it, Blackhawk. I was probably the one who shot you."

"Probably. I've decided to weigh in the circumstances and not hold it against you."

"That's real big of you. Now listen to me—"

"Frannie went home with Beth," he added, wanting to distract her. "She's okay. Shaky yet, but okay. She wanted to thank you, but you were busy."

"There we go." Will stepped back. "Your arm's in a lot better shape than your shirt. I'd say that's a loss." He held up the bloodstained linen and made Ally's stomach turn over. "Want me to go up and get you a fresh one before I go?"

"No. Thanks." Jonah lifted his arm, flexed. "Nice job. Haven't lost your touch."

"All in a day's work." Will picked up his discarded jacket. "You sure stand up, Ally. Could've been an awful mess out there tonight. But you sure stand up."

"All in a day's work."

"I'll lock up. 'Night."

Ally sat at the table, waited until she heard silence. "Okay, smart guy, what the hell were you thinking? You interfered with a police operation."

"Oh, I don't know. Maybe I was thinking that lunatic was going to kill you. It bothered me." He held out the brandy snifter. "How about a refill, since you drank mine."

"Fine. Sit here and swill brandy and look stoic." She shoved back, grabbed the glass, then gave in and wrapped her arms around his neck. "Don't *ever* scare me like that again."

"I won't if you won't. No, just stay right there a minute." He turned his face into her hair, breathed deep. "I'm going to see you stepping in front of that gun for a long time. That's hard."

"I know. I know it is."

"I'll deal with that, Ally, because that's the way it is." He drew her back, his eyes intense on hers. "There are some things you need to figure out if you can deal with. If you want to deal with."

"What are they?"

He rose to get the brandy himself, poured, set the bottle on the table. "Are there still cops in my place?"

"Other than me?"

"Yeah, other than you."

"No. We're clear."

"Then sit down."

"Sounds very serious." She pulled up her chair. "I'm sitting."

"My mother left when I was sixteen." He didn't know why he started there. It just seemed to be the spot. "I couldn't blame her, still don't. My father was a hard man, and she was tired of it."

"She left you with him?"

"I was self-sufficient."

"You were sixteen."

"Ally. I was never sixteen the way you were. And I had your father."

Everything inside her softened. "That's a lovely thing to say."

"It's just fact. He made me go to school. He came down on me when I needed it, which was most of the time. And he was the first person in my life to ever tell me I was worth anything. To ever see I might be. He's… I don't know anyone who comes up to him."

She reached across the table, took his hand. "I love him, too."

"Let me get through some of this." He squeezed her hand,

then drew his away. "I didn't go to college, even Fletch couldn't browbeat me into that. I took some business courses because it suited me. When I was twenty, my father died. Three packs of cigarettes a day and a general meanness catches up with you. It was long and ugly, and when it was over, the only thing I felt was relief."

"Is that supposed to make me think less of you?"

"There's a contrast here, and you see it as well as I do."

"Yeah, you had a lousy childhood. I had a great one. As fate would have it, we both got lucky and ended up with Boyd Fletcher as a father. Don't look at me like that. That's exactly what he is to you."

"I'm going to make something clear to you before this goes any farther. I wasn't a victim, Allison. I was a survivor, and used whatever methods worked. I stole and cheated and conned, and I don't apologize for it. Things would've turned out differently if I hadn't had your father hounding me. But they didn't."

"I think that was my point."

"Don't interrupt. I'm a businessman. I don't steal or cheat because I don't have to. That doesn't mean I don't play the game my way."

"A real tough guy aren't you? Blackhawk, you're a fraud. Cool customer, slick hands, icy stare. And this big, soft heart. Soft, hell, it's gooey."

Amused at the speechless shock on his face, she got up, sauntered to the fridge and hunted up an open bottle of white wine.

She wasn't tired anymore, she realized. She was revved.

"Do you think I didn't run you, pal? Run your friends, get the stories? You gather up your sick and wounded like a mama chick."

Enjoying herself now, Ally drew out the stopper, found

a glass. "Frannie—got her off the streets, got her clean, gave her work. Will—straightened him up, paid off his debts before he got his knees capped, gave him a suit and some dignity."

"None of that's relevant."

"I'm not finished." She poured the wine. "The iceman got Beth into a women's shelter, bought her kids presents from Santa Claus when she didn't have the money or the energy to deal with it. Jonah Blackhawk was buying Barbie dolls."

"I did not buy dolls." That was going just a little too far. "Frannie did. And it has nothing to do with this."

"Yeah, right. Then there's Maury, one of your line chefs." She sat down, wiggled into the chair and propped her feet up. "And the dough you lent him—and I use the word *lent* advisedly—to help his mother through a bad patch."

"Shut up."

She merely smiled, dipped a finger into her wine, licked it. "Sherry, the little busgirl, who's working her way through college. Who paid her tuition last semester when she couldn't scrape it together? Why, I believe it was you. And what about Pete the bartender's little problem last year when an uninsured driver totaled his car?"

"Investing in people is good business."

"That's your story, you stick to it."

Irritation and embarrassment warred for top gun inside him. He tossed his weight to the side of irritation. "You're ticking me off, Allison."

"*Ooooh*, really?" She leaned forward, leading with her chin. "Go ahead, hard case, slap me around and shut me up. Dare you."

"Be careful." He said it, meant it, then pushed to his feet. "This is irrelevant, and isn't getting us anywhere."

She crossed her ankles and made clucking noises.

"You're really asking for it."

"Yeah, yeah. I'm shaking. Sucker."

He cracked and lifted her right off the chair. "One more word. I swear, it's only going to take one more word."

She bit him, one quick nip on his already tender mouth. "Softy."

He pushed her aside and spun toward the door.

"Where you going?"

"To put on a damn shirt. I can't talk to you."

"Then I'll just have to rip it off you again. I've got a soft spot for wounded tough guys with gooey centers." And laughing, she launched herself at him, landed piggyback. "I'm crazy about you, Blackhawk."

"Go away. Go arrest somebody. I've had enough of cops for one day."

"You'll never get enough of me." She bit his earlobe, his shoulder. "Come on, shake me off."

He would have. He told himself he could have. It was just his bad luck he looked down and saw the scar in the floor. From a bullet meant for her.

He dragged her around, yanked her against him so hard, so fast, she swore her ribs knocked together. His mouth was on hers, fused there with a heat borne of desperation.

"Better. Much better. Here, Jonah. Now. We both need to make it right again. I need you to love me. Like our lives depended on it."

He was on the floor with her, without any thought but to prove to himself that she was whole and safe and alive beneath him.

The cool, hard surface of the floor might have been a feather bed, or clouds, or the jagged, unforgiving peaks of a mountain. Nothing mattered but that she was wrapped around him, that her breath was fast and hot against his skin, that her heart beat like wild wings against his.

All the fear, the tension, the ugliness poured out of her when he touched her. Her hands tangled with his, fighting to strip away boundaries. Until they were free to drive together.

When he filled her—temper, passion, desperation—it was like coming home.

His breath was in rags, his system spent, and still he rocked against her.

"Just hold me a minute more." She pressed her face against his shoulder. "Just hold me." But she felt the warm wetness on her fingers, and pulled away. "Damn it. You're bleeding again. Let me fix it."

"It's fine. It's all right."

"It'll only take a minute."

"Ally, leave it be."

The snap of his voice had her eyes narrowing. "Don't think you can step back from me now. Don't think you'll get away with it this time."

"Just get dressed." He pushed back his hair and began to follow his own orders.

"Fine." She snatched at clothes, dragged them on. "You want to go another round, we'll go another round. You stupid son of a bitch."

He heard the tremor in her voice, cursed her. Cursed himself. "Don't cry. That's playing dirty."

"I'm not crying. You think I'd cry over you?"

He could feel his heart start to shatter as he brushed a tear off her cheek with his thumb. "Don't."

She sniffled, flicked her hands over her face to dry it and sneered. "Sucker."

Fury whipped into his eyes and scalded her. She couldn't

have been more delighted. She got to her feet before he did, but it was close.

"You're in love with me." She punched her fist against his chest. "And you won't admit it. That doesn't make you tough, it makes you hardheaded."

"You weren't listening to me before."

"You weren't listening to me, either, so we're even."

"Listen now." He grabbed her face with both hands. "You have connections."

"Why, you insulting…" She wondered why the top of her head didn't fly off. "How dare you talk about my family's money at a time like this."

"I don't mean money." He jerked her up to her toes, then dropped her back on the flat of her feet again. "Now who's stupid? Money's nothing. I don't give a damn about your portfolio. I have my own. I'm talking about emotional connections. Foundations, roots, for God's sake."

"You have your own there, too. Frannie. Will. Beth. My father." She waved a hand, settling down again. "But I get you. You're saying, basically, that someone like me, who comes from the kind of place I come from, should hook herself up with a man who say, comes from a good, upstanding family. Probably upper-middle-class. He should have a good education, and hold a straight job. A profession. Like say a lawyer or a doctor. Is that the theme here?"

"More or less."

"Interesting. Yes, that's interesting," she said with a considering nod. "I can see the logic in that. Hey, you know who fits that bill to a tee? Dennis Overton. Remember him? Stalker, tire slasher, general pain in the ass?"

She'd turned it around and boxed him into his own corner. All he could do was steam.

"Don't cop to excuses, Blackhawk, if you haven't got

the guts to tell me how you feel about me, and what you want for us."

She flipped her hair back, tucked in her shirt. "My work is done here. See you around, pal."

He got to the door before she did. He was good at that. But this time he slapped a hand on it, held it closed while she glared at him. "You don't walk until we're finished."

"I said I was finished." She jerked on the door.

"I'm not. Shut up and listen."

"You tell me to shut up one more time, and—"

He shut her up. One hard, exasperated kiss. "I've never loved another woman. Never even came close. So cut me a damn break here."

Her heart did a lovely bounding leap. But she nodded, stepped back. "Okay. Spill it."

"You hit me between the eyes the first minute you walked in the room. I still can't see straight."

"Well." She backed up, slid onto a stool. "I'm liking this so far. Keep going."

"You see that? That right there." He stabbed a finger at her. "Anyone else would want to deck you."

"But not you. You love that about me."

"Apparently." He crossed to her, laid his hands on the bar on either side of her. "I love you, so that's it."

"Oh, I don't think so. Make me a deal."

"You want a deal? Here it is. You ditch the apartment and move in, officially, upstairs."

"Full gym and sauna privileges?"

Half the knots in his stomach loosened when he laughed. "Yeah."

"So far, I can live with it. What else are you offering me?"

"Nobody's ever going to love you like I do. I guarantee it. And nobody's ever going to put up with you. But I will."

"Same goes. But that's not enough."

Those wonderful eyes narrowed on her face. "What do you want?"

She rested her back against the bar. "Marriage."

Now those narrowed eyes darkened. "Do you mean that?"

"I say what I mean. Now I could ask you, but I have to figure that a guy who makes a habit of opening doors for women, and buying Christmas presents for little children—"

"Leave that part alone."

"Okay." But she sat up, brushed her knuckles over his cheek. "We'll just say I figure you've got enough of a traditional-guy streak to want to propose on your own. So, I'll let you." She linked her hands at the back of his neck. "I'm waiting."

"I'm just thinking. It's the middle of the night. We're in a bar and my arm's bleeding."

"So's your mouth."

"Yeah." He swiped at it with the back of his hand. "I guess that makes it close to perfect for you and me."

"Works for me. Jonah. You work for me."

He pulled the clip out of her hair, tossed it aside. "First tell me you love me. Use my name."

"I love you, Jonah."

"Then marry me, and let's see where it takes us."

"That's a deal."

# *Epilogue*

With a howl of outrage, Ally bolted up from the sofa. "Off side! Off side! What, are those refs blind? Did you see that?" Instead of kicking in the TV, which occurred to her, she settled for leaning down and pounding on Jonah's shoulder.

"You're just mad because your team's losing, and you're going to owe me."

"I don't know what you're talking about." She sniffed, pushing back her hair. "My team is *not* going to lose, despite corrupt and myopic officials." But it looked very dim for her side. She planted her hands on her hips. "Besides, must I remind you there is no bet because you don't have a license for gambling."

He skimmed his eyes down her long black robe. "You're not wearing your badge."

"Metaphorically, Blackhawk." She leaned over to kiss him. "I'm always wearing my badge." Then she narrowed her eyes. "You swear you didn't hear who won this game? You have no information?"

"Absolutely not."

But she didn't like the way he smiled at her. They'd missed the regular Monday night broadcast and were watching the hotly contested football game on videotape. "I don't know about you. You're slippery."

"We made a deal." He skimmed his hand up the sleeve of her robe, trailing his fingers over flesh. "I never go back on a deal." He reached for the remote, paused the screen. "Since you're up…" He held up his empty glass. "How about a refill?"

"I got it last time."

"You were up last time, too. If you'd sit down and stay down, you wouldn't get tagged."

Conceding his point, she took the glass. "Don't start the game until I get back."

"Wouldn't think of it."

She headed back to the kitchen. There were times she missed the apartment on top of the club. But even a couple of die-hard urbanites needed a little elbow room, she thought. And the house suited them. So did marriage, she thought with a contented sigh as she poured Jonah's habitual bottled water over ice.

There'd been a lot of changes in the eighteen months since they, well, closed the deal, she supposed. Good changes. The kind lives were built on. They were building strong, and they were building solid.

Sipping his water, she walked back to the great room and frowned when she found it empty. Then with a shake of her head, she set the glass down. She knew just where to find him.

She wound her way quietly through the house, and stopped at the door to the bedroom.

The winter moonlight streamed through the windows, glowing over him, and the infant he held in his arms. Love burst through her, a nova of feeling, then settled again to a steady warmth.

"You woke her up."

"She was awake."

"You woke her up," Ally repeated, crossing to him. "Because you can't keep your hands off her."

"Why should I?" He pressed his lips to his daughter's head. "She's mine."

"No question of that." Ally traced a finger over the baby's soft black hair. "She's going to have your eyes."

The idea of it was a staggering thrill. He looked down at that perfect little face, with those dark and mysterious eyes of the newborn. He could see his whole life in those eyes. Sarah's eyes.

"You can't tell at two weeks. The books say it takes longer."

"She's going to have your eyes," Ally repeated. She draped an arm around his waist and together they studied their miracle. "Is she hungry?"

"No. She's just a night person." And his, like the woman beside him was his. Two years before they hadn't existed for him. Now they were the world.

He turned his head, leaning down as Ally lifted her mouth. As the kiss sweetened, the baby stirred in his arms. He shifted, tucking Sarah's head on his shoulder with a natural grace that never failed to make Ally smile.

He'd taken to fatherhood as if he'd only been waiting for the moment. Then again, she thought, thinking of her own father, he'd had a wonderful teacher.

She angled her head, studied the two of them. "I guess she wants to watch the game now."

Jonah rubbed his cheek over his daughter's hair. "She mentioned it."

"She'll just fall asleep."

"So will you."

With a laugh, Ally took the blanket from the bassinet. "Give her up," she said, holding out her arms.

"No."

Ally rolled her eyes. "Okay, you get her till halftime, then it's my turn."

"Deal."

With the baby on his shoulder and his hand linked with the woman's he loved, he went out to enjoy the night.

\* \* \* \* \*

# HIDDEN STAR

To white knights and their damsels

# *Chapter 1*

Cade Parris wasn't having the best of days when the woman of his dreams walked into his office. His secretary had quit the day before—not that she'd been much of a prize anyway, being more vigilant about her manicure than maintaining the phone logs. But he needed someone to keep track of things and shuffle papers into files. Even the raise he offered out of sheer desperation hadn't swayed her to give up her sudden determination to become a country-and-western singing sensation.

So his secretary was heading off to Nashville in a second-hand pickup, and his office looked like the ten miles of bad road he sincerely hoped she traveled.

She hadn't exactly had her mind on her work the past month or two. That impression had been more than confirmed when he fished a bologna sandwich out of the file drawer. At least he thought the blob in the plastic bag was bologna. And it had been filed under *L*—for Lunch?

He didn't bother to swear, nor did he bother to answer the phone that rang incessantly on the empty desk in his reception area. He had reports to type up, and as typing wasn't one of his finer skills, he just wanted to get on with it.

Parris Investigations wasn't what some would call a thriving enterprise. But it suited him, just as the cluttered two-room office squeezed into the top floor of a narrow brick building with bad plumbing in North West D.C. suited him.

He didn't need plush carpets or polished edges. He'd grown up with all that, with the pomp and pretenses, and had had his fill of it all by the time he reached the age of twenty. Now, at thirty, with one bad marriage behind him and a family who continued to be baffled by his pursuits, he was, by and large, a contented man.

He had his investigator's license, a decent reputation as a man who got the job done, and enough income to keep his agency well above water.

Though actual business income was a bit of a problem just then. He was in what he liked to call a lull. Most of his caseload consisted of insurance and domestic work—a few steps down from the thrills he'd imagined when he set out to become a private investigator. He'd just cleaned up two cases, both of them minor insurance frauds that hadn't taken much effort or innovation to close.

He had nothing else coming in, his greedy bloodsucker of a landlord was bumping up his rent, the engine in his car had been making unsettling noises lately, his air conditioner was on the fritz. And the roof was leaking again.

He took the spindly yellow-leafed philodendron his double-crossing secretary had left behind and set it on the uncarpeted floor under the steady drip, hoping it might drown.

He could hear a voice droning into his answering machine. It was his mother's voice. Lord, he thought, did a man ever really escape his mother?

"Cade, dear, I hope you haven't forgotten the Embassy Ball. You know you're to escort Pamela Lovett. I had lunch with her aunt today, and she tells me that Pamela just looks marvelous after her little sojourn to Monaco."

"Yeah, yeah, yeah," he muttered, and narrowed his eyes at the computer. He and machines had poor and untrusting relationships.

He sat down and faced the screen as his mother continued to chatter: "Have you had your tux cleaned? Do make time to get a haircut, you looked so scraggly the last time I saw you."

And don't forget to wash behind the ears, he thought sourly, and tuned her out. She was never going to accept that the Parris lifestyle wasn't his lifestyle, that he just didn't want to lunch at the club or squire bored former debutantes around Washington and that his opinion wasn't going to change by dint of her persuasion.

He'd wanted adventure, and though struggling to type up a report on some poor slob's fake whiplash wasn't exactly Sam Spade territory, he was doing the job.

Mostly he didn't feel useless or bored or out of place. He liked the sound of traffic outside his window, even though the window was only open because the building and its scumsucking landlord didn't go in for central air-conditioning and his unit was broken. The heat was intense, and the rain was coming in, but with the window closed, the offices would have been as airless and stifling as a tomb.

Sweat rolled down his back, making him itchy and irritable. He was stripped down to a T-shirt and jeans, his long fingers fumbling a bit on the computer keys. He had to shovel his hair out of his face several times, which ticked him off. His mother was right. He needed a haircut.

So when it got in the way again, he ignored it, as he ignored the sweat, the heat, the buzz of traffic, the steady drip from the ceiling. He sat, methodically punching a key at a time, a remarkably handsome man with a scowl on his face.

He'd inherited the Parris looks—the clever green eyes that could go broken-bottle sharp or as soft as sea mist, depending on his mood. The hair that needed a trim was dark mink brown and tended to wave. Just now, it curled at his neck, over his ears, and was beginning to annoy him. His nose was straight, aristocratic and a little long, his mouth firm and quick to smile when he was amused. And to sneer when he wasn't.

Though his face had become more honed since the embarrassing cherubic period of his youth and early adolescence, it still sported dimples. He was looking forward to middle age, when, with luck, they'd become manly creases.

He'd wanted to be rugged, and instead was stuck with the slick, dreamy good looks of a *GQ* cover—for one of which he'd posed in his middle twenties, under protest and great family pressure.

The phone rang again. This time he heard his sister's voice, haranguing him about missing some lame cocktail party in honor of some big-bellied senator she was endorsing.

He thought about just ripping the damn answering machine out of the wall and heaving it, and his sister's nagging voice, out the window into the traffic on Wisconsin Avenue.

Then the rain that was only adding to the miserably thick heat began to drip on the top of his head. The computer blinked off, for no reason he could see other than sheer nastiness, and the coffee he'd forgotten he was heating boiled over with a spiteful hiss.

He leaped up, burned his hand on the pot. He swore viciously as the pot smashed, shattering glass, and spewing hot coffee in all directions. He ripped open a drawer, grabbed for a stack of napkins and sliced his thumb with the lethal edge of his former—and now thoroughly damned to perdition—secretary's nail file.

When the woman walked in, he was still cursing and bleeding and had just tripped over the philodendron set in the middle of the floor and didn't even look up.

It was hardly a wonder she simply stood there, damp from the rain, her face pale as death and her eyes wide with shock.

"Excuse me." Her voice sounded rusty, as if she hadn't used it in days. "I must have the wrong office." She inched backward, and those big, wide brown eyes shifted to the name printed on the door. She hesitated, then looked back at him. "Are you Mr. Parris?"

There was a moment, one blinding moment, when he couldn't seem to speak. He knew he was staring at her, couldn't help himself. His heart simply stood still. His knees went weak. And the only thought that came to his mind was *There you are, finally. What the hell took you so long?*

And because that was so ridiculous, he struggled to put a bland, even cynical, investigator's expression on his face.

"Yeah." He remembered the handkerchief in his pocket, and wrapped it over his busily bleeding thumb. "Just had a little accident here."

"I see." Though she didn't appear to, the way she continued to stare at his face. "I've come at a bad time. I don't have an appointment. I thought maybe…"

"Looks like my calendar's clear."

He wanted her to come in, all the way in. Whatever that first absurd, unprecedented reaction of his, she was still a potential client. And surely no dame who ever walked through Sam Spade's hallowed door had ever been more perfect.

She was blonde and beautiful and bewildered. Her hair was wet, sleek down to her shoulders and straight as the rain. Her eyes were bourbon brown, in a face that—though it could have used some color—was delicate as a fairy's. It was heart-shaped, the cheeks a gentle curve and the mouth was full, unpainted and solemn.

She'd ruined her suit and shoes in the rain. He recognized both as top-quality, that quietly exclusive look found only in designer salons. Against the wet blue silk of her suit, the canvas bag she clutched with both hands looked intriguingly out of place.

Damsel in distress, he mused, and his lips curved. Just what the doctor ordered.

"Why don't you come in, close the door, Miss…?"

Her heart bumped twice, hammer-hard, and she tightened her grip on the bag. "You're a private investigator?"

"That's what it says on the door." Cade smiled again, ruthlessly using the dimples while he watched her gnaw that lovely lower lip. Damned if he wouldn't like to gnaw on it himself.

And that response, he thought with a little relief, was a lot more like it. Lust was a feeling he could understand.

"Let's go back to my office." He surveyed the damage— broken glass, potting soil, pools of coffee. "I think I'm finished in here for now."

"All right." She took a deep breath, stepped in, then closed the door. She supposed she had to start somewhere.

Picking her way over the debris, she followed him into

the adjoining room. It was furnished with little more than a desk and a couple of bargain-basement chairs. Well, she couldn't be choosy about decor, she reminded herself. She waited until he'd sat behind his desk, tipped back in his chair and smiled at her again in that quick, trust-me way.

"Do you— Could I—" She squeezed her eyes tight, centered herself again. "Do you have some credentials I could see?"

More intrigued, he took out his license, handed it to her. She wore two very lovely rings, one on each hand, he noticed. One was a square-cut citrine in an antique setting, the other a trio of colored stones. Her earrings matched the second ring, he noted when she tucked her hair behind her ear and studied his license as if weighing each printed word.

"Would you like to tell me what the problem is, Miss…?"

"I think—" She handed him back his license, then gripped the bag two-handed again. "I think I'd like to hire you." Her eyes were on his face again, as intently, as searchingly, as they had been on the license. "Do you handle missing-persons cases?"

Who did you lose, sweetheart? he wondered. He hoped, for her sake and for the sake of the nice little fantasy that was building in his head, it wasn't a husband. "Yeah, I handle missing persons."

"Your, ah, rate?"

"Two-fifty a day, plus expenses." When she nodded, he slid over a legal pad, picked up a pencil. "Who do you want me to find?"

She took a long, shuddering breath. "Me. I need you to find me."

Watching her, he tapped the pencil against the pad. "Looks like I already have. You want me to bill you, or do you want to pay now?"

"No." She could feel it cracking. She'd held on so long—or at least it seemed so long—but now she could feel that branch she'd gripped when the world dropped out from under her begin to crack. "I don't remember. Anything. I don't—" Her voice began to hitch. She took her hands off the bag in her lap to press them to her face. "I don't know who I am. I don't know who I am." And then she was weeping the words into her hands. "I don't know who I am."

Cade had a lot of experience with hysterical women. He'd grown up with females who used flowing tears and gulping sobs as the answer to anything from a broken nail to a broken marriage. So he rose from his desk, armed himself with a box of tissues and crouched in front of her.

"Here now, sweetheart. Don't worry. It's going to be just fine." With gentle expertise, he mopped at her face as he spoke. He patted her hand, stroked her hair, studied her swimming eyes.

"I'm sorry. I can't—"

"Just cry it out," he told her. "You'll feel better for it." Rising, he went into the closet-size bathroom and poured her a paper cup of water.

When she had a lapful of damp tissues and three crushed paper cups, she let out a little jerky sigh. "I'm sorry. Thank you. I do feel better." Her cheeks pinkened a bit with embarrassment as she gathered up the tissues and mangled cups. Cade took them from her, dumped them in the wastebasket, then rested a hip on the corner of his desk.

"You want to tell me about it now?"

She nodded, then linked her fingers and began to twist them together. "I— There isn't that much to tell. I just don't remember anything. Who I am, what I do, where I'm from. Friends, family. Nothing." Her breath caught again, and she released it slowly. "Nothing," she repeated.

It was a dream come true, he thought, the beautiful woman without a past coming out of the rain and into his office. He flicked a glance at the bag she still held in her lap. They'd get to that in a minute. "Why don't you tell me the first thing you do remember?"

"I woke up in a room—a little hotel on Sixteenth Street." Letting her head rest back against the chair, she closed her eyes and tried to bring things into focus. "Even that's unclear. I was curled up on the bed, and there was a chair propped under the doorknob. It was raining. I could hear the rain. I was groggy and disoriented, but my heart was pounding so hard, as if I'd wakened from a nightmare. I still had my shoes on. I remember wondering why I'd gone to bed with my shoes on. The room was dim and stuffy. All the windows were closed. I was so tired, logy, so I went into the bathroom to splash water on my face."

Now she opened her eyes, looked into his. "I saw my face in the mirror. This ugly little mirror with black splotches where it needed to be resilvered. And it meant nothing to me. The face." She lifted a hand, ran it over her cheek, her jaw. "My face meant nothing to me. I couldn't remember the name that went with the face, or the thoughts or the plans or the past. I didn't know how I'd gotten to that horrid room. I looked through the drawers and the closet, but there was nothing. No clothes. I was afraid to stay there, but I didn't know where to go."

"The bag? Was that all you had with you?"

"Yes." Her hand clutched at the straps again. "No purse, no wallet, no keys. This was in my pocket." She reached into the pocket of her jacket and took out a small scrap of notepaper.

Cade took it from her, skimmed the quick scrawling writing.

Bailey, Sat at 7, right? MJ

"I don't know what it means. I saw a newspaper. To-day's Friday."

"Mmm. Write it down," Cade said, handing her a pad and pen.

"What?"

"Write down what it says on the note."

"Oh." Gnawing her lip again, she complied.

Though he didn't have to compare the two to come to his conclusions, he took the pad from her, set it and the note side by side. "Well, you're not M.J., so I'd say you're Bailey."

She blinked, swallowed. "What?"

"From the look of M.J.'s writing, he or she's a lefty. You're right-handed. You've got neat, simple penmanship, M.J.'s got an impatient scrawl. The note was in your pocket. Odds are you're Bailey."

"Bailey." She tried to absorb the name, the hope of it, the feel and taste of identity. But it was dry and unfamiliar. "It doesn't mean anything."

"It means we have something to call you, and someplace to start. Tell me what you did next."

Distracted she blinked at him. "Oh, I... There was a phone book in the room. I looked up detective agencies."

"Why'd you pick mine?"

"The name. It sounded strong." She managed her first smile, and though it was weak, it was there. "I started to call, but then I thought I might get put off, and if I just showed up... So I waited in the room until it was office hours, then I walked for a little while, then I got a cab. And here I am."

"Why didn't you go to a hospital? Call a doctor?"

"I thought about it." She looked down at her hands. "I just didn't."

She was leaving out big chunks, he mused. Going around his desk, he opened a drawer, pulled out a candy bar. "You didn't say anything about stopping for breakfast." He watched her study the candy he offered with puzzlement and what appeared to be amusement. "This'll hold you until we can do better."

"Thank you." With neat, precise movements, she unwrapped the chocolate bar. Maybe part of the fluttering in her stomach was hunger. "Mr. Parris, I may have people worried about me. Family, friends. I may have a child. I don't know." Her eyes deepened, fixed on a point over his shoulder. "I don't think I do. I can't believe anyone could forget her own child. But people may be worried, wondering what happened to me. Why I didn't come home last night."

"You could have gone to the police."

"I didn't want to go to the police." This time, her voice was clipped, definite. "Not until... No, I don't want to involve the police." She wiped her fingers on a fresh tissue, then began to tear it into strips. "Someone may be looking for me who isn't a friend, who isn't family. Who isn't concerned with my well-being. I don't know why I feel that way, I only know I'm afraid. It's more than just not remembering. But I can't understand anything, any of it, until I know who I am."

Maybe it was those big, soft, moist eyes staring up at him, or the damsel-in-distress nerves of her restless hands. Either way, he couldn't resist showing off, just a little.

"I can tell you a few things already. You're an intelligent woman, early-to-midtwenties. You have a good eye for color and style, and enough of a bankroll to indulge it with Italian shoes and silk suits. You're neat, probably organized. You prefer the understated to the obvious. Since you don't evade well, I'd say you're an equally poor liar. You've got a good head on your shoulders, you think things through. You don't panic easily. And you like chocolate."

She balled the empty candy wrapper in her hand. "Why do you assume all that?"

"You speak well, even when you're frightened. You thought about how you were going to handle this and went through all the steps, logically. You dress well—quality over flair. You have a good manicure, but no flashy polish. Your jewelry is unique, interesting, but not ornate. And you've been holding back information since you walked through the door because you haven't decided yet how much you're going to trust me."

"How much should I trust you?"

"You came to me."

She acknowledged that, rose and walked to his window. The rain drummed, underscoring the vague headache that hovered just behind her eyes. "I don't recognize the city," she murmured. "Yet I feel I should. I know where I am, because I saw a newspaper, the *Washington Post*. I know what the White House and the Capitol look like. I know the monuments—but I could have seen them on television, or in a book."

Though it was wet from incoming rain, she rested her hands on the sill, appreciated the coolness there. "I feel as though I dropped out of nowhere into that ugly hotel room. Still, I know how to read and write and walk and talk. The cabdriver had the radio on, and I recognized music. I recognized trees. I wasn't surprised that rain was wet. I smelled burned coffee when I came in, and it wasn't an unfamiliar odor. I know your eyes are green. And when the rain clears, I know the sky will be blue."

She sighed once. "So I didn't drop out of nowhere. There are things I know, things I'm sure of. But my own face means nothing to me, and what's behind the face is blank. I may have hurt someone, done something. I may be selfish and calculating, even cruel. I may have a husband I cheat on or neighbors I've alienated."

She turned back then, and her face was tight and set, a tough contrast to the fragility of lashes still wet from tears. "I don't know if I'm going to like who you find when you find me, Mr. Parris, but I need to know." She set the bag on his desk, hesitated briefly, then opened it. "I think I have enough to meet your fee."

He came from money, the kind that aged and increased and propagated over generations. But even with his background, he'd never seen so much in one place at one time. The canvas bag was filled with wrapped stacks of hundred-dollar bills—all crisp and clean. Fascinated, Cade took out a stack, flipped through. Yes, indeed, he mused, every one of the bills had Ben Franklin's homely and dignified face.

"I'd have to guess about a million," he murmured.

"One million, two hundred thousand." Bailey shuddered as she looked into the bag. "I counted the stacks. I don't know where I got it or why I had it with me. I may have stolen it."

Tears began to swim again as she turned away. "It could be ransom money. I could be involved in a kidnapping. There could be a child somewhere, being held, and I've taken the ransom money. I just—"

"Let's add a vivid imagination to those other qualities."

It was the cool and casual tone of his voice that had her turning back. "There's a fortune in there."

"A million two isn't much of a fortune these days." He dropped the money back in the bag. "And I'm sorry, Bailey, you just don't fit the cold, calculating kidnapper type."

"But you can check. You can find out, discreetly, if there's been an abduction."

"Sure. If the cops are involved, I can get something."

"And if there's been a murder?" Struggling to stay calm, she reached into the bag again. This time she took out a .38.

A cautious man, Cade nudged the barrel aside, took it from her. It was a Smith & Wesson, and at his quick check, he discovered it was fully loaded. "How'd this feel in your hand?"

"I don't understand."

"How'd it feel when you picked it up? The weight, the shape?"

Though she was baffled by the question, she did her best to answer thoroughly. "Not as heavy as I thought it should. It seemed that something that had that kind of power would have more weight, more substance. I suppose it felt awkward."

"The pen didn't."

This time she simply dragged her hands through her hair. "I don't know what you're talking about. I've just shown you over a million dollars and a gun. You're talking about pens."

"When I handed you a pen to write, it didn't feel awkward. You didn't have to think about it. You just took it and used it." He smiled a little and slipped the gun into his pocket, instead of the bag. "I think you're a lot more accustomed to holding a pen than a .38 Special."

There was some relief in that, the simple logic of it. But it didn't chase away all the clouds. "Maybe you're right. It doesn't mean I didn't use it."

"No, it doesn't. And since you've obviously put your hands all over it, we can't prove you didn't. I can check and see if it's registered and to whom."

Her eyes lit with hope. "It could be mine." She reached out, took his hand, squeezed it in a gesture that was thoughtless and natural. "We'd have a name then. I'd know my name then. I didn't realize it could be so simple."

"It may be simple."

"You're right." She released his hand, began to pace. Her movements were smooth, controlled. "I'm getting ahead of myself. But it helps so much, you see, so much more than I imagined, just to tell someone. Someone who knows how to figure things out. I don't know if I'm very good at puzzles. Mr. Parris—"

"Cade," he said, intrigued that he could find her economical movements so sexy. "Let's keep it simple."

"Cade." She drew in a breath, let it out. "It's nice to call someone by name. You're the only person I know, the only person I remember having a conversation with. I can't tell you how odd that is, and, right now, how comforting."

"Why don't we make me the first person you remember having a meal with? One candy bar isn't much of a breakfast. You look worn out, Bailey."

It was so odd to hear him use that name when he looked at her. Because it was all she had, she struggled to respond to it. "I'm tired," she admitted. "It doesn't feel as if I've slept very much. I don't know when I've eaten last."

"How do you feel about scrambled eggs?"

The smile wisped around her mouth again. "I haven't the faintest idea."

"Well, let's find out." He started to pick up the canvas bag, but she laid a hand over his on the straps.

"There's something else." She didn't speak for a moment, but kept her eyes on his, as she had when she first walked in. Searching, measuring, deciding. But there was, she knew, really no choice. He was all she had. "Before I show you, I need to ask for a promise."

"You hire me, Bailey, I work for you."

"I don't know if what I'm going to ask is completely ethical, but I still need your word. If during the course of your investigation you discover that I've committed a crime, I need your word that you'll find out everything you can, all the circumstances, all the facts, before you turn me over to the police."

He angled his head. "You assume I'll turn you in."

"If I've broken the law, I'll expect you to turn me over to the police. But I need all the reasons before you do. I need to understand all the whys, the hows, the who. Will you give me your word on that?"

"Sure." He took the hand she held out. It was delicate as porcelain, steady as a rock. And she, he thought, whoever she was, was a fascinating combination of the fragile and the steely. "No cops until we know all of it. You can trust me, Bailey."

"You're trying to make me comfortable with the name." Again, without thinking, in a move that was as innate as the color of her eyes, she kissed his cheek. "You're very kind."

Kind enough, she thought, that he would hold her now if she asked. And she so desperately wanted to be held, soothed, to be promised that her world would snap back into focus again at any moment. But she needed to stand on her own. She could only hope she was the kind of woman who stood on her own feet and faced her own problems.

"There's one more thing." She turned to the canvas bag again, slid her hand deep inside, felt for the thick velvet pouch, the weight of what was snugged inside it. "I think it's probably the most important thing."

She drew it out and very carefully, with what he thought of as reverence, untied the pouch and slid its contents into the cup of her palm.

The money had surprised him, the gun had concerned

him. But this awed him. The gleam of it, the regal glint, even in the rain-darkened room, held a stunning and sumptuous power.

The gem filled the palm of her hand, its facets clean and sharp enough to catch even the faintest flicker of light and shoot it into the air in bright, burning lances. It belonged, he thought, on the crown of a mythical queen, or lying heavily between the breasts of some ancient goddess.

"I've never seen a sapphire that big."

"It isn't a sapphire." And when she passed it to his hand, she would have sworn she felt the exchange of heat. "It's a blue diamond, somewhere around a hundred carats. Brilliant-cut, most likely from Asia Minor. There are no inclusions visible to the naked eye, and it is rare in both color and size. I'd have to guess its market worth at easily three times the amount of money in the bag."

He wasn't looking at the gem any longer, but at her. When she lifted her eyes to his, she shook her head. "I don't know how I know. But I do. Just as I know it's not all…it's not…complete."

"What do you mean?"

"I wish I knew. But it's too strong a feeling, an almost-recognition. I know the stone is only part of the whole. Just as I know it can't possibly belong to me. It doesn't really belong to anyone. Any one," she repeated, separating the word into two. "I must have stolen it."

She pressed her lips together, lifted her chin, squared her shoulders. "I might have killed for it."

# *Chapter 2*

Cade took her home. It was the best option he could think of, tucking her away. And he wanted that canvas bag and its contents in his safe as quickly as possible. She hadn't argued when he led her out of the building, had made no comment about the sleek little Jag parked in the narrow spot on the cracked asphalt lot.

He preferred using his nondescript and well-dented sedan for his work, but until it was out of the shop, he was stuck with the streamlined, eye-catching Jaguar.

But she said nothing, not even when he drove into a lovely old neighborhood with graceful shade trees and tidy flower-trimmed lawns and into the driveway of a dignified Federal-style brick house.

He'd been prepared to explain that he'd inherited it from a great-aunt who had a soft spot for him—which was true enough. And that he lived there because he liked the quiet and convenience of the established neighborhood in the heart of Washington.

But she didn't ask.

It seemed to Cade that she'd simply run down. Whatever energy had pushed her into going out in the rain, seeking his office and telling her story had drained out, leaving her listless.

And fragile again. He had to check the urge to simply gather her up and carry her inside. He could imagine it clearly—the stalwart knight, my lady's champion, carrying her into the safety of the castle and away from any and all dragons that plagued her.

He really had to stop thinking things like that.

Instead, he hefted the canvas bag, took her unresisting hand and led her through the graceful foyer, down the hall and directly into the kitchen.

"Scrambled eggs," he said, pulling out a chair for her and nudging her down to sit at the pedestal table.

"All right. Yes. Thank you."

She felt limp, unfocused, and terribly grateful to him. He wasn't peppering her with questions, nor had he looked particularly shocked or appalled by her story. Perhaps it was the nature of his business that made him take it all in stride, but whatever the reason, she was thankful for the time he was giving her to recoup.

Now he was moving around the kitchen in a casual, competent manner. Breaking brown eggs in a white bowl, popping bread in a toaster that sat on a granite-colored counter. She should offer to help, she thought. It seemed the right thing to do. But she was so dreadfully tired, and it was so pleasant to just sit in the big kitchen with rain drumming musically on the roof and watch him handle the simple task of making breakfast.

He was taking care of her. And she was letting him. Bailey closed her eyes and wondered if she was the kind of woman who needed to be tended to by a man, who enjoyed the role of the helpless female.

She hoped not, almost fiercely hoped not. Then wondered why such a minor, insignificant personality trait should matter so much, when she couldn't be sure she wasn't a thief or murderer.

She caught herself studying her hands, wondering about them. Short, neat, rounded nails coated in clear polish. Did that mean she was practical? The hands were soft, uncallused. It was doubtful she worked with them, pursued manual labor of any kind.

The rings… Very pretty, not bold so much as unique. At least it seemed they were. She knew the stones that winked back at her. Garnet, citrine, amethyst. How could she know the names of colored stones and not know the name of her closest friend?

Did she have any friends?

Was she a kind person or a catty one, generous or a fault-finder? Did she laugh easily and cry at sad movies? Was there a man she loved who loved her?

Had she stolen more than a million dollars and used that ugly little gun?

She jolted when Cade set her plate in front of her, then settled when he laid a hand on her shoulder.

"You need to eat." He went back to the stove, brought the cup he'd left there. "And I think tea's a better bet than coffee."

"Yes. Thank you." She picked up her fork, scooped up some eggs, tasted. "I like them." She managed a smile again, a hesitant, shy smile that touched his heart. "That's something."

He sat across from her with his mug of coffee. "I'm known throughout the civilized world for my scrambled eggs."

Her smile steadied, bloomed. "I can see why. The little dashes of dill and paprika are inspired."

"Wait till you taste my Spanish omelets."

"Master of the egg." She continued to eat, comforted by the easy warmth she felt between them. "Do you cook a lot?"

She glanced around the kitchen. Stone-colored cabinets and warm, light wood. An uncurtained window over a double sink of white porcelain. Coffeemaker, toaster, jumbled sections of the morning paper.

The room was neat, she observed, but not obsessively so. And it was a marked contrast to the clutter and mess of his office. "I never asked if you were married."

"Divorced, and I cook when I'm tired of eating out."

"I wonder what I do—eat out or cook."

"You recognized paprika and dill when you tasted them." Leaning back, he sipped his coffee and studied her. "You're beautiful." Her gaze flicked up, startled and, he noted, instantly wary. "Just an observation, Bailey. We have to work with what we know. You are beautiful—it's quiet, understated, nothing that seems particularly contrived or enhanced. You don't go for the flashy, and you don't take a compliment on your looks casually. In fact, I've just made you very nervous."

She picked up her cup, held it in both hands. "Are you trying to?"

"No, but it's interesting and sweet—the way you blush and eye me suspiciously at the same time. You can relax, I'm not hitting on you." But it was a thought, he admitted, a fascinating and arousing thought. "I don't think you're a pushover, either," he continued. "I doubt a man would get very far with you just by telling you that you have eyes like warm brandy, and that the contrast between them and that cool, cultured voice packs a hell of a sexual impact."

She lifted her cup and, though it took an effort, kept her gaze level with his. "It sounds very much like you're hitting on me."

His dimples flashed with charm when he grinned. "See, not a pushover. But polite, very polite and well mannered. There's New England in your voice, Bailey."

Staring, she lowered the cup again. "New England?"

"Connecticut, Massachusetts—I'm not sure. But there's a whiff of Yankee society upbringing in your voice, especially when it turns cold."

"New England." She strained for a connection, some small link. "It doesn't mean anything to me."

"It gives me another piece to work with. You've got class written all over you. You were born with it, or you developed it, either way it's there." He rose, took her plate. "And so's the exhaustion. You need to sleep."

"Yes." The thought of going back to that hotel room had her forcing back a shudder. "Should I call your office, set up another appointment? I wrote down the number of the hotel and room where I'm staying. You could call me if you find anything."

"You're not going back there." He had her hand again, drew her to her feet and began to lead her out of the kitchen. "You can stay here. There's plenty of room."

"Here?"

"I think it's best if you're where I can keep an eye on you, at least for the time being." Back in the foyer, he led her up the stairs. "It's a safe, quiet neighborhood, and until we figure out how you got your hands on a million two and a diamond as big as your fist, I don't want you wandering the streets."

"You don't know me."

"Neither do you. That's something else we're going to work on."

He opened the door to a room where the dim light flickered quietly through lace curtains onto a polished oak floor. A little seating area of button-back chairs and a piecrust table was arranged in front of a fireplace where a fern thrived in the hearth. A wedding-ring quilt was spread over a graceful four-poster, plumped invitingly with pillows.

"Take a nap," he advised. "There's a bath through there, and I'll dig up something for you to change into after you've rested."

She felt the tears backing up again, scoring her throat with a mixture of fear and gratitude and outrageous fatigue. "Do you invite all your clients into your home as houseguests?"

"No." He touched her cheek and, because he wanted to gather her close, feel how her head would settle on his shoulder, dropped his hand again. "Just the ones who need it. I'm going to be downstairs. I've got some things to do."

"Cade." She reached for his hand, held it a moment. "Thank you. It looks like I picked the right name out of the phone book."

"Get some sleep. Let me do the worrying for a while."

"I will. Don't close the door," she said quickly when he stepped out into the hall.

He pushed it open again, studied her standing there in the patterned light, looking so delicate, so lost. "I'll be right downstairs."

She listened to his footsteps recede before sinking down on the padded bench at the foot of the bed. It might be foolish to trust him, to put her life in his hands as completely as she had. But she did trust him. Not only because her world consisted only of him and what she'd told him, but because every instinct inside her told her this was a man she could depend on.

Perhaps it was just blind faith and desperate hope, but at the moment she didn't think she could survive another hour without both. So her future depended on Cade Parris, on his ability to handle her present and his skill in unearthing her past.

She slipped off her shoes, took off her jacket and folded it on the bench. Almost dizzy with fatigue, she climbed into bed and lay atop the quilt, and was asleep the moment her cheek met the pillow.

Downstairs, Cade lifted Bailey's prints from her teacup. He had the connections to have them run quickly and discreetly. If she had a record or had ever worked for the government, he'd have her ID'd easily.

He'd check with missing persons, see if anyone matching her description had been reported. That, too, was easy.

The money and the diamond offered another route. The theft of a gem of that size was bound to make news. He needed to verify the facts Bailey had given him on the stone, then do some research.

He needed to check the registration on the gun, too—and check his sources on recent homicides or shootings with a .38.

All those steps would be more effective if done in person. But he didn't want to leave her on her own just yet. She might panic and take off, and he wasn't going to risk losing her.

It was just as possible that she would wake up from her nap, remember who she was and go back to her own life before he had a chance to save her.

He very much wanted to save her.

While he locked the bag in his library safe, booted up his computer, scribbled his notes, he reminded himself that she might have a husband, six kids, twenty jealous lovers, or a criminal record as long as Pennsylvania Avenue. But he just didn't care.

She was his damsel in distress, and damn it, he was keeping her.

He made his calls, arranged to have the prints messengered over to his contact at the police station. The little favor was going to cost him a bottle of unblended Scotch, but Cade accepted that nothing was free.

"By the way, Mick, you got anything on a jewelry heist? A big one?"

Cade could clearly imagine Detective Mick Marshall pushing through his paperwork, phone cocked at his ear to block out the noise of the bull pen, his tie askew, his wiry red hair sticking up in spikes from a face set in a permanent scowl.

"You got something, Parris?"

"Just a rumor," Cade said easily. "If something big went down, I could use a link to the insurance company. Got to pay the rent, Mick."

"Hell, I don't know why you don't buy the building in the first place, then tear the rattrap down, rich boy."

"I'm eccentric—that's what they call rich boys who pal around with people like you. So, what do you know?"

"Haven't heard a thing."

"Okay. I've got a Smith & Wesson .38 Special." Cade rattled off the serial number as he turned the gun in his hand. "Run it for me, will you?"

"Two bottles of Scotch, Parris."

"What are friends for? How's Doreen?"

"Sassy as ever. Ever since you brought her over those damn tulips, I haven't heard the end of it. Like I got time to pluck posies before I go home every night. I ought to make it three bottles of Scotch."

"You find out anything about an important gem going missing, Mick, I'll buy you a case. I'll be talking to you."

Cade hung up the phone and stared malevolently at his computer. Man and machine were simply going to have to come to terms for this next bit of research.

It took him what he estimated was three times as long as it would the average twelve-year-old to insert the CD-ROM, search, and find what he was after.

Amnesia.

Cade drank another cup of coffee and learned more about the human brain than he'd ever wanted to know. For a short, uncomfortable time, he feared Bailey had a tumor. That he might have one, as well. He experienced a deep personal concern for his brain stem, then reconfirmed why he hadn't gone into medicine as his mother hoped.

The human body, with all its tricks and ticking time bombs, was just too scary. He'd much rather face a loaded gun than the capriciousness of his own internal organs.

He finally concluded, with some relief, that it was un-likely Bailey had a tumor. All signs pointed to hysterical amnesia, which could resolve itself within hours of the trauma, or take weeks. Months. Even years.

Which put them, he thought, solidly back at square one. The handy medical CD that had come with his computer indicated that amnesia was a symptom, rather than a disease, and that treatment involved finding and removing the cause.

That was where he came in. It seemed to Cade that a de-tective was every bit as qualified as a doctor to deal with Bailey's problem.

Turning back to his computer, he laboriously typed up his notes, questions and conclusions to date. Satisfied, he went back upstairs to find her some clothes.

She didn't know if it was a dream or reality—or even if it was her own dream or someone else's reality. But it was familiar, so oddly familiar…

The dark room, the hard slant of the beam of light from the desk lamp. The elephant. How strange—the elephant seemed to be grinning at her, its trunk lifted high for luck, its glinting blue eyes gleaming with secret amusement.

Female laughter—again familiar, and so comforting. Friendly, intimate laughter.

*It's got to be Paris, Bailey. We're not going to spend two weeks with you digging in the dirt again. What you need is romance, passion, sex. What you need is Paris.*

A triangle, gold and gleaming. And a room filled with light, bright, blinding light. A man who's not a man, with a face so kind, so wise, so generous, it thrills the soul. And the golden triangle held in his open hands, the offering of it, the power of it stunning, the impact of the rich blue of the stones nestled in each angle almost palpable. And the stones shining and pulsing like heartbeats and seeming to leap into the air like stars, shooting stars that scatter light.

The beauty of them sears the eyes.

And she's holding them in her hands, and her hands are shaking. Anger, such anger swirling inside her, and fear and panic and fury. The stones shoot out from her hands, first one, then two, winging away like jeweled birds. And the third is clutched to her heart by her open, protective hand.

Silver flashing, bolts of silver flashing. And the pounding of booming drums that shake the ground. Blood. Blood everywhere, like a hideous river spilling.

My God, it's wet, so red and wet and demon-dark.

Running, stumbling, heart thudding. It's dark again. The light's gone, the stars are gone. There's a corridor, and her heels echo like the thunder that follows lightning. It's coming after her, hunting her in the dark while the walls close in tighter and tighter.

She can hear the elephant trumpeting, and the lightning flashes closer. She crawls into the cave and hides like an animal, shivering and whimpering like an animal as the lightning streaks by her...

"Come on, sweetheart. Come on, honey. It's just a bad dream."

She clawed her way out of the dark toward the calm, steady voice, burrowed her clammy face into the broad, solid shoulder.

"Blood. So much blood. Hit by lightning. It's coming. It's close."

"No, it's gone now." Cade pressed his lips to her hair, rocked her. When he slipped in to leave her a robe, she'd been crying in her sleep. Now she was clinging to him, trembling, so he shifted her into his lap as if she were a child. "You're safe now. I promise."

"The stars. Three stars." Balanced between dream and reality, she shifted restlessly in his arms. "I've got to go to Paris."

"You did. I'm right here." He tipped her head back to touch his lips to her temple. "Right here," he repeated, waiting for her eyes to clear and focus. "Relax now. I'm right here."

"Don't go." With a quick shudder, she rested her head on his shoulder, just as he'd imagined. The pull on his heart was immediate, and devastating.

He supposed love at first sight was meant to be.

"I won't. I'll take care of you."

That alone was enough to ease her trembling. She relaxed against him, let her eyes close again. "It was just a dream, but it was so confusing, so frightening. I don't understand any of it."

"Tell me."

He listened as she struggled to remember the details, put them in order. "There was so much emotion, huge waves of emotions. Anger, shock, a sense of betrayal and fear. Then terror. Just sheer mindless terror."

"That could explain the amnesia. You're not ready to cope with it, so you shut it off. It's a kind of conversion hysteria."

"Hysteria?" The term made her chin lift. "I'm hysterical?"

"In a manner of speaking." He rubbed his knuckles absently over that lifted chin. "It looks good on you."

In a firm, deliberate movement that made his brow quirk, she pushed his hand from her face. "I don't care for the term."

"I'm using it in a strictly medical sense. You didn't get bopped on the head, right?"

Her eyes were narrowed now. "Not that I recall, but then, I'm hysterical, after all."

"Cute. What I mean is, amnesia can result from a concussion." He twirled her hair around his finger as he spoke, just to feel the texture. "I always thought that was bull or Hollywood stuff, but it says so right in the medical book. One of the other causes is a functional nervous disorder, such as—you'll excuse the term—hysteria."

Her teeth were gritted now. "I am not hysterical, though I'm sure I could be, if you'd care for a demonstration."

"I've had plenty of those. I have sisters. Bailey." He cupped her face in his hands in such a disarming gesture, her narrowed eyes widened. "You're in trouble, that's the bottom line. And we're going to fix it."

"By holding me in your lap?"

"That's just a side benefit." When her smile fluttered again and she started to shift away, he tightened his grip. "I like it. A lot."

She could see more than amusement in his eyes, something that had her pulse jumping. "I don't think it's wise for you to flirt with a woman who doesn't know who she is."

"Maybe not, but it's fun. And it'll give you something else to think about."

She found herself charmed, utterly, by the way his dimples flickered, the way his mouth quirked at the corner just enough to make the smile crooked. It would be a good mouth for a lover, quick, clever, full of energy. She could imagine too well just how it would fit against hers.

Perhaps because she couldn't imagine any other, couldn't remember another taste, another texture. And because that would make him, somehow, the first to kiss her, the thrill of anticipation sprinted up her spine.

He dipped her head back, slowly, his gaze sliding from her eyes to her lips, then back again. He could imagine it perfectly, and was all but sure there would be a swell of music to accompany that first meeting of lips.

"Want to try it?"

Need, rich and full and shocking, poured through her, jittering nerves, weakening limbs. She was alone with him, this stranger she'd trusted her life to. This man she knew more of than she knew of herself.

"I can't." She put a hand on his chest, surprised that however calm his voice his heart was pounding as rapidly as hers. Because it was, she could be honest. "I'm afraid to."

"In my experience, kissing isn't a scary business, unless we're talking about kissing Grandmother Parris, and that's just plain terrifying."

It made her smile again, and this time, when she shifted, he let her go. "Better not to complicate things any more than they are." With restless hands, she scooped her hair back, looked away from him. "I'd like to take a shower, if that's all right. Clean up a little."

"Sure. I brought you a robe, and some jeans you can roll up. The best I could come up with for a belt that would fit you was some clothesline. It'll hold them up and make a unique fashion statement."

"You're very sweet, Cade."

"That's what they all say." He closed off the little pocket of lust within and rose. "Can you handle being alone for an hour? There're a couple of things I should see to."

"Yes, I'll be fine."

"I need you to promise you won't leave the house, Bailey."

She lifted her hands. "Where would I go?"

He put his hands on her shoulders, waited until her gaze lifted to his. "Promise me you won't leave the house."

"All right. I promise."

"I won't be long." He walked to the door, paused. "And, Bailey? Think about it."

She caught the gleam in his eyes before he turned that told her he didn't mean the circumstances that had brought her to him. When she walked to the window, watched him get in his car and drive away, she was already thinking about it. About him.

Someone else was thinking about her. Thinking dark, vengeful thoughts. She had slipped through his fingers, and, with her, the prize and the power he most coveted.

He'd already exacted a price for incompetence, but it was hardly enough. She would be found, and when she was, she'd pay a much higher price. Her life, certainly, but that was insignificant.

There would be pain first, and great fear. That would satisfy.

The money he had lost was nothing, almost as insignificant as the life of one foolish woman. But she had what he needed, what was meant to belong to him. And he would take back his own.

There were three. Individually they were priceless, but together their value went beyond the imaginable. Already he had taken steps to recover the two she had foolishly attempted to hide from him.

It would take a little time, naturally, but he would have them back. It was important to be careful, to be cautious, to be certain of the recovery, and that whatever violence was necessary remained distant from him.

But soon two pieces of the triangle would be his, two ancient stars, with all their beauty and light and potency.

He sat in the room he'd had built for his treasures, those acquired, stolen or taken with blood. Jewels and paintings, statuary and precious pelts, gleamed and sparkled in his Aladdin's cave of secrets.

The altarlike stand he'd designed to hold his most coveted possession was empty and waiting.

But soon...

He would have the two, and when he had the third he would be immortal.

And the woman would be dead.

# *Chapter 3*

It was her body in the mirror, Bailey told herself, and she'd better start getting used to it. In the glass, fogged from her shower, her skin looked pale and smooth. Self-consciously she laid a hand against her breast.

Long fingers, short trimmed nails, rather small breasts. Her arms were a little thin, she noted with a frown. Maybe she should start thinking about working out to build them up.

There didn't seem to be any excess flab at the waist or hips, so perhaps she got some exercise. And there was some muscle tone in the thighs.

Her skin was pale, without tan lines.

What was she—about five-four? She wished she were taller. It seemed if a woman was going to begin her life at twentysomething, she ought to be able to pick her body type. Fuller breasts and longer legs would have been nice.

Amused at herself, she turned, twisted her head to study

the rear view. And her mouth dropped open. There was a tattoo on her butt.

What in the world was she doing with a tattoo of a—was that a unicorn?—on her rear end? Was she crazy? Body decoration was one thing, but on that particular part of the anatomy it meant that she had exposed that particular part of the anatomy to some needle-wielding stranger.

Did she drink too much?

Faintly embarrassed, she pulled on a towel and quickly left the misty bathroom.

She spent some time adjusting the jeans and shirt Cade had left her to get the best fit. Hung up her suit neatly, smoothed the quilt. Then she heaved a sigh and tunneled her fingers through her damp hair.

Cade had asked her to stay in the house, but he hadn't asked her to stay in her room. She was going to be jittery again, thinking about bags of money, huge blue diamonds, murder and tattoos, if she didn't find a distraction.

She wandered out, realizing she wasn't uncomfortable in the house alone. She supposed it was a reflection of her feelings for Cade. He didn't make her uncomfortable. From almost the first minute, she'd felt as though she could talk to him, depend on him.

And she imagined that was because she hadn't talked to anyone else, and had no one else to depend on.

Nonetheless, he was a kind, considerate man. A smart, logical one, she supposed, or else he wouldn't be a private investigator. He had a wonderful smile, full of fun, and eyes that paid attention. He had strength in his arms and, she thought, in his character.

And dimples that made her fingers itch to trace along them.

His bedroom. She gnawed on her lip as she stood in the

doorway. It was rude to pry. She wondered if she were rude, careless with the feelings and privacy of others. But she needed something, anything, to fill all these blank spots. And he had left his door open.

She stepped over the threshold.

It was a wonderfully large room, and full of him. Jeans tossed over a chair, socks on the floor. She caught herself before she could pick them up and look for a hamper. Loose change and a couple of shirt buttons tossed on the dresser. A gorgeous antique chest of drawers that undoubtedly held all sorts of pieces of him.

She didn't tug at the brass handles, but she wanted to.

The bed was big, unmade, and framed by the clean lines of Federal head- and footboards. The rumpled sheets were dark blue, and she didn't quite resist running her fingers over them. They'd probably smell of him—that faintly minty scent.

When she caught herself wondering if he slept naked, heat stung her cheeks and she turned away.

There was a neat brick fireplace and a polished pine mantel. A silly brass cow stood on the hearth and made her smile. There were books messily tucked into a recessed shelf. Bailey studied the titles soberly, wondering which she might have read. He went heavy on mysteries and true crime, but there were familiar names. That made her feel better.

Without thinking, she picked up a used coffee mug and an empty beer bottle and carried them downstairs.

She hadn't paid much attention to the house when they came in. It had all been so foggy, so distorted, in her mind. But now she studied the simple and elegant lines, the long, lovely windows, with their classic trim, the gleaming antiques.

The contrast between the gracious home and the second-rate office struck her, made her frown. She rinsed the mug in the sink, found the recycling bin for the bottle, then took herself on a tour.

It took her less than ten minutes to come to her conclusion. The man was loaded.

The house was full of treasures—museum-quality. Of that she was undeniably sure. She might not have understood the unicorn on her own rear end, but she understood the value of a Federal inlaid cherrywood slant-front desk. She couldn't have said why.

She recognized Waterford vases, Georgian silver. The Limoges china in the dining room display cabinet. And she doubted very much if the Turner landscape was a copy.

She peeked out a window. Well-tended lawn, majestic old trees, roses in full bloom. Why would a man who could live in such a style choose to work in a crumbling building in a stuffy, cramped office?

Then she smiled. It seemed Cade Parris was as much a puzzle as she was herself. And that was a tremendous comfort.

She went back to the kitchen, hoping to make herself useful by making some iced tea or putting something together for lunch. When the phone rang, she jumped like a scalded cat. The answering machine clicked on, and Cade's voice flowed out, calming her again: "You've reached 555-2396. Leave a message. I'll get back to you."

"Cade, this is becoming very irritating." The woman's voice was tight with impatience. "I've left a half a dozen messages at your office this morning, the least you can do is have the courtesy to return my calls. I sincerely doubt you're so busy with what you loosely call your clients to speak to your own mother." There was a sigh, long-suffering and loud. "I know very well you haven't contacted Pamela about arrangements for this evening. You've put me in a very awkward position. I'm leaving for Dodie's for bridge. You can reach me there until four. Don't embarrass me, Cade. By the way, Muffy's very annoyed with you."

There was a decisive click. Bailey found herself clearing her throat. She felt very much as if she'd received that cool, deliberate tongue-lashing herself. And it made her wonder if she had a mother who nagged, who expected obedience. Who was worried about her.

She filled the teakettle, set it on to boil, dug up a pitcher. She was hunting up tea bags when the phone rang again.

"Well, Cade, this is Muffy. Mother tells me she still hasn't been able to reach you. It's obvious you're avoiding our calls because you don't want to face your own poor behavior. You know very well Camilla's piano recital was last night. The least, the very least, you could have done was put in an appearance and pretended to have some family loyalty. Not that I expected any better from you. I certainly hope you have the decency to call Camilla and apologize. I refuse to speak to you again until you do."

Click.

Bailey blew out a breath, rolled her eyes. Families, she thought, were obviously difficult and complex possessions. Then again, perhaps she had a brother herself and was just as, well…bitchy, as the wasp-tongued Muffy.

She set the tea to steep, then opened the refrigerator. There were eggs, and plenty of them. That made her smile. There was also a deli pack of honey-baked ham, some Swiss, and when she discovered plump beefsteak tomatoes, she decided she was in business.

She worried over the choice of mustard or mayo for a time and whether the tea should be sweetened or unsweetened. Every little detail was like a brick in the rebuilding of herself. As she was carefully slicing tomatoes, she heard the front door slam, and her mood brightened.

But when she started to call out, the words stuck in her throat. What if it wasn't Cade? What if they'd found her? Come for her? Her hand tightened on the hilt of the knife as she edged toward the rear kitchen door. Fear, deep and uncontrollable, had sweat popping out in clammy pearls on her skin. Her heart flipped into her throat.

Running, running away from that sharp, hacking lightning. In the dark, with her own breath screaming in her head. Blood everywhere.

Her fingers tensed on the knob, turned it, as she prepared for flight or fight.

When Cade stepped in, a sob of relief burst out of her. The knife clattered on the floor as she launched herself into his arms. "It's you. It is you."

"Sure it is." He knew he should feel guilty that fear had catapulted her against him, but he was only human. She smelled fabulous. "I told you you're safe here, Bailey."

"I know. I felt safe. But when I heard the door, I panicked for a minute." She clung, wildly grateful to have him with her. Drawing her head back, she stared up at him. "I wanted to run, just run, when I heard the door and thought it could be someone else. I hate being such a coward, and not knowing what I should do. I can't seem…to think."

She trailed off, mesmerized. He was stroking her cheek as she babbled, his eyes intent on hers. Her arms were banded around his waist, all but fused there. The hand that had smoothed through her hair was cupped at the base of her neck now, fingers gently kneading.

He waited, saw the change in her eyes. His lips curved, just enough to have her heart quiver before he lowered his head and gently touched them to hers.

Oh, lovely… That was her first thought. It was lovely to be held so firmly, to be tasted so tenderly. This was a kiss, this sweet meeting of lips that made the blood hum lazily and the soul sigh. With a quiet murmur, she slid her hands up his back, rose on her toes to meet that patient demand.

When his tongue traced her lips, slipped between them, she shuddered with pleasure. And opened to him as naturally as a rose opens to the sun.

He'd known she would. Somehow he'd known she would be both shy and generous, that the taste of her would be fresh, the scent of her airy. It was impossible that he'd only met her hours before. It seemed the woman he held in his arms had been his forever.

And it was thrilling, hotly arousing, to know his was the first kiss she would remember. That he was the only man in her mind and heart to hold her this way, touch her this way. He was the first to make her tremble, his was the first name she murmured when needs swirled through her.

And when she murmured his name, every other woman he'd ever held vanished. She was the first for him.

He deepened the kiss gradually, aware of how easily he could bruise or frighten. But she came so suddenly alive in his arms, was so wildly responsive, her mouth hungry and hot, her body straining and pulsing against his.

She felt alive, brilliantly alive, aware of every frantic beat of her own heart. Her hands had streaked into his hair and were fisted there now, as if she could pull him inside her. He was filling all those empty places, all those frightening blanks. This was life. This was real. This mattered.

"Easy." He could barely get the word out, wished fervently he didn't feel obliged to. He was trembling as much as she, and he knew that if he didn't pull back, gain some control, he was going to take her exactly where they stood.

"Easy," he said again, and pressed her head to his shoulder so that he wouldn't be tempted to devour that ripe, willing mouth.

She vibrated against him, nerves and needs tangling, the echoes of sensations thumping through her system. "I don't know if it's ever been like that. I just don't know."

That brought him back to earth a little too abruptly. She didn't know, he reminded himself. He did. It had never been like that for him. "Don't worry." He pulled away, then rubbed his hands over her shoulders, because they were tense again. "You know that wasn't ordinary, Bailey. That ought to be enough for now."

"But—" She bit her lip when he turned and wrenched open the fridge. "I made— I'm making iced tea."

"I want a beer."

She winced at the brusque tone. "You're angry."

"No." He twisted off the cap, downed three long swallows. "Yes. With myself, a little. I pushed the buttons, after all." He lowered the bottle, studied her. She was standing with her arms crossed tight at her waist. His jeans bagged at her hips, his shirt drooped at her shoulders. Her feet were bare, her hair was tangled around her shoulders.

She looked absolutely defenseless.

"Let's just get this out, okay?" He leaned back against the counter to keep his distance. "I felt the click the minute you walked into the office. Never happened to me before, just click, there she is. I figured it was because you were a looker, you were in trouble and you'd come looking for me. I've got a thing about people in trouble, especially beautiful women."

He drank again, slower this time, while she watched him soberly, with great attention. "But that's not it, Bailey, or at least not all of it. I want to help you. I want to find out everything about you as much as you do. But I also want to make love with you, slow, really slow, so that every second's like an hour. And when we've finished making love, and you're naked and limp under me, I want to start all over again."

She had her hands crossed over her breasts now, to keep her bucking heart in place. "Oh" was all she could manage.

"And that's what I'm going to do. When you're a little steadier on your feet."

"Oh," she said again. "Well." She cleared her throat. "Cade, I may be a criminal."

"Uh-huh." Calm again, he inspected the sandwich makings on the counter. "So is this lunch?"

Her eyes narrowed. What sort of response was that from a man who'd just told her he wanted to make love with her until she was limp? "I may have stolen a great deal of money, killed people, kidnapped an innocent child."

"Right." He piled some ham on bread. "Yeah, you're a real desperado, sweetheart. Anybody can see that. You've got that calculating killer gleam in the eye." Then, chuckling, he turned to her. "Bailey, for God's sake, look at yourself. You're a polite, tidy woman with a conscience as wide as Kansas. I sincerely doubt you have so much as a parking ticket to your name, or that you've done anything wilder than sing in the shower."

It stung. She couldn't have said why, but the bland and goody-goody description put her back up. "I've got a tattoo on my butt."

He set the rather sloppy sandwich he'd put together down. "Excuse me?"

"I have a tattoo on my butt," she repeated, with a combative gleam in her eye.

"Is that so?" He couldn't wait to see it. "Well, then, I'll

have to turn you in. Now, if you tell me you've got something other than your ears pierced, I'll have to get my gun."

"I'm so pleased I could amuse you."

"Sweetheart, you fascinate me." He shifted to block her path before she could storm out. "Temper. That's a good sign. Bailey's not a wimp." She stepped to the right. So did he. "She likes scrambled eggs with dill and paprika, knows how to make iced tea, cuts tomatoes in very precise slices and knows how to tie a shank knot."

"What?"

"Your belt," he said with a careless gesture. "She was probably a Girl Scout, or she likes to sail. Her voice gets icy when she's annoyed, she has excellent taste in clothes, bites her bottom lip when she's nervous—which I should warn you instills wild lust in me for no sensible reason."

His dimples winked when she immediately stopped nibbling her lip and cleared her throat. "She keeps her nails at a practical length," he continued. "And she can kiss a man blind. An interesting woman, our Bailey."

He gave her hair a friendly tug. "Now, why don't we sit down, eat lunch, and I'll tell you what else I found out. Do you want mustard or mayo?"

"I don't know." Still sulking, she plopped down in a chair.

"I go for mustard myself." He brought it to the table, along with the fixings for her sandwich. "So what is it?"

She swiped mustard on bread. "What?"

"The tattoo? What is it?"

Embarrassed now, she slapped ham over mustard. "I hardly see that it's an issue."

"Come on." He grinned, leaning over to tug on her hair again. "A butterfly? A rosebud? Or are you really a biker chick in disguise, with a skull and crossbones hiding under my jeans?"

"A unicorn," she muttered.

He bit the tip of his tongue. "Cute." He watched her cut her sandwich into tidy and precise triangles, but refrained from commenting.

Because she wanted to squirm, she changed the subject. "You were going to tell me what else you've found out."

Since it didn't seem to do his blood pressure any good for him to paint mental images of unicorns, he let her off the hook. "Right. The gun's unregistered. My source hasn't been able to trace it yet. The clip's full."

"The clip?"

"The gun was fully loaded, which means it either hadn't been fired recently, or had been reloaded."

"Hadn't been fired." She closed her eyes, grasped desperately at relief. "I might not have used it at all."

"I'd say it's unlikely you did. Using current observations, I can't picture you owning an unregistered handgun, but if we get lucky and track it down, we may have a clearer picture."

"You've learned so much already."

He would have liked to bask in that warm admiration, but he shrugged and took a hefty bite of his sandwich. "Most of it's negative information. There's been no report of a robbery that involves a gem like the one you've been carrying, or that amount of cash. No kidnapping or hostage situations that the local police are involved in, and no open homicides involving the type of weapon we're dealing with in the last week."

He took another swallow of beer. "No one has reported a woman meeting your description missing in the last week, either."

"But how can that be?" She shoved her sandwich aside. "I have the gem, I have the cash. I *am* missing."

"There are possibilities." He kept his eyes on hers. "Maybe someone doesn't want that information out. Bailey, you said you thought the diamond was only part of a whole. And when you were coming out of the nightmare you talked about three stars. Stars. Diamonds. Could be the same thing. Do you think there are three of those rocks?"

"Stars?" She pressed her fingers to her temple as it started to ache. "Did I talk about stars? I don't remember anything about stars."

Because it hurt to think about it, she tried to concentrate on the reasonable. "Three gems of that size and quality would be unbelievably rare. As a set, even if the others were inferior in clarity to the one I have, they'd be beyond price. You couldn't begin to assess—" Her breath began to hitch, to come in gasps as she fought for air. "I can't breathe."

"Okay." He was up, shifting her so that he could lower her head between her knees, rub her back. "That's enough for now. Just relax, don't force it."

He wondered, as he stroked her back, just what she'd seen that put that kind of blind terror in her eyes.

"I'm sorry," she managed. "I want to help."

"You are. You will." He eased her up again, waiting as she pushed her hair back away from her pale cheeks. "Hey, it's only day one, remember?"

"Okay." Because he didn't make her feel ashamed of the weakness, she took a deep, cleansing breath. "When I tried to think, really think about what you were asking, it was like a panic attack, with all this guilt and horror and fear mixed together. My head started to throb, and my heart beat too fast. I couldn't get air."

"Then we'll take it slow. You don't get that panicky when we talk about the stone you have?"

She closed her eyes a moment, cautiously brought its image into her mind. It was so beautiful, so extraordinary. There was concern, and worry, yes. A layer of fear as well, but it was more focused and somehow less debilitating. "No, it's not the same kind of reaction." She shook her head, opened her eyes. "I don't know why."

"We'll work on that." He scooted her plate back in front of her. "Eat. I'm planning a long evening, and you're going to need fuel."

"What sort of plans?"

"I went by the library on my travels. I've got a stack of books on gems—technical stuff, pictures, books on rare stones, rare jewels, the history of diamonds, you name it."

"We might find it." The possibility cheered her enough to have her nibbling on her sandwich again. "If we could identify the stone, we could trace the owner, and then… Oh, but you can't."

"Can't what?"

"Work tonight. You have to go somewhere with Pamela."

"I do? Hell—" He pressed his fingers to his eyes as he remembered.

"I'm sorry, I forgot to mention it. Your mother called. I was in here, so I heard the message. She's upset that you haven't returned her calls, or contacted Pamela about the arrangements for tonight. She's going to be at Dodie's until four. You can call her there. Also, Muffy's very annoyed with you. She called shortly after your mother and she's very unhappy that you missed Camilla's piano recital. She isn't speaking to you until you apologize."

"I should be so lucky," he muttered, and dropped his hands. "That's a pretty good rundown. Want a job?" When she only smiled, he shook his head and rode on inspiration. "No, I'm serious. You're a hell of a lot more organized than my late, unlamented secretary. I could use some help around the office, and you could use the busywork."

"I don't even know if I can type."

"I know I can't, so you're already a step ahead. You can answer a phone, can't you?"

"Of course, but—"

"You'd be doing me a big favor." Calculating her weaknesses, he pressed his advantage. It was the perfect way to keep her close, keep her busy. "I'd rather not take the time to start advertising and interviewing secretaries right now. If you could help me out, a few hours a day, I'd really appreciate it."

She thought of his office, decided it didn't need a secretary so much as a bulldozer. Well, perhaps she could be of some use after all. "I'd be glad to help."

"Great. Good. Look, I picked up a few things for you while I was out."

"Things?"

"Clothes and stuff."

She stared as he rose and began to clear the plates. "You bought me clothes?"

"Nothing fancy. I had to guess at the sizes, but I've got a pretty good eye." He caught her worrying her lip again and nearly sighed. "Just a few basics, Bailey. As cute as you look in my clothes, you need your own, and you can't wear one suit day after day."

"No, I suppose I can't," she murmured, touched that he should have thought of it. "Thank you."

"No problem. It's stopped raining. You know what you could use? A little fresh air. Let's take a walk, clear your head."

"I don't have any shoes." She took the plates he'd put on the counter and loaded them into the dishwasher.

"I got you some sneakers. Six and a half?"

With a half laugh, she rewrapped the ham. "You tell me."

"Let's try them on and see."

She slid the tray into the dishwasher, closed the door. "Cade, you really have to call your mother."

His grin flashed. "Uh-uh."

"I told you she's upset with you."

"She's always upset with me. I'm the black sheep."

"Be that as it may." Bailey dampened a dishrag and methodically wiped the counters. "She's your mother, and she's waiting for your call."

"No, she's waiting so she can browbeat me into doing something I don't want to do. And when I don't do it, she'll call Muffy, my evil sister, and they'll have a grand old time ripping apart my character."

"That's no way to speak about your family—and you've hurt Camilla's feelings. I assume she's your niece."

"There are rumors."

"Your sister's child."

"No, Muffy doesn't have children, she has creatures. And Camilla is a whiny, pudgy-faced mutant."

She refused to smile, rinsed out the cloth, hung it neatly over the sink. "That's a deplorable way to speak about your niece. Even if you don't like children."

"I do like children." Enjoying himself now, he leaned on the counter and watched her tidy up. "I'm telling you, Camilla's not human. Now my other sister, Doro, she's got two, and somehow the youngest escaped the Parris curse. He's a great kid, likes baseball and bugs. Doro believes he needs therapy."

The chuckle escaped before she swallowed it. "You're making that up."

"Sweetheart, believe me, nothing I could invent about the Parris clan would come close to the horrible truth. They're selfish, self-important and self-indulgent. Are you going to mop the floor now?"

She managed to close her mouth, which had gaped at his careless condemnation of his own family. Distracted, she glanced down at the glossy ivory tiles. "Oh, all right. Where—"

"Bailey, I'm kidding." He grabbed her hand and tugged her out of the room just as the phone began to ring. "No," he said, before she could open her mouth. "I'm not answering it."

"That's shameful."

"It's self-preservation. I never agreed to this Pamela connection, and I'm not going to be pressured into it."

"Cade, I don't want you to upset your family and break a date on my account. I'll be fine."

"I said I didn't make the date. My mother did. And now, when I have to face the music, I can use you as an excuse. I'm grateful. So grateful I'm going to knock a full day off your fee. Here." He picked up one of the shopping bags he'd dropped by the front door and pulled out a shoe box. "Your glass slippers. If they fit, you get to go to the ball."

Giving up, she sat on the bottom landing and opened the box. Her brow cocked. "Red sneakers?"

"I liked them. They're sexy."

"Sexy sneakers." And she wondered as she undid the laces how she could be in such an enormous mess and find herself delighted over a silly pair of shoes. They slid on like butter, and for some reason made her want to laugh and weep at the same time. "Perfect fit."

"Told you I had a good eye." He smiled when she evened out the laces precisely, tied them into careful and neat bows. "I was right, very sexy." He reached down to draw her to her feet. "In fact, you make quite a package right now."

"I'm sure I do, when the only thing that fits are my shoes." She started to rise to her toes to kiss his cheek, then quickly changed her mind.

"Chicken," he said.

"Maybe." She held out her hand instead. "I'd really love to take a walk." She stepped through the door he opened, glanced up at him. "So is Pamela pretty?"

He considered, decided the straight truth might be to his advantage. "Gorgeous." He closed the door behind them, slipped an arm around Bailey's waist. "And she wants me."

The cool little hum of Bailey's response brought a satisfied smile to his lips.

# Chapter 4

Puzzles fascinated him. Locating pieces, shuffling them around, trying new angles until they slipped into place, was a challenge that had always satisfied him. It was one of the reasons Cade had bucked family tradition and chosen his particular line of work.

There was enough rebel in him that he would have chosen almost any line of work that bucked family tradition, but opening his own investigation agency had the added benefit of allowing him to call his own shots, solve those puzzles and right a few wrongs along the way.

He had very definite opinions on right and wrong. There were good guys and there were bad guys, there was law and there was crime. Still, he wasn't naive or simplistic enough not to understand and appreciate the shades of gray. In fact, he often visited gray areas, appreciated them. But there were certain lines that didn't get crossed.

He also had a logical mind that occasionally took recreational detours into the fanciful.

Most of all, he just loved figuring things out.

He'd spent a good deal of time at the library after he left Bailey that morning, scanning reams of microfiche, hunting for any snippet of news on a stolen blue diamond. He hadn't had the heart to point out to her that they had no idea where she came from. She might have traveled to D.C. from anywhere over the past few days.

The fact that she, the diamond and the cash were here now didn't mean that was where they had started out. Neither of them had any idea just how long her memory had been blank.

He'd studied up further on amnesia, but he hadn't found anything particularly helpful. As far as he could tell, anything could trigger her memory, or it could remain wiped clean, with her new life beginning shortly before she'd walked into his.

He had no doubt she'd been through or witnessed something traumatic. And though it might be considered one of those detours into the fanciful he was sometimes accused of having, he was certain she was innocent of any wrongdoing.

How could a woman with eyes like hers have done anything criminal?

Whatever the answers were, he was dead set on one thing—he meant to protect her. He was even ready to accept the simple fact that he'd fallen for her the moment he saw her. Whoever and whatever Bailey was, she was the woman he'd been waiting for.

So he not only meant to protect her—he meant to keep her.

He'd chosen his first wife for all the logical and traditional reasons. Or, he mused, he'd been fingered—calculatingly—by his in-laws, and also by his own family. And that soulless merger had been a disaster in its very reasonableness.

Since the divorce—which had ruffled everyone's feathers except those of the two people most involved—he'd dodged and evaded commitment with a master's consummate skill at avoidance.

He believed the reason for all that was sitting cross-legged on the rug beside him, peering myopically at a book on gemstones.

"Bailey, you need glasses."

"Hmm?" She had all but pressed her nose into the page.

"It's just a wild guess, but I'd say you usually wear reading glasses. If your face gets any closer to that book, you're going to be in it."

"Oh." She blinked, rubbed her eyes. "It's just that the print's awfully small."

"Nope. Don't worry, we'll take care of that tomorrow. We've been at this a couple hours. Want a glass of wine?"

"I suppose." Chewing on her bottom lip, she struggled to bring the text into focus. "The Star of Africa is the largest known cut diamond in existence at 530.2 carats."

"Sounds like a whopper," Cade commented as he chose the bottle of Sancerre he'd been saving for the right occasion.

"It's set in the British royal scepter. It's too big, and it's not a blue diamond. So far I haven't found anything that matches our stone. I wish I had a refractometer."

"A what?"

"A refractometer," she repeated, pushing at her hair. "It's an instrument that measures the characteristic property of a stone. The refractive index." Her hand froze as he watched her. "How do I know that?"

Carrying two glasses, he settled on the floor beside her again. "What's the refractive index?"

"It's the relative ability to refract light. Diamonds are singly refracting. Cade, I don't understand how I know that."

"How do you know it's not a sapphire?" He picked up the stone from where it sat like a paperweight on his notes. "It sure looks like one to me."

"Sapphires are doubly refracting." She shuddered. "I'm a jewel thief. That must be how I know."

"Or you're a jeweler, a gem expert, or a really rich babe who likes to play with baubles." He handed her a glass. "Don't jump to conclusions, Bailey. That's how you miss details."

"Okay." But she had an image of herself dressed all in black, climbing in second-story windows. She drank deeply. "I just wish I could understand why I remember certain things. Refractometers, *The Maltese Falcon*—"

*"The Maltese Falcon?"*

"The movie—Bogart, Mary Astor. You had the book in your room, and the movie jumped right into my head. And roses, I know what they smell like, but I don't know my favorite perfume. I know what a unicorn is, but I don't know why I've got a tattoo of one."

"It's a unicorn." His lips curved up, dimples flashing. "Symbol of innocence."

She shrugged that off and drank down the rest of her wine quickly. Cade merely passed her his own glass and got up to refill. "And there was this tune playing around in my head while I was in the shower. I don't know what it is, but I couldn't get rid of it." She sipped again, frowned in concentration, then began to hum.

"Beethoven's 'Ode to Joy,'" he told her. "Beethoven,

Bogart and a mythical beast. You continue to fascinate me, Bailey."

"And what kind of name is Bailey?" she demanded, gesturing expansively with her glass. "Is it my last name or my first? Who would stick a child with a first name like Bailey? I'd rather be Camilla."

He grinned again, wondered if he should take the wine out of her reach. "No, you wouldn't. Take my word for it."

She blew the hair out of her eyes and pouted.

"Tell me about diamonds."

"They're a girl's best friend." She chuckled, then beamed at him. "Did I make that up?"

"No, honey, you didn't." Gently, he took the half-empty glass from her, set it aside. Mental note, he thought—Bailey's a one-drink wonder. "Tell me what you know about diamonds."

"They sparkle and shine. They look cold, even feel cold to the touch. That's how you can easily identify glass trying to pass. Glass is warm, diamonds are cold. That's because they're excellent heat conductors. Cold fire."

She lay on her back, stretching like a cat, and had saliva pooling in his mouth. She closed her eyes.

"It's the hardest substance known, with a value of ten on Mohs' hardness scale. All good gem diamonds are white diamonds. A yellowish or brown tinge is considered an imperfection."

My, oh, my, she thought, and sighed, feeling her head spin. "Blue, green and red diamonds are very rare and highly prized. The color's caused by the presence of minor elements other than pure carbon."

"Good." He studied her face, the curved lips, closed eyes. She might have been talking of a lover. "Keep going."

"In specific gravity, diamonds range between 3.15 and

3.53, but the value for pure crystals is almost always 3.52. You need brilliancy and fire," she murmured, stretching lazily again.

Despite his good intentions, his gaze shifted, and he watched her small, firm breasts press against the material of his shirt. "Yeah, I bet."

"Uncut diamonds have a greasy luster, but when cut, oh, they shine." She rolled over on her stomach, bent her legs into the air and crossed her ankles. "This is characterized technically as adamantine. The name *diamond* is derived from the Greek word *adamas*, meaning 'invincible.' There's such beauty in strength."

She opened her eyes again, and they were heavy and clouded. She shifted, swinging her legs around until she was sitting, all but in his lap. "You're awfully strong, Cade. And so pretty. When you kissed me, it felt like you could gobble me right up, and I couldn't do a thing about it." She sighed, wiggled a bit to get comfortable, then confided, "I really liked it."

"Oh, boy." He felt the blood begin its slow, leisurely journey from head to loins and cautiously covered both the hands she had laid on his chest. "Better switch to coffee."

"You want to kiss me again."

"About as much as I'd like to take the next breath." That mouth of hers was ripe and willing and close. Her eyes were dreamy and dark.

And she was plowed.

"Let's just hold off on that."

Gently he started to ease her back, but she was busily crawling the rest of the way into his lap. In a smooth, agile movement, she wriggled down and hooked her legs around his waist.

"I don't think— Listen—" For a damsel in distress, she

had some pretty clever moves. He managed to catch her industrious hands again before she pulled his shirt off. "Cut that out. I mean it."

He did mean it, he realized, and accepted the new fact that he was insane.

"Do you think I'd be good in bed?" The question nearly had his eyes crossing and his tongue tied in knots. She, meanwhile, simply sighed, settled her head on his shoulder and murmured, "I hope I'm not frigid."

"I don't think there's much chance of that." Cade's blood pressure spiked while she nibbled delicately on his earlobe. Her hands snuck under his shirt and up his back with a light scraping of nails.

"You taste so good," she noted approvingly, her lips moving down his throat. "I'm awfully hot. Are you hot?"

With an oath, he turned his head, captured her mouth and devoured.

She was ripe with flavors, pulsing with heat. He let himself sink into her, drown in that hot, delicious mouth, while the humming purrs that rippled from her throat pounded through his system like diamonds cased in velvet.

She was pliant, almost fluid, in surrender. When she dipped her head back, offering her throat, no saint in heaven could have resisted it. He scraped his teeth over that smooth white column, listened to her moan, felt her move sinuously against him in invitation.

He could have taken her, simply laid her back on the books and papers and buried himself in her. He could almost feel that glorious slippery friction, the rhythm that would be theirs and only theirs.

And as much as he knew it would be right, it would be perfect, he knew it couldn't be either, not then, not there.

"I've never wanted anyone as much as I want you." He

plunged his hand into her hair, turning her head until their eyes met. "Damn it, focus for a minute. Look at me."

She couldn't see anything else. She didn't want anything else. Her body felt light as air, her mind empty of everything but him. "Kiss me again, Cade. It's like a miracle when you do."

Praying for strength, he lowered his brow to hers until he could steady his breathing. "Next time I kiss you, you're going to know just what's going on." He rose and lifted her into his arms.

"My head's spinning." Giggling, she let it fall back on his supporting arm.

"Whose isn't?" With what he considered really heroic control, he laid her on the couch. "Take a nap."

"'Kay." Obediently, she closed her eyes. "You'll stay here. I feel safe when you're here."

"Yeah, I'll be here." He dragged his hands through his hair and watched her drift off. They were going to laugh at this someday, he thought. Maybe when they had grandchildren.

Leaving her sleeping, he went back to work.

...She was digging in the dirt. The sun was a torch in a sapphire sky. The surrounding land was rocky and baked into muted shades of browns and reds and lavenders. Strong and pungent was the scent of sage from the pale green shrubs struggling out of cracks and crevices in the earth. With spade and hammer, she went about her work happily.

Under the narrow shade of a boulder, two women sat watching her. Her sense of contentment was strong, and stronger yet when she looked over and smiled at them.

One had a short cap of hair that glowed like copper and a sharp, foxy face. And, though her eyes were shielded by dark wraparound sunglasses, Bailey knew they were a deep, deep green.

The other had ebony hair, though it was tucked up now under a wide-brimmed straw hat with silly red flowers around the crown. Loose, the hair would fall past her shoulder blades, thick and wavy to the waist. It suited the magic of her face, the creamy complexion and impossibly blue eyes.

Bailey felt a wave of love just from looking at them, a bond of trust and a sense of shared lives. Their voices were like music, a distant song of which she could only catch snatches.

*Could go for a cold beer.*

*A cold anything.*

*How long do you think she'll keep at it?*

*For the rest of our lives. Paris next summer. Definitely.*

*Get her away from rocks long enough.*

*And the creeps.*

*Definitely.*

It made her smile that they were talking about her, cared enough to talk about her. She'd go to Paris with them. But for now, she chinked away at an interesting formation, hoping to find something worthwhile, something she could take back and study, then fashion into something pretty for her friends.

It took patience, and a good eye. Whatever she found today, she'd share with them.

Then, suddenly, the blue stones all but tumbled into her hand. Three perfect blue diamonds of spectacular size and luster. And it was with pleasure, rather than shock, that she examined them, turned them in her palms, then felt the jolt of power sing through her body.

The storm rolled in fast and mean, blocking the flaming sun, dark, grasping shadows shooting out and covering the landscape. Now there was panic, a great need to hurry. Hurry. Hurry. A stone for each of them, before it was too late. Before the lightning struck.

But it was already too late. Lightning stabbed the skin, sharp as a knife, and she was running, running blindly. Alone and terrified, with the walls closing in and the lightning stabbing at her heels...

She awoke with her breath heaving, shooting straight up on the sofa. What had she done? Dear God, what had she done? Rocking herself, her hands pressed to her mouth, Bailey waited for the shudders to pass.

The room was quiet. There was no thunder, no lightning, no storm chasing her. And she wasn't alone. Across the room, under the slant of light from a globe lamp, Cade dozed in a chair. He had a book open on his lap.

It calmed her just to see him there, papers scattered at his feet, a mug on the table beside him. His legs were stretched out, crossed comfortably at the ankles.

Even in sleep, he looked strong, dependable. He hadn't left her alone. She had to block an urge to go over, crawl into his lap and slide back to sleep cuddled with him. He pulled her, tugged at her emotions so strongly. It didn't seem to matter that she'd known him less than twenty-four hours. After all, she'd hardly known herself much longer.

Pushing at her hair, she glanced at her watch. It was just after three a.m., a vulnerable time. Stretching out again, she pillowed her head on her hands and watched him. Her memory of the evening was clear enough, no breaks, no jumps. She knew she'd thrown herself at him, and it both embarrassed and amazed her.

He'd been right to stop before matters got out of hand. She knew he was right.

But, oh, she wished he'd just taken her, there on the floor.

Taken her before she had all this time to think about the right and wrong of it, the consequences.

Some of this emptiness within her would be filled now, some of those undefinable needs met.

Sighing, she rolled to her back and stared up at the ceiling. But he'd been right to stop. She had to think.

She closed her eyes, not to seek sleep but to welcome memory. Who were the women she'd dreamed of? And where were they now? Despite herself she drifted off.

Cade woke the next morning stiff as a board. Bones popped as he stretched. He rubbed his hands over his face, and his palms made scratching sounds against the stubble. The moment his eyes cleared, he looked across the room. The couch was empty.

He might have thought he'd dreamed her, if not for the books and papers heaped all over the floor. The whole thing seemed like a dream—the beautiful, troubled woman with no past, walking into his life and his heart at the same time. In the morning light, he wondered how much he'd romanticized it, this connection he felt with her. Love at first sight was a romantic notion under the best of circumstances.

And these were hardly the best.

She didn't need him mooning over her, he reminded himself. She needed his mind to be clear. Daydreaming about the way she'd wrapped herself around him and asked him to make love with her simply wasn't conducive to logical thinking.

He needed coffee.

He rose and trying to roll the crick out of his neck, headed for the kitchen.

And there she was, pretty as a picture and neat as a pin. Her hair was smooth, brushed to a golden luster and pulled back with a simple rubber band. She was wearing the navy-and-white-striped slacks he'd bought her, with a white camp shirt tucked into the waist. With one hand resting on the counter, the other holding a steaming mug, she was staring out the window at his backyard where a rope hammock hung between twin maples and roses bloomed.

"You're an early riser."

Her hand shook in startled reaction to his voice, and then she turned, worked up a smile. Her heart continued to thud just a little too fast when she saw him, rumpled from sleep. "I made coffee. I hope you don't mind."

"Sweetheart, I owe you my life," he said in heartfelt tones as he reached for a mug.

"It seems I know how to make it. Apparently some things just come naturally. I didn't even have to think about it. It's a little strong. I must like it strong."

He was already downing it, reveling in the way it seared his mouth and jolted his system. "Perfect."

"Good. I didn't know if I should wake you. I wasn't sure what time you leave for your office, or how much time you'd need."

"It's Saturday, and the long holiday weekend."

"Holiday?"

"Fourth of July." While the caffeine pumped through his system, he topped off his mug. "Fireworks, potato salad, marching bands."

"Oh." She had a flash of a little girl sitting on a woman's lap as lights exploded in the night sky. "Of course. You'll be taking the weekend off. You must have plans."

"Yeah, I got plans. I plan for us to toddle into the office about midmorning. I can show you the ropes. Won't be able to do much legwork today, with everything shut down, but we can start putting things in order."

"I don't want you to give up your weekend. I'd be happy to go in and straighten up your office, and you could—"

"Bailey. I'm in this with you."

She set her mug down, linked her hands. "Why?"

"Because it feels right to me. The way I see it, what you can't figure out in your head, you do on instinct." Those sea-mist eyes roamed over her face, then met hers. "I like to think there's a reason you picked me. For both of us."

"I'm surprised you can say that, after the way I acted last evening. For all we know, I go out cruising bars every night and pick up strange men."

He chuckled into his mug. Better to laugh, he'd decided, than to groan. "Bailey, the way a single glass of wine affects you, I doubt you spent much time in bars. I've never seen anyone get bombed quite that fast."

"I don't think that's anything to be proud of." Her voice had turned stiff and cool, and it made him want to grin again.

"It's nothing to be ashamed of, either. And you didn't pick a strange man, you picked me." The amusement in his eyes flicked off. "We both know it was personal, with or without the alcohol."

"Then why didn't you…take advantage?"

"Because that's just what it would have been. I don't mind having the advantage, but I'm not interested in taking it. Want breakfast?"

She shook her head, waited until he'd gotten out a box of cereal and a bowl. "I appreciate your restraint."

"Do you?"

"Not entirely."

"Good." He felt the muscles of his ego expand and flex as he got milk out of the refrigerator. He poured it on, then added enough sugar to have Bailey's eyes widening.

"That can't be healthy."

"I live for risk." He ate standing up. "Later I thought we'd drive downtown, walk around with the tourists. You may see something that jogs your memory."

"All right." She hesitated, then took a chair. "I don't know anything about your work, really, your usual clientele. But it seems to me you're taking all of this completely in stride."

"I love a mystery." Then he shrugged and shoveled in more cereal. "You're my first amnesia case, if that's what you mean. My usual is insurance fraud and domestic work. It has its moments."

"Have you been an investigator very long?"

"Four years. Five, if you count the year I trained as an operative with Guardian. They're a big security firm here in D.C. Real suit-and-tie stuff. I like working on my own better."

"Have you ever…had to shoot at someone?"

"No. Too bad, really, because I'm a damn good shot." He caught her gnawing her lip and shook his head. "Relax, Bailey. Cops and P.I.s catch the bad guys all the time without drawing their weapon. I've taken a few punches, given a few, but mostly it's just legwork, repetition and making calls. Your problem's just another puzzle. It's just a matter of finding all the pieces and fitting them together."

She hoped he was right, hoped it could be just that simple, that ordinary, that logical. "I had another dream. There were two women. I knew them, I'm sure of it." When he pulled out a chair and sat across from her, she told him what she remembered.

"It sounds like you were in the desert," he said when she fell silent. "Arizona, maybe New Mexico."

"I don't know. But I wasn't afraid. I was happy, really happy. Until the storm came."

"There were three stones, you're sure of that?"

"Yes, almost identical, but not quite. I had them, and they were so beautiful, so extraordinary. But I couldn't keep them together. That was very important." She sighed. "I don't know how much was real and how much was jumbled and symbolic, the way dreams are."

"If one stone's real, there may be two more." He took her hand. "If one woman's real, there may be two more. We just have to find them."

It was after ten when they walked into his office. The cramped and dingy work space struck her as more than odd now that she'd seen how he lived. But she listened carefully as he tried to explain how to work the computer to type up his notes, how he thought the filing should be done, how to handle the phone and intercom systems.

When he left her alone to close himself in his office, Bailey surveyed the area. The philodendron lay on its side, spilling dirt. There was broken glass, sticky splotches from old coffee, and enough dust to shovel.

Typing would just have to wait, she decided. No one could possibly concentrate in such a mess.

From behind his desk, Cade used the phone to do his initial legwork. He tracked down his travel agent and, on the pretext of planning a vacation, asked her to locate any desert area where rockhounding was permitted. He told her he was exploring a new hobby.

From his research the night before, he'd learned quite a bit about the hobby of unearthing crystals and gems. The way Bailey had described her dream, he was certain that was just what she'd been up to.

Maybe she was from out west, or maybe she'd just visited there. Either way, it was another road to explore.

He considered calling in a gem expert to examine the diamond. But on the off chance that Bailey had indeed come into its possession by illegal means, he didn't want to risk it.

He took the photographs he'd snapped the night before of the diamond and spread them out on his desk. Just how much would a gemologist be able to tell from pictures? he wondered.

It might be worth a try. Tuesday, when businesses were open again, he mused, he might take that road, as well.

But he had a couple of other ideas to pursue.

There was another road, an important one, that had to be traveled first. He picked up the phone again, began making calls. He pinned Detective Mick Marshall down at home.

"Damn it, Cade, it's Saturday. I've got twenty starving people outside and burgers burning on the grill."

"You're having a party and didn't invite me? I'm crushed."

"I don't have play cops at my barbecues."

"Now you've really hurt my feelings. Did you earn that Scotch?"

"No match on those prints you sent me. Nothing popped."

Cade felt twin tugs of relief and frustration. "Okay. Still no word on a missing rock?"

"Maybe if you told me what kind of rock."

"A big glittery one. You'd know if it had been reported."

"Nothing's been reported, and I think the rocks are in your head, Parris. Now unless you're going to share, I've got hungry mouths to feed."

"I'll get back to you on it. And the Scotch."

He hung up, and spent some time thinking.

Lightning kept coming up in Bailey's dreams. There'd been thunderstorms the night before she came into his office. It could be as simple as that—one of the last things she remembered was thunder and lightning. Maybe she had a phobia about storms.

She talked about the dark, too. There'd been some power outages downtown that night. He'd already checked on that. Maybe the dark was literal, rather than symbolic.

He guessed she'd been inside. She hadn't spoken of rain, of getting wet. Inside a house? An office building? If whatever had happened to her had happened the night before she came to him, then it almost certainly had to have occurred in the D.C. area.

But no gem had been reported missing.

Three kept cropping up in her dreams, as well. Three stones. Three stars. Three women. A triangle.

Symbolic or real?

He began to take notes again, using two columns. In one he listed her dream memories as literal memories, in the other he explored the symbolism.

And the longer he worked, the more he leaned toward the notion that it was a combination of both.

He made one last call, and prepared to grovel. His sister Muffy had married into one of the oldest and most prestigious family businesses in the East. Westlake Jewelers.

When Cade stepped back into the outer office, his ears were still ringing and his nerves were shot. Those were the usual results of a conversation with his sister. But since he'd wangled what he wanted, he tried to take things in stride.

The shock of walking into a clean, ordered room and seeing Bailey efficiently rattling the keyboard on the computer went a long way toward brightening his mood.

"You're a goddess." He grabbed her hand, kissed it lavishly. "A worker of miracles."

"This place was filthy. Disgusting."

"Yeah, it probably was."

Her brows lowered. "There was food molding in the file cabinets."

"I don't doubt it. You know how to work a computer."

She frowned at the screen. "Apparently. It was like making the coffee this morning. No thought."

"If you know how to work it, you know how to turn it off. Let's go downtown. I'll buy you an ice cream cone."

"I've just gotten started."

"It can wait." He reached down to flick the switch, and she slapped his hand away.

"No. I haven't saved it." Muttering under her breath, she hit a series of keys with such panache, his heart swelled in admiration. "I'll need several more hours to put things in order around here."

"We'll come back. We've got a couple hours to kick around, then we've got some serious work to do."

"What kind of work?" she demanded as he hauled her to her feet.

"I've got you access to a refractometer." He pulled her out the door. "What kind of ice cream do you want?"

# Chapter 5

"Your brother-in-law owns Westlake Jewelers?"

"Not personally. It's a family thing."

"A family thing." Bailey's head was still spinning. Somehow she'd gone from cleaning molded sandwiches out of filing cabinets to eating strawberry ice cream on the steps of the Lincoln Memorial. That was confusing enough, but the way Cade had whipped through traffic, zipping around circles and through yellow lights, had left her dizzy and disoriented.

"Yep." He attacked his two scoops of rocky road. Since she'd stated no preference, he'd gotten her strawberry. He considered it a girl flavor. "They have branches all over the country, but the flagship store's here. Muffy met Ronald at a charity tennis tournament when she beaned him with a lob. Very romantic."

"I see." Or she was trying to. "And he agreed to let us use the equipment?"

"Muffy agreed. Ronald goes along with whatever Muffy wants."

Bailey licked her dripping cone, watched the tourists—the families, the children—clamber up and down the steps. "I thought she was angry with you."

"I talked her out of it. Well, I bribed her. Camilla also takes ballet. There's a recital next month. So I'll go watch Camilla twirl around in a tutu, which, believe me, is not a pretty sight."

Bailey choked back a chuckle. "You're so mean."

"Hey, I've seen Camilla in a tutu, you haven't. Take my word, I'm being generous." He liked seeing her smile, just strolling along with him eating strawberry ice cream and smiling. "Then there's Chip. That's Muffy's other mutant. He plays the piccolo."

"I'm sure you're making this up."

"I couldn't make it up, my imagination has limits. In a couple of weeks I have to sit front and center and listen to Chip and his piccolo at a band concert." He shuddered. "I'm buying earplugs. Let's sit down."

They settled on the smooth steps beneath the wise and melancholy president. There was a faint breeze that helped stir the close summer air. But it could do little about the moist heat that bounced, hard as damp bricks, up from the sidewalks. Bailey could see waves of it shimmer, like desert mirages, in the air.

There was something oddly familiar about all of it, the crowds of people passing, pushing strollers, clicking cameras, the mix of voices and accents, the smells of sweat, humanity and exhaust, flowers blooming in their plots, vendors hawking their wares.

"I must have been here before," she murmured. "But it's just out of sync. Like someone else's dream."

"It's going to come back to you." He tucked a stray strand of hair behind her ear. "Pieces already are. You know how to make coffee, use a computer, and you can organize an office."

"Maybe I'm a secretary."

He didn't think so. The way she'd rattled off information on diamonds the evening before had given him a different idea. But he wanted to weigh it awhile before sharing it. "If you are, I'll double your salary if you work for me." Keeping it light, he rose and offered her a hand. "We've got some shopping to do."

"We do?"

"You need reading glasses. Let's hit the stores."

It was another experience, the sprawling shopping center packed with people looking for bargains. The holiday sale was in full swing. Despite the heat, winter coats were displayed and discounted twenty percent, and fall fashions crowded out the picked over remains of summer wear.

Cade deposited her at a store that promised glasses within an hour and filled out the necessary forms himself while she browsed the walls of frames available.

There was a quick, warm glow that spread inside him when he listed her name as Bailey Parris and wrote his own address. It looked right to him, felt right. And when she was led into the back for the exam—free with the purchase of frames—he gave her a kiss on the cheek.

In less than two hours, she was back in his car, examining her pretty little wire-framed glasses, and the contents of a loaded shopping bag.

"How did you have time to buy all of this?" With a purely feminine flutter, she smoothed a hand over the smooth leather of a bone shoulder-strap envelope bag.

"It's all a matter of strategy and planning, knowing what you want and not being distracted."

Bailey peeked in a bag from a lingerie store and saw rich black silk. Gingerly she pulled the material out. There wasn't a great deal of it, she mused.

"You've got to sleep in something," Cade told her. "It was on sale. They were practically giving it away."

She might not have known who she was, but she was pretty sure she knew sleepwear from seduce-me wear. She tucked the silk back in the bag. Digging deeper, she discovered a bag of crystals. "Oh, they're lovely."

"They had one of those nature stores. So I picked up some rocks." He braked at a stop sign and shifted so that he could watch her. "Picked out a few that appealed to me. The smooth ones are... What do you call it?"

"Tumbling stones," she murmured, stroking them gently with a fingertip. "Carnelian, citrine, sodalite, jasper." Flushed with pleasure, she unwrapped tissue. "Tourmaline, watermelon tourmaline—see the pinks and the greens?— and this is a lovely column of fluorite. It's one of my favorites. I..." She trailed off, pressed a hand to her temple.

He reached in himself, took out a stone at random. "What's this?"

"Alexandrite. It's a chrysoberyl, a transparent stone. Its color changes with the light. See it's blue-green now, in daylight, but in incandescent light it would be mauve or violet." She swallowed hard because the knowledge was there, just there in her mind. "It's a multipurpose stone, but scarce and expensive. It was named for Czar Alexander I."

"Okay, relax, take a deep breath." He made the turn, headed down the tree-lined street. "You know your stones, Bailey."

"Apparently I do."

"And they give you a lot of pleasure." Her face had lit up, simply glowed, when she studied his choices.

"It scares me. The more the information crowded inside my head, the more it scared me."

He pulled into his driveway, turned to her. "Are you up to doing the rest of this today?"

She could say no, she realized. He would take her inside then, inside his house, where she'd be safe. She could go up to the pretty bedroom, close herself in. She wouldn't have to face anything but her own cowardice.

"I want to be. I will be," she added, and let out a long breath. "I have to be."

"Okay." Reaching over, he gave her hand a quick squeeze. "Just sit here. I'll get the diamond."

Westlake Jewelers was housed in a magnificent old building with granite columns and long windows draped in satin. It was not the place for bargains. The only sign was a discreet and elegant brass plate beside the arched front entrance.

Cade drove around the back.

"They're getting ready to close for the day," he explained. "If I know Muffy, she'll have Ronald here waiting. He may not be too thrilled with me, so... Yeah, there's his car." Cade shot his own into a space beside a sedate gray Mercedes sedan. "You just play along with me, all right?"

"Play along?" She wrinkled her brow as he dumped stones into her new handbag. "What do you mean?"

"I had to spin a little story to talk her into this." Reaching over, he opened Bailey's door. "Just go along."

She got out, walked with him to the rear entrance. "It might help if I knew what I was going along with."

"Don't worry." He rang the buzzer. "I'll handle it."

She shifted her now heavy bag on her shoulder. "If you've lied to your family, I think I ought to—" She broke off when the heavy steel door opened.

"Cade." Ronald Westlake nodded curtly. Cade had been right, Bailey thought instantly. This was not a happy man. He was average height, trim and well presented, in a dark blue suit with a muted striped tie so ruthlessly knotted she wondered how he could draw breath. His face was tanned, his carefully styled hair dark and discreetly threaded with glinting gray.

Dignity emanated from him like light.

"Ronald, good to see you," Cade said cheerily, and as if Ronald's greeting had been filled with warmth, he pumped his hand enthusiastically. "How's the golf game? Muffy tells me you've been shaving that handicap."

As he spoke, Cade eased himself inside, much, Bailey thought, like a salesman with his foot propped in a door. Ronald continued to frown and back up.

"This is Bailey. Muffy might have told you a little about her." In a proprietary move, Cade wrapped his arm around Bailey's shoulder and pulled her to his side.

"Yes, how do you do?"

"I've been keeping her to myself," Cade added before Bailey could speak. "I guess you can see why." Smoothly Cade tipped Bailey's face up to his and kissed her. "I appreciate you letting us play with your equipment. Bailey's thrilled. Sort of a busman's holiday for her, showing me how she works with stones." He shook her purse so that the stones inside rattled.

"You've never shown any interest in gems before," Ronald pointed out.

"I didn't know Bailey before," Cade said easily. "Now, I'm fascinated. And now that I've talked her into staying in the States, she's going to have to think about setting up her own little boutique. Right, sweetheart?"

"I—"

"England's loss is our gain," he continued. "And if one of the royals wants another bauble, they'll have to come here. I'm not letting you get away." He kissed her again, deeply, while Ronald stood huffing and tugging at his tie.

"Cade tells me you've been designing jewelry for some time. It's quite an endorsement, having the royal family select your work."

"It's sort of keeping it in the family, too," Cade said with a wink. "With Bailey's mama being one of Di's cousins. Was that third or fourth cousin, honey? Oh, well, what's the difference?"

"Third," Bailey said, amazed at herself not only for answering, but also for infusing her voice with the faintest of upper-class British accents. "They're not terribly close. Cade's making too much of it. It's simply that a few years ago a lapel pin I'd fashioned caught the eye of the Princess of Wales. She's quite a keen shopper, you know."

"Yes, yes, indeed." The tony accent had a sizable effect on a man with Ronald's social requirements. His smile spread, his voice warmed. "I'm delighted you could stop by. I do wish I could stay, show you around."

"We don't want to keep you." Cade was already thumping Ronald on the back. "Muffy told me you're entertaining."

"It's terribly presumptuous of Cade to interrupt your holiday. I would so love a tour another time."

"Of course, anytime, anytime at all. And you must try to drop by the house later this evening." Pumped up at the thought of entertaining even such a loose connection with royalty, Ronald began to usher them toward the jeweler's work area. "We're very select in our equipment, as well as our stones. The Westlake reputation has been unimpeachable for generations."

"Ah, yes." Her heart began to thud as she studied the equipment in the glass-walled room, the worktables, the saws, the scales. "Quite top-of-the-line."

"We pride ourselves on offering our clientele only the best. We often cut and shape our own gems here, and employ our own lapidaries."

Bailey's hand shook lightly as she passed it over a wheel. A lap, she thought, used to shape the stone. She could see just how it was done—the stone cemented to the end of a wooden stick, a dop, held against the revolving lap wheel with the aid of a supporting block adjacent to the wheel.

She knew, could hear the sounds of it. Feel the vibrations.

"I enjoy lap work," Bailey said faintly. "The precision of it."

"I'm afraid I only admire the craftsmen and artists. That's a stunning ring. May I?" Ronald took her left hand, examined the trio of stones arranged in a gentle curve and set in etched gold. "Lovely. Your design?"

"Yes." It seemed the best answer. "I particularly enjoy working with colored stones."

"You must see our stock sometime soon." Ronald glanced at his watch, clucked his tongue. "I'm running quite late. The security guard will let you back out when you're done. Please take all the time you want. I'm afraid the showroom itself is locked, time-locked, and you'll need the guard to open the rear door, as it engages from inside and out." He sent Bailey a professional-to-professional smile. "You'd understand how important security is in the business."

"Of course. Thank you so much for your time, Mr. Westlake."

Ronald took Bailey's offered hand. "Ronald, please. And it's my pleasure. You mustn't let Cade be so selfish of you. Muffy is very much looking forward to meeting her future sister-in-law. Be sure to drop by later."

Bailey made a strangled sound, easily covered by Cade's quick chatter as he all but shoved Ronald out of the work area.

"Sister-in-law?" Bailey managed.

"I had to tell them something." All innocence, Cade spread his hands. "They've been campaigning to get me married off again since the ink was dry on my divorce decree. And you being royalty, so to speak, puts you several societal steps up from the women they've been pushing on me."

"Poor Cade. Having women shoved at him right and left."

"I've suffered." Because there were dangerous glints in her eyes, he tried his best smile. "You have no idea how I've suffered. Hold me."

She slapped his hand away. "Is this all a big joke to you?"

"No, but that part of it was fun." He figured his hands would be safer in his pockets. "I guarantee my sister's been burning up the phone lines since I talked to her this morning. And now that Ronald's got a load of you—"

"You lied to your family."

"Yeah. Sometimes it's fun. Sometimes it's just necessary for survival." He angled his head. "You slipped right into the stream, sweetheart. That accent was a nice touch."

"I got caught up, and I'm not proud of it."

"You might make a good operative. Let me tell you, lying quick and lying well is one of the top requirements of the job."

"And the end justifies the means?"

"Pretty much." It was starting to irritate him, the disapproving ice in her voice. He had the feeling Bailey wasn't nearly as comfortable in gray areas as he was. "We're in, aren't we? And Ronald and Muffy are going to have a rousing success with their little party. So what's the problem?"

"I don't know. I don't like it." A lie, the simple fact of a lie, made her miserably uncomfortable. "One lie just leads to another."

"And enough of them sometimes lead to the truth." He took her bag, opened it and pulled out the velvet pouch, slid the diamond into his hand. "You want the truth, Bailey? Or do you just want honesty?"

"It doesn't seem like there should be a difference." But she took the stone from him. "All right, as you said, we're here. What do you want me to do?"

"Make sure it's real."

"Of course it's real," she said impatiently. "I know it's real."

He merely arched a brow. "Prove it."

With a huffing breath, she turned and headed for a microscope. She employed the dark-field illuminator, adjusting the focus on the binocular microscope with instinctive efficiency.

"Beautiful," she said after a moment, with a tint of reverence in her voice. "Just beautiful."

"What do you see?"

"The interior of the stone. There's no doubt it's of natural origin. The inclusions are characteristic."

"Let's see." He nudged her aside, bent to the microscope himself. "Could be anything."

"No, no. There are no air bubbles. There would be if it was paste, or strass. And the inclusions."

"Doesn't mean anything to me. It's blue, and blue means sapphire."

"Oh for heaven's sake, sapphire is corundum. Do you think I can't tell the difference between carbon and corundum?" She snatched up the stone and marched to another instrument. "This is a polariscope. It tests whether a gem is singly or doubly refracting. As I've already told you, sapphires are doubly refracting, diamonds singly."

She went about her work, muttering to herself, putting her glasses on when she needed them, slipping the eyepiece into the V of her blouse when she didn't. Every move competent, habitual, precise.

Cade tucked his hands in his back pockets, rocked back on his heels and watched.

"Here, the refractometer," she mumbled. "Any idiot can see the refractive index of this stone says diamond, not sapphire." She turned, holding up the stone. "This is a blue diamond, brilliant-cut, weighing 102.6 carats."

"All you need's a lab coat," he said quietly.

"What?"

"You work with this stuff, Bailey. I thought it might be a hobby, but you're too precise, too comfortable. And too easily annoyed when questioned. So my conclusions are that you work with stones, with gems. This type of equipment is as familiar to you as a coffeemaker. It's just part of your life."

She lowered her hand and eased herself back onto a stool. "You didn't do all this, go to all this trouble, so we could identify the diamond, did you?"

"Let's just say that was a secondary benefit. Now we have to figure whether you're in the gem or jewelry trade. That's how you got your hands on this." He took the diamond from her, studied it. "And this isn't the kind of thing you see for sale at Westlake or any other jeweler. It's the kind of thing you find in a private collection, or a museum. We've got a really fine museum right here in town. It's called the Smithsonian." He lowered the stone. "You may have heard of it."

"You think… I took it out of the Smithsonian?"

"I think someone there might have heard of it." He slipped the priceless gem casually into his pocket. "It'll have to wait until tomorrow. They'll be closed. No, hell, Tuesday." He hissed between his teeth. "Tomorrow's the Fourth, and Monday's a holiday."

"What should we do until Tuesday?"

"We can start with phone books. I wonder how many gemologists are in the greater metropolitan area?"

The reading glasses meant she could pore through all the books without risking a headache. And pore through them she did. It was, Bailey thought, something like rereading well-loved fairy tales. It was all familiar ground, but she enjoyed traveling over it again.

She read about the history of intaglio cutting in Mesopotamia, the gems of the Hellenistic period. Florentine engravings.

She read of famous diamonds. Of the Vargas, the Jonker, the Great Mogul, which had disappeared centuries before. Of Marie Antoinette and the diamond necklace some said had cost her her head.

She read technical explanations on gem cutting, on identification, on optical properties and formations.

They were all perfectly clear to her, and as smooth as the carnelian tumble stone she worried between her fingers.

How could it be, she wondered, that she remembered rocks and not people? She could easily identify and discuss the properties of hundreds of crystals and gems. But there was only one single person in the entire world she knew.

And even that wasn't herself.

She only knew Cade. Cade Parris, with his quick, often confusing mind. Cade, with his gentle, patient hands and gorgeous green eyes. Eyes that looked at her as though she could be the focus of his world.

Yet his world was so huge compared to hers. His was populated by people, and memories, places he'd been, things he'd done, moments he'd shared with others.

The huge blank screen that was her past taunted her.

What people did she know, whom had she loved or hated? Had anyone ever loved her? Whom had she hurt or been hurt by? And where had she been, what had she done?

Was she scientist or thief? Lover or loner?

She wanted to be a lover. Cade's lover. It was terrifying how much she wanted that. To sink into bed with him and let everything float away on that warm river of sensation. She wanted him to touch her, really touch her. To feel his hands on her, skimming over naked flesh, heating it, taking her to a place where the past meant nothing and the future was unimportant.

Where there was only now, the greedy, glorious now.

And she could touch him, feel the muscles bunch in his back and shoulders as he covered her. His heart would pound against hers, and she would arch up to meet him, to take him in. And then…

She jumped when the book slapped shut.

"Take a break," Cade ordered, shifting the book across the table where she'd settled to read. "Your eyes are going to fall out of your head."

"Oh, I…" Good God, she thought, goggling at him. She was all but trembling, brutally aroused by her own fantasy.

Her pulse was skidding along like skates on bumpy ice. "I was just—"

"Look, you're all flushed."

He turned to get the pitcher of iced tea from the refrigerator, and she rolled her eyes at his back. Flushed? She was flushed? Couldn't the man see she was a puddle just waiting to be lapped up?

He poured her a glass over ice, popped the top on a beer for himself. "We've done enough for one day. I'm thinking steaks on the grill. We'll see if you can put a salad together. Hey." He reached out to steady the glass he'd handed her. "Your hands are shaking. You've been overdoing it."

"No, I…" She could hardly tell him she'd just given serious thought to biting his neck. Carefully she removed her glasses, folded them, set them on the table. "Maybe a little. There's so much on my mind."

"I've got the perfect antidote for overthinking." He took her hand, pulled her to the door and outside, where the air was full of heat and the heady perfume of roses. "A half hour of lazy."

He took her glass, set it on the little wrought-iron table beside the rope hammock, put his beer beside it. "Come on, we'll watch the sky awhile."

He wanted her to lie down with him? Lie down cupped with him in that hammock, while her insides were screaming for release? "I don't think I should—"

"Sure you should." To settle the matter, he gave her a yank and tumbled into the hammock with her. It rocked wildly, making him laugh as she scrambled for balance. "Just relax. This is one of my favorite spots. There's been a hammock here as long as I can remember. My uncle used to nap in this red-and-white-striped one when he was supposed to be puttering around the garden."

He slid his arm under her, took one of her nervous hands in his. "Nice and cozy. You can see little pieces of sky through the leaves."

It was cool there, shaded by the maples. She could feel his heart beating steadily when he laid their joined hands on his chest.

"I used to sneak over here a lot. Did a lot of dreaming and planning in this hammock. It was always peaceful over here, and when you were swinging in a hammock in the shade, nothing seemed all that urgent."

"It's like being in a cradle, I suppose." She willed herself to relax, shocked to the core at how much she wanted to roll on top of him and dive in.

"Things are simpler in a hammock." He toyed with her fingers, charmed by their grace and the glitter of rings. He kissed them absently and made her heart turn over in her chest. "Do you trust me, Bailey?"

At that moment, she was certain that, whatever her past, she'd never trusted anyone more. "Yes."

"Let's play a game."

Her imagination whirled into several erotic corners. "Ah…a game?"

"Word association. You empty your mind, and I'll say a word. Whatever pops into your head first, you say it."

"Word association." Unsure whether to laugh or scream, she closed her eyes. "You think it'll jog my memory."

"It can't hurt, but let's just think of it as a lazy game to play in the shade. Ready?"

She nodded, kept her eyes closed and let herself be lulled by the swing of the hammock. "All right."

"City."

"Crowded."

"Desert."

"Sun."

"Work."

"Satisfaction."

"Fire."

"Blue."

When she opened her eyes, started to shift, he snuggled her closer. "No, don't stop and analyze, just let it come. Ready? Love."

"Friends." She let out a breath, found herself relaxing again. "Friends," she repeated.

"Family."

"Mother." She made a small sound, and he soothed it away.

"Happy."

"Childhood."

"Diamond."

"Power."

"Lightning."

"Murder." She let out a choked breath and turned to bury her face against his shoulder. "I can't do this. I can't look there."

"Okay, it's all right. That's enough." He stroked her hair, and though his hand was gentle, his eyes were hot as they stared up through the shady canopy of leaves.

Whoever had frightened her, made her tremble with terror, was going to pay.

While Cade held Bailey under the maple trees, another stood on a stone terrace overlooking a vast estate of rolling hills, tended gardens, jetting fountains.

He was furious.

The woman had dropped off the face of the earth with his property. And his forces were as scattered as the three stars.

It should have been simple. He'd all but had them in his

hands. But the bumbling fool had panicked. Or perhaps had simply become too greedy. In either case, he'd let the woman escape, and the diamonds had gone with her.

Too much time had passed, he thought, tapping his small, beautifully manicured hand on the stone railing. One woman vanished, the other on the run, and the third unable to answer his questions.

It would have to be fixed, and fixed soon. The timetable was now destroyed. There was only one person to blame for that, he mused, and stepped back into his lofty office, picked up the phone.

"Bring him to me" was all he said. He replaced the receiver with the careless arrogance of a man used to having his orders obeyed.

# Chapter 6

Saturday night. He took her dancing. She'd imagined hunkering down at the kitchen table with books and a pot of strong coffee as soon as dinner was over. Instead, he swept her out of the house, before she'd finished wiping off the counters, barely giving her enough time to run a brush through her hair.

She needed a distraction, he'd told her. She needed music. She needed to experience life.

It was certainly an experience.

She'd never seen anything like it. That she knew. The noisy, crowded club in the heart of Georgetown vibrated with life, shook from floor to ceiling with voices and busy feet. The music was so loud she couldn't hear her own thoughts, and the stingy little table Cade managed to procure for them in the middle of it all was still sticky from the last patron's pitcher of beer.

It astonished her.

Nobody seemed to know anyone else. Or they knew each other well enough to make love standing up in public. Surely the hot, wiggling moves done body against body on the tiny dance floor were nothing less than a mating ritual.

He bought her club soda, stuck to the same harmless drink himself, and watched the show. More, he watched her watch the show.

Lights flashed, voices echoed, and no one seemed to have a care in the world.

"Is this what you usually do on the weekend?" She had to shout into his ear, and she still wasn't certain he would hear her over the crash and din of guitars and drums.

"Now and again." Hardly ever, he thought, studying the ebb and flow of the tide of singles at the bar. Certainly not a great deal since his college days. The idea of bringing her here had been an impulse, even an inspiration, he thought. She could hardly brood and worry under these conditions. "It's a local group."

"I've been duped?" she repeated doubtfully.

"No, no, this band is a local group." He chuckled, scooted his chair closer to hers, slid his arm around her shoulders. "Down-and-dirty rock. No country, no soft crap, no pap. Just kick ass. What do you think?"

She struggled to think, to tune in to the hard, pulsating and repetitive rhythm. Over the driving ocean of music, the band was shouting about dirty deeds and doing them dirt-cheap.

"I don't know, but it sure isn't the 'Ode to Joy.'"

He laughed at that, long and loud, before grabbing her hand. "Come on. Dance with me."

Instant panic. Her palm went damp, her eyes grew huge. "I don't think I know how to—"

"Hell, Bailey. There's not enough room out there to do

more than break a couple of Commandments. That doesn't take any practice."

"Yes, but…" He was dragging her toward the dance floor, snaking his way through tables, bumping into people. She lost count of the number of feet they must have trod on. "Cade, I'd rather just watch."

"You're here to experience." He yanked her into his arms, gripped her hips in an intimate and possessive way that had her breath locking in her throat. "See? One Commandment down." And suddenly his body was moving suggestively against hers. "The rest is easy."

"I don't think I've ever done this." The lights circling and flashing overhead made her dizzy. Giddy. "I'm sure I'd remember."

He thought she was probably right. There was something entirely too innocent about the way she fumbled, the way the color rushed to her cheeks. He slid his hands over her bottom, up to her waist. "It's just dancing."

"I don't think so. I've probably danced before."

"Put your arms around me." He levered her arms around his neck himself. "And kiss me."

"What?"

"Never mind."

His face was close, and the music was filling her head. The heat from his body, from all the bodies pressed so close against them, was like a furnace. She couldn't breathe, she couldn't think, and when his mouth swooped down on hers, she didn't care.

Her head pounded with the backbeat. It was unmercifully hot, the air thick with smoke and body heat, scented with sweat and liquor and clashing perfumes. All of that faded away. She swayed against him while her lips parted for his and the strong, male essence of him filled her.

"If we'd stayed home, we'd be in bed." He murmured it against her lips, then skimmed his mouth to her ear. She was wearing the perfume he'd bought for her. The scent of it was unreasonably intimate. "I want you in bed, Bailey. I want to be inside you."

She closed her eyes, burrowed against him. Surely no one had said such things to her before. She couldn't have forgotten this wild thrill, this wild fear. Her fingers slipped up into the untidy hair that waved over his collar. "Before, when I was in the kitchen, I—"

"I know." He flicked his tongue over her ear, spread fire everywhere. "I could have had you. Did you think I couldn't see that?" To torment them both, he skimmed his lips along her throat. "That's why we're here instead of home. You're not ready for what I need from you."

"This doesn't make any sense." She thought she murmured it, but he heard her.

"Who the hell cares about sense? This is now." He caught her chin, brought her face to his again. "We're now." And kissed her until her blood bubbled and burst in her head. "It can be hot." He bit her bottom lip until she was ready to sink to the floor. "Or sweet." Then laved it tenderly with his tongue. "It can be fun." He spun her out, then whipped her back into his arms with such casual grace that she blinked. "Whatever you want."

Her hands were braced on his shoulders, her face was close to his. Lights revolved around them, and music throbbed. "I think… I think we'd be safer with the fun. For the time being."

"Then let's have it." He whipped her out again, spun her in two fast circles. His eyes lit with amusement when she laughed.

She caught her breath as her body rammed into his again. "You've had lessons."

"Sweetheart, I may have hooked cotillion more times than I want to admit, but some things stuck."

They were moving again, somehow magically, through the thick throng of dancers. "Cotillion? Isn't that white gloves and bow ties?"

"Something like that." He skimmed his hands up her sides, just brushed her breasts. "And nothing like this."

She missed a step, rapped back solidly into what she first took for a steel beam. When she glanced back, she saw what appeared to be one massive muscle with a glossy bald head, a silver nose ring and a gleaming smile.

"I beg your pardon," she began, but found she had breath for nothing else as the muscle whirled her to the right.

She found herself jammed in the middle of a pack of dancers with enthusiastically jabbing elbows and bumping hips. They hooted at her in such a friendly manner, she tried to pick up the beat. She was giggling when she was bumped back into Cade's arms.

"It is fun." Elemental, liberating, nearly pagan. "I'm dancing."

The way her face glowed, her voice rang with delighted laughter, had a grin flashing on his face. "Looks that way."

She waved a hand in front of her face in a useless attempt to fan away the heat. "I like it."

"Then we'll do it again." The volume eased down, the beat smoothed into a hum. "Here comes a slow one. Now all you have to do is plaster yourself all over me."

"I think I already am."

"Closer." His leg slid intimately between hers, his hands cruised low on her hips.

"Oh, God." Her stomach filled with frantic butterflies. "That has to be another Commandment."

"One of my personal favorites."

The music was seductive, sexy and sad. Her mood changed with it, from giddiness to longing. "Cade, I don't think this is smart." But she'd risen to her toes, so their faces were close.

"Let's be reckless. Just for one dance."

"It can't last," she murmured as her cheek pressed against his.

"Shh. For as long as we want."

Forever, she thought, and held tight. "I'm not an empty slate. I've just been erased for a while. Neither of us might like what's written there when we find it."

He could smell her, feel her, taste her. "I know everything I need to know."

She shook her head. "But I don't." She drew back, looked into his eyes. "I don't," she repeated. And when she broke away and moved quickly through the crowd, he let her go.

She hurried into the restroom. She needed privacy, she needed to get her breath back. She needed to remember that, however much she might want it, her life had not begun when she walked into a cramped little office and saw Cade Parris for the first time.

The room was nearly as packed as the dance floor, with women primping at the mirrors, talking about men, complaining about other women. The room smelled thickly of hair spray, perfume and sweat.

In one of the three narrow sinks, Bailey ran the water cold, splashed it on her overheated face. She'd danced in a noisy nightclub and screamed with laughter. She'd let the man she wanted touch her intimately, without a care for who saw it.

And she knew as she lifted her face and studied the reflection in the spotty mirror that none of those things were usual for her.

This was new. Just as Cade Parris was new. And she didn't know how any of it would fit into the life that was hers.

It was happening so quickly, she thought, and dug into her purse for a brush. The purse he'd bought her, the brush he'd bought her, she thought, while emotion swamped her. Everything she had right now, she owed to him.

Was that what she felt for him? A debt, gratitude? Lust?

Not one of the women crowded into the room with her was worried about things like that, she thought. Not one of them was asking herself that kind of question about the man she'd just danced with. The man she wanted, or who wanted her.

They would all go back out and dance again. Or go home. They would make love tonight, if the mood was right. And tomorrow their lives would simply move on.

But she had to ask. And how could she know the answer when she didn't know herself? And how could she take him, or give herself to him, until she did know?

Get yourself in order, she told herself, and methodically ran the brush through her tumbled hair. Time to be sensible, practical. Calm. Satisfied her hair was tidy again, she slipped the brush back into her bag.

A redhead walked in, all legs and attitude, with short-cropped hair and wraparound shades. "Son of a bitch grabbed my butt," she said to no one in particular, and strode into a stall, slammed the door.

Bailey's vision grayed. Clammy waves of dizziness had her clutching the lip of the sink. But her knees went so weak she had to lean over the bowl and gulp for air.

"Hey, hey, you okay?"

Someone patted her on the back, and the voice was like bees buzzing in her head. "Yes, just a little dizzy. I'm all right. I'm fine." Using both hands, she cupped cold water, splashed it again and again on her face.

When she thought her legs would hold her, she snatched paper towels and dried her dripping cheeks. As wobbly as a drunk, she staggered out of the restroom and back into the screaming cave that was the club.

She was bumped and jostled and never noticed. Someone offered to buy her a drink. Some bright soul offered boozily to buy her. She passed through without seeing anything but blinding lights and faceless bodies. When Cade reached her, she was sheet white. Asking no questions, he simply picked her up, to the cheering approval of nearby patrons, and carried her outside.

"I'm sorry. I got dizzy."

"It was a bad idea." He was cursing himself viciously for taking her to a second-rate nightclub with rowdy regulars. "I shouldn't have brought you here."

"No, it was a wonderful idea. I'm glad you brought me. I just needed some air." For the first time, she realized he was carrying her, and wavered between embarrassment and gratitude. "Put me down, Cade. I'm all right."

"I'll take you home."

"No, is there somewhere we can just sit? Just sit and get some air?"

"Sure." He set her on her feet, but watched her carefully. "There's a café just down the street. We can sit outside. Get some coffee."

"Good." She held tightly on to his hand, letting him lead the way. The bass from the band inside the club all but shook the sidewalk. The café a few doors down was nearly as crowded as the club had been, with waiters scurrying to deliver espressos and lattes and iced fruit drinks.

"I came on pretty strong," he began as he pulled out a chair for her.

"Yes, you did. I'm flattered."

Head cocked, he sat across from her. "You're flattered?"

"Yes. I may not remember anything, but I don't think I'm stupid." The air, however close and warm, felt glorious. "You're an incredibly attractive man. And I look around, right here..." Steadying herself, she did just that, scanning the little tables crammed together under a dark green awning. "Beautiful women everywhere. All over the city where we walked today, inside that club, right here in this café. But you came on to me, so I'm flattered."

"That's not exactly the reaction I was looking for, or that I expected. But I guess it'll do for now." He glanced up at the waiter who hustled to their table. "Cappuccino?" he asked Bailey.

"That would be perfect."

"Decaf or regular?" the waiter chirped.

"Real coffee," Cade told him, and leaned closer to Bailey. "Your color's coming back."

"I feel better. A woman came in the ladies' room."

"Did she hassle you?"

"No, no." Touched by his immediate instinct to defend, she laid a hand over his. "I was feeling a little shaky, and then she walked in. Sort of swaggered in." It made her lips curve. "And for a minute, I thought I knew her."

He turned his hand over, gripped hers. "You recognized her?"

"No, not her, precisely, though I thought... No, it was the type, I suppose you'd say. Arrogant, cocky, striking. A tall redhead in tight denim, with a chip on her shoulder."

She closed her eyes a moment, let out a long breath, opened them again. "M.J."

"That was the name on the note in your pocket."

"It's there," Bailey murmured, massaging her temples. "It's there somewhere in my head. And it's important. It's vital, but I can't focus on it. But there's a woman, and she's part of my life. And, Cade, something's wrong."

"Do you think she's in trouble?"

"I don't know. When I start to get a picture—when I can almost see her—it's just this image of utter confidence and ability. As if nothing could possibly be wrong. But I know there is something wrong. And it's my fault. It has to be my fault."

He shook his head. Blame wouldn't help. It wasn't the angle they needed to pursue. "Tell me what you see when you start to get that picture. Just try to relax, and tell me."

"Short, dark red hair, sharp features. Green eyes. But maybe those are yours. But I think hers are green, darker than yours. I could almost draw her face. If I knew how to draw."

"Maybe you do." He took a pen and pad out of his pocket. "Give it a try."

With her lip caught between her teeth, she tried to capture a sharp, triangular face. With a sigh, she set the pen down as their coffee was served. "I think we can safely assume I'm not an artist."

"So we'll get one." He took the pad back, smiled at the pathetic sketch. "Even I could do better than this, and I scraped by with a C my one dismal semester of art. Do you think you can describe her, the features?"

"I can try. I don't see it all clearly. It's like trying to focus a camera that's not working quite right."

"Police artists are good at putting things together."

She slopped coffee over the rim of her cup. "The police? Do we have to go to the police?"

"Unofficial, don't worry. Trust me."

"I do." But the word *police* rang in her head like alarm bells. "I will."

"We've got something to go on. We know M.J.'s a woman, a tall redhead with a chip on her shoulder. Mary Jane, Martha June, Melissa Jo. You were with her in the desert."

"She was in the dream." Sun and sky and rock. Contentment. Then fear. "Three of us in the dream, but it won't come clear."

"Well, we'll see if we can put a likeness together, then we'll have somewhere to start."

She stared down into her foamy coffee, thinking her life was just that, a cloud concealing the center. "You make it sound easy."

"It's just steps, Bailey. You take the next step, and see where that goes."

She nodded, stared hard into her coffee. "Why did you marry someone you didn't love?"

Surprised, he leaned back, blew out a breath. "Well, that's quite a change in topic."

"I'm sorry. I don't know why I asked that. It's none of my business."

"I don't know. Under the circumstances, it seems a fair enough question." He drummed his fingers restlessly on the table. "You could say I got tired, worn down by family pressure, but that's a cop-out. Nobody held a gun to my head, and I was over twenty-one."

It annoyed him to admit that, he realized. To be honest with Bailey was to face the truth without excuses. "We liked each other well enough, or at least we did until we got married. A couple of months of marriage fixed that friendship."

"I'm sorry, Cade." It was easy to see the discomfort on his face, his unhappiness with the memory. And though she envied him even that unhappiness, she hated knowing she'd helped put it there. "There's no need to go into it."

"We were good in bed," he went on, ignoring her. And kept his eyes on hers when she shrank back, drew in and away from him. "Right up until the end, the sex was good. The trouble was, toward the end, which was a little under two years from the beginning, it was all heat and no heart. We just didn't give a damn."

Couldn't have cared less, he remembered. Just two bored people stuck in the same house. "That's what it came down to. There wasn't another man, or another woman. No passionate fights over money, careers, children, dirty dishes. We just didn't care. And when we stopped caring altogether, we got nasty. Then the lawyers came in, and it got nastier. Then it was done."

"Did she love you?"

"No." He answered immediately, then frowned, looked hard at nothing and again tried to be honest. And the answer was sad and bruising. "No, she didn't, any more than I loved her. And neither one of us worried about working too hard on that part of it."

He took money from his wallet, dropped it on the table and rose. "Let's go home."

"Cade." She touched his arm. "You deserved better."

"Yeah." He looked at the hand on his arm, the delicate fingers, the pretty rings. "So did she. But it's a little late for that." He lifted her hand so that the ring gleamed between them. "You can forget a lot of things, Bailey, but can you forget love?"

"Don't."

He'd be damned if he'd back off. Suddenly his entire miserable failure of a marriage was slapped into his face. He'd be damned. "If a man put this on your finger, a man you loved, would you forget? Could you?"

"I don't know." She wrenched away, rushed down the sidewalk toward his car. When he whirled her around, her eyes were bright with anger and fears. "I don't *know*."

"You wouldn't forget. You couldn't, if it mattered. This matters."

He crushed his mouth to hers, pressing her back against the car and battering them both with his frustration and needs. Gone was the patience, the clever heat of seduction. What was left was all the raw demand that had bubbled beneath it. And he wanted her weak and clinging and as desperate as he. For just that moment.

For just the now.

The panic came first, a choke hold that snagged the air from her throat. She couldn't answer this vivid, violent need. Simply wasn't prepared or equipped to meet it and survive.

So she surrendered, abruptly, completely, thoughtlessly, part of her trusting that he wouldn't hurt her. Another praying that he couldn't. She yielded to the flash of staggering heat, the stunning power of untethered lust, rode high on it for one quivering moment.

And knew she might not survive even surrender.

She trembled, infuriating him. Shaming him. He was hurting her. He almost wanted to, for wouldn't she remember if he did? Wasn't pain easier to remember than kindness?

He knew if she forgot him it would kill him.

And if he hurt her, he would have killed everything worthwhile inside him.

He let her go, stepped back. Instantly she hugged her arms over her chest in a defensive move that slashed at him. Music and voices lifted in excitement and laughter flowed down the sidewalk behind him as he stared at her, spotlighted like a deer caught in headlights.

"I'm sorry."

"Cade—"

He lifted his hands, palms out. His temper rarely flashed, but he knew better than to reach for reason until it had settled again. "I'm sorry," he repeated. "It's my problem. I'll take you home."

And when he had, when she was in her room and the lights were off, he lay out in the hammock, where he could watch her window.

It wasn't so much examining his own life, he realized, that had set him off. He knew the highs and lows of it, the missteps and foolish mistakes. It was the rings on her fingers, and finally facing that a man might have put one of them on her. A man who might be waiting for her to remember.

And it wasn't about sex. Sex was easy. She would have given herself to him that evening. He'd seen it when he walked into the kitchen while she was buried in a book. He'd known she was thinking of him. Wanting him.

Now he thought he'd been a fool for not taking what was there for him. But he hadn't taken it because he wanted more. A lot more.

He wanted love, and it wasn't reasonable to want it. She was adrift, afraid, in trouble neither of them could identify. Yet he wanted her to tumble into love with him, as quickly and completely as he'd tumbled into love with her.

It wasn't reasonable.

But he didn't give a damn about reason.

He'd slay her dragon, whatever the cost. And once he had, he'd fight whoever stood in his way to keep her. Even if it was Bailey herself who stood there.

When he slept, he dreamed. When he dreamed, he dreamed of dragons and black nights and a damsel with golden hair who was locked in a high tower and spun straw into rich blue diamonds.

And when she slept, she dreamed. When she dreamed, she dreamed of lightning and terror and of running through the dark with the power of gods clutched in her hands.

## Chapter 7

Despite the fact that she'd slept poorly, Bailey was awake and out of bed by seven. She concluded that she had some internal clock that started her day at an assigned time, and couldn't decide if that made her boring or responsible. In either case, she dressed, resisted the urge to go down the hall and peek into Cade's room and went down to make coffee.

She knew he was angry with her. An icy, simmering anger that she hadn't a clue how to melt or diffuse. He hadn't said a word on the drive back from Georgetown, and the silence had been charged with temper and, she was certain, sexual frustration.

She wondered if she had ever caused sexual frustration in a man before, and wished she didn't feel this inner, wholly female, pleasure at causing it in a man like Cade.

But beyond that, his rapid shift of moods left her baffled and upset. She wondered if she knew any more about human nature than she did of her own past.

She wondered if she knew anything at all about the male of the species.

Did men behave in this inexplicable manner all the time? And if they did, how did a smart woman handle it? Should she be cool and remote until he'd explained himself? Or would it be better if she was friendly and casual, as if nothing had happened?

As if he hadn't kissed her as if he could swallow her whole. As if he hadn't touched her, moved his hands over her, as though he had a right to, as though it were the most natural thing in the world for him to turn her body into a quivering mass of needs.

Now her own mood shifted from timid to annoyed as she wrenched open the refrigerator for milk. How the hell was she supposed to know how to behave? She had no idea if she'd ever been kissed that way before, ever felt this way, wanted this way. Just because she was lost, was she supposed to meekly go in whichever direction Cade Parris pointed her?

And if he pointed her toward the bed, was she supposed to hop in?

Oh, no, she didn't think so. She was a grown woman, capable of making her own decisions. She wasn't stupid and she wasn't helpless. She'd managed to hire herself a detective, hadn't she?

Damn it.

Just because she had no precedents for her own behavior, that didn't mean she couldn't start setting some here and now.

She would not be a doormat.

She would not be a fool.

She would not be a victim.

She slapped the milk carton down on the counter,

scowled out the window. It was Cade's bad luck that she happened to spot him sleeping in the hammock just as her temper peaked.

He wouldn't have dozed so peacefully if he could have seen the way her eyes kindled, the way her lips peeled back in a snarl.

Fueled for battle, Bailey slammed out of the house and marched across the lawn.

She gave the hammock one hard shove.

"Who the hell do you think you are?"

"What?" He shot rudely awake, gripping the sides of the hammock for balance, his brain musty with sleep. "What? Don't you remember?"

"Don't get smart with me." She gave the hammock another shove as he struggled to sit up. "I make my own decisions, I run my own life—such as it is. I hired you to help me find out who I am and what happened to me. I'm not paying you to sulk because I won't hop into bed with you when you have an itch."

"Okay." He rubbed his eyes, finally managed to focus on the stunning and furious face bent over him. "What the hell are you talking about? I'm not sulking, I—"

"Don't tell me you're not sulking," she shot back. "Sleeping out in the backyard like a hobo."

"It's my yard." It irritated him to have to point it out. It irritated him more to be dragged out of sleep into an argument before his mind could engage.

"Taking me dancing," she continued, stalking away and back. "Trying to seduce me on the dance floor, then having a snit because—"

"A snit." That stung. "Listen, sweetheart, I've never had a snit in my life."

"I say you did, and don't call me sweetheart in that tone of voice."

"Now you don't like my tone." His eyes narrowed dangerously, to sharp green slits that threatened retaliation. "Well, let's try a brand-new tone and see how you—" He ended with an oath when she jerked the hammock and flipped him out on his face.

Her first reaction was shock, then an immediate urge to apologize. But as the air turned blue around her, she snapped herself back, jerked her chin up in the air and marched off.

He'd hit the ground with a thud, and he was sure he'd heard his own bones rattle. But he was on his feet again quickly enough, limping a little, but fast enough to snag her before she reached the door.

He yanked her around to face him. "What bug got up your—"

"You deserved it." The blood was roaring in her head, her heart was pounding, but she wasn't going to back down.

"What the hell for?"

"For…whatever."

"Well, that sure covers it."

"Just get out of my way. I'm going for a walk."

"No," he said precisely, "you're not."

"You can't tell me what to do."

He estimated he was close to twice her weight and had a good eight inches in height on her. His lips curved grimly. "Yes, I can. You're hysterical."

That snapped it. "I certainly am not hysterical. If I were hysterical, I'd scratch that nasty smile off your face, and poke those smug eyes out, and—"

To simplify matters, he simply picked her up and carried her inside. She wiggled, sputtered, kicked a little, but he managed to drop her into a kitchen chair. Putting his hands on her shoulders, his face close to hers, he gave one pithy order.

"Stay."

If he didn't have coffee, immediately, he was going to die. Or kill someone.

"You're fired."

"Fine, great, whoopee." He let her fume while he poured coffee and downed it like water. "God, what a way to start the day." He grabbed a bottle of aspirin, fought with the childproof cap while the headache that was brewing insidiously burst into full-blown misery.

"I'm not going to tolerate having a woman yell at me before my eyes are open. Whatever's got you going, sweetheart, you just hold on to it until I—" He cursed again, slamming the stubborn cap on the edge of the counter, where it held firm.

His head was throbbing, his knee wept where it had hit the ground, and he could easily have chewed through the plastic to get to the aspirin.

Swearing ripely, he grabbed a butcher knife out of the wooden block on the counter and hacked at the bottle until he'd decapitated it. His face tight with fury, he turned with the bottle in one hand, the knife in the other. His teeth were clenched.

"Now you listen…" he began.

Bailey's eyes rolled back in her head, and she slid from the chair onto the floor in a dead faint before he could move.

"Sweet God." The knife clattered on the floor, and aspirin rolled everywhere as the mangled bottle hit the tiles. He gathered her up, and for lack of anything better, laid her on the kitchen table while he dampened a cloth. "Come on, Bailey, come around, sweetheart."

He bathed her face, chafed her wrists and cursed himself. How could he have shouted at her that way, manhandled her like that, when she was so fragile? Maybe he'd go out and kick some puppies, stomp on some kittens, for his next act.

When she moaned and shifted, he pressed her limp hand to his lips. "That's the way. All the way back." Her eyes fluttered open while he stroked her hair. "It's okay, Bailey. Take it easy."

"He's going to kill me." Her eyes were open, but blind. She clutched at Cade's shirt as terror strangled her breath. "He's going to kill me."

"No one's going to hurt you. I'm right here."

"He's going to kill me. He's got a knife. If he finds me, he'll kill me."

He wanted to gather her up, soothe it all away, but she'd trusted him to help. He kept his voice very calm, uncurled her fingers from his shirt and held them. "Who's got the knife, Bailey? Who's going to kill you?"

"He…he…" She could see it, almost see it, the hand hacking down, the knife flashing again and again. "There's blood everywhere. Blood everywhere. I have to get away from the blood. The knife. The lightning. I have to run."

He held her still, kept his voice calm. "Where are you? Tell me where you are."

"In the dark. Lights are out. He'll kill me. I have to run."

"Run where?"

"Anywhere." Her breath was coming so fast, the force of it scored her throat like nails. "Anywhere, away. Somewhere away. If he finds me—"

"He's not going to find you. I won't let him find you." He cupped her face firmly in his hands so that her eyes met his. "Slow down now. Just slow down." If she kept panting like that, she was going to hyperventilate and faint on him again. He didn't think he could handle it. "You're safe here. You're safe with me. Understand that?"

"Yes. Yes." She closed her eyes, shuddered hard. "Yes. I need air. Please, I need some air."

He picked her up again, carried her outside. He set her on the padded chaise on the patio, sat beside her. "Take it slow. Remember, you're safe here. You're safe."

"Yes, all right." With an effort, she evened out the air that seemed to want to clog and burst in her lungs. "I'm all right."

Far from it, he thought. She was sheet white, clammy and shivering. But the memory was close, and he had to try to dislodge it. "No one's going to hurt you. Nothing's going to touch you here. You hang on to that and try to tell me everything you remember."

"It comes in blips." She struggled to breathe past the pressure in her chest. "When you had the knife…" Fear clawed through her again with razored talons.

"I scared you. I'm sorry." He took her hands, held them. "I wouldn't hurt you."

"I know." She closed her eyes again, let the sun beat hot on the lids. "There was a knife. A long blade, curved. It's beautiful. The bone handle is deeply carved. I've seen it— maybe I've used it."

"Where did you see it?"

"I don't know. There were voices, shouting. I can't hear what they're saying. It's like the ocean, all sound, roaring, violent sound." She pressed her hands to her ears, as if she could block it out. "Then there's blood, everywhere there's blood. All over the floor."

"What kind of floor?"

"Carpet, gray carpet. The lightning keeps flashing, the knife keeps flashing."

"Is there a window? Do you see lightning through the window?"

"Yes, I think…" She shivered again, and the scene fighting to form in her mind went blank. "It's dark. Everything went dark, and I have to get away. I have to hide."

"Where do you hide?"

"It's a little place, hardly room, and if he sees, I'll be trapped. He has the knife. I can see it, his hand on the hilt. It's so close, if he turns—"

"Tell me about the hand," Cade said, interrupting her gently. "What does the hand look like, Bailey?"

"It's dark, very dark, but there's a light bouncing around. It almost catches me. He's holding the knife, and his knuckles are white. There's blood on them. On his ring."

"What kind of ring, Bailey?" His eyes stayed intent on her face, but his voice remained calm and easy. "What does the ring look like?"

"It's heavy gold, thick band. Yellow gold. The center stone's a ruby cabochon. On either side there are small diamonds, brilliant-cut. Initials. *T* and *S* in a stylized sweep. The diamonds are red with blood. He's so close, so close, I can smell it. If he looks down. If he looks down and sees me. He'll kill me, slice me to pieces, if he finds me."

"He didn't." Unable to bear it any longer, Cade drew her up, held her. "You got away. How did you get away, Bailey?"

"I don't know." The relief was so huge—Cade's arms around her, the sun warm at her back, his cheek pressed to her hair—she could have wept. "I don't remember."

"It's all right. That's enough."

"Maybe I killed him." She drew back, looked into Cade's face. "Maybe I used the gun that was in the bag and shot him."

"The gun was fully loaded, Bailey."

"I could have replaced it."

"Sweetheart, in my professional opinion, you wouldn't know how."

"But if I—"

"And if you did—" he took her shoulders now, gave her a quick shake "—it was to protect yourself. He was armed, you were terrified, and it sounds as if he'd already killed someone. Whatever you did to survive was right."

She shifted away, looked out over the yard, past the flowers, the leafy old trees, the tidy fence line. "What kind of person am I? There's a very real possibility I saw someone murdered. I did nothing to stop it, nothing to help."

"Be sensible, Bailey. What could you have done?"

"Something," she murmured. "I didn't get to a phone, call the police. I just ran."

"And if you hadn't, you'd be dead." He knew by the way she winced that his tone had been harsh. But it was what she needed. "Instead, you're alive, and bit by bit, we're putting it together."

He rose, paced away, so that he wouldn't give in to the temptation just to cuddle her. "You were in a building of some sort. In a room with gray carpet, probably a window. There was an argument, and someone had a knife. He used it. His initials could be *T.S.* He came after you, and it was dark. More than likely it was a blackout and the building had lost power. A section of North West D.C. lost power for two hours the night before you hired me, so we've got somewhere to look. You knew the building well enough to head for cover. I'd say you belonged there. You live or work there."

He turned back, noting that she was watching him, paying close attention. Her hands were steady in her lap again.

"I can check if there was a knifing reported that night, but I've been watching the papers, and there hasn't been any press on it."

"But it was days ago now. Someone must have found—found a body, if there was one."

"Not if it was a private home, or an office that shut down for the long weekend. If there'd been someone else there, other people in the building when it happened, it would have been reported. Odds are you were alone."

It made his stomach crawl to think of it—Bailey alone in the dark with a killer.

"The storm didn't hit until after ten."

It was logical, and the simple movement from theory to fact calmed her. "What do we do now?"

"We'll drive around the area that lost power, starting at the hotel where you ended up."

"I don't remember getting to the hotel, whether I walked or took a cab."

"You either walked, took a bus or the metro. I've already checked on cabs. None of the companies dropped off a fare within three blocks of the hotel that night. We're going to move on the assumption that you were on foot, dazed, too shaken to think of hopping a bus, and since the metro only runs until midnight, that's too close to call."

She nodded, looked down at her hands. "I'm sorry I shouted at you before. You didn't deserve it, after everything you've done for me."

"I deserved it." He tucked his hands in his pockets. "I refuse to accept the term *snit* but I'll allow the phrase *out of sorts.*" He enjoyed seeing her lips curve in one of her hesitant smiles as she lifted her head.

"I suppose we both were. Did I hurt you when I knocked you down?"

"My ego's going to be carrying a bruise for a while. Otherwise, no." He angled his head. There was a quick cockiness in the movement, and in the eyes that glinted at hers. "And I didn't try to seduce you on the dance floor, Bailey. I did seduce you on the dance floor."

Her pulse stuttered a bit. He was so outrageously gorgeous, standing there in the bright morning sun, rumpled, his dark hair thick and untidy, the dimples denting his cheeks and his mouth arrogantly curved. No woman alive, Bailey thought, could have stopped her mouth from watering.

And she was certain he knew it.

"Your ego seems to function well enough, bruised or not."

"We can always stage a reenactment."

Her stomach fluttered at the thought, but she worked up a smile. "I'm glad you're not angry with me anymore. I don't think I handle confrontations very well."

He rubbed his elbow, where he'd lost several layers of skin on impact. "You seemed to do well enough. I'm going to clean up, then we'll take ourselves a Sunday drive."

There were so many kinds of buildings, Bailey thought as Cade tooled around the city. Old ones, new ones, crumbling row houses and refurbished homes. Tall office buildings and squat storefronts.

Had she ever really noticed the city before? she wondered. The sloping stone walls, the trees rising up from the sidewalks. Belching buses with whining air brakes.

Was it always so humid in July? Was the summer sky always the color of paper? And were the flowers always so luscious in the public spaces tucked around statues and along the streets?

Had she shopped in any of these stores, eaten in any of these restaurants?

The trees took over again, tall and stately, lining both sides of the road, so that it seemed they were driving through a park, rather than the middle of a crowded city.

"It's like seeing everything for the first time," she murmured. "I'm sorry."

"Doesn't matter. Something will either click or it won't."

They passed gracious old homes, brick and granite, then another strip of shops, smart and trendy. She made a small sound, and though she was hardly aware of it herself, Cade slowed. "Something click?"

"That boutique. Marguerite's. I don't know."

"Let's take a look." He circled around, backtracked, then pulled into a narrow lot that fronted several upscale shops. "Everything's closed, but that doesn't mean we can't window-shop." Leaning over, he opened her door, then climbed out his own.

"Maybe I just liked the dress in the window," she murmured.

It was very lovely, just a sweep of rose-petal silk with thin straps of glittery rhinestones that continued down to cross under the bodice.

The display was completed by a tiny silver evening bag and impossibly high heels in matching silver.

The way it made her smile, Cade wished the shop was open, so that he could buy it for her. "It's your style."

"I don't know." She cupped her hands to the glass, peered through them for the simple delight of looking at pretty things. "That's a wonderful cocktail suit in navy linen. Oh, and that red dress is just fabulous. Bound to make you feel powerful and accomplished. I really should start wearing bolder colors, but I always wimp out with pastels."

*Try this green, Bailey. It's got punch. There's nothing more tiring than a clothes coward.*

*How long do I have to stand around while you two play with clothes? I'm starving.*

*Oh, stop bitching. You're not happy unless you're feeding your face or buying new jeans. Bailey, not that tedious beige. The green. Trust me.*

"She talked me into it," Bailey murmured. "I bought the green suit. She was right. She always is."

"Who's right, Bailey?" He didn't touch her, afraid that even an encouraging hand on her shoulder would jar her. "Is it M.J.?"

"No, no, not M.J. She's annoyed, impatient, hates to waste time. Shopping's such a waste of time."

Oh, her head hurt. It was going to explode any moment, simply burst off her shoulders. But the need was greater, the need to latch on to this one thing. This one answer. Her stomach rolled, threatened to heave, and her skin went clammy with the effort of holding off nausea.

"Grace." Her voice broke on the name. "Grace," she said again as her knees buckled. "Her name's Grace. Grace and M.J." Tears sprang to her eyes, rolled down her cheeks as she threw her arms around Cade's neck. "I've been here. I've been to this shop. I bought a green suit. I remember."

"Good. Good job, Bailey." He gave her a quick swing.

"No, but that's all." She pressed a hand to her forehead. The pain was screaming now. "That's all I remember. Just being in there with them, buying a suit. It's so foolish. Why should I remember buying a suit?"

"You remember the people." He smoothed his thumbs over her temples. He could all but feel the headache raging inside. "They're important to you. It was a moment, something shared, a happy time."

"But I can't remember them. Not really. Just feelings."

"You're breaking through." He pressed his lips to her brow, drew her back toward the car. "And it's happening quickly now." He eased her down on the seat, hooked her safety belt himself. "And it hurts you."

"It doesn't matter. I need to know."

"It matters to me. We'll get you something for that headache, and some food. Then we'll start again."

Arguments wouldn't sway him. Bailey had to admit that fighting Cade and a blinding headache was a battle she was doomed to lose. She let him prop her up in bed, dutifully swallowed the aspirin he gave her. Obediently she closed her eyes as he instructed, then opened them again when he brought up a bowl of chicken soup.

"It's out of a can," he told her, fussing with the pillows behind her back. "But it should do the job."

"I could eat in the kitchen, Cade. It was a headache, not a tumor. And it's almost gone."

"I'm going to work you hard later. Take the pampering while you can get it."

"All right, I will." She spooned up soup. "It's wonderful. You added thyme."

"For that little hint of France."

Her smile faded. "Paris," she murmured. "Something about Paris." The headache snuck back as she tried to concentrate.

"Let it go for now." He sat beside her. "I'd say your subconscious is letting you know you're not all the way ready yet to remember. A piece at a time will do."

"I suppose it'll have to." She smiled again. "Want some soup?"

"Now that you mention it." He leaned forward, let her

feed him, and didn't take his eyes from hers. "Not too shabby."

She took another spoonful herself, tasted him. Marvelous. "As handy as you are in the kitchen, I'm surprised your wife let you get away."

"Ex-wife, and we had a cook."

"Oh." She fed him again, slowly taking turns. "I've been trying to figure out how to ask without seeming rude."

He slipped her hair behind her ear. "Just ask."

"Well, this lovely house, the antiques, the fancy sports car… Then there's your office."

His mouth twitched. "Something wrong with my office?"

"No. Well, nothing a bulldozer and a construction crew couldn't cure. It just doesn't compute with the rest."

"I've got a thing about my business paying for itself, and that office is about all it can afford so far. My investigative work pays the bills and just a little more. On a personal level, I'm rolling in it." His eyes laughed into hers. "Money, that is. If that's what you're asking."

"I guess it was. You're rich, then."

"Depends on your definition, or if you mean me personally or the entire family. It's shopping centers, real estate, that sort of thing. A lot of doctors and lawyers and bankers down through the ages. And me, I'm—"

"The black sheep," she finished for him, thrilled that he was just that. "You didn't want to go into the family business. You didn't want to be a doctor or a lawyer or a banker."

"Nope. I wanted to be Sam Spade."

Delighted, she chuckled. "*The Maltese Falcon.* I'm glad you didn't want to be a banker."

"Me, too." He took the hand she'd laid on his cheek, pressed his lips to it and felt her quiver of response.

"I'm glad I found your name in the phone book." Her voice thickened. "I'm glad I found you."

"So am I." He took the tray from between them, set it aside. Even if he'd been blind, he thought, he would have understood what was in her eyes just then. And his heart thrilled to it. "I could walk out of here and leave you alone now." He trailed a finger across her collarbone, then let it rest on the pulse that beat rabbit-quick at her throat. "That's not what I want to do."

It was her decision, she knew. Her choice. Her moment. "That's not what I want, either." When he cupped her face in his hands, she closed her eyes. "Cade, I may have done something horrible."

His lips paused an inch from hers. "I don't care."

"I may have— I may be—" Determined to face it, she opened her eyes again. "There may be someone else."

His fingers tightened. "I don't give a damn."

She let out a long breath, and took her moment. "Neither do I," she said, and pulled him to her.

# Chapter 8

This was what it felt like to be pressed under a man's body. A man's hard, needy body. A man who wanted you above all else.

For that moment.

It was breathless and stunning, exciting and fresh. The way he combed his fingers through her hair as his lips covered hers thrilled her. The fit of mouth against mouth, as if the only thing lips and tongues were made for were to taste a lover. And it was the taste of him that filled her—strong and male and real.

Whatever had come before, whatever came after, this mattered now.

She stroked her hands over him, and it was glorious. The shape of his body, the breadth of shoulders, the length of back, the narrowing of waist, the muscles beneath so firm, so tight. And when her hands skimmed under his shirt, the smooth, warm flesh beneath fascinated.

"Oh, I've wanted to touch you." Her lips raced over his face. "I was afraid I never would."

"I've wanted you from the first moment you walked in the door." He drew back only enough to see her eyes, the deep, melting brown of them. "Before you walked in the door. Forever."

"It doesn't make any sense. We don't—"

"It doesn't matter. Only this." His lips closed over hers again, took the kiss deeper, tangling their flavors together.

He wanted to go slowly, draw out every moment. It seemed he'd waited for her all his life, so now he could take all the time in the world to touch, to taste, to explore and exploit. Each shift of her body beneath his was a gift. Each sigh a treasure.

To have her like this, with the sun streaming through the window, with her hair flowing gold over the old quilt and her body both yielding and eager, was sweeter than any dream.

They belonged. It was all he had to know.

To see her, to unfasten the simple shirt he'd picked for her, to open it inch by inch to pale, smooth flesh was everything he wanted. He skimmed his fingertips over the curve of her breast, felt her skin quiver in response, watched her eyes flicker dark, then focus on his.

"You're perfect." He cupped her, and she was small and firm and made for his palm.

He bent his head, rubbed his lips where the lace of her bra met flesh, then moved them up, lazily up her throat, over her jaw, and back to nip at her mouth.

No one had kissed her like this before. She knew it was impossible for anyone else to have taken such care. With a soft sigh, she poured herself into the kiss, murmuring when he shifted her to slip the shirt away, trembling when he slid the lace aside and bared her breasts to his hands.

And his mouth.

She moaned, lost, gloriously lost, in a dark maze of sensations. Soft here, then rough, cool, then searing, each feeling bumped gently into the next, then merged into simple pleasure. Whichever way she turned, there was something new and thrilling. When she tugged his shirt away, there was the lovely slippery slide of his flesh against hers, the intimacy of it, heart to heart.

And her heart danced to the play of his lips, the teasing nip of teeth, the slow torture of tongue.

The air was like syrup, thick and sweet, as he slid her slacks over her hips. She struggled to gulp it in, but each breath was shallow and short. He was touching her everywhere, his hands slick and slow, but relentlessly pushing her higher and stronger until the heat was immense. It kindled inside her like a brushfire.

She moaned out his name, clutching the quilt and dragging it into tangles as her body strained to reach for something just beyond her grasp. As she arched desperately against him, he watched her. Slid up her body again until his lips were close to hers, and watched her. Watched her as, with quick, clever fingers, he tore her free.

It was his name she called when the heat reached flash point, and his body she clung to as her own shuddered.

That was what he'd wanted.

His name was still vibrating on her lips when he crushed them with his, when he rolled with her over the bed in a greedy quest to take and possess. Blind with need, he tugged at his jeans, trembling himself when she buried her mouth against his throat, strained against him in quivering invitation.

She was more generous than any fantasy. More generous than any wish. More his than any dream.

With sunlight pouring over the tangled sheets, she arched to him, opened as if she'd been waiting all her life for him. His heart pounded in his head as he slipped inside her, moved to fill her.

Shock froze him for a dazed instant, and every muscle tensed. But she shook her head, wrapped herself around him and took him in.

"You" was all she said. "Only you."

He lay still, listening to her heart thudding, absorbing the quakes of her body with his. Only him, he thought, and closed his eyes. She'd been innocent. Untouched. A miracle. And his heart was tugged in opposing directions of guilt and pure selfish pleasure.

She'd been innocent, and he'd taken her.

She'd been untouched, until he touched.

He wanted to beg her to forgive him.

He wanted to climb out on the roof and crow.

Not certain either would suit the situation, he gently tested the waters.

"Bailey?"

"Hmm?"

"Ah, in my professional opinion as a licensed investigator, I conclude it's extremely unlikely you're married." He felt the rumble of her laughter, and lifted his head to grin down at her. "I'll put it in my report."

"You do that."

He brushed the hair from her cheek. "Did I hurt you? I'm sorry. I never considered—"

"No." She pressed her hand over his. "You didn't hurt me. I'm happy, giddy. Relieved." Her lips curved on a sigh. "I never considered, either. I'd say we were both surprised." Abruptly her stomach fluttered with nerves. "You're not... disappointed? If you—"

"I'm devastated. I really hoped you'd be married, with six kids. I really only enjoy making love with married women."

"No, I meant… Was it—was I—was everything all right?"

"Bailey." On a half laugh, he rolled over so that she could settle on his chest. "You're perfect. Absolutely, completely perfect. I love you." She went very still, and her cheek stayed pressed to his heart. "You know I do," he said quietly. "From the moment I saw you."

Now she wanted to weep, because it was everything she wanted to hear, and nothing she could accept. "You don't know me."

"Neither do you."

She lifted her head, shook it fiercely. "That's exactly the point. Joking about it doesn't change the truth."

"Here's the truth, then." He sat up, took her firmly by the shoulders. "I'm in love with you. In love with the woman I'm holding right now. You're exactly what I want, what I need, and sweetheart—" he kissed her lightly "—I'm keeping you."

"You know it's not that simple."

"I'm not asking for simple." He slid his hands down, gripped hers. "I'm asking you to marry me."

"That's impossible." Panicked, she tugged on her hands, but he gripped them calmly and held her in place. "You know that's impossible. I don't know where I come from, what I've done. I met you three days ago."

"That all makes sense, or would, except for one thing." He drew her against him and shot reason to hell with a kiss.

"Don't do this." Torn to pieces, she wrapped her arms around his neck, held tight. "Don't do this, Cade. Whatever my life was, right now it's a mess. I need to find the answers."

"We'll find the answers. I promise you that. But there's one I want from you now." He drew her head back. He'd expected the tears, knew they'd be shimmering in her eyes and turning them deep gold. "Tell me you love me, Bailey, or tell me you don't."

"I can't—"

"Just one question," he murmured. "You don't need a yesterday to answer it."

No, she needed nothing but her own heart. "I can't tell you I don't love you, because I can't lie to you." She shook her head, pressed her fingers to his lips before he could speak. "I won't tell you I do, because it wouldn't be fair. It's an answer that has to wait until I know all the others. Until I know who the woman is who'll tell you. Give me time."

He'd give her time, he thought when her head was nestled on his shoulder again. Because nothing and no one was taking her from him, whatever they found on the other side of her past.

Cade liked to say that getting to a solution was just a matter of taking steps. Bailey wondered how many more there were left to climb. She felt she'd rushed up a very long staircase that day, and when reaching the landing been just as lost as ever.

Not entirely true, she told herself as she settled down at the kitchen table with a notepad and pencil. Even the urge to make a list of what she knew indicated that she was an organized person, and one who liked to review things in black and white.

*Who is Bailey?*

A woman who habitually rose at the same hour daily. Did that make her tedious and predictable, or responsible? She liked coffee black and strong, scrambled eggs, and her steaks medium rare. Fairly ordinary tastes. Her body was trim, not particularly muscular, and without tan lines. So, she wasn't a fitness fanatic or a sun-worshiper. Perhaps she had a job that kept her indoors.

Which meant, she thought with some humor, she wasn't a lumberjack or a lifeguard.

She was a right-handed, brown-eyed blonde, and was reasonably sure her hair color was natural or close to what she'd been born with.

She knew a great deal about gemstones, which could mean they were a hobby, a career, or just something she liked to wear. She had possession of a diamond worth a fortune that she'd either stolen, bought—highly unlikely, she thought—or gained through an accident of some sort.

She'd witnessed a violent attack, possibly a murder, and run away.

Because that fact made her temple start to throb again, she skipped over it.

She hummed classical music in the shower and liked to watch classic film noir on television. And she couldn't figure out what that said about her personality or her background.

She liked attractive clothes, good materials, and shied away from strong colors unless pushed.

It worried her that she might be vain and frivolous.

But she had at least two female friends who shared part of her life. Grace and M.J., M.J. and Grace. Bailey wrote the names on the pad, over and over, hoping that the simple repetition would strike a fresh spark.

They mattered to her, she could feel that. She was frightened for them and didn't know why. Her mind might be blank, but her heart told her that they were special to her, closer to her than anyone else in the world.

But she was afraid to trust her heart.

There was something else she knew that Bailey didn't want to write down, didn't want to review in black and white.

She'd had no lover. There'd been no one she cared for enough, or who cared for her enough, for intimacy. Perhaps in the life she led she'd been too judgmental, too intolerant, too self-absorbed, to accept a man into her bed.

Or perhaps she'd been too ordinary, too boring, too undesirable, for a man to accept her into his.

In any case, she had a lover now.

Why hadn't the act of lovemaking seemed foreign to her, or frightening, as it seemed it would to the uninitiated? Instead, with Cade, it had been as natural as breathing.

Natural, exciting and perfect.

He said he loved her, but how could she believe it? He knew only one small piece of her, a fraction of the whole. When her memory surfaced, he might find her to be the very type of woman he disliked.

No, she wouldn't hold him to what he'd said to this Bailey, until she knew the whole woman.

And her feelings? With a half laugh, she set the pencil aside. She'd been drawn to him instantly, trusted him completely the moment he took her hand. And fallen in love with him while she watched him stand in this kitchen, breaking brown eggs into a white bowl.

But her heart couldn't be trusted in this case, either. The closer they came to finding the truth, the closer they came to the time when they might turn from each other and walk away.

However much she wished it, they couldn't leave the canvas bag and its contents in his safe, forget they existed and just be.

"You forgot some things."

She jolted, turned her head quickly and looked into his face. How long, she wondered, had he been standing behind her, reading her notes over her shoulder, while she was thinking of him?

"I thought it might help me to write down what I know."

"Always a good plan." He walked to the fridge, took out a beer, poured her a glass of iced tea.

She sat feeling foolish and awkward, her hands clutched in her lap. Had they really rolled naked on a sun-washed bed an hour before? How was such intimacy handled in a tidy kitchen over cold drinks and puzzles?

He didn't seem to have a problem with it. Cade sat across from her, propped his feet on an empty chair and scooted her pad over. "You're a worrier."

"I am?"

"Sure." He flipped a page, started a new list. "You're worrying right now. What should you say to this guy, now that you're lovers? Now that you know he's wildly in love with you, wants to spend the rest of his life with you?"

"Cade—"

"Just stating the facts." And if he stated them often enough, he figured she'd eventually accept them. "The sex was great, and it was easy. So you worry about that, too. Why did you let this man you've known for a weekend take you to bed, when you've never let another man get that close?" His eyes flicked up, held hers. "The answer's elementary. You're just as wildly in love with me, but you're afraid to face it."

She picked up her glass, cooled her throat. "I'm a coward?"

"No, Bailey, you're not a coward, but you're constantly worried that you are. You're a champion worrier. And a woman, I think, who gives herself very little credit for her strengths, and has very little tolerance for her weaknesses. Self-judgmental."

He wrote that down as well, while she frowned at the words on the page. "It seems to me someone in my situation has to try to judge herself."

"Practical, logical." He continued the column. "Now, leave the judging to me a moment. You're compassionate, responsible, organized. And a creature of habit. I'd say you hold some sort of position that requires those traits, as well as a good intellect. Your work habits are disciplined and precise. You also have a fine aesthetic sense."

"How can you be so sure?"

"Bailey, forgetting who you are doesn't change who you are. That's your big flaw in reasoning here. If you hated brussels sprouts before, it's likely you're still going to hate them. If you were allergic to cats, you're still going to sneeze if you pet a kitten. And if you had a strong, moral and caring heart, it's still beating inside you. Now let me finish up here."

She twisted her head, struggling to read upside down. "What are you putting down?"

"You're a lousy drinker. Probably a metabolism thing. And I think at this point, we could have some wine later, so I can take full advantage of that." He grinned over at her. "And you blush. It's a sweet, old-fashioned physical reaction. You're tidy. You hang up your towels after you shower, you rinse off your dishes, you make your bed every morning."

There were other details, he thought. She wiggled her foot when she was nervous, her eyes went gold when she was aroused, her voice turned chilly when she was annoyed.

"You've had a good education, probably up north, from your speech pattern and accent. I'd say you concentrated on your studies like a good girl and didn't date much. Otherwise you wouldn't have been a virgin up to a couple hours ago. There, you blushed again. I really love when you do that."

"I don't see the point in this."

"There's that cool, polite tone. Indulge me," he added, then sipped his beer. "You've got a slim body, smooth skin. You either take care of both or you were lucky genetically. By the way, I like your unicorn."

She cleared her throat. "Thank you."

"No, thank you," he said, and chuckled. "Anyway, you have or make enough money to afford good clothes. Those classic Italian pumps you were wearing go for about two hundred and fifty at department-store prices. And you had silk underwear. I'd say the silk undies and the unicorn follow the same pattern. You like to be a little daring under the traditional front."

She was just managing to close her gaping mouth. "You went through my clothes? My underwear?"

"What there was of them, and all in the name of investigation. Great underwear," he told her. "Very sexy, simple, and pricey. I'd say peach silk ought to look terrific on you."

She made a strangled sound, fell back on silence. There was really nothing to say.

"I don't know the annual income of your average gemologist or jewelry designer—but I'll lay odds you're one or the other. I'm leaning toward the scientist as vocation, and the designer as avocation."

"That's a big leap, Cade."

"No, it's not. Just another step. The pieces are there. Wouldn't you think a diamond like the one in the safe would require the services of a gemologist? Its authenticity would have to be verified, its value assessed. Just the way you verified and assessed it yesterday."

Her hands trembled, so she put them back in her lap. "If that's true, then it ups the likelihood that I stole it."

"No, it doesn't." Impatient with her, he tapped the pencil sharply against the pad. "Look at the other facts. Why can't you see yourself? You wouldn't steal a stick of gum. Doesn't the fact that you're riddled with guilt over the very thought you might have done something illegal give you a clue?"

"The fact is, Cade, I have the stone."

"Yeah, and hasn't it occurred to you, in that logical, responsible, ordered mind of yours, that you might have been protecting it?"

"Protecting it? From—"

"From whoever killed to get their hands on it. From whoever would have killed you if he had found you. That's what plays, Bailey, that's what fits. And if there are three stones, then you might very well know where the others are, as well. You may be protecting all of them."

"How?"

He had some ideas on that as well, but didn't think she was ready to hear them. "We'll work on that. Meanwhile, I've made a few calls. We've got a busy day ahead of us tomorrow. The police artist will come over in the morning, see if she can help you put images together. And I managed to snag one of the undercurators, or whatever they're called, at the Smithsonian. We have a one-o'clock appointment tomorrow."

"You got an appointment on a holiday?"

"That's where the Parris name and fortune come in handy. Hint at funding, and it opens a lot of musty old doors. And we'll see if that boutique opens for the holiday sale hunters, and find out if anyone remembers selling a green suit."

"It doesn't seem like we're doing enough."

"Sweetheart, we've come a long way in a short time."

"You're right." She rose, walked to the window. There was a wood thrush in the maple tree, singing its heart out. "I can't begin to tell you how grateful I am."

"I'll bill you for the professional services," he said shortly. "And I don't want gratitude for the rest of it."

"I have to give it, whether or not you take it. You made this bearable, more than that. I don't know how many times you made me smile or laugh or just forget it all for little spaces of time. I think I'd have gone crazy without you, Cade."

"I'm going to be there for you, Bailey. You're not going to be able to shake me loose."

"You're used to getting what you want," she murmured.

"I wonder if I am. It doesn't feel as if that's true."

"That's something you can change."

He was right. That was a matter of patience, perseverance, control. And perhaps wanting the right things. She wanted him, wanted to think that one day she could stand here, listening to the wood thrush sing of summer while Cade drowsed in the hammock. It could be their house instead of his. Their life. Their family.

If it was the right thing, and she could persevere.

"I'm going to make you a promise." She followed the impulse and turned, letting her heart be reckless. He was so much what she needed, sitting there with his jeans torn at the knee, his hair too long, his feet bare. "If, when this is over, when all the steps have been taken, all the pieces are in place to make the whole…if I can and you still want me, I'll marry you."

His heart stuttered in his chest. Emotion rose up to fill his throat. Very carefully, he set the bottle aside, rose. "Tell me you love me."

It was there, in her heart, begging to be said. But she shook her head. "When it's all over, and you know everything. If you still want me."

"That's not the kind of promise that suits me. No qualifications, Bailey. No whens, no ifs. Just you."

"It's all I can give you. It's all I have."

"We can go into Maryland on Tuesday, get a license. Be married in a matter of days."

He could see it. The two of them, giddy in love, rousing some sleepy-eyed country J.P. out of bed in the middle of the night. Holding hands in the living room while an old yellow dog slept on a braid rug, the J.P.'s wife played the piano and he and the woman he loved exchanged vows.

And sliding the ring onto her finger, feeling her slide one on his, was the link that would bind them.

"There are no blood tests in Maryland," he continued. "Just a couple of forms, and there you are."

He meant it. It staggered her to see in those deep green eyes that he meant nothing less than he said. He would take her exactly as she was. He would love her just as she stood.

How could she let him?

"And what name would I put on the form?"

"It doesn't matter. You'll have mine." He gripped her arms, drew her against him. In all his life, there had been no one he needed as much. "Take mine."

Just take, she thought when his lips covered hers. Take what was offered—the love, the safety, the promise. Let the past come as it would, let the future drift, and seize the moment.

"You know it wouldn't be right." She pressed her cheek to his. "You need to know as much as I do."

Maybe he did. However much the fantasy of a reckless elopement appealed, creating a fake identity for Bailey, it wasn't the answer either one of them needed. "Could be fun." He struggled to lighten the mood. "Like practice for the real thing." He pulled her back to arm's length, studied her face. Delicate, troubled. Lovely. "You want orange blossoms, Bailey? A white dress and organ music?"

Because her heart sighed at the image, she managed to smile. "I think I might. I seem to be a traditional soul."

"Then I should buy you a traditional diamond."

"Cade—"

"Just speculating," he murmured, and lifted her left hand. "No, however traditional your soul, your taste in jewelry is unique. We'll find something that suits. But I should probably take you to meet the family." His eyes lifted to hers, and he laughed. "God help you."

Just a game, she thought, just pretend. She smiled back at him. "I'd love to meet your family. See Camilla do pirouettes in her tutu."

"If you can get through that and still want to marry me, I'll know you're hopelessly in love with me. They'll put you through the gauntlet, sweetheart. A very sophisticated, silk-edged gauntlet. Where did you go to school, what does your father do, does your mother play bridge or tennis? And by the way, what clubs do you belong to, and did I run into you on the slopes last season at St. Moritz?"

Instead of making her unhappy, it made her laugh. "Then I'd better find out the answers."

"I like making them up. I took a cop to Muffy's tenth-anniversary bash. Couldn't get out of it. We told everyone she was the niece of the Italian prime minister, educated in a Swiss boarding school and interested in acquiring a pied-à-terre in D.C."

Her brows drew together. "Oh, really?"

"They all but drooled on her. Not nearly the reaction we'd have gotten with the truth."

"Which was?"

"She was a uniformed cop who grew up in New York's Little Italy and transferred to Washington after her divorce from a guy who ran a pasta place off Broadway."

"Was she pretty?"

"Sure." His grin flashed. "Gorgeous. Then there was the lounge singer in Chevy Chase who—"

"I don't think I want to know." She turned away, picked up her empty glass and made a business out of rinsing it out. "You've dated a lot of women, I suppose."

"That depends on your definition of 'a lot.' I could probably run a list of names, ages, physical descriptions and last known addresses. Want to type it up for me?"

"No."

Delighted, he nuzzled the back of her neck. "I've only asked one woman to marry me."

"Two," she corrected, and set the now sparkling glass on the counter with a snap.

"One. I didn't ask Carla. That just sort of evolved. And now she's happily married—as far as I can tell—to a corporate lawyer and the proud mama of a bouncing baby girl named Eugenia. So it hardly counts anyway."

She bit her lip. "You didn't want children?"

"Yes, I did. I do." He turned her around, kissed her gently. "But we're not naming any kid of ours Eugenia. Now what do you say we think about going out for dinner, someplace quiet, where we can neck at the table? Then we can watch the fireworks."

"It's too early for dinner."

"That's why I said we should think about it." He scooped her up. "First we have to go upstairs and make love again."

Her pulse gave a pleasant little jump as she curled her arms around his neck. "We have to?"

"It'll pass the time. Unless you'd rather play gin rummy?"

Chuckling, she traced a line of kisses up his neck. "Well, if those are my only choices..."

"Tell you what, we can play strip gin rummy. We can both cheat and that way— Hell." He was halfway up the stairs with her, and nicely aroused, when the doorbell sounded. "Hold that thought, okay?" He set her down, and went to answer.

One peek through the side panel of wavy glass framing the door had him groaning. "Perfect timing, as always." With a hand on the knob, he turned, looked at Bailey. "Sweetheart, the woman on the other side of this door is my mother. I realize you expressed a mild interest in meeting my family, but I'm giving you this chance, because I love you. I really do. So I'm advising you to run, hide, and don't look back."

Nerves fluttered, but she straightened her shoulders. "Stop being silly and open the door."

"Okay, but I warned you." Bracing himself, he pulled the door open and fixed a bright, welcoming smile on his face. "Mother." As was expected, he kissed her smooth, polished cheek. "What a nice surprise."

"I wouldn't have to surprise you if you'd ever return my calls." Leona Parris stepped into the foyer.

She was, Bailey realized with a stunned first glance, a striking woman. Surely, with three grown children and several grandchildren, she had to be at least fifty. She could have passed for a sleek thirty-five.

Her hair was a lush sable brown with hints of golden highlights and fashioned in a perfect and elegant French twist that complemented a face of ivory and cream, with cool green eyes, straight nose and sulky mouth. She wore an elegant tailored bronze-toned suit that nipped at her narrow waist.

The topaz stones at her ears were square-cut and big as a woman's thumb and earned Bailey's instant admiration.

"I've been busy," Cade began. "A couple of cases, and some personal business."

"I certainly don't want to hear about your cases, as you call them." Leona set her leather bag on the foyer table. "And whatever your personal business is, it's no excuse for neglecting your family duties. You put me in a very awkward position with Pamela. I had to make your pathetic excuses."

"You wouldn't have had to make excuses if you hadn't set it up in the first place." He could feel the old arguments bubbling inside him, and he struggled not to fall into the familiar, too-predictable traps. "I'm sorry it put you in an awkward position. Do you want some coffee?"

"What I want, Cade, is an explanation. At Muffy's garden party yesterday—which you also failed to attend—Ronald told me some wild tale about you being engaged to some woman I've never heard of with a connection to the Princess of Wales."

"Bailey." Because he'd all but forgotten her, Cade turned, offered an apologetic smile and held out a hand. "Bailey, come meet my mother."

Oh, good God, was all that came into Bailey's head as she descended the stairs.

"Leona Parris, meet Bailey, my fiancée."

"Mrs. Parris." Bailey's voice trembled a bit as she offered a hand. "How wonderful to meet you. Cade has told me so much about you."

"Really?" Attractive, certainly, Leona mused. Well-groomed, if a bit understated. "He's told me virtually nothing about you, I'm afraid. I don't believe I caught your full name."

"Bailey's only been in the States for a few months." Cade barreled in, all cheer and delight. "I've been keeping her to myself." He slipped an arm around Bailey's shoulders, squeezed possessively. "We've had a whirlwind courtship, haven't we, sweetheart?"

"Yes," Bailey said faintly. "A whirlwind. You could say that."

"And you're a jewelry designer." Lovely rings, Leona noted. Unique and attractive. "A distant cousin of the Princess of Wales."

"Bailey doesn't like to drop names," Cade said quickly. "Sweetheart, maybe you ought to make those calls. Remember the time difference in London."

"Where did you meet?" Leona demanded.

Bailey opened her mouth, struggling to remember if they'd spun this part of the lie for Ronald. "Actually—"

"At the Smithsonian," Cade said smoothly. "In front of the Hope Diamond. I was researching a case, and Bailey was sketching designs. She looked so intent and artistic. It took me twenty minutes of fast-talking and following her around—remember how you threatened to call the security guard, sweetheart? But I finally charmed her into having a cup of coffee with me. And speaking of coffee—"

"This is just ridiculous," Bailey said, interrupting him. "Absolutely ridiculous. Cade, this is your mother, and I'm just not having it." She turned, faced Leona directly. "We did not meet in the Smithsonian, and the Princess of Wales is not my cousin. At least I seriously doubt it. I met Cade on Friday morning, when I went to his office to hire him. I needed a private investigator because I have amnesia, a blue diamond and over a million dollars in cash."

Leona waited ten humming seconds while her foot tapped. Then her lips firmed. "Well, I can see neither of you intends to tell the simple truth. As you prefer to make up outrageous fabrications, I can only presume that you're perfectly suited to one another."

She snatched up her bag and marched to the door with outraged dignity in every step. "Cade, I'll wait to hear from you when you decide to grant me the courtesy of the simple truth."

While Bailey simply stared, Cade grinned like a fool at the door his mother had closed with a snap.

"I don't understand. I did tell her the truth."

"And now I know what they mean by 'the truth shall set you free.'" He let out a whooping laugh, swung her back up into his arms. "She's so ticked off now she'll leave me alone for a week. Maybe two." He gave Bailey an enthusiastic kiss as he headed for the stairs. "I'm crazy about you. Who would have thought telling her the real story would have gotten her off my back?"

Still laughing, he carried her into the bedroom and dropped her on the mattress. "We've got to celebrate. I've got some champagne chilled. I'm going to get you drunk again."

Pushing her hair out of her face, she sat up. "Cade, she's your mother. This is shameful."

"No, it's survival." He leaned over, gave her a smacking kiss this time. "And, sweetheart, we're both black sheep now. I can't tell you how much more fun that's going to be for me."

"I don't think I want to be a black sheep," she called as he headed out again.

"Too late." His laughter echoed back to her.

# Chapter 9

They did make it out to dinner. But they settled for grilled burgers and potatoes fried in peanut oil at a country fair in rural Maryland. He'd thought about a romantic little restaurant, then a fight through the teeming crowds downtown for the huge fireworks display.

Then inspiration had struck. Ferris wheels and shooting galleries. Live music, whirling lights, the flash of fireflies in a nearby field, with fireworks to top it off.

It was, he thought, the perfect first date.

When he told her just that, while she clung to him with screams locked in her throat on the whizzing car of the Tilt-A-Whirl, she laughed, shut her eyes tight and hung on for her life.

He wanted to ride everything, and he pulled her along from line to line, as eager as any of the children tugging on an indulgent parent's hand. She was spun, shaken, twirled and zoomed until her head revolved and her stomach flopped.

Then he tilted her face upward for inspection, declared that since she wasn't turning green yet they could do it all again.

So they did.

"Now, you need a prize," he decided as she staggered off the Octopus.

"No more cotton candy. I'm begging you."

"I was thinking more of an elephant." He hooked an arm around her waist and headed toward the shooting gallery. "That big purple one up there."

It was three feet tall, with a turned-up trunk and toenails painted a bright pink. An elephant. The thought of elephants made her smile bloom brilliantly.

"Oh, it's wonderful." She grinned, fluttered her lashes at Cade. "I want it."

"Then it's my job to get it for you. Just stand back, little lady." He plunked down bills, chose his weapon. Cheery-faced rabbits and ducks rolled by, with the occasional wolf or bear rearing up at odd moments to threaten. Cade sighted the air gun and fired.

Bailey grinned, then applauded, then gaped as wildlife died in droves. "You didn't miss once." She goggled at him. "Not once."

Her wide-eyed admiration made him feel like a teenager showing off for the prom queen. "She wants the elephant," he told the attendant, then laughed when she launched herself into his arms.

"Thank you. You're wonderful. You're amazing."

Since each statement was punctuated by eager kisses, he thought she might like the floppy-eared brown dog, as well. "Want another?"

"Man, you're killing me here," the attendant muttered, then sighed as Cade pulled out more bills.

"Want to give it a try?" Cade offered the rifle to Bailey.

"Maybe." She bit her lip and studied her prey. It had looked simple enough when Cade did it. "All right."

"Just sight through the little V at the end of the barrel," he began, stepping behind her to adjust her stance.

"I see it." She held her breath and pulled the trigger. The little pop had her jolting, but the ducks swam on, and the rabbits continued to hop. "Did I miss?"

"Only by a mile or so." And he was dead certain the woman had never held a gun in her life. "Try again."

She tried again, and again. By the time she'd managed to nip a few feathers and ruffle some fur, Cade had put twenty dollars back in the attendant's grateful hands.

"It looked so easy when you did it."

"That's okay, sweetheart, you were getting the hang of it. What'd she win?"

The attendant perused his lowest row of prizes, generally reserved for children under twelve, and came up with a small plastic duck.

"I'll take it." Delighted, she tucked it in the pocket of her slacks. "My first trophy."

With hands linked, they strolled the midway, listening to the screams, the distant music of a bluegrass band, the windy whirl of rides. She loved the lights, the carnival colors, bright as jewels in the balmy night. And the smells of frying oil, of spun sugar and spiced sauces.

It seemed so easy, as if there couldn't be any trouble in the world—only lights and music and laughter.

"I don't know if I've ever been to a country carnival before," she told him. "But if I have, this one is the best."

"I still owe you a candlelight dinner."

She turned her head to smile at him. "I'll settle for another ride on the Ferris wheel."

"Sure you're up to it?"

"I want to go around again. With you."

She stood in line, flirted with a toddler who kept his head on his father's shoulder and peeked at her with huge blue eyes. She wondered if she was good with children, if she'd ever had a chance to be. And, laying her head on Cade's shoulder, dreamed a little.

If this was just a normal night in normal lives, they could be here together like this. His hand would be in hers, just like this, and they wouldn't have a care in the world. She'd be afraid of nothing. Her life would be as full and rich and bright as a carnival.

What was wrong with pretending it was, and could be, for just one night?

She climbed into the rocking car beside him, snuggled close. And rose into the sky. Beneath, people swarmed across the grass. Teenagers strutted, older couples strolled, children raced. The scents rose up on the wind, an evocative mix she could have breathed in forever.

The downward rush was fast and exciting, making her hair fly out and her stomach race to catch up. Tilting her head upward, she closed her eyes and prepared for the upward swing.

Of course, he kissed her. She'd wanted that, too, that sweet, innocent meeting of lips as they circled over the high summer grass, with the lights around them a rainbow gleam.

They circled again as the first fireworks spewed gold across a black sky.

"It's beautiful." She settled her head on his shoulder. "Like jewels tossed in the sea. Emeralds, rubies, sapphires."

The colors shot upward, fountained and faded on a booming crash. Below, people applauded and whistled, filled the air with noise. Somewhere a baby wailed.

"He's frightened," she murmured. "It sounds like gun-shots, or thunder."

"My father used to have an English setter who'd hide under his bed every Fourth." Cade toyed with her fingers as he watched the show. "Trembled for hours once the fire-works got going."

"It's so loud, scary if you don't know what it is." A bril-liant flash of gold and sparkling diamonds erupted as they topped the wheel in a rush. Her heart began to race, her head to throb. It was the noise, that was all. The noise, and the sickening way the car rocked as the Ferris wheel jerked to a halt to unload passengers.

"Bailey?" He drew her closer, watching her face. She was trembling now, her cheeks white, her eyes dark.

"I'm all right. Just a little queasy."

"We'll be off soon. Just a couple more cars."

"I'm all right." But the lights flashed again, shattering the sky. And the image rolled into her head like thunder.

"He threw up his hands." She managed a whisper. She couldn't see the lights now, the colored diamonds scattered across the sky. The memory blinded her to everything else. "Threw them up to try to grab the knife. I couldn't scream. I couldn't scream. I couldn't move. There was only the desk light. Just that one beam of light. They're like shad-ows, and they're screaming, but I can't. Then the lightning flashed. It's so bright, just that one instant, so bright the room's alight with it. And he... Oh, God, his throat. He slashed his throat."

She turned her face into Cade's shoulder. "I don't want to see that. I can't bear to see that."

"Let it go. Just hold on to me and let it go. We're get-ting off now." He lifted her out of the car, all but carried her across the grass. She was shuddering as if the air had turned icy, and he could hear sobs choking her. "It can't hurt you now, Bailey. You're not alone now."

He wound his way through the field where cars were parked, swore each time a boom of gunpowder made her jerk. She curled up in the seat, rocking herself for comfort while he skirted the hood and got quickly behind the wheel.

"Cry it out," he told her, and turned the key. "Scream if you want to. Just don't let it eat at you like this."

Because he didn't make her feel ashamed, she wept a little, then rested her throbbing head against the seat as he drove down the winding road and back toward the city.

"I keep seeing jewels," she said at length. Her voice was raw, but steady. "Beautiful gemstones. Floods of them. Lapis and opals, malachite and topaz. All different shapes, cut and uncut. I can pick out each one. I know what they are, how they feel in my hand. There's a long piece of chalcedony, smooth to the touch and sword-shaped. It sits on a desk like a paperweight. And this lovely rutilated quartz with silvery threads running through it like shooting stars. I can see them. They're so familiar."

"They make you happy, comfortable."

"Yes, I think they do. When I think of them, when they drift back into my head, it's pleasant. Soothing. There's an elephant. Not this one." She hugged the plush toy against her for comfort. "Soapstone, carved with a jeweled blanket over its back and bright blue eyes. He's so regal and foolish."

She paused a moment, tried to think past the headache pounding in her temples. "There are other stones, all manner of others, but they don't belong to me. Still, they soothe. It doesn't frighten me at all to think of them. Even the blue diamond. It's such a beautiful thing. Such a miracle of nature. It's amazing, really, that just the right elements, the right minerals, the right pressure and the right amount of time can join together to create something so special.

"They're arguing about them. About it," she continued, squeezing her eyes shut to try to bring it back. "I can hear them, and I'm angry and feeling righteous. I can almost see myself marching toward that room where they're arguing, and I'm furious and satisfied. It's such an odd combination of feelings. And I'm afraid, a little. I've done something... I don't know."

She strained toward it, fisting her hands. "Something rash or impulsive, or even foolish. I go to the door. It's open, and their voices echo outside. I go to the door, and I'm trembling inside. It's not all fear, I don't think it's just fear. Some of it's temper. I close my hand over the stone. It's in my pocket, and I feel better with my hand on it. The canvas bag's there, on the table by the door. It's open, too, and I can see the money inside. I pick it up while they shout at each other."

The lights as they slipped from suburb to city made her eyes water. She closed them again. "They don't know I'm there. They're so intent on each other, they don't notice me. Then I see the knife in his hand, the curved blade gleaming. And the other one throws up his hands to grab it. They struggle over it, and they're out of the light now, struggling. But I see blood, and one of the shadows staggers. The other moves in. He doesn't stop. Just doesn't stop. I'm frozen there, clutching the bag, watching. The lights go off, all at once, and it's totally dark. Then the lightning flashes, fills the sky. It's suddenly so bright. When he slices the knife again, over his throat, he sees me. He sees me, and I run."

"Okay, try to relax." The traffic was murder, choked and impatient. He couldn't take her hand, draw her close, comfort her. "Don't push it now, Bailey. We'll deal with this at home."

"Cade, they're the same person," she murmured, and let out a sound somewhere between a moan and a laugh. "They're the same."

He cursed the clogged streets, hunted for an opening and shot around a station wagon with inches to spare. "The same as what?"

"Each other. They're the same person. But that can't be. I know that can't be, because one's dead and one isn't. I'm afraid I'm going crazy."

Symbols again, he wondered, or truth? "How are they the same?"

"They have the same face."

She carried the stuffed elephant into the house, clutching it to her as if it were a lifeline to reality. Her mind felt musty, caught between dreams, with a sly headache hovering at the corners waiting to pounce.

"I want you to lie down. I'll make you some tea."

"No, I'll make it. I'll feel better if I'm doing something. Anything. I'm sorry. It was such a wonderful evening." In the kitchen, she set the smiling elephant on the table. "Until."

"It was a wonderful evening. And whatever helps jiggle more pieces in place is worth it. It hurts you." He took her shoulders. "And *I'm* sorry, but you have to get through the rest of it to get where we want to be."

"I know." She lifted a hand to his, squeezed briefly, then turned to put the kettle on the stove. "I'm not going to fall apart, Cade, but I'm afraid I may not be stable." Pressing her fingers to her eyes, she laughed. "Funny statement coming from someone who can't remember her own name."

"You're remembering more all the time, Bailey. And you're the most stable woman I've ever met."

"Then I'm worried about you, too, and your choice of women."

She set cups precisely on their saucers, concentrating on the simple task. Tea bags, spoons, sugar bowl.

In the maple tree, the wood thrush had given over to a whippoorwill, and the song was like liquid silver. She thought of honeysuckle burying a chain-link fence, perfuming the evening air while the night bird called for his mate.

And a young girl weeping under a willow tree.

She shook herself. A childhood memory, perhaps, bittersweet. She thought those vignettes of the past would be coming more quickly now. And she was afraid.

"You have questions." She set the tea on the table, steadied herself and looked at him. "You're not asking them because you're afraid I'll crumble. But I won't. I wish you'd ask them, Cade. It's easier when you do."

"Let's sit down." He pulled out a chair for her, took his time stirring sugar into his tea. "The room has gray carpet, a window, a table by the door. There's a desk lamp. What does the desk look like?"

"It's a satinwood library desk, George III." She set her cup back down with a rattle. "Oh, that was clever. I never expected you to ask about the desk, so I didn't think, and it was just there."

"Concentrate on the desk, Bailey. Describe it for me."

"It's a beautiful piece. The top is crossbanded with rosewood that's inlaid with boxwood lines. The sides, even the kneehole, are inlaid with ovals. One side has a long drawer paneled with false fronts. It opens to shelves. It's so clever. The handles are brass, and they're kept well polished."

Baffled, she stared into her tea. "Now I sound like an antique dealer."

No, he thought, just someone who loves beautiful things. And knows that desk very well.

"What's on the desk?"

"The lamp. It's brass, too, with a green glass shade and an old-fashioned chain pull. And there are papers, a neat stack of papers aligned with the corner of the desk. A leather blotter is in the center, and a *briefke* sits there."

"A what?"

"A *briefke*, a little cup of paper for carrying loose stones. They're emeralds, grass green, of varying cuts and carats. There's a jeweler's loupe and a small brass scale. A glass, Baccarat crystal, with ice melting in the whiskey. And… and the knife…" Her breath was strangling, but she forced it free. "The knife is there, carved bone handle, curved blade. It's old, it's beautiful."

"Is someone at the desk?"

"No, the chair's empty." Easier to look away from the knife, to look somewhere else. "It's a dark, pewter-gray leather. Its back is to the window. There's a storm." Her voice hitched. "There's a storm. Lightning, lashing rain. They're shouting over the thunder."

"Where are they?"

"In front of the desk, facing each other."

He pushed her cup aside so that he could take her hand. "What are they saying, Bailey?"

"I don't know. Something about a deposit. Take the deposit, leave the country. It's a bad deal. Too dangerous. His mind's made up."

She could hear the voices. The words were bouncing out of the static of sound, harsh angry phrases.

*Double-crossing son of a bitch.*

*You want to deal with him, you go ahead. I'm out of it.*

*Both of us. Together. No backing out.*

*You take the stones, deal with him. Bailey's suspicious. Not as stupid as you think.*

*You're not walking out with the money and leaving me twisting in the wind.*

"He shoves him back. They're fighting, pushing, shoving, punching. It frightens me how much they hate each other. I don't know how they can despise each other so much, because they're the same."

He didn't want to take her through what had happened next. He had the scene now, the steps. "How are they the same?"

"The same face. Same eyes, dark eyes, dark hair. Everything. Mirror images. Even their voices, the same pitch. They're the same man, Cade. How can they be the same man, unless it didn't happen that way at all—and I've lost not only my memory, but my mind?"

"You're not looking at the simple, Bailey. At the simple and the obvious." His smile was grim, his eyes glowed. "Twins."

"Twins? Brothers?" Everything in her, every part of her being, was repelled. She could only shake her head, and continued to shake it until the movement was frantic. "No, no, no." She couldn't accept that. Wouldn't. "That's not it. That can't be it."

She pushed back from the table abruptly, her chair scraping harshly on the tile. "I don't know what I saw." Desperate now to block it out, she grabbed her cup, slopping tea on the table before she carried it to the sink and dumped it down the drain. "It was dark. I don't know what I saw."

Didn't want to know what she'd seen, Cade concluded. Wasn't ready to know. And he wasn't willing to risk playing analyst until she'd regrouped.

"Put it away for now. It's been a rough day, you need some rest."

"Yes." Her mind was screaming for peace, for oblivion. But she was terrified of sleep, and the dreams that would come with it. She turned, pressed herself against him. "Make love with me. I don't want to think. I just want you to love me."

"I do." He met her seeking mouth with his. "I will."

He led her out of the kitchen, stopping on the way to kiss, to touch. At the base of the stairs, he unbuttoned her blouse, skimmed his hands up her narrow rib cage, then cupped her breasts.

On a broken gasp, she clutched her hands in his hair and dragged his mouth down to hers.

He'd wanted to be gentle, tender. But her lips were wild and desperate. He understood that it was the wild and desperate she needed. And let himself go.

He tore the bra aside, watched the shock and arousal flare in her eyes. When his hands possessed this time, they were greedy and rough.

"There's a lot I haven't shown you." He sought the delicate curve between neck and shoulder. Bit. A lot no one had shown her, he thought with a wild spurt of sheer lust. "You may not be ready."

"Show me." Her head fell back, and her pulse scrambled like frightened birds. And fear was suddenly liberating. "I want you to."

He dragged her slacks down her hips, and plunged his fingers inside her. Her nails bit into his shoulders as she rocked on that swift, stunning peak. The whimper in her throat became a cry that was both fear and joy.

His breath hissed out as he watched her fly up, fly over. The dazed shock in her eyes brought him a dark thrill. She was helpless now, if he wanted her helpless.

And he did.

He peeled away layers of clothes, his hands quick and sure. When she was naked and quivering, his lips curved.

He traced his thumbs over her nipples until her eyes fluttered closed.

"You belong to me." His voice was thick, rough, compelling. "I need to hear you say it. For now, you belong to me."

"Yes." She would have told him anything. Promised her soul, if that was what he asked of her. This was no lazy river now, but a flood of heaving sensations. She wanted to drown in them. "More."

He gave more. His mouth raced down her body, then fixed greedily on the core of heat.

She swayed, quaked, exploded. Colors burst in her head—carnival lights and jewels, stars and rainbows. Her back pressed into the railing, and her hands gripped at it for balance while her world spun like a carousel gone mad.

Then pleasure, the sharp edge of it tipped toward pain. At that point, between glory and devastation, her body simply shattered.

He pulled her into his arms, darkly pleased that she was limp. Leaving her clothes where they lay, cradling her, he mounted the steps. His bed this time, he thought with a restless, lustful need to claim her there.

He fell to the bed with her, let the fire inside him rage.

It was unbearable. Glorious. His hands, his mouth, destroyed her, rebuilt her. Sweat dewed her skin, slickening it. And, when he'd dragged his clothes away, slickening his. Her body arched and bucked, straining for more, moving eagerly against each new demand.

When he yanked her to her knees, she wrapped herself around him eagerly, bowing back when his head lowered once more to suckle her breast. And when her head touched the mattress, her body bridged, he buried himself deep inside her.

Her moan was low and throaty, a mindless sound as he

gripped her hips, braced them. With his own heart screaming in his chest, he drove them both hard and fast. No thoughts, no doubts, nothing but the hot, frenzied joining.

There was moonlight on her face, glinting in her hair, glowing on her damp skin. Even as his vision grayed, he fixed the picture of her in his mind. Locked it there, as the dark pleasure peaked and he emptied himself into her.

He waited until he was sure she slept. For a time, he simply watched her, bewitched by her and what they'd brought to each other. No woman he'd touched, no woman who had touched him, had ever reached so deep inside him, held his heart so close and fast.

He'd demanded that she tell him she belonged to him. It was no less true that he belonged to her. The miracle of it humbled him.

He touched his lips to her temple. When he left her, she was sprawled on her stomach, one arm flung out where he had lain beside her. He hoped exhaustion would tranquilize her dreams. He left the door open so that he could hear if she cried out in sleep, or called for him.

He took time to brew a pot of coffee and carried it with him into the library. He gave his computer one grim sneer before booting it up. The clock in the corner chimed midnight, then bonged the half hour before he found his rhythm.

In hardly twice the time it would have taken a ten-year-old hacker, the information he was searching for flashed up on the screen.

Gem experts. The greater metropolitan area.

He scrolled through, keeping his senses alert with caffeine, fumbled for a moment in engaging the printer for hard copy.

Boone and Son.

Kleigmore Diamond Consultants.

Landis Jewelry Creations.

His computer provided him with more detailed information than the phone book. For once he blessed technology. He scanned the data, names, dates, then continued to scroll.

Salvini.

Salvini. His eyes narrowed as he skimmed the data. Appraisers and gemologists. Estate jewelry and antiquities a specialty. Established in 1952 by Charles Salvini, now deceased.

Certified and bonded. Consultants to museums and private collectors. Personalized designs, repairs and remounting. All work done on premises.

A Chevy Chase address, he mused. The location was close enough. The firm was respected, had earned a triple-A rating. Owners Thomas and Timothy Salvini.

T.S., he thought on a quick spurt of excitement. Brothers. Bingo.

# *Chapter 10*

"Just take your time."

Bailey took a deep breath and struggled to be as calm and precise as Cade wanted. "Her nose is sharper than that. I think."

The police artist's name was Sara, and she was young and patient. Skilled, Bailey had no doubt, or Cade wouldn't have called on her. She sat at the kitchen table with her sketch pad and pencils, a cup of steaming coffee at her elbow.

"More like this?" With a few quick strokes, Sara honed down the nose.

"Yes, I think so. Her eyes are bigger, sort of tilted up."

"Almond-shaped?" Sara whisked the gum eraser over the pencil strokes, adjusted for size and shape.

"I suppose. It's hard to see it all in my head."

"Just give me impressions." Sara's smile was easy and relaxed. "We'll go from there."

"It seems the mouth is wide, softer than the rest of the face. Everything else is angles."

"Quite a face," Cade commented as Sara sketched. "Interesting. Sexy."

As Bailey continued to instruct, he studied the image. Angular face, carelessly short hair with long, spiky bangs, with dark, dramatically arched eyebrows peeking through. Exotic and tough, he decided, and tried to hook a personality with the features.

"That's very close to what I remember." Bailey took the sketch Sara offered. She knew this face, she thought, and looking at it brought competing urges to smile and to weep.

M.J. Who was M.J., and what had they shared?

"You want to take a break?" Cade asked and lowered his hands to Bailey's shoulders to rub away the tension.

"No, I'd like to keep at it. If you don't mind," she said to Sara.

"Hey, I can do this all day. Long as you keep the coffee coming." She held her empty mug up to Cade, with a quick smile that told Bailey they knew each other well.

"You— Ah, it's interesting work," Bailey began.

Sara tossed a long ginger-colored braid behind her back. Her outfit was both cool and casual, denim cutoffs and a plain white tank, the combination straight-up sexy.

"It's a living," she told Bailey. "Computers are slowly putting me out of business. It's amazing what they can do with imaging. But a lot of cops and P.I.'s still prefer sketches." She took her refilled mug back from Cade. "Parris here, he'll do most anything to avoid a computer."

"Hey, I'm getting the hang of it."

Sara snickered. "When you do, I'll be making my living doing caricatures in bars." She shrugged, sipped, then picked up a fresh pencil. "Want to try for the other?"

"Yes, all right." Telling herself not to focus on just how

well Cade and Sara knew each other, Bailey closed her eyes and concentrated.

*Grace.* She let the name cruise through her mind, bring up the image.

"Soft," she began. "There's a softness to her face. It's very beautiful, almost unbelievably so. It's an oval face, very classic. Her hair's ink black, very long. It sort of spills down her back in loose waves. No bangs, just a flow of dark, thick silk. Her eyes are wide, heavy-lidded and thickly lashed. Laser-blue eyes. The nose is short and straight. Think perfect."

"I'm starting to hate her," Sara said lightly, and made Bailey smile.

"It must be hard to be wildly beautiful, don't you think? People only look at the surface."

"I think I could live with it. How about the mouth?"

"Lush. Full."

"Natch."

"Yes, that's good." Excitement began to drum. The sketch was coming together quickly. "The eyebrows are a little fuller, and there's a mole beside the left one. Just here," Bailey said, pointing to her own face.

"Now I really hate her," Sara muttered. "I don't want to know if she's got the body to match this face. Tell me she's got Dumbo ears."

"No, I'm afraid not." Bailey smiled at the sketch and felt warm and weepy again. "She's just beautiful. It startles the eye."

"She looks familiar."

At Sara's careless comment, Bailey tensed. "Does she? Really?"

"I'd swear I've seen this face before." Pursing her lips, Sara tapped her pencil against the sketch. "In a magazine, maybe. She looks like someone who'd model—pricey perfume or face cream. You got a million-dollar face, you'd be crazy not to use it."

"A model." Bailey bit her lip, fought to remember. "I just don't know."

Sara tore off the sheet, handed it to Cade. "What do you think?"

"A heart-stopper," he said after a moment. "The gene fairy was in one hell of a good mood when she was born. I can't place it, though, and that's a face no man with a pulse would forget."

Her name is Grace, Bailey told herself. And she's more than beautiful. She's not just a face.

"Good work, Sara." Cade laid the two sketches together on the counter. "Got time for one more?"

Sara took a quick look at her watch. "I've got about a half hour to spare."

"The man, Bailey." Cade crouched down until they were eye to eye. "You know what he looks like now."

"I don't—"

"You do." He said it firmly, though his hands were gentle on her arms. "It's important. Just tell Sara how you see him."

It would hurt, Bailey realized. Her stomach muscles were already clenched at the thought of letting that face back into her head. "I don't want to see him again."

"You want the answers. You want it over. This is a step. You've got to take the steps."

She closed her eyes, shifted. Her head began to throb as she put herself back in that room with the gray carpet and the storm-lashed window.

"He's dark," she said quietly. "His face is long, narrow. It's tight with anger. His mouth is grim with temper. It's thin and strong and stubborn. His nose is slightly hooked. Not unattractive, but strong again. It's a very strong face. His eyes are deep-set. Dark. Dark eyes."

Flashing with fury. There was murder in them. She shuddered, hugged her elbows and fought to concentrate.

"Hollowed cheeks and high forehead. His eyebrows are dark and straight. So's his hair. It's well cut, full at the top, very precisely trimmed around the ears. It's a very handsome face. The jaw spoils it a little, it's soft, slightly weak."

"Is that him, Bailey?" Cade put a hand on her shoulder again, squeezed lightly in support.

Braced, she opened her eyes and looked at the sketch. It wasn't precise. It wasn't perfect. The eyes should be a bit farther apart, the mouth slightly fuller. But it was enough to have her trembling.

"Yes, it's very like him." Mustering all her control, she rose slowly. "Excuse me," she murmured, and walked out of the room.

"The lady's terrified," Sara commented, sliding her pencils back in their case.

"I know."

"Are you going to tell me what kind of trouble she's in?"

"I'm not sure." Cade dipped his hands in his pockets. "But I'm close to finding out. You did good work, Sara. I owe you."

"I'll bill you." She gathered her tools and rose. She kissed him lightly, studied his face. "I don't think you're going to be calling me up for a night on the town anymore."

"I'm in love with her," he said simply.

"Yeah, I got that." She shouldered her bag, then touched his cheek. "I'm going to miss you."

"I'll be around."

"You'll be around," she agreed. "But those wild and wacky days are over for you, Parris. I like her. Hope you work it out." With a last wistful smile, she turned. "I know the way out."

He walked her out anyway, and closing the door, realized

he was indeed shutting off a part of his life. The freedom of coming and going as he pleased, with whom he pleased. Late nights in a club, with the prospect of friendly, unfettered sex to follow. Responsible to no one but himself.

He glanced up the stairs. She was up there. Responsibility, stability, commitment. One woman from now throughout the rest of his life—a troubled woman, one who had yet to say the words he needed to hear, to make the promises he needed made.

He could still walk away, and she wouldn't blame him. In fact, he was sure that was exactly what she'd expected. It made him wonder who had left her before.

With a shake of his head, he climbed the stairs to her without the slightest regret.

She was standing in the bedroom, looking out the window. Her hands were clasped in front of her, her back was to the door.

"Are you all right?"

"Yes. I'm sorry, I was rude to your friend. I didn't even thank her."

"Sara understands."

"You've known her a long time."

"A few years, yeah."

Bailey swallowed. "You've been together."

Cade lifted a brow, decided against moving to her. "Yeah, we've been together. I've been with other women, Bailey. Women I've liked, cared for."

"Knew." She turned on the word, and her eyes were fierce.

"Knew," he agreed with a nod.

"This is out of sync." She dragged her hands through her hair. "You and me, Cade, it's out of sync with the rest of it. It should never have happened."

"It did happen." He stuck his hands in his pockets, because they'd tensed, wanted to fist. "Are you going to stand there and tell me you're upset because you've met a woman I've slept with? Because I didn't come to you the same way you came to me?"

"Blank." The word shot out of her like a bullet. "You didn't come to me blank. You have family, friends, lovers. A life. I have nothing but pieces that don't fit. I don't care if you've slept with a hundred women." Her voice snapped on that, then whispered fiercely on the rest. "It's that you remember them. Can remember them."

"You want me to tell you they don't matter?" His temper began to inch up, nudged by panic. She was pulling back, pulling away. "Of course they mattered. I can't blank out my past for you, Bailey."

"I wouldn't want you to." She covered her face with her hands for a moment as she fought for even a slippery grip on control. She'd made up her mind. Now she just had to be strong enough to follow through. "I'm sorry. Your private life before I came into it isn't my business, or even the point. The point is, you had one, Cade."

"So did you."

"So did I." She nodded, thinking that was precisely what frightened her. "I never would have gotten this close to finding it without you. But I realize I should have gone to the police straightaway. I've only complicated things by not doing so. But that's what I'm going to do now."

"You don't trust me to finish this?"

"That's not the issue—"

"Damn right it's not," he told her. "This isn't about going to the cops. It's about you and me. You think you can walk out of here and away from what's between us." His hands shot out of his pockets, grabbed her arms. "Think again."

"Someone's dead. I'm involved." Her teeth threatened to chatter as she fought to keep her eyes level with his. "And I shouldn't have involved you."

"It's too late for that now. It was too late the minute you walked into my office. You're not shaking me off." When his mouth crushed down on hers, the kiss tasted of frustration and fury. He held her close, blocking any choice, ravaging her mouth until her hands went limp on his shoulders.

"Don't," she managed when he lifted her off her feet. But that, too, was too late. She was pressed beneath him on the bed, every sense scrambling and screaming as his hands streaked over her.

"I don't give a damn what you forget." Eyes dark and reckless, he dragged at her clothes. "You'll remember this."

He spun her out of control, out of time, out of place. There was a wildness and willfulness here that she'd never experienced and couldn't resist. His mouth closed over her breast, stabbing pleasure through her. Even as she sucked in air to moan, his fingers pierced her and drove her ruthlessly to peak.

She cried out, not in alarm, not in protest, but with the staggered thrill of being plunged beyond reason. Her nails bit into his back, her body moved like lightning under his. She opened herself to him recklessly. The only thought in her head was, *Now, now, now.*

He drove himself into her hard and deep, felt her clutch convulsively around him as she flew over the new crest. It was mindless, desperate. It was wrong. It was irresistible.

He gripped her hands in his, watched pleasure chase shock across her face. The animal inside him had broken free, and it clawed at both of them. So his mouth was rough as it savaged hers. And he pistoned himself inside her until she wept out his name and what was left of his mind shattered.

Empty, hollowed out, he collapsed on her. Her body shuddered under his as a catchy whimper sounded in her throat. Her hands lay, palm out and limp, on the rumpled spread. His mind began to clear enough for shame.

He'd never taken a woman so roughly. Never given a woman so little choice. He rolled away from her, stared at the ceiling, appalled by what he'd found inside himself.

"I'm sorry." It was pathetic, that phrase. The uselessness of it scraped at him as he sat up, rubbed his hands over his face. "I hurt you. I'm sorry. There's no excuse for it." And, finding none, he rose and left her alone.

She managed to sit up, one hand pressed to her speeding heart. Her body felt weak, tingly and still pulsingly hot. Her mind remained fuzzy around the edges, even as she patiently waited for it to clear. The only thing she was certain of was that she had just been savaged. Overwhelmed by sensation, by emotion, by him.

It had been wonderful.

Cade gave her time to compose herself. And used the time to formulate his next steps. It was so difficult to think around fury. He'd been angry before. Hurt before. Ashamed before. But when she came down the stairs, looking tidy and nervous, those three emotions threatened to swamp him. "Are you all right?"

"Yes. Cade, I—"

"You'll do what you want." He interrupted her in a voice that was both cool and clipped. "And so will I. I apologize again for treating you that way."

She felt her stomach sink to her knees. "You're angry with me."

"With both of us. I can deal with myself, but first I have to deal with you. You want to walk out."

"It's not what I want." There was a plea for understanding in her voice. "It's what's right. I've made you an accessory to God knows what."

"You hired me."

She let out an impatient breath. How could he be so blind and stubborn? "It hasn't been a professional relationship, Cade. It barely started as one."

"That's right. It's personal, and you're not walking out on me out of some misguided sense of guilt. You want to walk for other reasons, we'll get into them after this is done. I love you." There was chilly fury over the words that only deepened the emotion behind them. "If you don't, can't or won't love me, I'll have to live with it. But walking out at this point's just not an option."

"I only want—"

"You want to go to the cops." He paused a moment, hooked his thumbs in his front pockets to keep his hands from reaching for her. "That's fine, it's your choice. But meanwhile, you hired me to do a job, and I'm not finished. Whatever your personal feelings, or mine, I intend to finish. Get your purse."

She wasn't sure how to handle him now. Then again, she realized, had she ever known? Still, this cold, angry man standing in front of her was much more of a stranger than the one she had first seen in a cluttered, messy office only days before.

"The appointment at the Smithsonian," she began.

"I've postponed it. We have somewhere else to go first."

"Where?"

"Get your purse," he repeated. "We're taking this next step my way."

He didn't speak on the drive. She recognized some of the buildings. They'd ridden past them before. But when he drove out of D.C. and into Maryland, her nerves began to jump.

"I wish you'd tell me where we're going." The trees were too close to the road, she thought, panicky. Too green, too big.

"Back," he said. "Sometimes you've just got to open the door and look at what's on the other side."

"We need to talk to the curator at the museum." Her throat was closing. She'd have bartered her soul for a glass of water. "We should turn around and go back to the city."

"You know where we're going?"

"No." The denial was sharp, desperate. "No, I don't."

He only flicked a glance at her out of sharp green eyes. "The pieces are there, Bailey."

He turned left, off the main drag, listening to her breathing coming short and labored. Ruthlessly he repressed his instinct to soothe. She was stronger than he'd pretended she was. He could admit that. And she would get through this. He'd help her get through it.

If the place was being watched, he was bringing her out in the open. He had to weigh the possibility of that against doing his job. She'd hired him to solve the puzzle, he reminded himself. And this, he was sure, was the last piece.

She couldn't continue to live in the safe little world he'd provided for her. It was time, for both of them, to move forward.

Setting his jaw, he pulled into the lot at Salvini.

"You know where we are."

Her skin was clammy. In long, restless strokes, she rubbed her damp palms over the knees of her slacks. "No, I don't."

The building was brick, two stories. Old, rather lovely, with tall display windows flanked by well-established azaleas that would bloom beautifully in the spring. There was an elegance to the place that shouldn't have made her shudder.

There was a single car in the lot. A BMW sedan, dark blue. Its finish gleamed in the sunlight.

The building stood alone, taking up the corner, while behind it, across a vast parking lot, a trendy strip mall seemed to be doing a brisk holiday business.

"I don't want to be here." Bailey turned her head, refusing to look at the sign that topped the building in large, clear letters.

SALVINI

"They're closed," she continued. "There's no one here. We should go."

"There's a car in the lot," Cade pointed out. "It won't hurt to see."

"No." She snatched her hand away from his, tried to bury herself in the corner of the seat. "I'm not going in there. I'm not."

"What's in there, Bailey?"

"I don't know." Terror. Just terror. "I'm not going in."

He would rather have cut out his heart than force her to do what he intended. But, thinking of her, he got out of the car, came around to her side, opened the door. "I'll be with you. Let's go."

"I said I'm not going in there."

"Coward." He said it with a sneer in his voice. "Do you want to hide the rest of your life?"

Fury sparkled off the tears in her eyes as she ripped the seat belt free. "I hate you for this."

"I know," he murmured, but took her arm firmly and led her to the building's front entrance.

It was dark inside. Through the window he could see little but thick carpet and glass displays where gold and stones gleamed dully. It was a small showroom, again elegant, with a few upholstered stools and countertop mirrors where customers might sit and admire their choices.

Beside him, Bailey was shaking like a leaf.

"Let's try the back."

The rear faced the strip mall, and boasted delivery and employee entrances. Cade studied the lock on the employee door and decided he could handle it. From his pocket he took out a leather roll of tools.

"What are you doing?" Bailey stepped back as he chose a pick and bent to his work. "Are you breaking in? You can't do that."

"I think I can manage it. I practice picking locks at least four hours a week. Quiet a minute."

It took concentration, a good touch, and several sweaty minutes. If the alarm was set, he figured, it would go off when he disengaged the first lock. It didn't, and he changed tools and started on the second.

A silent alarm wasn't out of the question, he mused as he jiggled tumblers. If the cops came, he was going to have a lot of explaining to do.

"This is insane." Bailey took another step in retreat. "You're breaking into a store in broad daylight. You can't do this, Cade."

"Did it," he said with some satisfaction as the last tumbler fell. Fastidiously he replaced his tools in the roll, pocketed them. "An outfit like this ought to have a motion alarm in place, as well."

He stepped through the door. In the dim light, he saw the alarm box beside the doorway. Disengaged.

He could almost hear another piece fall into place.

"Careless of them," he murmured. "With the way crime pays."

He took Bailey's hand and pulled her inside. "Nobody's going to hurt you while I'm around. Not even me."

"I can't do this."

"You're doing it." Keeping her hand firm in his, he hit the lights.

It was a narrow room, more of an entranceway with a worn wooden floor and plain white walls. Against the left wall were a watercooler and a brass coatrack. A woman's gray raincoat hung on one of the hooks.

It had called for thunderstorms the previous Thursday, he thought. A practical woman such as Bailey wouldn't have gone to work without her raincoat. "It's yours, isn't it?"

"I don't know."

"Coat's your style. Quality, expensive, subtle." He checked the pockets, found a roll of breath mints, a short grocery list, a pack of tissues. "It's your handwriting," he said, offering her the list.

"I don't know." She refused to look at it. "I don't remember."

He pocketed the list himself, and led her into the next room.

It was a workroom, a smaller version of the one at Westlake. He recognized the equipment now, and deduced that if he took the time to pick the locks on the drawers of a tall wooden cabinet, he would find loose stones. The flood of gems Bailey had described from her dreams. Stones that made her happy, challenged her creativity, soothed her soul.

The worktable was wiped spotlessly clean. Nothing, not the thinnest chain of gold links, was out of place.

It was, he thought, just like her.

"Someone keeps their area clean," he said mildly. Her hand was icy in his as he turned. There were stairs leading up. "Let's see what's behind door number two."

She didn't protest this time. She was too locked in terror to form the words. She winced as he flooded the stairway with light and drew her up with him.

On the second level, the floors were carpeted in pewter gray. Nausea swam in her stomach. The hallway was wide enough for them to walk abreast, and there were gleaming antique tables set at well-arranged spots. Red roses were fading in a silver vase. And the scent of their dying sickened her.

He opened a door, nudged it wider. And knew at first glance that it was her office.

Nothing was out of place. The desk, a pretty, feminine Queen Anne gleamed with polish and care under the light coating of weekend dust. On it was a long, milky crystal, jagged at one end, like a broken blade of a sword. She'd called it chalcedony, he remembered. And the smooth multiangled rock nearby must be the rutilated quartz.

On the walls were dreamy watercolors in thin wooden frames. There was a small table beside a love seat that was thickly upholstered in rose-toned fabric and set off with pale green pillows. On the table stood a small glass vase with drooping violets and pictures framed in polished silver.

He picked up the first. She was about ten, he judged, a little gangly and unformed, but there was no mistaking those eyes. And she'd grown to closely resemble the woman who sat beside her in a porch glider, smiling into the camera.

"It's your past, Bailey." He picked up another photo. Three woman, arms linked, laughing. "You, M.J. and Grace. Your present." He set the picture down, picked up another. The man was golden, handsome, his smile assured and warm.

Her future? he wondered.

"He's dead." The words choked out of her, slicing her heart on the journey. "My father. He's dead. The plane went down in Dorset. He's dead."

"I'm sorry." Cade set the photo down.

"He never came home." She was leaning against the desk, her legs trembling, her heart reeling as too many images crowded their way inside. "He left on a buying trip and never came back. We used to eat ice cream on the porch. He'd show me all the treasures. I wanted to learn. Lovely old things. He smelled of pine soap and beeswax. He liked to polish the pieces himself sometimes."

"He had antiques," Cade said quietly.

"It was a legacy. His father to him, my father to me. Time and Again. The shop. Time and Again. It was so full of beautiful things. He died, he died in England, thousands of miles away. My mother had to sell the business. She had to sell it when…"

"Take it slow, and easy. Just let it come."

"She got married again. I was fourteen. She was still young, she was lonely. She didn't know how to run a business. That's what he said. She didn't know how. He'd take care of things. Not to worry."

She staggered, caught herself. Then her gaze landed on the soapstone elephant with the jeweled blanket on her desk. "M.J. She gave it to me for my birthday. I like foolish things. I collect elephants. Isn't that odd? You picked an elephant for me at the carnival, and I collect them."

She passed a hand over her eyes, tried to hang on. "We laughed when I opened it. Just the three of us. M.J. and Grace and I, just a few weeks ago. My birthday's in June. June nineteenth. I'm twenty-five."

Her head spun as she struggled to focus on Cade. "I'm twenty-five. I'm Bailey James. My name's Bailey Anne James."

Gently Cade eased her into a chair, laid his hand on hers. "Nice to meet you."

# *Chapter 11*

"It's mixed up in my head." Bailey pressed her fingers to her eyes. Visions were rocketing in, zooming through, overlapping and fading before she could gain a firm hold.

"Tell me about your father."

"My father. He's dead."

"I know, sweetheart. Tell me about him."

"He—he bought and sold antiques. It was a family business. Family was everything. We lived in Connecticut. The business started there. Our house was there. He—he expanded. Another branch in New York, one in D.C. His father had established the first one, then my father had expanded. His name was Matthew."

Now she pressed her hand to her heart as it swelled and broke. "It's like losing him all over again. He was the center of the world to me, he and my mother. She couldn't have any more children. I suppose they spoiled me. I loved them so much. We had a willow tree in the backyard. That's where I went when my mother told me about the crash. I went out and sat under the willow tree and tried to make him come back."

"Your mother came and found you?" He was guessing now, prompting her gently through her grief.

"Yes, she came out, and we sat there together for a long time. The sun went down, and we just sat there together. We were lost without him, Cade. She tried, she tried so hard to hold the business together, to take care of me, the house. It was just too much. She didn't know how. She met—she met Charles Salvini."

"This is his building."

"It was." She rubbed her mouth with the back of her hand. "He was a jeweler, specialized in estate and antique pieces. She consulted with him on some of our stock. That's how it started. She was lonely, and he treated her very well. He treated me very well. I admired him. I think he loved her very much, I really do. I don't know if she loved him, but she needed him. I suppose I did, too. She sold what was left of the antique business and married him."

"Was he good to you?"

"Yes, he was. He was a kind man. And like my father, he was scrupulously honest. Honesty in business, in personal matters, was vital. It was my mother he wanted, but I came with the package, and he was always good to me."

"You loved him."

"Yes, it was easy to love him, to be grateful for what he did for me and my mother. He was very proud of the business he'd built up. When I developed an interest in gems, he encouraged it. I apprenticed here, in the summers, and after school. He sent me to college to study. My mother died while I was away in college. I wasn't here. I was away when she died."

"Honey." He gathered her close, tried to soothe. "I'm sorry."

"It was an accident. It happened very fast. A drunk driver, crossed the center line. Hit her head-on. That was it." Grief was fresh again, raw and fresh. "Charles was devastated. He never really recovered. He was older than she by about fifteen years, and when she died, he lost interest in everything. He retired, went into seclusion. He died less than a year later."

"And you were all alone?"

"I had my brothers." She shuddered, gripped Cade's hands. "Timothy and Thomas. Charles's sons. My stepbrothers." She let out a broken sob. "Twins." Her hands jerked in his. "I want to go now. I want to leave here."

"Tell me about your brothers," he said calmly. "They're older than you."

"I want to go. I have to get out."

"They worked here," Cade continued. "They took over the business from your stepfather. You worked here with them."

"Yes, yes. They took over the business. I came to work here when I graduated from Radcliffe. We're family. They're my brothers. They were twenty when their father married my mother. We lived in the same house, we're family."

"One of them tried to kill you."

"No. No." She covered her face again, refused to see it. "It's a mistake. I told you, they're my brothers. My family. We lived together. We work together. Our parents are dead, and we're all that's left. They're impatient or brusque sometimes, but they'd never hurt me. They'd never hurt one another. They couldn't."

"They have offices here? In this building, on this floor?"

She shook her head, but her gaze shifted to the left. "I want you to sit right here. Stay right here, Bailey."

"Where are you going?"

"I need to look." He cupped her face, kept his eyes level with hers. "You know I have to look. Stay here."

She let her head fall back against the cushion, closed her eyes. She would stay. There was nothing she needed to see. Nothing she needed to know. She knew her name now, her family. Wasn't that enough?

But it played back in her head, with an echoing crack of lightning that made her moan.

She hadn't moved when Cade came back into the room, but she opened her eyes. And when she did, she saw it on his face.

"It's Thomas," she said hollowly. "It's Thomas who's dead in his office down the hall."

He didn't wonder that she had blocked out what she'd seen. The attack had been vicious and violent. To witness the cause of the effect in the room he'd just left would have been horrifying. But to watch, from a few feet away, knowing it was one brother savagely slaying another, would have been unspeakable.

"Thomas," she repeated, and let tears fall. "Poor Thomas. He wanted to be the best in everything. He often was. They were never unkind to me. They ignored me a great deal of the time, as older brothers would, I suppose. I know they resented that Charles left me a part of the business, but they tolerated it. And me."

She paused, looked down at her hands. "There's nothing we can do for him, is there?"

"No. I'll get you out of here." He took her hand, helped her to her feet. "We'll call this in."

"They planned to steal the Three Stars of Mithra."

She stood her ground. She could bear it, she promised herself, and she needed to say it all. "We'd been commissioned to verify and assess the three diamonds. Or I had, actually, since that's my field. I often do consults with the Smithsonian. The stars were going to be part of their gem display. They're originally from Persia. They're very old and were once set in a triangle of gold, held in the open hands of a statue of Mithra."

She cleared her throat, spoke calmly now, focused, practical. "He was the ancient Persian god of light and wisdom. Mithraism became one of the major religions of the Roman Empire. He was supposed to have slain the divine bull, and from the bull's dying body sprang all the plants and animals."

"You can tell me in the car."

He urged her to the door, but she simply couldn't move until she'd said it all. "The religion wasn't brought to Rome until 68 B.C., and it spread rapidly. It's similar to Christianity in many respects. The ideals of brotherly love." Her voice broke, forced her to swallow. "The Three Stars were thought to be a myth, a legend spawned by the Trinity, though some scholars believed firmly in their existence, and described them as symbols of love, knowledge and generosity. It's said if one possesses all three, the combination of these elements will bring power and immortality."

"You don't believe that."

"I believe they're powerful enough to bring about great love, great hate, great greed. I found out what my brothers were doing. I realized Timothy was creating duplicates in the lab." She scrubbed at her eyes. "Maybe he could have hidden something like that from me if he'd been more methodical, more careful, but he was always the more impatient of the two, the more reckless." Now her shoulders slumped as she remembered. "He's been in trouble a few times, for assault. His temper is very quick."

"He never hurt you?"

"No, never. He may have hurt my feelings from time to time." She tried a smile, but it faded quickly. "He seemed to feel that my mother had only married his father so that the two of us could be taken care of. It was partially true, I suppose. So it was always important to me to prove myself."

"You proved yourself here," Cade said.

"Not to him. Timothy was never one to praise. But he was never overly harsh, not really. And I never thought he or Thomas would be dishonest. Until we were commissioned to assess the Stars."

"And that was more than they could resist."

"Apparently. The fakes wouldn't fool anyone for very long, but by the time the stones were found out, my brothers would have the money and be gone. I don't know who was paying them, but they were working for someone."

She stopped on the stairs, stared down. "He chased me down here. I was running. It was pitch-dark. I nearly fell down these stairs. I could hear him coming after me. And I knew he'd kill me. We'd shared Christmas dinner every year of my life since I was fourteen. And he would kill me, the same horrible way he'd killed Thomas. For money."

She clutched the railing as she slowly walked down to the lower level. "I loved him, Cade. I loved both of them." At the base of the steps, she turned, gestured to a narrow door. "There's a basement down there. It's very small and cramped. There's where I ran. There's a little nook under the steps, with a lattice door. I used to explore the building when I was young, and I liked sitting in that nook, where it was quiet. I'd study the gem books Charles gave me. I don't suppose Timothy knew it was there. If he'd known, I'd be dead."

She walked into the sunlight.

"I honestly don't remember how long I stayed in there, in the dark, waiting for him to find me and kill me. I don't know how I got to the hotel. I must have walked part of the way, at least. I don't drive to work. I live only a few blocks from here."

He wanted to tell her it was done now, but it wasn't. He wanted to let her rest her head on his shoulder and put it behind her. But he couldn't. Instead, he took her hands, turned her to face him.

"Bailey. Where are the other two stars?"

"The—" She went dead pale, so quickly he grabbed her certain she would faint. But her eyes stayed open, wide and shocked.

"Oh, my God. Oh, my God, Cade, what have I done? He knows where they live. He knows."

"You gave them to M.J. and Grace." Moving fast, he wrenched open the car door. The cops would have to wait. "Tell me where."

"I was so angry," she told him as they sped through afternoon traffic. "I realized they were using me, my name, my knowledge, my reputation, to authenticate the gems. Then they would switch them and leave me—leave the business my stepfather had built—holding the bag. Salvini would have been ruined, after all Charles had done to build it. I owed him loyalty. And, damn it, so did they."

"So you beat them to it."

"It was impulse. I was going to face them down with it, but I wanted the Stars out of reach. At least I thought they shouldn't all be in one place. As long as they were, they could be taken. So I sent one to M.J. and one to Grace, by different overnight couriers."

"Dear Lord, Bailey, you put priceless diamonds in the mail?"

She squeezed her eyes shut. "We use special couriers regularly for delivering gems." Her voice was prim, vaguely insulted. She'd already told herself she'd been unbelievably rash. "All I could think was that there were two people in the world I could trust with anything. I didn't consider they'd be put in danger. I never realized how far it could go. I was certain that when I confronted my brothers, told them I'd separated the diamonds for safekeeping and would be making arrangements to have the diamonds delivered to the museum, that would have to be the end of it."

She hung onto the door as his tires spun around a corner. "It's this building. We're on the third floor. M.J. and I have apartments across from each other."

She was out of the car before he'd fully stopped, and racing toward the entrance. Cursing, he snatched his keys out of the ignition and sprinted after her. He caught her on the stairs. "Stay behind me," he ordered. "I mean it."

Both the lock and the jamb on apartment 324 were broken. Police tape was slashed across it. "M.J." was all she could manage as she pushed at Cade and reached for the knob to M.J.'s apartment.

"There you are, dearie." A woman in pink stretch pants and fluffy slippers scuffed down the hall. "I was getting worried about you."

"Mrs. Weathers." Bailey's knuckles turned white on the knob as she turned. "M.J. What's happened to M.J.?"

"Such a hullabaloo." Mrs. Weathers fluffed her helmet of blond hair and gave Cade a measuring smile. "You don't expect such things in a nice neighborhood like this. The world is going to hell in a handbasket, I swear."

"Where's M.J.?"

"Last I saw, she was running off with some man. Clattering down the steps, swearing at each other. That was after all the commotion. Glass breaking, furniture smashing. Gunshots." She nodded briskly several times, like a bird bobbing for juicy worms.

"Shot? Was M.J. shot?"

"Didn't look shot to me. Mad as a wet hen, and fired up."

"My brother. Was she with my brother?"

"No, indeed. Hadn't even seen this young man before. I'da remembered, I can tell you. He was one tall drink of water, had his hair back in one of those cute little ponytails, and had eyes like steel. Dent in his chin, just like a movie star. I got a good look at him, seeing as he nearly knocked me over."

"When did this happen, Mrs. Weathers?"

She fastened her gaze on Cade's face at the question, beamed and offered a hand. "I don't believe we've been introduced."

"I'm Cade, a friend of Bailey's." He flashed a grin back at her while impatience twisted his stomach. "We've been away for a few days and wanted to catch up with M.J."

"Well, I haven't seen hide nor hair of her since Saturday, when she went running out. Left the door of her apartment wide-open—or I thought she had till I saw it was broken. So I peeked in. Her place was a wreck. I know she's not the housekeeper you are, Bailey, but it was upside down and sideways, and..." She paused dramatically. "There was a man laid out cold on the floor. Big bruiser of a man, too. So I skedaddled back to my apartment and called the police. What else could I do? I guess he'd come to and cleared out by the time they got here. Lord knows I didn't put a toe out the door until the cops came knocking, and they said he was gone."

Cade slipped an arm around Bailey's waist. She was starting to tremble. "Mrs. Weathers, I wonder if you might have an extra key to Bailey's apartment. She left it back at my place, and we need to pick up a few things."

"Oh, is that the way of it?" She smiled slyly, fluffed her hair again and admonished Bailey. "And high time, too. Holing yourself up here, night after night. Now, let's see. I just watered Mr. Hollister's begonias, so I've got my keys right here. Here you are."

"I don't remember giving you my key."

"Of course you did, dearie, last year when you and the girls went off to Arizona. I made a copy, just in case." Humming to herself, she unlocked Bailey's door. Before she could push it open and scoot in, Cade outmaneuvered her.

"Thanks a lot."

"No trouble. Can't imagine where that girl got off to," she said, craning her neck to see through the crack in the door of Bailey's apartment. "I told the police how she was running off on her own steam. Oh, and now that I think about it, Bailey, I did see your brother."

"Timothy," Bailey whispered.

"Can't say which one for sure. They look like clones to me. He came by, let's see." She tapped a finger on her front teeth, as if to jiggle the thought free. "Must have been Saturday night. I told him I hadn't seen you, that I thought you might have taken a holiday. He looked a little perturbed. Let himself right in, then closed the door in my face."

"I didn't realize he had a key, either," Bailey murmured, then realized she'd left her purse behind when she ran. She wondered how foolishly useless it would be to change her locks. "Thank you, Mrs. Weathers. If I miss M.J. again, will you tell her I'm looking for her?"

"Of course, dearie. Now, if you—" She frowned as Cade gave her a quick wink, slid Bailey inside and shut the door in her face.

It was just as well he had. One glance around told him his tidy Bailey didn't usually leave her apartment with cushions ripped open and drawers spilled out.

Apparently Salvini hadn't been content to search the place, he'd wanted to destroy it. "Messy amateur," Cade murmured, running a hand up and down her back.

It was the same madness, she realized. The same violent loss of control she'd seen when he grabbed the antique knife Thomas used for a letter opener off the desk. When he used it.

These were only things, she reminded herself. No matter how dear and cherished, they were only things.

She'd seen for herself just what Timothy could do to people. "I have to call Grace. She'd have gone to Grace if she could."

"Did you recognize who M.J. was with from the description?"

"No. I don't know anyone like that, and I know most of M.J.'s friends." She waded through the destruction of her living room and reached the phone. Her message light was blinking, but she ignored it and hastily punched in numbers. "It's her machine," Bailey murmured, and strained while the throaty voice recited the announcement. Then: "Grace, if you're there, pick up. It's urgent. I'm in trouble. M.J.'s in trouble. I don't know where she is. I want you to go to the police, give them the package I sent you. Call me right away."

"Give her my number," Cade instructed.

"I don't know it."

He took the phone himself, recited it, then handed the receiver back to Bailey.

It was a calculated risk, revealing Bailey's whereabouts, but the diamond was going into safekeeping and he didn't want to put up any impediments to Grace being able to reach them. "It's life-and-death, Grace. Don't stay in the house alone. Get to the police. Don't talk to my brother, whatever you do. Don't let him in the house. Call me, please, please, call me."

"Where does she live?"

"In Potomac." Bailey told him when he gently took the receiver away and hung it up. "She may not be there at all. She has a place up in the country, western Maryland. That's where I sent the package. There's no phone there, and only a few people know she goes there. Other times she just gets in the car and drives until she sees someplace that suits her. She could be anywhere."

"How long does she usually stay out of touch?"

"No more than a few days. She'd call me, or M.J." With an oath, she pounced on the message machine. The first voice to flow out was Grace's.

"Bailey, what are you up to? Is this thing real? Are we giving smuggling a try? Look, you know how I hate these machines. I'll be in touch."

"Four o'clock on Saturday." Bailey hung on to that. "She was all right at four o'clock on Saturday, according to the machine."

"We don't know where she called from."

"No, but she was all right on Saturday." She punched to get the next message. This time it was M.J.

"Bailey, listen up. I don't know what the hell's going on, but we're in trouble. Don't stay there, he might come back.

I'm in a phone booth outside some dive near—" There was swearing, a rattle. "Hands off, you son of a—" And a dial tone.

"Sunday, two a.m. What have I done, Cade?"

Saying nothing, he punched in the next message. It was a man's voice this time. "Little bitch, if you hear this, I'll find you. I want what's mine." There was a sob, choked off. "He cut my face. He had them slice up my face because of what you did. I'm going to do the same to you."

"It's Timothy," she murmured.

"I figured as much."

"He's lost his mind, Cade. I could see it that night. Something snapped in him."

He didn't doubt it, not after what he'd seen in Thomas Salvini's office. "Is there anything you need from here?" When she only looked around blankly, he took her hand. "We'll worry about that later. Let's go."

"Where?"

"A quiet spot where you can sit down and tell me everything else. Then we'll make a call."

The park was shady and green. Somehow, the little bench under the spreading trees seemed to block out the punch of the oppressive July heat. It hadn't rained in days, and humidity hung like a cloud of wasps in the air.

"You need to have yourself under control when we go to the cops," Cade told her. "You have to have your mind clear."

"Yes, you're right. And I need to explain everything to you."

"I'm putting the pieces together well enough. That's what I do."

"Yeah." She looked down at her hands, felt useless. "That's what you do."

"You lost your father when you were ten. Your mother did her best, but didn't have a head for business. She struggled to keep a house, raise a daughter alone and run an antique business. Then she met a man, an older man, successful, competent, financially solvent and attractive, who wanted her and was willing to accept her daughter into his family."

She let out an unsteady breath. "I suppose that's it, cutting to the bottom line."

"The child wants a family, and accepts the stepfather and stepbrothers as such. That's it, too, isn't it?"

"Yes. I missed my father. Charles didn't replace him, but he filled a need. He was good to me, Cade."

"And the stepbrothers' noses were a little out of joint at the addition of a little sister. A pretty, bright, willing-to-please little sister."

She opened her mouth to deny it, then closed it again. It was time to face what she'd tried to ignore for years. "Yes, I suppose. I stayed out of their way. I didn't want to make waves. They were both in college when our parents married, and when they came back and were living at home again, I was off. I can't say we were close, but it seemed—I always felt we were a blended family. They never teased or abused me, they never made me feel unwelcome."

"Or welcome?"

She shook her head. "There wasn't any real friction until my mother died. When Charles withdrew into himself, pulled back from life so much, they took over. It seemed only natural. The business was theirs. I felt I'd always have a job with the company, but I never expected any percentage. There was a scene when Charles announced I'd have twenty percent. He was giving them forty each, but that didn't seem to be the point to them."

"They hassled you?"

"Some." Then she sighed. "They were furious," she admitted. "With their father, with me. Thomas backed off fairly quickly, though. He was more interested in the sales-and-accounting end than the creative work, and he knew that was my area of expertise. We got along well enough. Timothy was less content with the arrangement, but he claimed I'd get tired of the routine, find some rich husband and leave it all up to them anyway."

It still hurt to remember that, the way he'd sneered at her. "The money Charles left me is in trust. It dribbles out to me until I reach thirty. It's not a great deal, but more than enough. More than necessary. He put me through college, he gave me a home, he gave me a career I love.

"And when he sent me to college, he gave me M.J. and Grace. That's where I met them. We were in the same dorm the first semester. By the second, we were rooming together. It was as if we'd known each other all our lives. They're the best friends I've ever had. Oh, God, what have I done?"

"Tell me about them."

She steadied herself, and tried. "M.J.'s restless. She changed her major as often as some women change hairstyles. Took all sorts of obscure courses. She'd bomb tests or ace them, depending on her mood. She's athletic, impatient, generous, fun, tough-minded. She tended bar her last year at college for a lark, claimed she was so good at it she'd have to have her own place. She bought one two years ago. M.J.'s. It's a pub off Georgia Avenue, near the District line."

"I've missed it."

"It's kind of a neighborhood bar. Regulars, some Irish music on the weekends. If things get rowdy, she takes care of it herself most of the time. If she can't intimidate or outyell someone, she can drop-kick them around the block. She's got a black belt in karate."

"Remind me not to cross her."

"She'd like you. She can take care of herself, that's what I keep telling myself. No one can take care of herself better than M. J. O'Leary."

"And Grace?"

"She's beautiful, you saw that from the sketch. That's what most people see, and they don't see anything else. She uses that when she likes—despises it, but uses it."

Watching pigeons flutter and strut, Bailey let the memories come. "She was orphaned young, younger than I, and was raised by an aunt in Virginia. She was expected to behave, to be a certain way, a certain thing. A Virginia Fontaine."

"Fontaine? Department stores."

"Yes, money, lots of old money. At least old enough to have that luster a century or so of prestige provides. Because she was beautiful, wealthy and from a fine family, it was expected that she would be properly educated, associate with the right people and marry well. Grace had other ideas."

"Didn't she pose for...?" He trailed off, cleared his throat.

Bailey simply lifted a brow. "For a centerfold, yes, while she was still in college. The Ivy League Miss April. She did it without blinking an eye, with the idea of scandalizing her family and, as she put it, exploiting the exploiters. She came into her own money when she was twenty-one, so she didn't give a damn what her proper family thought."

"I never saw the picture," Cade said, wondering if he should be feeling regret or gratitude, under the circumstances. "But it created quite a stir."

"That's just what she was after." Bailey's lips curved again. "Grace liked creating stirs. She modeled for a while, because it amused her. But it didn't satisfy her. I think she's still looking for what will satisfy her. She works very hard for charities, travels on whims. She calls herself the last of the dilettantes, but it's not true. She does amazing work for underprivileged children, but won't have it publicized. She has tremendous compassion and generosity for the wounded."

"The bartender, the socialite and the gemologist. An unlikely trio."

It made her smile. "I suppose it sounds that way. We— I don't want to sound odd, but we recognized each other. It was that simple. I don't expect you to understand."

"Who'd understand better?" he murmured. "I recognized you."

She looked up then, met his eyes. "Knowing who I am hasn't solved anything. My life is a mess. I've put my friends in terrible danger, and I don't know how to help them. I don't know how to stop what I've started."

"By taking the next step." He lifted her hand, brushed a kiss over the knuckles. "We go back to the house, get the canvas bag, and contact a pal of mine on the force. We'll find your friends, Bailey."

He glanced up at the sky as clouds rolled over the sun. "Looks like we're finally going to get that rain."

Timothy Salvini swallowed another painkiller. His face throbbed so deeply it was difficult to think. But thinking was just what he had to do. The man who had ordered his face maimed, then ordered it tended by his personal physician, had given him one last chance.

If he didn't find Bailey and at least one of the diamonds by nightfall, there was nowhere on earth he could hide.

And fear was a deeper throb than pain.

He didn't know how it could have gone so horribly wrong. He'd planned it out, hadn't he? Handled the details when Thomas buried his head in the sand. He was the one who'd been contacted, approached. Because he was the one with the brains, he reminded himself. He was the one who knew how to play the games.

And he was the one who'd made the deal.

Thomas had jumped at it at first. Half of ten million dollars would have set his twin up nicely, and would have satisfied his own craving for real wealth.

Not the dribs and drabs of their business income, however successful the business. But real money, money to dream on.

Then Thomas had gotten cold feet. He'd waited until the eleventh hour, when everything was falling into place, and he'd been planning to double-cross his own flesh and blood.

Oh, he'd been furious to see that Thomas had planned on taking the million-plus deposit and leaving the country, leaving all the risk and the responsibility of pulling everything off on him.

Because he was afraid, Salvini thought now. Because he was worried about Bailey, and what she knew. Grasping little bitch had always been in the way. But he'd have handled her, he'd have taken care of everything, if only Thomas hadn't threatened to ruin everything.

The argument had simply gotten out of control, he thought, rubbing a hand over his mouth. Everything had gotten out of control. The shouting, the rage, the flashing storm.

And somehow the knife had just been there, in his hand.

Gripped in his hand, and already slicked with blood before he realized it.

He hadn't been able to stop himself. Simply hadn't been able to stop. He'd gone a little mad for a moment, he admitted. But it had been all the stress, the sense of betrayal, the fury at being duped by his own brother.

And she'd been there. Staring at him with those huge eyes. Staring at him out of the dark.

If not for the storm, if not for the dark, he'd have found her, taken care of her. She'd been lucky, that was all, just lucky. He was the one with the brains.

It wasn't his fault. None of it was his fault.

But he was taking the blame for all of it. His life was on the line because of his brother's cowardice and the schemes of a woman he'd resented for years.

He was certain she'd shipped off at least one of the stones. He'd found the receipt for the courier in the purse she'd left in her office when she fled from him. Thought she was clever, he mused.

She'd always thought she was the clever one. Little Miss Perfect, ingratiating herself with his father, coming back from her fancy college years with honors and awards. Honors and awards meant nothing in business. Shrewdness did. Guts did. Canniness did.

And Timothy Salvini had all three.

He would have had five million dollars, too, if his brother hadn't bumbled and alerted Bailey then lost his nerve and tried to double-cross their client.

Client, he thought, gingerly touching his bandaged cheek. It was more like master now, but that would change, too.

He would get the money, and the stone, find the others. And then he would run far, and he would run fast. Because

Timothy Salvini had looked the devil in the eye. And was smart enough to know that once the stones were in the devil's hand, his minion would be of no more use.

So he was a dead man.

Unless he was smart.

He'd been smart enough to wait. To spend hours waiting outside that apartment building for Bailey to come home. He'd known she would. She was a creature of habit, predictable as the sunrise. And she hadn't disappointed him.

Who would have thought that someone so...ordinary could have ruined all his plans? Separating the stones, shipping them off in different directions. Oh, that had been unexpectedly clever of her. And extremely inconvenient for him.

But his job now was to concentrate on Bailey. Others were concentrating on the other women. He would deal with that in time, but for now his patience had paid off.

It had been so easy, really. The fancy car had pulled up, Bailey had leaped out. And the man had followed, in too much of a hurry to lock the car door. Salvini had located the registration in the glove box, noted the address.

Now he was breaking the window on the rear door of the empty house, and letting himself inside.

The knife he'd used to kill his brother was tucked securely in his belt. Much quieter than a gun, and just as effective, he knew.

# Chapter 12

"Mick's a good cop," Cade told Bailey as he pulled into the drive. "He'll listen, and he'll clear away the red tape to get to the answers."

"If I'd gone straight to them—"

"You wouldn't be any farther along than you are now," Cade said, interrupting her. "Maybe not as far. You needed time. What you'd been through, Bailey." It sickened him to think about it. "Give yourself a break." He hissed through his teeth as he remembered how ruthlessly he'd pulled her through the building where it had all happened. "I'm sorry I was so hard on you."

"If you hadn't pushed me, I might have kept backing away from it. Avoiding everything. I wanted to."

"It was catching up with you. It was hurting you." He turned, cupped her face. "But if you hadn't blocked it out, you might have gone straight back to your apartment. Like a homing pigeon, calling in your friends. He would have found you. All of you."

"He'd have killed me. I didn't want to face that. Couldn't, I suppose. I've thought of him as my brother for over ten years, even defended him and Thomas to M.J. and Grace. But he would have killed me. And them."

When she shuddered, he nodded. "The best thing you did for all three of you was to get lost for a while. No one would look for you here. Why would they?"

"I hope you're right."

"I am right. Now the next step is to bring in the cops, get them to put out an APB on Salvini. He's scared, he's hurting and he's desperate. It won't take them long."

"He'll tell them who hired him." Bailey relaxed a little. "He isn't strong enough to do otherwise. If he thinks he can make some sort of deal with the authorities, he'll do it. And Grace and M.J.—"

"Will be fine. I'm looking forward to meeting them." He leaned over, opened her door. Thunder rumbled, making her look up anxiously, and he squeezed her hand. "We'll all go to the pub, toss back a few."

"It's a date." Brightening by the image, she got out, reached for his hand. "When this is over, maybe you can get to know me."

"Sweetheart, how many times do I have to tell you? I knew you the minute you walked in my door." He jingled his keys, stuck one in the lock.

It was blind instinct, and his innate need to protect, that saved his life.

The movement was a blur at the corner of his eye. Cade twisted toward it, shoving Bailey back. The quick jerk of his body had the knife glancing down his arm, instead of plunging into his back.

The pain was immediate and fierce. Blood soaked through his shirt, dripped onto his wrist, before he managed to strike out. There was only one thought in his mind— Bailey.

"Get out!" he shouted at her as he dodged the next thrust of the knife. "Run!"

But she was frozen, shocked by the blood, numbed by the horrid replay of another attack.

It all happened so quickly. She was certain she'd no more than taken a breath. But she saw her brother's face, both cheeks bandaged with gauze, a gouge over his left brow.

Murder in his eyes, again.

He lunged at Cade. Cade pivoted, gripped Timothy's knife hand at the wrist. They strained against each other, their faces close as lovers', the smell of sweat and blood and violence fouling the air.

For a moment, they were only shadows in the dim foyer, their breath coming harsh and fast as thunder bellowed.

She saw the knife inch closer to Cade's face, until the point was nearly under his chin, while they swayed together on the bloody wood of the foyer, like obscene dancers.

Her brother would kill again, and she would stand and watch.

She lunged.

It was a mindless, animal movement. She leaped onto his back, tore at his hair, sobbing, cursing him. The sudden jolt sent Cade stumbling backward, his hand slipping, his vision graying around the edges.

With a howl of pain as she dug her fingers into his wounded face, Salvini threw her off. Her head rapped hard on the banister, sent stars circling in her head, flashing like lightning. But then she was up and back at him like vengeance.

It was Cade who pulled her away, threw her back out

of the path of the knife that whistled by her face. Then the force of Cade's leap sent both him and his quarry crashing into a table. They grappled on the floor, panting like dogs. The uppermost thought in Cade's mind was to live long enough to keep Bailey safe. But his hands were slippery with blood and wouldn't keep a firm hold.

Using all his strength, he managed to twist Timothy's knife hand, veering the blade away from his own heart, then pushed away.

When he rolled weakly upright, he knew it was over.

Bailey was crawling to him, sobbing his name. He saw her face, the bruise just blooming on her cheekbone. He managed to lift a hand to it.

"You're supposed to leave the heroics to me." His voice sounded thready, faraway, to his own ears.

"How bad are you hurt? Oh, God, you're bleeding so much." She was doing something with the fire in his arm, but it didn't seem to matter. Turning his head, he looked into Salvini's face. The eyes were on him, dimming but still aware.

Cade coughed his throat clear. "Who hired you, you bastard?"

Salvini smiled slowly. It ended in a grimace. His face was bloody, the bandages torn aside, his breathing thin. "The devil" was all he said.

"Well, say hello to him in hell." Cade struggled to focus on Bailey again. Her brows were drawn together in concentration. "You need your glasses for close work, honey."

"Quiet. Let me stop the bleeding before I call for an ambulance."

"I'm supposed to tell you it's just a flesh wound, but the truth is, it hurts like hell."

"I'm sorry. So sorry." She wanted to lay her head on his shoulder and weep, just weep. But she continued to make a thick pad out of what she'd torn from his shirt and pressed it firmly against the long, deep gash. "I'll call for an ambulance as soon as I finish bandaging this. You're going to be fine."

"Call Detective Mick Marshall. Be sure to ask for him, use my name."

"I will. Be quiet. I will."

"What in the world is going on here?"

The voice made him wince. "Tell me I'm hallucinating," he murmured. "Tell me, and I'm begging you, tell me that's not my mother."

"Good God, Cade, what have you done? Is this blood?"

He closed his eyes. Dimly he heard Bailey, in a firm, no-nonsense voice, order his mother to call an ambulance. And, gratefully, he passed out.

He came to in the ambulance, with Bailey holding his hand, rain pattering briskly on the roof. And again in the ER, with lights shining in his eyes and people shouting. Pain was like a greedy beast biting hunks out of his arm.

"Could I have some drugs here?" he asked, as politely as possible, and went out again.

The next time he surfaced, he was in a bed. He remained still, eyes closed, until he tested the level of pain and consciousness. He gave the pain a six on a scale of ten, but he seemed to be fully awake this time.

He opened his eyes, and saw Bailey. "Hi. I was hoping you'd be the first thing I'd see."

She got up from the chair beside the bed to take his hand. "Twenty-six stitches, no muscle damage. You lost a lot of blood, but they pumped more into you." Then she sat on the edge of the bed and indulged in a good cry.

She hadn't shed a tear since she fought to stop the bleeding as he lay on the floor. Not during the ambulance ride, speeding through the wet streets while lightning and thunder strode across the sky.

Or during the time she spent pacing the hospital corridors, or during the headachy ordeal of dealing with his parents. Not even when she struggled to tell the police what had happened.

But now she let it all out.

"Sorry," she said when she'd finished.

"Rough day, huh?"

"As days go, it was one of the worst."

"Salvini?"

She looked away toward the window where the rain ran wet. "He's dead. I called the police. I asked for Detective Marshall. He's outside waiting for you to wake up, and for the doctors to clear him in." She stood, straightened the sheets. "I tried to tell him everything, to make it clear. I'm not sure how well I did, but he took notes, asked questions. He's worried about you."

"We go back some. We'll straighten it out, Bailey," he told her, and reached for her hand again. "Can you hold up a little longer?"

"Yes, as long as it takes."

"Tell Mick to get me out of here."

"That's ridiculous. You've been admitted for observation."

"I've got stitches in my arm, not a brain tumor. I'm going home, drinking a beer and dumping this on Mick."

She angled her chin. "Your mother said you'd start whining."

"I'm not whining, I'm..." He trailed off, narrowed his eyes as he sat up. "What do you mean, my mother? Wasn't I hallucinating?"

"No, she came over to give you a chance to apologize, which apparently you never do."

"Great, take her side."

"I'm not taking her side." Bailey caught herself, shook her head. Could they actually be having this conversation at such a time? "She was terrified, Cade, when she realized what had happened, that you were hurt. She and your father—"

"My father? I thought he was off fly-fishing in Montana."

"He just got home this morning. They're in the waiting room right now, worried to death about you."

"Bailey, if you have one single ounce of affection for me, make them go away."

"I certainly will not, and you should be ashamed of yourself."

"I'll be ashamed later. I've got stitches." It wasn't going to work. He could see that plainly enough. "All right, here's the deal. You can send my parents in, and I'll square things with them. Then I want to see the doctor and get sprung. We'll talk to Mick at home and square things there."

Bailey folded her arms. "She said you always expect to have your own way." With that, she turned and marched to the door.

It took a lot of charm, arguments and stubbornness, but in just over three hours, Cade was sinking onto his own sofa. It took another two, with the distraction of Bailey fussing over him, to fill Mick in on the events since Thursday night.

"You've been a busy boy, Parris."

"Hey, private work isn't eating doughnuts and drinking coffee, pal."

Mick grunted. "Speaking of coffee." He glanced toward Bailey. "I don't mean to put you out, Miss James."

"Oh." She got to her feet. "I'll make a fresh pot." She took his empty mug and hurried off.

"Smooth, Mick, very smooth."

"Listen." Mick leaned closer. "The lieutenant's not going to be happy with two corpses and two missing diamonds."

"Buchanan's never happy."

"He doesn't like play cops like you on principle, but there's a lot of bad angles on this one. Your lady friend waiting four days to report a murder's just one of them."

"She didn't remember. She'd blocked it out."

"Yeah, she says. And me, I believe her. But the lieutenant…"

"Buchanan has any trouble with it, you send him my way." Incensed, Cade pushed himself up and ignored the throbbing in his arm. "Good God, Mick, she watched one of her brothers murder the other, then turn on her. You go to the scene, look at what she looked at, then tell me you'd expect a civilian to handle it."

"Okay." Mick held up a hand. "Shipping off the diamonds."

"She was protecting them. They'd be gone now, if she hadn't done something. You've got her statement and mine. You know exactly how it went down. She's been trying to complete the circle since she came to me."

"That's how I see it," Mick said after a moment, and glanced down at the canvas bag by his chair. "She's turned everything over. There's no question here about self-defense. He broke a pane out in the back door, walked in, waited for you."

Mick threaded a hand through his wiry hair. He knew how easily it could have gone down another way. How easily he could have lost a friend. "Thought I told you to put in an alarm."

Cade shrugged. "Maybe I will, now that I've got something worth protecting."

Mick glanced toward the kitchen. "She's, ah, choice."

"She's certainly mine. We need to find M. J. O'Leary and Grace Fontaine, Mick, and fast."

"We?"

"I'm not going to sit on my butt."

Mick nodded again. "All we've got on O'Leary is there was a disturbance in her apartment, what looks like a whale of a fight, and her running off with some guy wearing a ponytail. Looks like she's gone to ground."

"Or is being held there," Cade murmured, casting a glance over his shoulder to make certain Bailey was still out of earshot. "I told you about the message on Bailey's recorder."

"Yeah. No way to trace a message, but we'll put a flag out on her. As for Fontaine, I've got men checking her house in Potomac, and we're hunting down her place up in the mountains. I should know something in a couple hours."

He rose, hefted the bag, grinned. "Meanwhile, I get to dump this on Buchanan, watch him tap-dance with the brass from the Smithsonian." He had to chuckle, knowing just how much his lieutenant hated playing diplomat with suits. "How much you figure the rocks are worth?"

"So far, at least two lives," Bailey said as she carried in a tray of coffee.

Mick cleared his throat. "I'm sorry for your loss, Miss James."

"So am I." But she would live with it. "The Three Stars of Mithra don't have a price, Detective. Naturally, for insurance purposes and so forth, the Smithsonian required a professional assessment of market value. But whatever dollar value I can put on them as a gemologist is useless, really. Love, knowledge and generosity. There is no price."

Not quite sure of his moves, Mick shifted his feet. "Yes, ma'am."

She worked up a smile for him. "You're very kind and very patient. I'm ready to go whenever you are."

"Go?"

"To the station. You have to arrest me, don't you?"

Mick scratched his head, shifted his feet again. It was the first time in his twenty-year career that he'd had a woman serve him coffee, then politely ask to be arrested. "I'd have a hard time coming up with the charge. Not that I don't want you to stay available, but I figure Cade's got that handled. And I imagine the museum's going to want to have a long talk with you."

"I'm not going to jail?"

"Now she goes pale. Sit down, Bailey." To ensure that she did, Cade took her hand with his good one and tugged.

"I assumed, until the diamonds were recovered... I'm responsible."

"Your brothers were responsible," Cade corrected.

"I have to go with that," Mick agreed. "I'm going to take a rain check on the coffee. I may need to talk to you again, Miss James."

"My friends?"

"We're on it." He gave Cade a quick salute and left.

"Timothy can't hurt them now," she murmured. "But whoever hired him—"

"Only wants the diamonds, not your friends. Odds are Grace is up in her mountain hideaway, and M.J. is out busting some guy's chops."

It almost made her smile. "You're right. We'll hear from them soon. I'm sure of it. I'd know if something had happened to them. I'd feel it." She poured a cup of coffee, then left it sitting untouched. "They're the only family I have left. I suppose they're the only family I've had for a long time. I just pretended otherwise."

"You're not alone, Bailey. You know that."

No, she wasn't alone. He was there, waiting. "You should lie down, Cade."

"Come with me."

She turned, caught the fresh cockiness of his grin. "And rest."

"I'm not tired."

Her smile faded, and her eyes went dark and serious. "You saved my life."

He thought of the way she'd leaped onto Salvini's back, biting and scratching like a wildcat. "I'd say it was a toss-up as to who saved whom."

"You saved my life," she said again, slowly. "The minute I walked into yours. I'd have been lost without you. Today, you shielded me, fought for me. Risked your life to protect mine."

"I've always wanted to slay the dragon for the damsel. You gave me the chance."

"It's not white knights or Sam Spade." Her voice went rough with emotion. "It was real blood pouring out of you. My brother who turned a knife on you."

"And you," he reminded her. "You're not responsible for what he did, and you're too smart to believe you are."

"I'm trying to be." She turned away for a moment, until she had her courage in place. "If it had gone the other way, if it had been you who died, who else could I blame? I came to you. I brought this to you."

"It's my job." He rose, winced only a little. "Are you going to have a problem with that? What I do for a living? The risks involved with it?"

"I haven't thought that far." She turned back, faced him. "What you've done for me comes first. I'll never be able to repay you for a moment of it."

In an impatient movement, he scooped the hair out of his face. "You're going to tick me off here, Bailey."

"No, I'm going to say what I have to say. You believed me, right from the first. You took me into your home. You bought me a hairbrush. Something so simple, hundreds of others would have overlooked it. You listened to me and promised to help. You kept your promise. And today it almost killed you."

His eyes went sharp. "Do you want me to tell you I'd die for you? I suppose I would. Would I kill for you? Without question. You're not a fantasy to me, Bailey. You're what made reality snap into place."

Her heart fluttered into her throat and swelled. He was angry with her again, she noted. His eyes were impatient in his bruised face. His arm was bandaged from elbow to shoulder and had to be painful.

And he was hers, without question, for the taking.

"I guess I'm trying to figure out why."

"You want to be reasonable where reason doesn't fit. It's not a piece of the puzzle, Bailey. It's the whole puzzle." Frustrated, he dragged a hand through his hair again. "Love was the first Star, wasn't it? And so is this."

That simple, she realized. That powerful. Pressing her lips together, she took a step toward him. "I'm Bailey James," she began. "I'm twenty-five and live in Washington, D.C. I'm a gemologist. I'm single."

She had to stop, pace herself before she babbled. "I'm neat. One of my closest friends says neatness is a religion to me, and I'm afraid she may be right. I like everything in its place. I like to cook, but don't often, as I live alone. I like old movies, especially film noir."

He was grinning at her now, but she shook her head. There had to be more to her than that. "Let me think," she muttered, impatient with herself. "I have a weakness for Italian shoes. I'd rather do without lunch for a month than a nice pair of pumps. I like good clothes and antiques. I prefer buying one good thing than several inferior ones. That same friend calls me a retail snob, and it's true. I'd rather go rockhounding than visit Paris, though I wouldn't mind doing both."

"I'll take you."

But she shook her head again. "I'm not finished. I have flaws, a lot of flaws. Sometimes I read very late into the night and fall asleep with the light on and the TV going."

"Well, we'll have to fix that."

He stepped toward her, but she stepped back, held up a hand. "Please. I squint without my reading glasses, and I hate wearing them because I'm vain, so I squint quite a lot. I didn't date much in college, because I was shy and studious and boring. My only sexual experience has come about recently."

"Is that so? If you'd shut up, you could have another sexual experience."

"I'm not done." She said it sharply, like a teacher chastising a rowdy student. "I'm good at my work. I designed these rings."

"I've always admired them. You're so pretty when you're serious, Bailey. I've got to get my hands on you."

"I'm not without ambition," she continued, sidestepping his grab for her. "I intend to be successful in what I do. And I like the idea of making a name for myself."

"If you're going to make me chase you around the sofa, at least give me a handicap. I've got stitches."

"I want to be important to someone. I want to know I matter. I want to have children and cook Thanksgiving dinner. I want you to understand that I've tried to be sensible about this, because that's the way I am. I'm precise and I'm practical and I can be very tedious."

"I've never spent such a boring weekend in my entire life," he said dryly. "I could barely keep my eyes open." When she chuckled, he outmaneuvered her and pulled her into his arms. And swore as pain radiated straight up to his shoulder.

"Cade, if you've opened those stitches—"

"You're so precise and practical, you can sew me back up." He lifted her chin with his fingers, smiled. "Are you finished yet?"

"No. My life isn't going to be settled until M.J. and Grace are back and I know they're safe and the Three Stars are in the museum. I'll worry until then. I'm very good at worrying, but I believe you already know that."

"I'll write it down in case it slips my mind again. Now, why don't you take me upstairs and play doctor?"

"There's one more thing." When he rolled his eyes, she drew in a breath. "I love you very much."

He went very still, and the fingers on her chin tightened. Emotions poured through him, sweet and potent as wine. There might not be stars in her eyes, he thought. But her heart was in them. And it belonged to him.

"Took you long enough to get to it."

"I thought it was the best place to finish."

He kissed her for a long, gentle time. "It's a better place to start," he murmured.

"I love you, Cade," she repeated, and touched her lips to his again. "Life starts now."

# *Epilogue*

One Star was out of his reach, for the time being. He'd known the moment it was placed in the hands of the authorities. He hadn't raged or cursed the gods. He was, after all, a civilized man. He had only sent his quivering messenger away with a single icy stare.

Now, he sat in his treasure room, gliding his finger over the stem of a golden goblet filled with wine. Music poured liquidly through the air, soothing him.

He adored Mozart, and gently followed the strains of the music with his hand.

The woman had caused him a great deal of trouble. Salvini had underestimated her, had claimed she was nothing more than a token, a pet of his late father's. With some brains, of course, and undeniable skill, but no courage. A quiet mouse of a woman, he'd been told, who closed herself off with her rocks and minded her own business.

The mistake had been to trust Salvini's estimation of Bailey James.

But he wouldn't make that mistake again. He chuckled to himself. He wouldn't be required to, as Ms. James and her protector had dealt so finally with Timothy Salvini.

And with that convenience, there was nothing to link him with the stones, with the deaths. And nothing to stop him from completing his plan—with some adjustments, of course. He could be flexible when it was necessary.

Two Stars were still free, still lost or wandering. He could see them if he closed his eyes, pulsing with light, waiting for him to take them, unite them with the third. Embrace their power.

He would have them soon enough. Whoever stood in his way would be removed.

It was a pity, really. There had been no need for violence. No need for a single drop of blood to be spilled. But now that it had, well…

He smiled to himself and drank deep of warm red wine. Blood, he thought, would have blood.

Three women, three stones, three Stars. It was almost poetic. He could appreciate the irony of it. And when the golden triangle was complete, when the Three Stars of Mithra were his alone, and he could stroke them as they sat on the altar, he would think of the women who'd tried to turn his destiny aside.

He would remember them with some fondness, even admiration.

He hoped he could arrange for them all to die poetically.

\* \* \* \* \*